A LADY
FOLLOWS

A LADY
FOLLOWS

HOLLY NEWMAN

A TOM DOHERTY ASSOCIATES BOOK
NEW YORK

A LADY FOLLOWS

Copyright © 1999 by Holly Newman

This book is printed on acid-free paper.

A Forge Book
Published by Tom Doherty Associates, Inc.
175 Fifth Avenue
New York, NY 10010

Forge® is a registered trademark of Tom Doherty Associates, Inc.

Newman, Holly.
    A lady follows / Holly Newman.—1st ed.
        p.   cm.
    "A Tom Doherty Associates book."
    ISBN 0-312-86871-5 (alk. paper)
    I. Title.
PS3564.E91616L33   1999
813'.54—dc21   98-41785
                                              CIP

First Edition: February 1999

Printed in the United States of America

0   9   8   7   6   5   4   3   2   1

For Marjorie Manning Thompson,

a loving mother who shared with her daughter
a love for history.

ACKNOWLEDGMENTS

I OWE PARTICULAR thanks to Denise Little for introducing me to old diaries, journals, and memoirs that provide rich, detailed word pictures of peoples' experiences. After I was hooked and wanted more, she showed me catalogues from university presses in the United States that were finding and reprinting old journals. I herald this preservation work, for these pieces of writing are yesterday's word cameras, and need to be preserved as lovingly and carefully as old photographs.

Though I'd like to own every piece of research material I use (particularly diaries and journals), that is not feasible, so I've come to depend on and appreciate the staffs of the Inter-Library Loan desks at Phoenix Public Library and Maricopa County Library.

And last but certainly not least, my thanks go Diane Stuckart, Gail Selinger, Ed Dixon, Sharon Geyer, Betty Webb, and Sharon Magee for encouragement, advice, and critiques.

A LADY
FOLLOWS

1

"THAT'S IT. THAT'S the last of it, Mrs. Harper." Walter Christian wiped his large hands on his canvas apron and walked toward her, leaving his eldest son to tie down the osnaburg sheets covering the big Conestoga freight wagon that stood before his general store. "But I sure don't feel right about this."

Carolina Harper looked at the rotund merchant. Though the early morning air retained a hint of the night's coolness, his bald head glistened and sweat gathered on his brow, pooling at the edges of grizzled eyebrows drawn together in concern. "I know," she said softly, smiling at the man who had helped her organize and prepare her caravan. "But I do."

He dragged his shirtsleeve across his forehead, then shook his head. "Ain't the best time, neither. There's strong rumors of war with Mexico."

She nodded. Talk of war grew stronger and louder as each passing day more travelers from the east came to Westport, Missouri, bringing with them new tales, rumors, and conclusions.

It wasn't that she was unafraid of war or did not believe in its inevitability. She did believe and she was terrified. But she didn't fear the horrors of war for herself. She'd lost the ability to care what happened to herself when she lost first her son, David, and then her husband, Edward, within days of each other.

No, she risked the harshness of the trail and the threat of war for the lives of three children, her young, motherless cousins.

Her uncle Elliott Reeves had ever been a likeable ne'er-do-well. Anxious to get into trade like his brother-in-law, ten years ago he'd joined a summer caravan to Santa Fe with a wagonload of odds and ends he'd assembled to sell. To the family's surprise, he sold at a large profit, then promptly married and settled in New Mexico.

From returning merchant caravans, the family heard of his successes and failures. But lately the family had heard unsettling stories. They heard he'd been imprisoned for angering a powerful military officer. Later they heard his wife had died. Those who passed the latter information along laughed about the machinations Elliott Reeves went through to take care of his children.

The merchants' careless laughter had spurred Carolina to travel down the Santa Fe Trail. The conviction—the need—to care for and protect these motherless children gnawed at her insides by day and plagued her dreams by night. She hadn't been able to save her son, but she could save other children. She drew a deep breath.

"Every day entire families set out from here, or Independence, destined for Oregon, yet there are equally strong rumors of war with England over the Oregon Territory," she said.

Christian snorted. "Don't you believe it. President Polk will finagle us outta that one, negotiate some compromise or other with ol' John Bull. But those rumors outta Texas and Mexico," he frowned, tucking his chin into his thick neck, "they look mighty serious."

"Mr. Christian, at one time or another we all are faced with duties that might weigh easier on another day. I am well aware that crossing the Santa Fe Trail is a hardship, even without those rumors of war. But it is expressly *because* of those rumors that my duty, and my mission, lie in New Mexico. I must go," Carolina finished with quiet dignity.

His lips pressed tightly together, air whistling through his nose as he sighed, but he made no further comment and Carolina liked him the better for it.

"Thank you for all your help. And your concern. But, please, be easy in your mind. With Colonel Kearney readying his Army of the West at Fort Leavenworth, and the large caravans ahead on the trail, situated in between these two large contingents, I'm certain our journey to Santa Fe shall be a safe one."

"Just be sure you join up with any trains you meet going your direction," he said gruffly.

She nodded as she pulled on her black leather riding gloves. "We hope to catch the caravans at Council Grove. But if we are to do so, we must get on our way now. They have several days on us as it is."

She turned to wave at Mr. Gaspard, the guide Mr. Christian had contracted for her, to let him know they could leave. Almost immediately her Mexican ox and mule drivers called out to their teams, and harnesses jingled. Mr. Christian's son gave her a leg up onto her horse. Carolina settled her right leg around the standing head of the sidesaddle and adjusted her skirts. She glanced around to see Sibby, her longtime servant, and Pedro Perales, whose services her mother had pressed upon her, mounting their mules. Satisfied, she turned back to Mr. Christian.

He shooed his son away and came to stand by Carolina's horse, one large hand reaching out to stroke the mare's neck. "You sure you can't wait a couple weeks to go with the Magoffin caravan? I hear Sam Magoffin is taking that pretty li'l wife of his. Be female company for you."

Carolina Harper laughed at Walter Christian's persistence. "No, Mr. Christian. Have done. All my goods are packed, the men are hired. My mind is made up, we leave this morning. But I am touched by your concern."

He sighed heavily once again. "I wouldn't feel right with my Maker if I didn't try. A man's got his duty, too," he said gruffly.

"I know," she said softly, moved by his sincerity. "And you have done yours admirably." She reached out to grasp his hand. "Goodbye, and thank you again. Give my best to your wife as well. And, please, when you go to St. Louis next month, give what assurances you can to my mother and stepfather. Tell my mother I promise to write her a journal account of my travels to rival *Commerce of the Prairies,* Josiah Gregg's published journal!"

He laughed and nodded wearily. "Godspeed, child."

Carolina waved, turned her horse west, and followed her guide, wagons, and servants on the Santa Fe Trail out of Westport, Missouri.

CIVILIZATION PUSHED EVER westward, clogging the road out of Westport with people and wagon teams going about their business in the area. For two hours Carolina's little caravan progressed slowly and Carolina's concentration needed to focus on her horse and her riding. Dogs ran out from homesteads, barking. Barefoot children skipped after the teams or watched their passing with commingled expressions of envy and dreams for tomorrow. Men leaned on gun barrels and spat tobacco wads into the dust. Women, their faces shielded by large bonnets and their arms full of baskets or babies, bent their heads to whisper together. A woman riding sidesaddle on the trail was a three-day wonder, fodder for the evening's gossip.

Carolina smiled and nodded pleasantly as she passed them, glad she'd decided to ride horseback this first day rather than ride in one of the Dearborn wagons. There would be days enough ahead for the wagon. This day she wanted to savor the start of an adventure.

Adventure?

She frowned at the turn of her thoughts. It was nothing of the sort; even if her friend Dorcas Carr had deemed it so when they had discussed the journey.

Dorcas Carr may call it adventure; she came from an adventuring family and was too often surrounded by even more adventuring men. Therein lay her problem. Married to Judge William Chiles Carr, and sister to the Bent brothers of the Bent, St. Vrain Company and Bent's Fort on the Arkansas River, the St. Louis matron established her elegant parlor as a crossroads and a lectern to the principles of Manifest Destiny that swept the country.

Mrs. Carr had warned her that war with Mexico was imminent, and the tenor of the minds of the people in parts of New Mexico was already harsh against Anglos. Americans periodically fled Taos for safety at the Bent, St. Vrain ranchero on Ponil Creek, or farther, to Bent's Fort. Mrs. Carr worried for her brother Charles Bent's safety and that of his family, as they lived in Taos. Charles met the world boldly and was not a man for caution.

Ultimately, it was Mrs. Carr's concerns for her brother's family that spurred Carolina down the trail. She had relatives in New Mexico, too. It was for their sake that Carolina journeyed—she hoped ahead of disaster—to New Mexico.

By noon Carolina's little caravan passed beyond the last outpost of settled land. Quickly the landscape changed. Trees gave way to scrub, and scrub gave way to tall grass. With fewer trees, no obstacles remained to break the wind's course across the landscape, it rippled the silver-green waist-high grass and bent wildflowers, hiding their glory.

Sibby kicked her mule to come alongside Carolina's dun-colored mare. "It be mighty like the ocean, Miz Carolina, stretch'n' as far as a body can see," she said.

Awe, and another emotion Carolina couldn't identify, wavered in Sibby's voice. Carolina couldn't fault Sibby's description. It *was* like looking out across ocean waves, vast and endless.

To Carolina, ocean journeys called for great commitment. They called for an acknowledgment of God's divine creation and an acknowledgment of the blessings he gave man in order for man to pass from one land to another in small wooden vessels at the mercy of wind and tide. Crossing the prairie would be no different.

From Mrs. Carr's parlor, Carolina had heard traders, soldiers, and politicians speak of the vast plains beyond Missouri's borders. They described the western plains as the land of Indians, wild animals, and inhospitable climate. They called it the land of purgatory before heaven. Their harsh words clothed feverish desire, for beyond the plains, they assured her, lay America's future.

The memory of their assurances sent cold chills down Carolina's spine. The Spanish and, after Mexico's freedom from Spanish rule, the Mexicans had claimed much of the western lands. The northwest lands were claimed by England and France. By what right did the United States dispute those territory claims? Or prove their own? Territorial disputes could generate innocent bloodshed for those caught in the path of greed or blind idealism.

A philosophy printed in journalistic organs and fervently discussed that could soon lead to bloodshed pervaded American thought: The United States should extend from the Atlantic Coast to the Pacific Coast.

Manifest Destiny!

The idea swept the country faster and stronger than any storm of nature's devising.

Letters from Santa Fe echoed Mrs. Carr's fears of impending war. Carolina thought apprehensively about her young cousins, Maria, Alfredo, and little Luz. Santa Fe was far away. So very far away. How would either side judge those born of both worlds? From her experience, she bitterly knew that to be wholly neither left one open to cruel mercies.

"Yes, Sibby," she acknowledged on a long, freeing exhale. "It is like the ocean. And on the other side is another world."

Sibby rubbed the side of her nose with a long brown finger. "This place, this Santy Fe, they don't speak English, Pedro, he say."

"No. They speak Spanish."

"That's what he say." She paused and frowned. "He say he teach me, if it be all right with you," she added in a rush.

"Sibby!" Carolina said, her pensive expression clearing into a smile. "I think that's a marvelous idea! Why should I mind?"

Sibby's thin shoulders lifted in a shrug. "Some folks would think it a mite strange."

Carolina laughed. "Nonsense. It is practical and I'm ashamed I did not think of that myself. Goodness knows, I haven't spoken Spanish since my father's death and could use the practice. I'll help you and myself by speaking Spanish, too. I shall need your help with Uncle Elliot's children and I do not know how well they may speak English. I should say your learning Spanish is a necessity."

Sibby nodded. "That's what Pedro say, too, and I guess I can see that. I'll try, but I ain't bright like other folks. Don't have nothin' to build on."

"What nonsense! You should not think book learning equivalent to intelligence. It doesn't work that way no matter what the great universities would say. And we shall have plenty of time to learn the language. It will take us at least five to six weeks to reach New Mexico."

Sibby whistled softly through her teeth. "And all the miles, they be like this?" she asked, sweeping her arm in an arc to encompass as far as their eyes could see.

"From what I've heard tell and read, most are." Carolina watched fear flow across Sibby's face. "What is it?"

Sibby laughed as she shook her head. "Why, t'ain't nothin'. Just more a my nonsense. Pay me no mind, Miz Carolina. I jest get the willies at stuff I cain't understand."

Carolina laughed. "You are not alone, Sibby. But I cannot allow my own fear to stand in the way of my duty."

"I understands, Miz Carolina. Truly I docs," Sibby said in a rush. She slapped the reins back and forth against the mule's neck to quicken his pace next to Carolina's horse. "And you're right good to me and I knows you wouldn't allow nothin' to happen to me if you could stop it." They rode in silence for a moment, then Sibby turned again to Carolina, her voice rushed. "But I heard tales, too. In the washhouse. Jeremy Tuttle, he come by and told us 'bout reg'lar Injun attacks agin' people headin' toward Santy Fe.

They takes the hair right off'n their head! Sometimes they take the women and sometimes the children and works 'em right hard and changes 'em so that they's as wild as the Injuns, and then their own folk won't take to 'em no more." Sibby's voice settled into a hushed whisper, her eyes wide. She kicked her heels and slapped the reins against the mule's neck again as if to urge her mount to outrun the demons she'd conjured.

"Sibby! That's enough!" Carolina said, horrified at the tenor of Sibby's mind. "Yes, there have been stories of Indian atrocities. There have also been stories of danger from wild animals, other men, and Mother Nature's whims. In all, I doubt the dangers are any more than one would experience crossing a real ocean."

Her voice mellowed. "Life is full of possibilities, Sibby, both good and bad," she said on a drawn-out sigh. "And right now, with the large number of caravans taking the trail to Santa Fe, the probabilities are safety for us, while in Santa Fe my cousins face a possibility of their world tearing asunder. I don't trust my uncle Elliott to watch out for them properly. My mother's youngest brother has ever been impetuous, and a barn burner as far as dealing with other people. Being an Anglo in a country of Mexicans, well, I fear he is bound to get himself in trouble. He has already been imprisoned once. He has no more sense than that mule you're riding." She laughed. "Probably less. Never has had. If you must fear something, fear the situation in New Mexico. It is a powder keg awaiting the right spark." She paused to look down the trail they would follow. "We must get there as quickly as possible," she said softly. "We must!"

Carolina urged her horse into a canter to catch up with Mr. Gaspard at the head of their train.

He touched his hat as she reined in next to him. "Ma'am," he said.

"How far do you think we'll be able to travel today, Mr. Gaspard?"

"Should be a good day, Mrs. Harper. Probably fifteen, twenty miles. We'll be calling a halt soon to noon it, get past the worst heat, let the oxen and mules rest, then probably pull on to nigh dark." He looked at her, his silver-gray eyes shining with life from within a badly scarred face. "Don't start fretting about not catching any caravans in Council Grove. Bound to be one or two heading our way and if not, we'll just sit a spell and wait."

"Do you think there is any reasonable hope of catching the big caravan in Council Grove?"

Gaspard scratched the side of his head, knocking his stained tan hat askew. "Depends. But if you want my honest opinion, I'd say no."

"Why?"

"Well, now, this is just supposition from an ol' coon like me, but I'd say certain parties in that train will be pushing to go as fast as might be. Seeing as how folks are talking war, it'd be in their best interests."

"What do you mean?"

"About twenty-five of those wagons are owned by Speyer and Armijo," he said dryly.

"Armijo!"

"Yep. The governor of New Mexico himself. He ain't above playing both ends against the middle." He chuckled and winked at her.

"But surely that would be the safest caravan to be with! They are bound to be allowed into Santa Fe."

"If they make it that far."

"What do you mean?"

"If the rumors I heard tell are true, those wagons aren't filled with calico and fancy geegaws. They're filled with ammunition and weapons."

"Weapons!" Carolina frowned, her dark brows pulling together. "But, I don't understand. With the threat of war as imminent as it appears, how could anyone sell them arms?"

Gaspard laughed. "Business is business, ma'am. But, like I say, they may not make New Mexico. I shouldn't be surprised a bit to find our military on their tail when word gets out of their cargo."

"And will word get out?" she asked, intrigued.

He grinned. "Though business is business, ma'am, there's also duty to one's country. And to one's self."

"By that you mean," she said slowly, "that whoever sold them the goods might also notify the military of their shipment?"

"And thought loyal for it, too."

She nodded, her lips twisting into a grimace. "And would they also have the opportunity to resell the goods once the army captured them?"

Gaspard leaned forward on the saddle horn, shifting his weight. Saddle leather creaked. "You've got a fine understanding of commerce, ma'am. A right fine understanding," he said, settling back into his saddle.

"I see."

"Excuse me, ma'am, but I'd best be searching out a spot to noon it. Best save any long jawing for evening."

Carolina glanced up swiftly. "Oh, yes, of course, Mr. Gaspard. I didn't mean to detain you from your work," she said absently, her mind still occupied with considering what she had learned.

"Not a trouble, ma'am. Just it's time to earn my keep." He pulled down the brim of his hat, then flicked the brim in salute before urging his horse into a canter.

May 28, 1846, on the trail out of Westport.

*I promised you a faithful record of my journey and so today,
the first day on the trail, I begin.*

*We traveled farther today than Mr. Gaspard had planned.
I'm afraid I pestered him to push on. We made over twenty
miles, he said. But he was also quick to warn me we cannot
expect every day to be as fortuitous.*

*And what should I tell you of this first day and its
beginnings? Westport, our point of departure, is a fascinating
little community. Its existence sprang from the Kansas
Landing on the Missouri River. Here adventurers and
homesteaders, all looking for a new start in life in the western
territories, gather. All manner of accent, and worse grammar,
may be heard on its dusty streets, and everywhere the eyes are
greeted by a panoply of color and style. Blanketed and painted
Indians, Mexicans in slashed pantaloons with large silver
buttons, mountain men in buckskins, bullwhackers with their
bowie knives strapped to their waists, soldiers in blue, farmers
in homespun, and rivermen wearing bits and pieces of
costumes—all manner of men walked the streets.*

Many merchants have established emporiums in this new little town and trade is brisk in outfitting westward caravans. There are also many settlers and Indians about. I am told the Shawnee and Kansa Indians who live in the area are peaceful. No such assurances are given with regards to the settlers! I have remained vigilant.

I took your advice and in Westport took my custom to Mr. Christian. He is a dear man and proved very helpful. He and his wife, Anna, even opened the doors of their home for me to stay with them for the few days required to organize my venture. That was a blessing after staying in Colonel Longford's hotel in Independence. Four hundred guests! There were people coming and going at all hours of the day and night. It was not a restful establishment.

When I finally convinced Mr. Christian I was serious in my intention to travel to Santa Fe, he found me a trail guide. Rest assured Mr. Christian did try to dissuade me from my course; but he saw the depth of my commitment and refrained from pressing too hard. He is a good man and I can see why Mr. Davies respects him.

And how is Mr. Davies? I hope my stepfather is not too disgruntled with me. I know his intentions were always the best; however, I did not journey to St. Louis to be a part of the St. Louis social whirl. I can't forget David or Edward, and the pain of past remembrances spouts upward from the depths of my soul to douse what enjoyment I might find in your pleasant, growing metropolis.

But we have spoken enough of this in the past and there is too much else worthy to take up the pages of this copybook.

The trail. What might I tell you of the trail? Remember how we used to say the gentlemen were given to hyperbole whenever they waxed eloquent about the trail? Already I perceive we were wrong! Their descriptions did little to begin to describe its actuality, and this I tell you after less than twenty-four hours traveling down it.

Around Westport there are woods; but these woods quickly give way to scrub and then to the prairie. The prairie is almost entirely comprised of silvery-green waist-high grass for as far as the eye can see. Here and there lone trees appear, like the Lone Elm, a well-known trail marker. Also found in odd patches are wild roses, plum, grape, and other flowering plants I cannot identify, all struggling against the endless grass for nourishment from the land.

I began the journey riding my little dun-colored mare, anxious to miss nothing. But after our afternoon stop, an incessant wind chased Sibby and me into one of the wagons for more comfortable travel. Windborne dust and dirt scoured my complexion despite my veil, and penetrated the fabric of my riding habit, weighing the seams with dirt particles. When we left Westport I thought it odd that Mr. Gaspard should prefer donning leather clothing in this summer heat; however, this afternoon showed me the wisdom of his choice! Leather affords greater protection than wool!

Mr. Gaspard tells me the prairie wind is common. It's hot, and strong, and bends the prairie grass before it in undulating waves. With the wind rippling the long grass Sibby likens the prairie horizon to an ocean, and I can see where she is right. But, unlike the ocean, which leaves no trail, no history of who's come and gone, enough wagons have gone before us over the years to Santa Fe that their passing has left scars on the land forming a visible road. Though I am content with Mr. Gaspard as guide, I see now that following the trail would not have been as difficult a proposition as I feared and if necessary we could do without the man.

I can almost hear that little catch in your throat as you read this! Do not worry. Getting rid of Mr. Gaspard is not our intent.

I suppose here I should tell you what and who make up my little party. I have become a merchant! We have four yoke of oxen pulling an almost new Conestoga wagon loaded with

*trade goods. The wagon's sky-blue body is nearly as bright as
when first painted and its red running gear shows only the
scrapes and scars of minimal use. It is beautiful! I purchased it
from a widow whose husband passed away before they could
begin their journey to the Oregon territory. The poor woman
was anxious to sell so she could return to the bosom of her
family in Cincinnati. My heart went out to her, as well you
might imagine. Her need gave me the courage to put action to
my desire to discover a way to travel to Santa Fe since no
caravan would accept my money as passenger because I am a
lone woman traveling with servants. As a member of the
merchant fraternity, no such restriction applies!*

*Mr. Christian had two thick mackinaw blankets placed
between the white sheets stretched over the ribs of the
Conestoga wagon. These will protect the merchandise from
rain and later be resaleable in Santa Fe. One benefit, he told
me, of using them between the sheets is they remain hidden
from customs inspectors and therefore may be sold without
paying duty! I am not a proponent of such dishonest dealings;
however, if I should confess all to the Mexican authorities,
what effect will this have on those who come after me? Maybe
I should just consider keeping the blankets. If they are as
valuable as Mr. Christian said, certainly Uncle Elliott's family
would like them.*

*I know one of your concerns is how I am financing this
trip. Mr. Christian has been helpful in arranging all the
details and has taught me much as to how people think in the
west. It is, to my mind, very different from our eastern cities. I
used the proceeds from the sale of the Louisiana estate to buy,
with the help of Mr. Christian, the Conestoga wagon and the
goods packed inside it. I have promised those who lead me
down the trail that they are to receive a share of the profits on
the sale of the goods we're carrying as their pay. Mr. Christian
calls this passing on the risk of the venture to my fellow*

*travelers. He assures me this is a common business
arrangement. He also believes this will ensure their loyalty to
me and our enterprise.*

*In addition to our large wagon, we have three Dearborn
wagons packed with luggage and supplies, each wagon pulled
by three teams of mules. It is to one of these wagons Sibby and
I retreated when the winds proved the stronger. Our
wagoneers are all Mexican drivers anxious to return to their
country. They are a jovial group, but much given to
swearing—a circumstance that nearly causes a perpetual pink
to stain my cheeks. It is my hope that their colorful language
will be tempered as we journey together.*

*Pedro is helping a fifth Mexican herd our loose stock after
us. Though he has been in your service for twenty-five years
and I protested your offer of his services, I now freely confess I
am thankful for his company. Every day he does me a
thousand silent little services without my asking until I fear I
should become an indolent lady of leisure if I weren't traveling
the trail. And I have seen, in just the day we have traveled
together, that the Mexican drivers speak respectfully to him.
Of course, he does have a grand air about him, what with his
silver hair and drooping mustache.*

*Mr. Gerard Gaspard is captain of our party. Mr. Christian
told me Mr. Gaspard's father was a Frenchman who
immigrated to the United States at the time of the great
French troubles in the last century. Mr. Gaspard, he said, has
been traipsing the wilderness roads for nearly twenty years. I
well believe this.*

*I think Mr. Gaspard is more comfortable on the trail than in
civilization. He scarce said a dozen words to me before we left
Westport; but since then the gentleman has proved to be a
fount of information and observation on the human condition.
His speech is plain, though not, I feel, unlettered, and
physically, I shall truthfully tell you, the man is*

*unprepossessing. Quite frightening on first acquaintance. His
long and scraggly hair is nearly white and falls forward across
his brow and cheek to obscure a nasty, jagged scar that pulls
the skin around his left eye downward. The scar then curves
down and back toward the base of his left ear, which I noticed,
when he pushed hair away from his eyes, is missing the lobe.
Mr. Christian said his scars are the result of an encounter
with a bear. I shudder at the thought! However, the encounter
must have been at least a year or more in the past, for the
puckered scar is more white than red and as such stands out
from his tanned complexion.*

*But do not think, from my description, that I am traveling
with some wild-eyed mountain man. Nothing could be farther
from the truth. There is a natural friendliness, shrewdness,
and sincerity in the man I find reassuring. And a
youthfulness quite at odds with his white hair, scars, and sun-
weathered visage! I wonder at his age. I swear he could be
anywhere from five and thirty to five and fifty! Whenever I
look into his shrewd gray eyes I swear he is older, but when he
laughs, they turn silver-gray and he looks twenty years
younger.*

*All in all I am quite pleased with my little party. But lest
you think the small numbers I have quoted here are all that
shall be traveling together, I will assuage your fears. For forty
miles we travel in parallel with wagons bound for Oregon and
California. Beyond, it is our plan to rendezvous with several
large caravans that left Westport before we did. Mr. Gaspard
assures me our best hope of meeting them will be to look for
them at Council Grove, some one hundred and fifty miles
down the trail; however, if we do not find them there, if they
have indeed gone before us, then we shall remain at Council
Grove until other caravans come in this direction.*

*Today we have made an auspicious beginning. I look
forward to my continuing days on the trail with faith and
confidence.*

May 29, 1846. Day two.
A thick, early morning fog delayed our departure today. Too
quickly I see why Mr. Gaspard says we cannot expect to travel
the distance we did yesterday! It was an eerie fog, like being in
the middle of dyed combed cotton without a sense of direction.
All around me I could hear the voices of men and the sounds
of animals, but until I was within ten feet of either, I couldn't
see them.
A young child from the immigrant wagon train wandered
off into this dense blue-gray swirl. A little girl of two years. I
heard the mother's frantic cries and the shouts of the men as
they went in search. Finally I heard the child crying and that
is how she was mercifully found. One of the dogs that travel
with them found her and in its exuberance knocked her
down. That released her wails and brought people running.
I felt so helpless, standing in the middle of my camp,
blinded by fog. My heart beat harder as my mind and soul
went out to that mother, frantic for the life of her child. To lose
a child is dying while the heart beats. This morning, again, I
died. I slipped into that fathomless well of nothingness, away
from all senses. There, this time, I might have stayed, if it
hadn't been for the dogs finding the child.
Enough.
It is for three alive children I journey to Santa Fe. If any
shadow should rest upon my soul it is for those wagons bound
for Oregon and California. The wagons belong to—

"MRS. HARPER!"

Carolina looked up from the densely written pages of her journal to see Mr. Gaspard's lean figure silhouetted against her tent
canvas, the campfire glowing behind him.

"Yes, Mr. Gaspard?" she called out.

"Mrs. Harper, the folks camped a half mile north have asked if
you'd join them this evening. For a wedding."

"A wedding?" She tightly curled her fingers around the edge of her lap desk.

"Yes, ma'am."

Carolina exchanged glances with Sibby. A wedding? Weddings were for those who could feel, who could care, she thought hysterically as she fought against the sudden tightness in her throat. She compressed her lips, then signaled for Sibby to open the tent flap for Mr. Gaspard while she restored her journal to the hinged compartment of her lap desk and set the box and inkstand on the floor. She wiped her hands down the front of her apron and rose to her feet as Mr. Gaspard took his hat off and ducked his head to enter. He stopped suddenly, his body pitching forward, when he saw the painted oiled-canvas carpet Pedro had laid down for a floor. He rocked backward to keep from stepping on the carpet.

Carolina laughed at his expression and his contortions devised to avoid soiling the carpet. "Yes. I know it does seem a bit pretentious. But, please, don't worry about it. Come in."

Gaspard shook his head. "It isn't for me to judge, ma'am. Just not something I've ever seen anyone do. Probably easier on the feet when we get to the buffalo grass country," he said, glancing down at her stockinged feet.

Carolina flushed and twitched her skirts to resettle them over her feet. "You were explaining about a wedding, Mr. Gaspard?"

"Yes, ma'am. They're having a wedding and afterward planning a chivaree loud enough to be heard back in Independence. Seems the bride saw you riding today and is asking you to attend. Her pa says she's hankering for the largest wedding this side of the Mississippi."

"But here? On the trail?" She shook her head, bemused. "When there is so much possibility of death or illness? What kind of a way to start a marriage is that? Why didn't they get married in Independence before they left? Or wait until Oregon is achieved?"

A slow smile twisted his scarred features into a parody of good humor. "Well, now, I'd venture to say they waited on purpose for the trail."

Carolina crossed her arms and grabbed her elbows, cupping them in the palms of her hands.

"This wedding was probably planned for the trail, to be a milestone for their journey. It sure won't be something folks'll forget soon."

She reluctantly laughed. Behind her she heard Sibby clucking her tongue. "No, Mr. Gaspard, I'd have to agree with you there." She ran her hands up her arms as she paused to think. She had never been comfortable at large parties where she didn't know anyone. And for a couple to invite a complete stranger to their wedding . . .

"Ma'am," Mr. Gaspard said into the growing silence, "these immigrants, they've got a long, hard road ahead of them. Many'll die before they reach Oregon and others be born. Things like weddings, well, that sorta gives them hope for the future." His voice sounded rougher, almost as if it held back anger, or some other equally strong emotion.

Carolina looked up at him, chagrined. Her arms fell to her sides. "All right, Mr. Gaspard. And you are right, it is not for me to judge. I am embarrassed that I did." She raised a hand to lightly touch her temple with her fingertips, then shook her head. "No matter. If I attend this wedding, will you stand my escort?" she asked, then quickly turned her head away and bit her lip at her temerity. Fool! she angrily thought, Do not be what the Harpers would have you be! She turned back to look at Gaspard.

One long finger stroked the puckered scar on his cheek. "Well, now, ma'am, I'd be honored."

She blinked at him for a moment in surprise, then recovered. "I shall be just a moment, then," she said crisply as she reached behind her back to untie the strings of the apron she wore. Mr. Gaspard nodded and turned to leave the tent.

"Sibby, where are my shoes?" she asked as her fingers struggled to untie a knot that a moment ago had been a bow. "And could you fetch me that little straw hat I bought in Independence?" She yanked hard at the recalcitrant apron string and heard a rip as it gave way, but she paid no heed as she tossed the apron aside and sat back down on her camp stool to draw on her shoes when Sibby placed them in front of her.

"Imagine, Miz Carolina," Sibby said, clucking her tongue as she sorted through packs, "wanting to be married out here! It don't make no sense!"

"I don't know," Carolina said. "Perhaps Mr. Gaspard has the right of it. A wedding is a time for a new beginning. I remember I thought so once. Unfortunately, we don't often get the chance for new beginnings," she said. She laughed at the wistfulness she heard in her own voice. She stood up and took the small hat from Sibby's hand and looked in the hand mirror Sibby held out for her so she could pin the hat on her dark curls. "Don't wait up, Sibby. Tomorrow will be another long day," she advised. She tilted her head as she looked in the mirror. "Some things never change, do they?"

"Beg pardon?"

"Or perhaps this is what Manifest Destiny, that phrase that has been so bandied about, truly means: bringing civilization to the wilderness in our habits, like putting on a new hat to attend a wedding."

Sibby shook her head. "I'm sorry, but I cain't understand."

Carolina sighed. "I am merely laughing at myself and my little hat. Here we are, miles from any settlement, and I'm putting on a frivolous piece of millinery designed for nothing more than ornamentation. Good night, Sibby," she said softly. She turned and lifted the tent flap to go out into the night.

3

CAROLINA PACKED THE last of the midday-meal cooking utensils into the wooden box hung off the side of the wagon, then straightened, rolled her shoulders backward, and stretched her neck from side to side, moaning softly at the relief that little bit of stretching did her body. She was certain the worst of the aches and pains came from her activities at the immigrants' camp last evening. She hadn't danced so much or so hard since. . . . She shook her head and firmly closed the drawer where she had that memory tucked away.

Some memories were too old. Memories of a gay, frivolous life in New Orleans before she married Edward Harper could well belong to another person. She sighed as she tucked damp wayward strands of hair back into the bun Sibby had contrived for her hair that morning. She turned from the wagon to see Mr. Gaspard striding toward her. She settled her hands into her apron as she waited for him.

He was an odd man, she thought, not one she could readily comprehend. He'd surprised her by becoming quite voluble with the Oregon immigrants. He'd seemed younger, too, as if another man lived behind that scarred visage. And that story he told the immigrant children!

"Mrs. Harper. We're going to settle here awhile longer, I'm thinking until late afternoon, then pull on until dark," he said when he stopped before her, his long-fingered hands resting on his hips.

Carolina looked at him in surprise. Just that morning he'd said they'd have another good day for traveling. "All right, but why? I'm finished with packing up and Sibby's fetching water from the stream to refill our barrels now. Is something wrong?"

"No, ma'am. The day's gotten hotter than I expected. It'll just be easier on the stock and us." He stared off at the animal picket lines as he talked. "This air is wet enough to wring out and with this heat, well, ma'am, that saps strength sooner than no water."

"Oh. That—"

"Don't worry. We'll still make the miles today, like I promised you," he said shortly, still not looking at her.

"I'm certain, I—"

"Should pass the Oregon trail cutoff, then we'll be on our own, probably until Council Grove," he finished.

"Thank you, Mr. Gaspard," she said in a rush. When she paused, she was surprised he didn't continue. He seemed so brusque, as if he didn't wish to talk to her, or listen to her reactions to his decisions. He certainly wasn't looking at her. His attitude troubled her, for this was not behavior she was accustomed to from him.

"We'll be ready whenever you deem it appropriate," she finished stiffly. She turned away before he could turn back to her to see traces of disappointment on her face. She didn't know why his briskness should bother her. It wasn't rude, or specifically directed toward her. It was, in truth, a part of his plainspoken nature as far as she'd witnessed in their short acquaintance.

Perhaps he remembered his behavior from the previous evening and wished to counteract whatever impressions she'd formed. Some men could not reconcile gentler behavior in themselves. With the children of the immigrant train she had seen in Mr. Gaspard a different person. A stranger. He'd been entertaining and playful and deliberately mysterious. The children had loved it.

And so had she.

He turned to walk back toward the men who gathered beneath a lone, straggly tree near the animal picket line.

She sighed and climbed up into the wagon to fetch her lap desk. She would use the time to finish the aborted entry to her journal from last evening.

She spread a quilt out on the grass by one of the wagon's wheels on the wagon's shadowed side, then sat down on the quilt and leaned back, using the wheel for a back rest. Carefully she set her filled inkstand out of the way of accidental mishap.

Carolina brushed the end of the pen quill against her chin as she thought of what more to tell her mother, then she smiled and began to write.

May 30, 1846, somewhere on the trail. Afternoon, day three.
We have stopped to "noon it," which means we have
established a temporary camp in the middle of the day for
cooking a midday meal and waiting out the worst heat of the
day. For the next couple of hours time will stretch lazily.
Many men will doze in whatever shade they may find, their
snores joining a chorus of cicadas and bees in the afternoon
quiet. At least there is enough of a breeze today to keep the
mosquitoes at bay. There is a feeling of dampness in the air. If
there were any more I dare swear I could wring water from my
skirts. I wonder if it will rain.
The heat makes staying in the wagon unbearable. I've
settled down outside the wagon, leaning back against one of
the wagon wheels and wondering what the future brings.
Idle ideas.

First, I must tell you about last evening and why this journal stopped so abruptly.

I attended a wedding last night. Here, on the prairie, with stars for a cathedral ceiling! And quite the most glorious cathedral I have ever seen.

A young girl of fifteen married a tongue-tied youth of eighteen. To look at these children I wonder, was I ever so young? If I was it has long faded from memory. Though I had no acquaintance with them, tears slipped down my cheeks as I watched the simple ceremony. To see their shared faith in the future stirred the ashes of my own faith. The coals aren't as cold as I'd supposed and I'm not sure yet how I feel about that.

But that is for another day's musing.

Jordanna Bates, the bride, is the daughter of Elisha Bates, a carpenter whose entire family—wife, sons, daughters, parents, and brother—are immigrating to Oregon. The groom, until two months ago apprenticed to a blacksmith, is Thaddeus Cline. Young Mr. Cline is as big as one would suppose all blacksmiths to be. He seems a good man, too. His master died and left the lad a small capital, which he has invested in journeying to Oregon.

The young couple met on the riverboat packet going up the Missouri River from St. Louis to Independence, a matter of three weeks ago! Mr. Bates told me it was love at first sight. (Love at first sight? I'm sure I didn't know how to respond so I merely nodded politely, albeit weakly.)

The Bates family sent invitations to the wedding to all within a half hour's ride of their camp. There weren't many women, but all who came must have left exhausted. I know I did.

Aside from the Bates women, I doubt there were ten other women guests while the men numbered at least fifty. It was a jovial wedding, full of laughter and cheers. Mr. Gaspard suggested to me that the wedding serves as a symbol for the

immigrants of their chosen new life. As I looked around at
their faces illuminated by the campfires, I hoped this wedding
would be an omen of good fortune for their lives. I pray they
all survive their journey with their enthusiasm intact. And I
pray their new home is kind to them. Perhaps Mr. Polk can
settle with the British equitably. For their sakes, I pray for this
as well.

I met the little girl who was lost yesterday. She is a plump
little blue-eyed blond angel who now clings to her mother's
skirts. The young mother clung to her as well, carrying her
around despite her advancing second pregnancy. She will give
birth soon. All I could think when I looked at her is that she
has great courage. Far more than I would!

Among the immigrants were a fiddler and banjo player.
They kept everyone dancing and singing about the campfires
until they dropped, then led the boisterous chivaree when the
young couple would retire. My own voice is hoarse today and
my sides ache from laughter. I don't know when last I had
such fun!

Mr. Gaspard served as my escort to the wedding. The man
is scrupulously polite to me; however, I get the impression he
doesn't quite approve of me. Though what there is to approve
of or not, I do not know. Nonetheless, for all his wild
appearances the man knows proper behavior. I wonder where
he learned it?

The wedding did serve to reveal another aspect of Mr.
Gaspard's personality. One that took me quite by surprise.

Upon arriving at the immigrant camp, a swarm of children
surrounded Mr. Gaspard demanding to know how he came by
his scars. I blushed to hear them ask! Oh, for the sweet
innocence of youth! I should never have had the courage.

The scars are a result, he told the children, of an encounter
with a bear. But he at first declined to relate the story, for his
tale, he said, was not as dramatic as the legend of Hugh

Glass's mauling by a bear and being left dead by his two
companions. This did not satisfy the children, nor do I think
Mr. Gaspard expected them to be satisfied. The children
begged and pleaded and pulled on his arms. Mr. Gaspard
made a show of hesitating, yet I noted a broad mountain man
dialect beginning to color his voice and slowly grow stronger
and stronger as he spoke with the children. I knew then he had
every intention of telling his tale. The dialect was as much a
part of the story as the story itself and increased the
entertainment of his young listeners.

He is truly a man of many parts! Here is the story he told
the children, with as much of the dialectic color as I am able to
transcribe.

"Well, now, I ken tell that yarn, bein' amongst a passle o'
nice folks. But it's a mite long," he said, drawing out his
words with a show of hesitation.

The children again clamored for the tale and promised,
without prompting, to listen attentively. After that solemn
promise, I found myself regarding them with doubt for
certainly their need to volunteer that promise came from a
history of restive behavior! It was not but a moment, though,
before all my attention centered on Mr. Gaspard's tale, as did
the children's attention.

"It war the wettest spring this ol' coon ever see'd. I don't
ken what war wetter, me or nature," he said, settling down in
front of the fire and reaching into his possibles bag for an
ample pinch of tobacco for his pipe. "Without dry wood ner
buffler patties for a cookin' fyir I ate nothing' but pemmican.
And it sure warn't long before this hyar meat bag," he said,
patting his stomach, "war rumblin' and twistin' in knots like
some ol' rope. Then one mornin' up come the sun. It been so
long since I see'd her I near as not didn't recognize her. Nature
couldn't dry soon enough fer me, that war fer sartin. I war
that restive I dreamed even of a fyir and a mug a coffee while I
war wide awake.

"I war as low as a man could get, and that's a fact. Low and careless." He stopped to shake his head. *"Never get so low as to get careless. 'Member that. This wilderness, well, she's a mite stingy with her second chances. I figure I got lucky. "Suddenly I heared a buzzin'. A honey bee kinda buzzin'. I follered the buzzin' sound to a tree must a been long since hit by lightnin' fer half war dead and half green strugglin' to recover lost glory. It war now a bee tree.*

"My meat bag started grumblin' and howlin' louder than them bees just a thinkin' about that honey in thyar. I determined that this ol' coon was gonna get him some.

"I gathered up the driest tinder I could find to light. It warn't much, a piece hyar or thyar underneath rocks or a pile of leaves. But it didn't have to be a lot, nor real dry, 'cause I wanted somethin' only dry enough to light but wet enough to smoke real good, get them bees woozylike.

"It took grit, but I finally got a good smoker goin'. When thyar warn't any buzzin' comin' from the tree I reached in to get the prize. My mouth war watering in anticipation. All that sweet honey after days of jerked meat!

"As I pulled ma arm out, my hand sticky with the rich prize, I felt a shadow cover my body. I turned to find this great she-byar rearin' up on hind legs. Her mouth war wide open in a snarl revealin' gums dashed full a teeth. Long and sharp ones that'd put a mountain lion to shame."

The children oohed and aahed. One of the littlest ones cuddled closer to her big sister. Mr. Gaspard nodded and took a long draw on his pipe.

"The devil war in her dark eyes, and that's a fact," he continued. *"She reckoned that thyar honey tree fer her personal property, that war double dang sure. She swatted me with her paw afore I could move, her claws rakin' ma face and nigh takin' ma ear off. In that moment ma hyar turned all white. I knew I war goin' beaver.*

"Lucky fer me, I still had ma rifle in ma left hand. In the

mountains, see, a man learns not to get too far from his rifle
and knife. Now you 'member that. I swung ma rifle up, an'
with honey dripping from my right hand, I fired as that she-
byar looked to pounce on this pore chile again. The bullet
caught her in her open mouth and went right on into her
brain. She died right as she war comin' at me. I rolled out of
the way as she fell. I almost didn't make it. I felt the air whistle
through ma hyar at her passin'. Whew, but that war close!

"It warn't until she war dead that I realized I'd been hurt
bad. Blood streamed down my face, an invite fer wolves to
come visitin'. I crawled to the creek bank to clean it off, then
packed the wounds with mud and willow bark.

"It warn't long afore my face and ear war on fire, my head
poundin' as loud and hard as a smithy's hammer. But I had to
get that byar pelt afore any other varmints come by, four
legged or two.

"That war the only idear that kept me goin'. It kept buzzin'
in my head same as them bees. I jest kept at it until it war off.
I took a hunk of byar meat off fer to eat and drug that thyar
fur and this hyar battered chile away."

Mr. Gaspard dolefully shook his head. "My mule'd run off,
but I knowed she couldn't go far on account of her hobble. So I
went lookin' fer her. I must a been a mite touched by then fer I
came to yellin' 'Jezebel!' all over the area until I couldn't yell
nor run no more. I sunk to the ground, not knowin' if I'd ever
get up agin."

At this point Mr. Gaspard fell silent. He puffed on his pipe
and stared into the fire. Then he took his pipe tamp from his
possible pouch at his side and tamped down on the tobacco in
his pipe and rose as to leave. The children shrieked in protest
and demanded to know what happened next.

He grinned. When next he spoke his voice was devoid of
any of the mountain man dialect. Far from it! It took on a
genteel accent!

"A hunting party of Lakota Indians found me," he simply said, then he walked off, grabbed one of the older women about the waist, and whirled her into a dance!

I don't know who was more disappointed in the stark ending of his tale, me or the children. I think it was me, even if the children were more vociferous in their protest. There has to be more to the story. What about the Indians? Were they friendly? Did they help him? I've decided to make learning the rest of the tale one of my goals for this journey!

4

THE LATE-AFTERNOON breeze rippled the silvered grass in undulating waves clear to the horizon. Wagon after wagon followed the path of narrow, rutted parallels created by countless wagons and animals before them. Their passing churned up dust in billows that hung in the air.

Carolina rode directly ahead of her party. A quarter mile north a long span of white covered wagons traveled in parallel, their beginning and end lost from view as if they began and ended in forever. Their trailing dust made Carolina's eyes burn and her chest ache despite the enveloping veil she wore. She reined in her horse and unfastened the water pouch from her saddle. She poured a dab of water onto her handkerchief. She loosened the ties of the veil that fell forward from her hat and were tied securely about her neck. She tossed the veil back over the brim and touched the cool, water-soaked cloth against her cheeks and nose to refresh wind-chapped skin and inhale dampness to soothe her nose and lungs. Everything smelled of parched earth.

The veil had muted the late-afternoon sun. Without the veil the world possessed a white-hot glare. She squinted her eyes against the white brightness. Ahead, she saw something different in the landscape. Something man-made. She urged her horse into a walk. It was a sign, a crude arrow. But was it of promise or warning? Curious, she kicked her horse into a canter.

OREGON.

The leaning, weathered sign pointed to a divergence in the trail. The white-capped wagons that had traveled parallel to her caravan veered gently away to the northwest from that point. Carolina watched wagon after wagon pass the sign, their inhabitants exhibiting renewed excitement for their destination. She smiled and waved farewell to them as they passed. How odd to consider how close she'd come to some of them in the short time they traveled together, and yet how much they remained strangers. The Oregon immigrants' goals differed, but did their dreams? She knew their fear and their excitement at leaving everything they'd known behind. She felt it pounding in her chest every day. It made her feel alive again in ways she didn't always understand.

A heavyset man on horseback approached her. She recognized him as Mr. Bates.

"Afternoon, Mrs. Harper!" he called out as he rode closer.

"Mr. Bates," she acknowledged.

He looked down at the sign, then took a big breath and sighed. "This is it." He looked northwest, following the line of wagons that had gone before him with his eyes. "I don't know if you can understand or not, Mrs. Harper, but it ain't seemed real until now."

"I assure you, Mr. Bates, I do understand."

He turned back toward her. "It's a big gamble, uprooting the family and all, but my pa did it, moved us from Connecticut to Ohio when I were no taller than this here grass, and his granddaddy did it afore that, comin' from England to the colonies. I cain't be no less a man than them," he said, and Carolina knew he repeated a litany.

"No, I don't suppose you can," she said softly. She saw that uncertainty filled him. Her heart went out to this man and his family.

"I figure it's in the family blood," he went on. He frowned for a moment. "Kinda like an itch that needs scratchin', I guess. I'm glad, though, that my little Jordanna found herself a good man. I was worrit about taking her up there at her age, without being spoken for."

"Mr. Cline seems truly taken with her."

Mr. Bates brightened. "Yes. Yes, that's a fact. A father couldn't wish for better. Mrs. Bates, she says it's a sign from God. Oregon's our promised land." He looked back toward the wagons moving northwest.

"I'd best be going," he finally said, turning back to look at her. "Are you sure you won't come with us? Leave off this New Mexico nonsense? Them Mex, they ain't like regular folk, y'know. Cain't be the place for a gently reared woman such as yourself."

Carolina swallowed a laugh and studiously contrived to keep her face and voice neutral. Where did these odd prejudices spring from? "I must go to Santa Fe, Mr. Bates, but I thank you for your kind offer. I have family in Santa Fe. I shall be fine."

"Well, if'n you're sure . . ."

"I'm sure." She nodded her head toward the northwest-bound wagons. The sunlight had turned golden and the wagons cast long shadows. "You'd best catch up before your good wife worries that you've changed your mind!" she said with a teasing laugh.

"Yes, guess I'd best." He touched his hat in farewell. "Pleasure meetin' you, Mrs. Harper. Best of luck to you." He kicked his heels into his horse and rode off.

"And to you, too, Mr. Bates!" she called after him. "And to you, too," she repeated softly to herself as she watched him ride away. A sudden wind kicked up more dust, hazing the distance, obscuring her view of the wagons and Mr. Bates as if they had been no more than a dream.

She turned her horse toward the west. Ahead lay another trail. No sign indicated its destination. She studied the landscape. The road appeared less distinct than the road to Oregon, for the trail consisted of flattened grass with bare spots, not dusty bare ruts. That difference in appearance brought back Mr. Bates's words to her. The journey hadn't seemed real until now. She sighed and re-settled her veil down over her face, tying it securely behind her neck. Her mare shifted her weight and raised her head. Carolina turned her head in the same direction.

Her caravan had approached faster than she'd anticipated. Mr. Gaspard was almost at her side.

"From here on out, Mrs. Harper, don't ride ahead," he said, frowning, his scraggly brows pulled close over his eyes.

"Mr. Gaspard?" Carolina tossed her head up and stiffened her spine for she couldn't suppress a feeling of pique.

"It's best we all stay together. No wandering off for any purpose. We've got more than a hundred miles to go to get to Council Grove, where we'll hitch up with another caravan. We're a small party. Some might find that easy pickings."

"You mean some Indians?"

"Them, among others," he agreed as his eyes scanned the horizon. He turned back to look at her. "Especially if anyone were foolish enough to go out riding alone."

"I see." Carolina's eyes drifted toward the line of wagons heading northwest.

"Yes, ma'am. From now on, we're on our own."

Carolina nodded and turned her horse back toward her wagons.

May 30, 1846. Continued, night.

Today we parted company with the Oregon immigrants. The trail divided at a simple, weathered sign that said 'Oregon' and pointed away to the northwest. I have a jumble of feelings about parting with the good people in those immigrant wagon trains. But I was touched when Mr. Bates suggested I should accompany them to Oregon. He is quite certain Santa Fe will prove uncivilized. He didn't see any incongruity in suggesting Oregon as an alternative destination! Bless him. All of them shall be in my prayers.

Yes, in my prayers. Those glowing coals among the ashes

*have rekindled a desire to feel again. I only wonder if it's too
late.*

*Tonight Sibby and I are sleeping in the wagon. Mr.
Gaspard assures me a wild thunderstorm is approaching.
Even now I can hear the wind building in ferocity ahead of the
rain. Flashes of lightning augment my lantern light and a
growling thunder lingers. The air smells sharply of rain and
lightning. I close my eyes and inhale deeply, savoring the
clean smell so unlike the cities with their poor drainage and
befouled streets. Heat, dirt, and long days not withstanding, I
am falling in love with the trail.*

*It is, however, cramped for space in this wagon. I am quite
spoiled by my tent, but we shall be more cozy in here and less
likely to feel the worst effects of the storm. I have my little
lantern to write by. Sibby is asleep. I am content.*

THE ROCKING WAGON lulled Carolina's senses. Sleep stole over
her, only to be abruptly chased away by a rock or rut in the road
jarring the wagon, then sleep would creep forward again. Across
from her, Sibby nodded, grumbling without opening her eyes
when another road obstacle hit the wagon's wheels and sent
them swaying. Carolina's mind drifted lazily from idea to memory to projection into the future. It wasn't difficult to trace the
road she'd traveled in her mind to lead her to the road she traveled in body. With yellow fever claiming David, her baby, followed so quickly by her husband's suicide, she'd been left
without purpose.

She acknowledged that the pain of her losses still threatened to
overwhelm her. If a year ago anyone had told her she could feel
such numbing emptiness she would have laughed at them. She
had not thought herself to be a woman who would allow the vi-
cissitudes of life to defeat her, but some days . . .

Still, she would not, could not, live a meaningless life. Nor a life
dependent on others as her in-laws, her stepfather, and her mother

would have her do. There was work for her, a purpose, in New Mexico.

She would not let those children down as she had David.

A shrill whistle cut through the steady lulling sounds of jingling harness chains and creaking wood.

"Jorge! No!"

Carolina roused herself from preoccupation with the past. "What's going on?" She stretched and leaned forward to peer out the Dearborn's canvas bonnet past her driver's shoulder. Bright afternoon sunlight glared white. She blinked, squinted, and raised her hand to shield her eyes.

"No! You damn fool, follow the others!"

It was Mr. Gaspard's voice. Curious, Carolina tried to see Gaspard. "Jorge, what does Mr. Gaspard want? Who's he yelling at?"

"No sé, señora." He flicked the reins against the mules' backs and called out to each like a mother to her child.

"Quicksand! Rein in, man!"

"What? Where?" Carolina struggled to climb over a box of supplies to get to the wagon seat. Her heavy skirts caught on a jagged edge. "Oh, damnation," she muttered as she stopped to release the fabric.

"Miz Carolina!" protested Sibby.

Carolina ignored her. Something was wrong with the mules. They moved awkwardly, no longer in tandem. A mule squealed and tossed its head as a loud sucking caught at its hooves. The wagon lurched. Carolina stared at the earth the mules had sunk into past their knees, earth that just a moment ago had appeared dry, hard packed, and covered with dainty, innocent flowers. And they were still sinking. Her mouth went dry.

"Ay, Dios Mío!" Jorge threw down the reins and leapt from the wagon.

"Jorge!" Carolina scrambled onto the wagon box. Sibby screamed and threw her apron over her head.

Bubbles and a slurping, sucking sound mingled with distant

shouts and swears. Creaking loudly in protest, the wagon began a gentle slide. Carolina grabbed the reins and slapped them against the mules' backs, but knew the futility of the action. The wagon settled up to its front wheel hubs in a mud sinkhole.

Carolina acknowledged a somersaulting tension in her stomach as she realized how fortunate they were that it was not a true quicksand pit. Still, the mud was deep enough and cloying enough to make escape problematic.

The mules squealed and thrashed about in their traces. Carolina knew they'd do more damage to themselves than the mud would if they kept it up. She looked around. The land appeared dry and firm except where the mules and wagon had sunk into the cloying mud soup. She hung on to the edge of the wagon seat as she twisted around to look behind them. Jorge stood on a small elevated ridge of rocky land looking down at the wagon. Mr. Gaspard rode hard toward him, his course erratic as he adroitly avoided other sinkhole prospects.

When Gaspard reached Jorge's ridge of firm land he tightly reined in his horse, wheeling in a circle before bringing the animal to a stiff-legged stop. Off the horse even as the animal landed with all four hooves on the ground, he grabbed Jorge by his shirt and pulled him forward, the two of them nearly nose to nose. His words to the driver were too low and guttural for Carolina to hear, strain as she might. It was obvious to the company, however, that the preternaturally unruffled Gaspard was in a foul temper. He slugged Jorge in the jaw. Carolina bit back a cry of surprise as the Mexican stumbled backward, blood trickling from a split lip.

"You damn Mex!" Gaspard yelled, emphatically spacing out his words. "You ever leave Mrs. Harper in danger again and I'm the one going to be counting coup in these here parts."

The cold fury in Gaspard's voice and on his face set promise to his words. "Now fetch the spare Conestoga tongue," he continued, his voice dropping so that Carolina had to strain to hear him, "and do it fast or I'm going to have you dancing to dodge bullets 'n' knives."

Jorge stumbled toward the big Conestoga. He nodded vigorously, his dark eyes wide with fright, as he blotted his bleeding lip on his shirtsleeve.

Gaspard whistled shrilly and waved the other men to come help. Though he was too far away to hear, Carolina clearly saw an intensity in the man that had all eyes fixed upon him. Curious, she watched him.

He stripped off his leathers.

Carolina felt heat rise in her cheeks. She turned around quickly to look at the mules harnessed to the wagon, but not before she'd seen the broad expanse of his chest covered with springy dark hair, and an edge of white skin as he started to remove his breeches.

She had had no idea Mr. Gaspard would shed all his leathers, or that he should omit wearing all other garments under the leathers! She licked her lips as she struggled to overcome her prurient shock. Mr. Gaspard would likely not take kindly to feminine vapors.

With his hat still on his head and a length of rope coiled over his shoulder, Gaspard walked toward the wagon. As the wagon had already disturbed the mud, it didn't take him long to lose his footing and join the wagon in the ooze. Carolina heard the mud squelch and watched him nearly swim through the mud toward her. The strain was evident in his grimly set jaw. Beads of sweat gathered on his brow. When he reached the wagon's side he was clothed in mud to his waist with large streaks splattered up to his shoulders and across his chest.

Sibby screeched and flung her apron over her head again.

"Mrs. Harper," he said, his breath labored, "I'm going to unhitch the mules. They got their traces all tangled and their heads full of fear. They aren't worth a lick to us right now. When they're out, I'll see how far this mud hole extends. Then we'll decide if we're going to push or pull the wagon out of it. But don't you worry, ma'am. I'll get you out."

Carolina couldn't believe that would be possible. "Wouldn't it be advisable to abandon the wagon here?"

He shook his head. "No, ma'am. There's no need. Seems this sinkhole has got a hard bottom; that's a blessing to us. You won't be in danger if you do as I say. It'll just take some time, is all."

"Oh-h-h-h!" Sibby moaned loudly. "I don't wanna die!"

"Hush, Sibby!" Carolina said, waving her to silence while she watched Mr. Gaspard approach the mules.

"I ain't ready for my Maker!"

"Sibby! Listen to Mr. Gaspard!" Carolina said, finally turning to look at her.

"Please, Miz Carolina." She grabbed Carolina's arm. Caught off balance, Carolina fell against Sibby and the two of them fell against the side of the wagon with a jolt that caused the wagon to slide farther. Sibby screamed. From outside the wagon, Carolina heard Mr. Gaspard curse and a mule bray.

"Sibby!" Carolina snapped. She pulled herself free. "We're not going to die if we do as he says!" She crawled over Sibby to go back to the front of the wagon. "Mr. Gaspard, can I do anything to help?"

"Well, ma'am," Gaspard paused as he fumbled with a harness buckle slippery with mud and looked over his shoulder at her, "I think it best you just sit calmly right there. Wagons get stuck in sinkholes regularly on the trail. It's a damn nuisance—begging your pardon, ma'am—but it ain't a disaster."

Carolina brushed back a strand of hair that had pulled free from her bun and raised an eyebrow at his offhand manner.

Fully clothed, Pedro waded into the mud heading toward the mules. He crooned to them as he came up to their heads. Behind him, a driver brought the team from another Dearborn to the edge of the boggy ground. Over by the Conestoga, Jorge struggled to unlash the heavy spare wagon tongue from where it was stored, hanging from the bottom of the wagon.

Gaspard released the last buckle harnessing the mules to the wagon. "Hee-yah!" he yelled, slapping the rump of the nearest mule. The animal jumped, stiff-legged, forward. Pedro pulled on the team's halters. Gaspard swatted the mule again. When the mules realized they were no longer hitched to the wagon, they tossed their heads and renewed their struggles with the mud. Pedro and Gaspard urged them forward; Pedro from their heads with endearments, Gaspard at their tails with curses. When their front hooves pulled free of the grasping mud, they bucked to kick their rear hooves free, spattering Carolina and Gaspard with mud. The mules tossed their heads and whinnied, bucking again while trying to trot off in different directions.

Gaspard leaned forward, hands braced on his knees, as he watched Pedro calming the mules. He took a couple of deep breaths and shook his head vigorously, as if to clear it of pain or memory. Carolina bit her lower lip, a frown pulling her dark brows together. Mr. Gaspard demanded more of himself than he did of anyone.

He straightened abruptly and waved to the men to come help. They came slowly, shuffling toward the sinkhole, tossing leather chaps, vests, and tobacco pouches aside on dry ground.

"Come on, you no-good, rag-tail bunch of mule chasers! Shake the lead out or I'll put some lead in your backsides!" Gaspard yelled. "Jorge! Bring that tongue here. We'll lever the wagon up, then push her back out."

"Oh, Miz Carolina," Sibby said, rising up from the wagon floor to peer out the wagon's canvas bonnet, "they's all gonna die!"

"Nonsense, Sibby. Stop that at once," Carolina said briskly, not bothering to look at her woman.

"They'll be leavin' us in this devil's hell. I knows it!" Sibby grabbed on to Carolina again.

Carolina winced as her shoulder hit the corner of a large trunk. "Sibby! Stop it!"

"Sweet Jesus, save us!" Sibby yelled, trembling.

Carolina pried Sibby's fingers from her arm, then turned to grab the woman's shoulders to shake her. "Stop it! Stop it, I say!"

"Oh, Lord, what's gonna become of us?" Carolina sobbed, drawing away and folding in on herself.

"If you're going to use the Lord's name then do it properly," Carolina snapped. "Pray that we get out of this mud hole without injury. Don't whine. I can't abide whining."

"Mrs. Harper!"

Carolina scrambled back toward the wagon seat. "Yes, Mr. Gaspard."

"I'm afraid I'm going to have to ask you ladies to sit steady now for a mite. We cain't get the wagon moving backward if you're rocking it."

"Yes, of course. I'm sorry, Mr. Gaspard," Carolina assured him, blushing to her hairline. She turned toward Sibby. "Now's a good time for some of those quiet prayers, Sibby," she said softly.

"Yes'm," Sibby said on a sniff. She dabbed her eyes with her apron, then squeezed them shut while her lips moved in silent prayer. Carolina turned back to watch the men.

They wedged the Conestoga wagon tongue under her wagon at an angle. Four men lifted while two men pushed the wagon backward, their efforts accompanied by a loud slurping sound as the mud struggled to retain possession of the wagon. Then the men moved the wagon tongue closer and repeated the procedure. Slowly the wagon moved backward out of the muck.

The wind died as the men worked, denying them respite from their arduous labor. Carolina felt perspiration drip down the side of her face. She wiped it away with a damp handkerchief. Again the tongue was repositioned, the wagon lifted, and shifted backward another foot. A droning buzz in the air added counterpoint to the grunts and curses of the men as they worked. Carolina slapped the side of her face, and realized Mr. Gaspard's mosquitoes had found them. Again they shifted the tongue, lifted, and slid the wagon back. Carolina fought an urge to scratch and slapped at another droning irritant.

The wagon moved again, this time to the lip of the sinkhole. And there it stayed.

"Come on, boys, put your backs into it!" Gaspard cajoled. The wagon creaked and groaned under the pressure, but it did not move. The air rang blue with curses. Two of the men slipped and fell face first into the mud. The wagon fell forward so suddenly the drop caused Carolina to bite her tongue.

Outside the wagon she heard excited screeching and Spanish chattering. Carolina scrambled out onto the wagon seat. One of the big wheels had trapped one of the men and he was drowning in mud!

Quickly, Gaspard had the men reposition the wagon tongue and lift again. The wagon fell as they pulled the man out, his arm hanging limply at his side.

"My God!" Carolina whispered, then she recovered her wits. "Sibby, one of the men has been hurt. We must help," she said as she swung back into the wagon and bent down to unlace her boots.

"What's you doin'? What's you mean?"

"Hurry!" Carolina stripped off her boots and stockings and, after checking to be certain none of the men were peering into the wagon, she shimmied out of her petticoat.

"Miz Carolina!"

"Come on, Sibby!" Carolina climbed over the wagon seat, stepped onto the running board, and jumped down into the mud. The mud felt cold as it oozed up between her toes and slid up her legs. She tried to take a step toward where they'd carried the fallen man, but she couldn't pull her leg up high enough. She slipped, mud sliding up her arms as she tried to catch herself.

"Mrs. Harper!" protested Gaspard. He sloshed through the mud toward her, his nude body clothed in caking golden-brown mud.

She gasped and looked hurriedly away, then scolded herself for acting the ninny. After all, she had been a married woman. If Mr. Gaspard was not embarrassed to be without clothes, then it behooved her to remain unembarrassed as well. Carolina kept her eyes on his face as she grasped his proffered arm and allowed her-

self to be half pulled, half propelled out of the mud toward the dry
land.

Behind her, Carolina heard Sibby's squeals as the woman tentatively lowered herself into the mud to follow her mistress. Carolina smiled to herself. That was like the Sibby she was
accustomed to. Pride swelled her heart and mind.

May 31, 1846. The Narrows. Day four.
I have learned many things these four days we have been
traveling.
   I have learned I am a selfish, arrogant woman.
   This is not a pretty realization, nor one done lightly. I have
been so wound up in journeying to Santa Fe to handle what I
see as my Christian duty to my little cousins that I've failed to
consider how my actions could effect those about me. I have
pushed Mr. Gaspard and my little caravan to travel longer
and farther every day. So consumed have I been with speed
that I've failed to consider the cost. It is a cost in human
energy and heart, food, and livestock health.
   We encountered a mud sinkhole today. It captured the
wagon I rode in up to the wagon bed. It was a grasping,
sucking mud pulling us into it like some great leviathan of the
deep. It was frightening that in its innocent appearance it
should possess such power. The poor mules became frantic in
their fear. Pedro and Mr. Gaspard had to unharness them from
the wagon, for their fright made them useless in the task of
extricating us. By using a stout piece of lumber, the spare
Conestoga wagon tongue, the men were able to lever the
wagon free and push it to the edge of the sinkhole. From there,
ropes tied from the wagon to another team of mules were used
to pull the wagon completely clear.
   This entire incident was not without its mishap. Hector
Garcia, one of the mule drivers, suffered a dislocated shoulder.
He is lucky his entire arm is not broken; it may have been the

properties of the mud itself that prevented more serious harm. Mr. Gaspard applied a rough-and-ready method to reset the man's shoulder. Hector screamed like he was dying, but he did not pass out, owing, I am certain, to the quantity of alcohol Mr. Gaspard encouraged the man to drink for medicinal purposes before he applied his ungentle yet effective treatment.

The efforts involved in freeing the wagon were herculean. If we were not upon the trail and miles from the last vestiges of civilization, I am convinced the wagon would have been abandoned. After we were free of the sinkhole and cleansed of the mud, I asked Mr. Gaspard why he went to such effort to free the wagon. Mr. Gaspard told me nothing is easily or quickly abandoned on the trail. Every piece of wood, scrap of cloth, and crust of food is jealously guarded, for all too soon it may prove to be the last such item standing between an individual and death.

In all the times people have spoken to me of the dangers of the trail, I'll own they have never communicated its reality so effectively as that simple statement coupled with the proof of the effort the men were willing to exert to save the wagon. Sweat dripped off creased brows, veins stood out on corded necks, and muscles bulged until I thought they should burst under the strain. Even Sibby, who as I have previously written has been beset by fears, rallied at the last to brave the mud and help tend the injured man. I am very lucky and humbled in my traveling companions.

5

THE NIGHT PEARLED gray with approaching dawn as Carolina came out of her tent, a folded length of linen in her arms. She shivered against the lingering night chill. Though the morning campfire drew her, she savored the slight chill for its own sake. She knew that too soon she'd be hot and damp with sweat under the day's fierce sun.

Seeing her approach, Pedro poured a mug of coffee and handed it to her. She murmured her thanks as she tucked the linen under her arm so she could wrap both hands around the steaming mug.

"Do you know where Sibby is?" she asked between sips.

Pedro shrugged. "*No sé, señora.*"

Carolina's gaze traveled the circle of their camp. "She's probably down by the stream," she offered, more to herself than to Pedro. "But perhaps it *would* be best if you helped me."

"Señora?"

"I want to bind Hector's arm close to his body. If he's to heal quickly he has to keep the arm still. The temptation to use it will be too great if it's not bound to his side."

"Hector, he will not like that," Pedro said, dolefully shaking his head.

"I don't suppose anyone would. No matter. It must be done," she said, setting her coffee mug down by the fire. "Follow me. We'd best get to it."

She led the way to where the mule and ox drivers lounged on the grass by the big Conestoga wagon smoking cigarillos and finishing their coffee. Pedro reluctantly followed. Carolina knelt down beside the sinewy old Mexican with a sling around his neck. He leaned back on his good arm and held his corn-husk cigarillo in the sling hand.

"When you're finished with your cigarillo I need to take a look at your arm."

He gingerly raised his hand to his lips, wincing in exaggerated pain, and took a long inhale on his cigarillo. *"Por que?"* the man grunted as he blew smoke out his nose and into her face.

Carolina closed her eyes against the acrid cloud, then she slowly and deliberately waved the smoke away. Furious at the deliberate affront, Pedro began yelling in Spanish, but Carolina held up her hand to abruptly stem Pedro's passion. When she opened her eyes again, there was no sympathy or compassion in her gaze for the injured driver. Hector Garcia looked away as he shifted position to sit up straighter.

Carolina stared coldly at Garcia as she grabbed the cigarillo from between his fingers and ground it into the dirt.

"Aiyee!" the man yelled, scrambling for the crushed butt.

She slapped her hand down over the cigarillo. "I said I want to look at your arm," she said evenly though her heart raced and in her stomach thousands of frantically beating butterfly wings made her nauseous.

He glared at her.

"Excuse me, ma'am," Mr. Gaspard said congenially as he came to stand beside her. Then he looked down at Garcia and grabbed him by his shirt front and hauled him upright. Garcia yowled in pain.

"Mrs. Harper wants to preserve your miserable hide," Gaspard told him with hard-edged pleasantry.

"*Pero, señor! Señor, por favor!* She take my cigarillo!"

"You don't blow smoke in a lady's face."

"Señor! I meant no disrespect," babbled Garcia.

"Apologize to Mrs. Harper," Gaspard said, twisting his hand tighter in the man's shirt front.

"Señora!" Garcia squeaked. He tried to twist his head to see her. "*Señora, por favor! Lo siento mucho. Madre de Dios!* The pain in my shoulder, it make me crazy. *Por favor, señora!*"

"Mr. Gaspard, please!" Carolina protested weakly. It would have made a better impression on this man and the other drivers if Gaspard could have left well enough alone. Though she did wonder just what Garcia thought Mr. Gaspard was going to do to him.

Gaspard looked down at her. "Mrs. Harper?" He eased his grip on Garcia's shirt front. The man sagged down, almost falling against him.

Carolina sighed, then set her jaw and rose to her feet. "The arm should be held rigidly to give the shoulder time to heal. If it is bound to his body, that will reduce any occurrence of accidental movement. I've brought a length of linen to support it," she said, unfolding the cloth.

Gaspard nodded. He helped her position the cloth against Garcia's body and wrap it over his injured arm and under his good arm. When the arm was tightly secured against Garcia's side, Carolina stepped back to survey their handiwork.

"That should hold it. If you wear the arm supported in this manner," she told Garcia, "in two or three days it will be well enough to remove the binding and continue with only a sling until the shoulder is completely healed. In the meantime, you will help herding the livestock. On foot," she said crisply.

"But, my wagon!" Garcia protested.

"Pedro will drive your wagon."

"Pedro! *Pero—*"

"And with each step you take you will remember that I do not accept anyone questioning my instructions. Nor do I like cigarillo smoke," she finished, her tone soft but implacable. "Do you understand?"

Hector Garcia looked from Carolina to Mr. Gaspard and back. "*Sí*, señora," he said.

She nodded, and turned to walk back toward the campfire. Mr. Gaspard fell into step beside her.

Carolina folded her arms across her stomach. The butterflies were still there, though their numbers seemed to have lessened. She took several deep breaths, then noticed Mr. Gaspard looking at her, his brows drawn together in concern. One corner of her mouth curved upward in a wry smile. "I'm all right."

He snorted, but refrained from any other comment.

"Have you seen Sibby?" she asked him as they approached the main campfire. She bent down to retrieve her coffee mug. When he didn't answer immediately she looked up at him. He had an odd expression on his face, almost one of disbelief. She raised one eyebrow, a slight frown tightening her mouth.

"I think she's down by the stream," he finally said. "That's where I saw her heading at first light."

Carolina nodded as she grabbed the coffeepot handle with her apron and refilled her cup. "Would you care for any, Mr. Gaspard?"

"Thank you, ma'am."

"How much delay did we suffer by yesterday's excitement?"

He shook his head. "Not much. We should still reach Council Grove by June fourth."

She looked at him in surprise. "Of course, that means barring any more mishaps," she said dryly.

"Yes," he agreed, "barring any more mishaps. And if we break camp in good time every day."

"Ah! There's Sibby!" she said when she saw her maid climb the bank from the stream. "Sibby! Where have you been? Hurry up! We must get packing!" she called out. Carolina threw the dregs of

her coffee on the ground. "We'll not hold you up, Mr. Gaspard,"
she promised before she hurried into her tent.

June 1, 1846. Early morning, day five.
> *I haven't much time to write this morning for even now the
> mule and ox drivers are hitching their teams to the wagons.
> But I am stealing a few moments. I had an interesting
> situation arise this morning, one for which there was probably
> no right way to react. It brought forcibly to mind the
> limitations I face as a woman merchant.*
>
>   *Hector Garcia, the driver who dislocated his shoulder
> yesterday, questioned an instruction I gave him and
> deliberately blew cigarillo smoke in my face. I was so angry! I
> have not felt that much anger since the Harper family
> insinuated that I was the cause of Edward's erratic behavior.
> Strangely, now as then, I maintained a rigid outward
> demeanor while inside my body shivered like willows in the
> wind. Before I could think I grabbed the cigarillo from his
> hand and ground it into the dirt. I know, I know, that was not
> wise. My stomach quivered abominably when I came to my
> senses and realized what I had just done, but I braved it out,
> determined to have the man do as I say. I realized if I did not,
> if I backed down, I should lose all the respect of the men and
> that is not a circumstance I want! There are too many miles
> yet between us and Santa Fe.*
>
>   *But just as quickly as all this flowed through my mind and
> I became comfortable in my actions, Mr. Gaspard thrust
> himself into the situation. He grabbed Garcia by his shirt front
> and hauled him to his feet, then he told him that he owed me
> respect. But now, I wonder, if these men owe me anything. I
> have not demonstrated any ability to lead. I brazened it out,
> nonetheless, and even declared the man should walk today
> instead of ride. Only time will tell, I suppose, as to the effect of
> this morning's activities. Santa Fe remains a long way away.*

Though I have made Mr. Gaspard captain of our enterprise, I must take a more active role.

I am still worried about Sibby. Her behavior is not as I would expect. This morning I could not find her for nearly an hour. These extended periods of absence in the morning are becoming common. Sometimes I worry for her state of mind and if I shall ever see her again.

Ah! I hear harnesses jingling. We must be nearly ready to leave. I've decided to ride today so I'd best check on my mare.

June 3, 1846. Day seven.

The bloom is scarce off the rose and already my good intentions falter. We have traveled the trail seven days and I have not maintained my promise to keep a faithful daily record of all that transpires. But what is there to report? This prairie rolls on and on. Excitement at the prospect of this journey has given way to reality. I see neither the romance nor the adventure of trekking across this unchanging landscape. One day is much like the next and the one before in all aspects. Hot, dirty, and long.

As I read over what I have just written I fear I sound melancholy, as if already I regret my decisions. No, I do not. What I believe is my affliction is a healthy tonic dose of truth. Oh, that such truths could truly be bottled and peddled across the land! I have not set myself a trivial task to journey to New Mexico. It is a task fraught with complication and difficulty. But I digress. Neither do I mean to set myself up as some philosopher! My contract with you is to write of the sights and events so you might vicariously experience my journey. I should leave the pondering of greater issues to others more qualified to wear the mantle.

We make steady progress, but the days are long and monotonous. To my dismay I find I can neither read nor write while riding in the wagon without queasiness besetting my stomach, so the hours pass slowly, leaving me entirely to the less than tender mercies of my thoughts and memories. Oh, how they whip me! Again I am plagued with doubts and filled with guilt. Could I have somehow done something differently that would have stayed the hand of God from taking my son from me and driving my husband to his final end? In my thoughts, I know the answer is no, but in my heart . . . ah, that is where the truth lies.

I rode my mare most of yesterday, but the dry wind has scoured my complexion so that today I retreated to my wagon with grease upon my face. It is not that I believe the grease cures the wind's ravages; but I do believe it provides my skin respite, an opportunity, perhaps, to become accustomed to wind. Mr. Gaspard tells me I should be grateful to the wind, or see it as the lesser of two evils. When the winds die down, which he assures me happens frequently, the prairie becomes alive with thousands of mosquitoes. Much more so than we experienced the day my wagon was caught in the mud. My skin itches at the mere thought!

I have come to accept the fact we shall not catch the spring caravan at Council Grove. The journey to Council Grove from Independence, Missouri, normally takes ten to twelve days. Though we are traveling faster than most caravans and should be in Council Grove tomorrow, we could not have hoped to get there in fewer than seven or eight days. And most likely, with the threat of war, the big caravans probably left Council Grove even before we started on our journey. Nonetheless, we press forward. Mr. Gaspard assures me the traffic to Santa Fe will be heavy enough this year, consequently we are bound to encounter other groups to travel with.

Despite the sameness of our days Sibby is restless and full of fears. She was a rock for me in my time of trials and sorrows. She helped me regain my will to live! No, more than that, she helped me see that my life could have meaning. I find

I have a difficult time reconciling the woman I knew then with the woman who is my traveling companion now. She is plagued by nightmares and startles as easily as a deer. I have had to be quite firm with her on several occasions lest she dissolve into hysteria. Something is troubling her, something beyond a new adventure. I wish she would trust me to help her. I perhaps have not been as patient as I might be. And her continued reticence fuels my impatience. In truth, as of late I have been prone to irritation and hurtful comments. I do not understand what causes this behavior in me. It is not how I would view myself, nor do I feel it could be caused by Sibby's behavior alone. Something churns within my mind and heart. I must pray for patience and guidance.

June 4, 1846. Morning, day eight.
We will be foregoing our afternoon "nooning it" time in favor of pressing on to our immediate destination: Council Grove. Mr. Gaspard assures me we can be at this preeminent meeting ground for Santa Fe caravans by midafternoon. The time and the miles underfoot cannot come too quickly!

I have mercifully recovered from my odd mood of last evening. I can never recall being in that unusual humor before. I think the fault lies with becoming too full of my own company. I wish Sibby were more sensible. We used to talk for hours, now we hardly say ten words all day. I know Sibby did not want to make this trip, that she has been frightened of it. I suppose I never considered how fear could twist someone up so inside. But I'm learning because I'm afraid. I'm afraid of losing a friend. I am glad, however, to see Sibby talking to others if she won't talk to me. Pedro gives her Spanish lessons and several of the drivers laughingly contribute to her lessons and her vocabulary. Of course, all they wish to teach are the words not suitable for polite company. In listening to them I find I remember more

*than I thought I ever knew! It is all I can do to maintain a
calm demeanor and act as if I do not understand. I believe
I've been successful. Except for Mr. Gaspard. He knows I
understand and takes enjoyment out of my attempts to
pretend I don't!*

*So, what do I do when time hangs heavy and I have no one
to converse with and nothing new to relate to you of our
journey? I sew and knit some. I've repaired shirts, jackets, and
vests for the men of this company, but there is only so much to
repair. I am not a woman to be idle. It plagues me more than
fear. Or perhaps, idleness breeds fear for the mental demons
that creep out to beleaguer me. I'm not certain.*

*Pedro has come to dismantle my tent. We will soon be
breaking camp. Strangely I feel a welling excitement within
me to rival that of any child's anticipation for a trip or special
gift. I consider Council Grove another milestone for our
journey, our first major milestone since the road cut-off to the
Oregon territory. Though I know now that we shall not meet
the major caravans at Council Grove, I find I do hope for at
least one other caravan going in our direction. Apart from the
dangers of this journey, worse I believe is the boredom. I look
forward to new faces.*

THE DARK GREEN on the horizon heralded the thick timbers at
Council Grove; thin spirals of white smoke said at least one other
party of travelers occupied the area. Carolina rode forward alongside Mr. Gaspard at the head of the caravan.

"It looks as if we will not be staying long at Council Grove waiting for another caravan to come," she said.

"No," he agreed, but a frown creased his brow.

"What's the matter?"

"That's a good-sized enterprise. The only companies that big to
leave Missouri ahead of us should have been well down the trail
by now."

"Maybe it's not just one company."

"Maybe," he said laconically.

"Well, even if it is one company, what is your worry?"

"I don't know. Maybe accident or illness. Maybe trouble."

Carolina laughed. "Well, I do pay you to be careful, but I'm beginning to think you take your job too seriously," she teased.

He turned his cool gray eyes upon her and suddenly they had the appearance of whetted steel as sharp as her Green River knife and as likely to cut right through her. "The trail's not something to take lightly at any time."

Carolina looked at him closely, a slight frown pulling her brows together. "Mr. Gaspard, I am not saying it is. I am merely saying you are too skittish and surely that has as many contraindications as a complete lack of care for one's surroundings and circumstances. It leads to jumping at shadows," she said in as equitable a tone as she could manage. Mr. Gaspard's manner irritated her. "I will ride ahead and—"

"No!" he said firmly, shooting her a frowning glance from beneath furrowed brows.

"Nonsense. I—"

He grabbed her horse's reins.

Carolina looked at him in surprise. "I beg your pardon!" she said quellingly.

"Remember what I told you when we passed the Oregon turnoff?" he asked softly. "Don't ride ahead of the caravan. For any reason."

"Yes, normally." She shook her head. "But you are not making sense, Mr. Gaspard. This is just Council Grove." She could feel her temper gathering.

He held her reins firmly. "Mrs. Harper, I'm not different from you in what I want and expect from others. Right now I feel like you did when Garcia blew cigarillo smoke in your face."

"I don't understand."

"As captain of this enterprise, when I give an order I expect it to be obeyed without question," he said, releasing her reins and leaning back in his saddle, one hand resting on his hip.

"I agree. But . . . Oh." She stopped, her mind ahead of her words.

"For the well being of this enterprise," he continued solemnly.

She cocked her head to the side as she considered him. "All right, Mr. Gaspard," she said, though she wondered why he should choose this moment to make his point. She frowned, then cast a sideways glance in his direction. "When different parties join together for the sake of safety in traveling," she said slowly, "what happens?"

"You mean in the way of governance?"

"Yes."

They rode together in silence for a moment. "A captain is elected to lead the entire enterprise," he finally said. "Normally it is the captain of the largest caravan."

"So we may be led by someone other than yourself."

"Yes, ma'am."

"And do we owe this person unquestioning allegiance?"

Gaspard stared at the white smoke plumes rising in the air above the Council Grove area. "Now, ma'am, you come to the crux of the problem. Unquestioning allegiance implies trust, and trust is a very special and fragile commodity on the prairie."

"But?"

He sighed. "It's too often abused or forgotten. Out here, every man, or woman, has to think of himself first in order to survive. With that necessity, where does trust belong?" He shook his head. "Hell, I'm sounding like one of those damn philosophers who sit back in their plush homes and write about life in the west. As if they knew. I promise you this, though, while I may not be captain of our travels after today, I'll watch after you and yours same as I've been doing. I just ask that you let me do the deciding when and where we're to place trust. I know the trail, and I know the kinda people who go down this trail."

"Why is that important?"

"Damn it, woman, there you go again."

"But why is it so difficult to give me an answer?"

"This isn't an immigrant trail. It's a commerce trail and where there's money involved, well, ma'am, that breeds a different kinda man."

"I see. I'll own I had not thought of the trail in quite that context." She thought about the immigrants she'd met. They had to trust each other, for their success depended in great part upon cooperation. But what of the merchant caravans? If there wasn't the threat of trouble from Indians, would one help another? Her stepfather was a St. Louis merchant. Though he had many friends in the business, they were not close friends and when misfortune overtook one or another confederate, the trait of the society was to distance itself from the unfortunate. Mr. Gaspard himself was a loner. Who better than a loner to understand other loners?

"All right, Mr. Gaspard. I will keep my trust with you. But for my peace, when I ask *why*, I would like an answer. It is not a matter of questioning your decisions, it is a matter of understanding them. For me."

"I'm not accustomed to accounting for myself," he said brusquely, scowling at her.

"And I am not your wife or a woman from whom you may demand unquestioning obedience. I am your employer."

He stared at her for a long silent moment, then he took off his hat and wiped his forehead with the back of his hand as he laughed. "I guess when a man's not used to a woman boss, that takes a bit of reminding."

"Truce?"

He resettled his hat on his head. "Truce."

Looking again toward Council Grove, Carolina could see that their approach had been noticed. Two men on horseback were riding toward them.

"Well, I'll be." Gaspard murmured.

Carolina looked at him, but his eyes were on the approaching men. She saw his cold visage melt. A slow, lopsided smile pulled at his scarred face and crinkled the corners of his gray eyes. She looked back toward the riders approaching them. One of them waved his hand in salute, then broke into a gallop toward them, whooping at the top of his lungs. "Gerry! Hey, Gerry, you old sorry excuse for a two-legged varmint!"

The man rode straight at them, only sawing his reins to the side and pulling up on his horse when Carolina thought disaster was imminent. Her horse crow-jumped nervously as the man swung his horse alongside Gaspard. His horse reared and pawed the ground, pulling its head up. Good-humoredly the man brought the animal under control and patted its neck. Carolina was amazed the horse could rear so high, for the man on its back was a broad-shouldered giant.

"Jed!" Gaspard exclaimed. He reached out to clasp arms with the other man. "I heard you'd taken a train this spring. I thought you'd be nearly to the Cimarron cutoff by now."

The man called Jed let his smile slip. "We shoulda been by now, but dammit—begging your pardon, ma'am," he said, acknowledging Carolina's presence with a tip of his hat, "if we haven't had the devil's worse luck. Come on to camp and I'll tell you about it. But what have you got here for yourself, you sly old dog?" he said, winking and jerking his head in Carolina's direction.

"Don't go to point, Rawlins," Gaspard said dryly. He turned his head toward Carolina. "Mrs. Harper, this ill-mannered lout is Jedediah Rawlins. Jed, this is Mrs. Harper."

Rawlins tipped his hat. "Pleased to meet you, ma'am. Sorry for the horseplay. Gerry and I go way back."

"No offense taken, Mr. Rawlins," she said.

Rawlins hailed the man who was still walking his horse toward them, then he turned back to Carolina and Gaspard to introduce them to Egan Bush, his wagon master. Then the four of them continued on toward the camp, Carolina's wagons coming steadily behind them.

As they rode into the Council Grove area Carolina looked about, judging the size of the camp. The camp was situated on a hill edged by a thick grove of trees. She counted twenty-two Murphy wagons and six Dearborns. Beyond them, grazing in the plentiful grass, must have been over one hundred horses, mules, and oxen. A sound of squawking drew Carolina's attention. Her eyebrows rose in surprise at seeing a small flock of chickens.

She heard a laugh from beside her. Mr. Rawlins stood at her side ready to lift her off her horse.

"My wife is a fanatic about her chickens," he said as he helped her down.

"Singing Waters is with you, then?" Gaspard asked as he took the reins to Carolina's horse.

"She scarcely lets me out of her sight." He turned toward Carolina. "Come, I'll introduce you. Or would you rather wait for Mr. Harper?"

"Mr. Harper is not with us. He is deceased."

"Oh, I'm sorry. I . . ." He looked in confusion toward Gaspard.

Gaspard paused in leading the horses away. "Mrs. Harper is my employer."

Seeing the shock on Rawlins's face, Carolina laughed. "When our camp has been set up and our stock tended to, perhaps we may all sit together for a time and trade stories," she suggested.

"I'll look forward to it, ma'am. I certainly will."

June 4, 1846. Evening.

We arrived at Council Grove a little past midday to discover, to my delight, that another enterprise camped in the area. It is a fair-sized party of some twenty-eight wagons. It is captained by Jedediah Rawlins, who Mr. Gaspard knows quite well. Mr. Rawlins is a big lion of a man. He would be a man to respect and perhaps fear if one did not see the twinkle of mischief in

*his outwardly bland light brown eyes. He is also, I must add
in true honesty, one of the most handsome men I have seen in
over six months. The New Orleans belles would swoon!*

*Mr. Rawlins has with him his wife, an Indian woman
named Singing Waters, who is of the Cheyenne tribe. She is
heavily pregnant. I have not asked her directly, for she is
exceedingly shy around me, but I believe her to be in her
eighth month. Her shyness, Mr. Gaspard tells me, stems from
her experience with the attitudes of white women toward
Indians, particularly Indian women who have married white
men. They have been quite cruel. Can you believe that once
when she went to wash some of Mr. Rawlins's clothes in a
stream, the white women there before her hurried away and
later sent their menfolk to Mr. Rawlins, telling him not to
have his "dirty squaw" come anywhere near their women!
And that is not the only incidence he related. She has been so,
so browbeaten by the reaction of white people to her that
whenever Mr. Rawlins must go to a city or town, she camps
alone, several miles away, until he is done with his business.
Hearing Mr. Gaspard's recitation of some of Singing Waters'
experiences set my blood to boiling. Sometimes I swear
members of the fairer sex embarrass me. I shall make a firm
endeavor to befriend her.*

*Before supper Sibby and I washed some clothes in the creek
as did several of the men from our party. Singing Waters did
not join us, though I noted her quietly headed in that direction
with clothes in her arms after I returned to camp. Those
wounds she suffered from the behavior of others may not be
visible, but they scar fiercely. I must do something to heal
those wounds!*

*Writing of women in the party reminds me of Sibby's
reaction to our new companions. She seems much calmer, even
happier. I am beginning to wonder if it was not the smallness
of our party that has had her tied in knots. She is even now
helping with the injured man, and talking to me again!*

Oh! I have not told you of the injured man as of yet. He is the reason the Rawlins caravan remains in Council Grove. His name is Ralph Grady.

Mr. Grady was working on repairs to one of the wagons— several were damaged in quagmires and mud sinkholes at the Narrows—when the wagon support broke and the wagon fell on him, crushing his abdomen, hip, and leg. His injuries are too severe for the man to recover; but he is a tough old codger and has been hanging on to life by a thread for three days now. It is evident that the man is in a great deal of pain. It will be a mercy when he dies.

Between the difficulties Mr. Rawlins's caravan encountered at the Narrows, the necessity to make repairs and prepare additional replacement wagon parts, and now Mr. Grady's injury, Mr. Rawlins's enterprise lags two weeks behind in their travel. Pedro tells me there is much grumbling among the men for the delay. Many of the teamsters have brought merchandise of their own to sell in Santa Fe. They are worried that the delay will cause them to greet a glutted market when they finally do arrive. Scowling faces and small knots of men talking in whispers are not conducive to a successful enterprise. I think their fears shall prove hollow. With Mexico on the brink of war with the United States, New Mexican citizens will eagerly buy all they can for fear the conduit shall be closed indefinitely.

However, I cannot help feeling guilty that, except for Mr. Grady, their misfortune is our fortune. Beyond Council Grove Mr. Gaspard would not lead my caravan without the safety of larger numbers.

Enough. I should tell you of the sights! That is my charter.

Here at Council Grove there is a half-mile band of timber running through the area that is full of oak, walnut, ash, hickory, and elm. Through this timber band runs Council Grove Creek, a principal branch of the Neosho River. The land on either side of the stream looks to be excellent farming acreage should one day the Indians' title to the land ever cease. There are rolling prairie hills and verdant valleys full of wild grapes hard by.

This afternoon I took a walk upon one of these hills. Mr. Gaspard suggested the walk so he might have an opportunity to impress upon the gentlemen of Mr. Rawlins's enterprise that I am not a woman for whom they are to entertain any flirtatious notions. He seemed to feel this was important. After meeting Mr. Rawlins, I do not think he would hire any man who was not as good as his bond; but I did not argue with Mr. Gaspard, for idle hands . . . Besides, a walk suited me. I sat for a time atop one of the hills studying the horizon in all four directions. There is an awesome beauty to the land, and the air is so fresh and clean I understand why men first came here.

6

THE CAMP ROSE early, the men off in teams felling hickory and ash trees for wood necessary to repair damaged wagons and supply spare wagon parts. But early or late, Carolina would have been hard pressed to say the time of day exactly, for the sky remained an even leaden gray. The air smelled of impending rain. Watching them from a distance, Carolina detected a certain frenzy in the actions of the men. They obviously hoped to finish the greater part of their work before the rains fell.

Her eyes swept the camp. Sibby could not be found. Again.

Irritation hardened the line of Carolina's jaw. She resolved she would deal with Sibby later. At the moment she wanted to visit Mr. Grady's tent and see if she could help Singing Waters in her care of the man.

Carolina stopped at the opening to the tent and peered inside. Singing Waters knelt beside Grady, changing his bandages, her beautiful face contorted with sorrow.

"Is there anything I can do to help?" Carolina softly asked.

Singing Waters looked up, her expression smoothing out until a gentle smile lifted the corner of her lips, then faded again. She rocked back on her heels, arching her back. Then she pointed to the bandages on Grady's crushed hip. She shook her head and sighed. "They stick."

"Shall I get some hot water?"

A fleeting smile returned. She nodded.

Carolina smiled back and left. As she walked down to the stream to fill a bucket, she wondered again where Sibby could be hiding herself. And why. Her frown deepened as she carried the water back to the cooking area. She filled a large pot with water and balanced it on a sturdy tripod of three rocks in the midst of the fire. While the water heated she braced her hands on her hips and again looked around the camp for Sibby.

"Sibby! Sibby!" she called out. She walked the inside perimeter of the camp. "Sibby! Where are you!" She knew her voice was rising in inflection, anger giving way to a slowly building fear. She heard a strange, muffled sound.

Carolina tried to regulate her breathing. She needed to be calm. She walked slowly in the direction of the sound and stopped not far from her own tent. She listened to the sounds around and in the camp. When the strange sound came again, she recognized it as a muffled sob. Quietly, she followed the sound to its source.

Sibby!

She found her behind a tent curled into a ball, her face wet with tears.

"Sibby! What is it? What's the matter?" Carolina asked as she twitched her skirts aside so she could sit on the ground next to her. She drew her maid toward her until Sibby's head rested on her lap. She stroked her forehead with one hand while the other searched her apron pocket for a handkerchief to blot her tears.

All the anger and frustration leached out of Carolina. "Tell me," she whispered, her heart aching for the unknown agony within Sibby.

Sibby clung to her, her thin shoulders shaking. "Oh, Miz Carolina! I been bad, and, and the Lord, he's punishing me!" she said on a hiccuping wail, her tears flowing freely again.

"What? Sibby, what are you talking about?" She pushed Sibby up to a sitting position. "Here, take my handkerchief," she said earnestly as she searched her maid's face. "Now stop crying," she pleaded. She drew Sibby toward her to wrap her arms around her in a hug. She patted and rubbed her back soothingly. "Sh-h-h. Stop crying. Whatever it is, we can see it through. Let me help."

Sibby buried her face in the handkerchief and just shook her head. "You-ou-ou cain't help," she hiccuped.

"Tell me Sibby."

"I'm, I'm increasing!" she cried.

Carolina stopped rubbing Sibby's back. *A child. David.* Pain ripped through her. Strange, she'd thought herself beyond pain. She wrapped her arms tightly around Sibby, but in her mind, it wasn't Sibby she held. She felt a pudgy little body full of scarcely contained energy. She smelled nursery soap and dirt.

She closed her eyes against the memory, then opened them and put her hands on Sibby's shoulders. She pushed her up so she could see her tear-streaked face. "You're with child?" she asked gently. A fragment within her hoped she'd misunderstood.

Gloomily Sibby nodded, her lower lip trembled, then she wailed again and shoved the handkerchief back up to her eyes.

"Gracious," Carolina murmured faintly, her mind racing. "When? Who? One of the men in our party?"

Sibby shook her head. "N-no," she gulped. "It were, it were J-J-Jeremy Tuttle."

"From St. Louis. Oh, dear. Then that means you're at least six weeks along."

Sibby nodded miserably.

"If you were sweet on Jeremy you should have told me! You could have stayed with my mother and stepfather!"

Sibby shook her head. "Th-that's what's so bad. I didn't care none for Jeremy more'n a friend, b-but he jest kept after me about this trip and all the dangers. Hearin' everything, I, I knew I couldn't let you go by yourself, you needed me, but he made me so skairt that I, that I . . ."

"That you turned to him for comfort."

Sibby nodded, her lip quivering again.

Carolina sighed. "Oh, was there never such a coil," she murmured to herself as she stared off at the dark cloud shapes above Sibby's head.

Sibby came because I needed her. The thought made her throat tight. Did she deserve such loyalty?

"We will work this out. And you are right," Carolina said, smiling and looking at Sibby's tear-streaked face. "I *do* need you. Just now I was looking for you to ask for your help. . . . Oh, my gracious! The water!" she exclaimed. She got to her feet and pulled Sibby up with her.

"That length of linen we used to bind up Garcia's arm, has it been cleaned?"

"Yes'm," Sibby said, blinking rapidly and sniffing to dry the tears.

"Find it, please, and bring it to Mr. Grady's tent. Singing Waters wants to change his bandages and I think that linen might prove useful. I've heated some water, which I'll take to her now. We'll talk more later," Carolina promised as she backed away. She turned and ran toward the fire.

The water boiled furiously. Carolina used an iron hook to remove the pot from the fire, then she wrapped the corner of her apron around the pot handle so she could carry it.

She was ten feet away from the tent when she heard the scream.

Carolina ran, the boiling water she carried sloshing out of the pot, scalding her hands and splashing down her dress. Inside, the tent smelled of death. A blanket covered Grady's body. Singing Waters crouched in a corner, her eyes wide. In front of her stood a hissing black and white animal. A skunk.

Foaming saliva dripped from its mouth.

Blood dripped from Singing Waters' hand.

Carolina gasped. The animal turned and leapt toward her. She screamed, and threw the boiling water at it. The animal squealed in high-pitched rage. It twisted in midair, then darted past Carolina and out of the tent.

Stunned, she watched it run past her. *The animal was rabid!* Slowly her head turned back to look at Singing Waters. And it had bitten Singing Waters!

Dimly Carolina heard Sibby yelling and the sound of men's shouts and running feet. Trembling, she put her arm around Singing Waters and drew her to her feet, her eyes fixed upon the blood beginning to coagulate on Singing Waters' hand.

"Come, we must get that wound cleaned out," she said shakily.

Singing Waters just turned her head to look at her, her eyes bleak.

Carolina swallowed past the sudden lump in her throat and took a deep breath against the weight in her chest. "Come on. It will be all right," she said. But her voice rose in a question for which they both knew the answer. Determinedly she propelled her forward.

At the tent entrance they were met by Egan Bush. He took one look at Singing Waters's hand and crossed himself, muttering, "Damn phoby cat."

Behind him came Jedediah Rawlins. He pushed Bush aside. His dark, weathered complexion visibly palled when he saw Singing Waters' hand. "Oh my God!" he whispered.

"Move, please," Carolina said. "We must get the wound clean. Sibby! Fetch some water." She fell into the businesslike mein that had stood her in good stead during those last few months in New Orleans: during the yellow fever epidemic, her baby's illness and death, her husband's increasing insanity and final suicide.

Today it helped her keep the horror away from her consciousness. Rabies!

The men silently backed away from the tent entrance. Rawlins put his arm around his wife, his face wet.

Singing Waters drew a long shuddering breath, then she raised

her head. "I make poultice to put on bite. You help?" she asked
Carolina.

"All I can," she said. Tears rolled down her cheeks.

June 5, 1846, Council Grove.

*It is late and I am tired to the depths of my soul, but sleep
eludes me. I expect it will for hours yet as it has often enough
in the months past. Rain pounds down upon the wagon
canvas above my head in rhythm with the pounding in my
head. I thought perhaps writing of today might help.
Unfortunately I don't know where to begin. And I'm half
afraid fresh tears will fall to stain and blur whatever I do
write. Yet, for all of that, I am numb.*

It is probably best to baldly begin.

Today, a hydrophobic skunk bit Singing Waters.

*How simple that sounds, so innocuous, as if one were
saying that today their cat scratched them. But it isn't simple,
nor forgettable.*

*It all happened so fast. Perhaps if I hadn't spent so much
time with Sibby I might have been there. I might have been
able to do something! Anything! I might have been able to
prevent death from hovering over this gentle woman's head!*

*My heart is breaking. Why is it always the innocent? Why
is it never those of us who are less than perfect? Are we to be
somehow saved by another's suffering? If that is so, I would
not be saved.*

*These words and more have run through my head all day.
Could I have made a difference?*

*I volunteered to heat some water so Singing Waters and I
could change Grady's bandage. While the water heated I went
looking for Sibby. As I have mentioned elsewhere in this
journal, Sibby has made a habit of disappearing for a time
every morning. This morning I was determined to find her
and call her to task for her disappearances. I found her crying*

behind a tent. It seems the woman was caught by Jeremy Tuttle before we left St. Louis and is increasing. My poor brain foundered on this knowledge; but that is another tale which I shall have to go into another time. My mind is too unsettled.

After I calmed Sibby I got the pot of water and walked toward the tent where Mr. Grady lay at death's door. I was almost to the tent when I heard Singing Waters scream.

I ran into the tent. From Singing Waters' hand dripped blood. In front of her stood a skunk with frothing spittle dripping from its mouth. I think I screamed, or something. I don't recall; but then the animal turned toward me. In terror I threw the boiling water on it. The animal shrieked and escaped from the tent.

From what Singing Waters told me later, I gather that Grady had just died. She was pulling the blanket over him in white man fashion, she said, when the skunk, who had evidently come into the tent while she was ministering to Grady, bit her hand. She hadn't seen him or smelled him.

I must admit that I was surprised that the animal did not leave his odiferous mark. Mr. Bush, however, told me that hydrophobic skunks, phoby cats, he called them, aren't afraid, which is generally the reason a skunk sprays. They're in a mad frenzy. He said anytime you see a skunk in the daytime, it's probably a phoby cat because skunks are nighttime animals. The knowledge that the skunk is probably still alive somewhere has everyone in camp nervous.

Everyone except Singing Waters.

After her initial shock she became frighteningly serene. I do not know or understand Indian beliefs but she is accepting of her fate. Her only hope centers on her unborn child. For the child's sake she hopes the dreaded madness is held away until after the baby is born. Mr. Bush says the rabies madness may come in four days or in four months, there is no way of

*predicting. He says if the skunk is rabid, and he has few
doubts on that score, there is no maybe about Singing Waters
getting the madness.*

*I swear, thinking of the madness, waiting for the madness
tears one's soul asunder as surely as the bear tore open Mr.
Gaspard's face. And it leaves those left behind just as scarred,
though the scars lie hidden in the mind. This night my scars
are scraped raw. Can I be strong for Singing Waters? From
what well within myself can I draw? And I must draw
strength for myself and others.*

*Just thinking of Singing Waters' strength makes my eyes
glassy again.*

*I have cried so much today my head aches, my throat hurts,
and my nose is sore. I haven't cried this much since David
died. No more. Exhaustion steals over me. I shall relate more
of today's events at another writing.*

Oh, Singing Waters!

June 7, 1846, by the Little Arkansas.
*For two days our party has been shrouded in melancholy as
thick as an early morning prairie fog. While there is a
modicum of relief in the knowledge one is not alone in
melancholia, a surfeit of the condition defeats a party and
causes each obstacle one encounters to loom larger than its
reality should allow. Such has happened to us.*

*Our unhappy state has been exacerbated by Mother
Nature, which has increased everyone's frustration and
irritability until all are heartily sick of everyone else's
company.*

*All except Singing Waters. She is sad, yes. But what
person who has been condemned to death is not? Yet there
exists such nobility in her stature and expression that those of
European royalty would be hard pressed to duplicate it. I fear
if I were the one condemned as she is, I should rage at deaf*

*heaven and go mad in my mind before the madness of the
devil's curse could take me.*

*From what Mr. Gaspard has told me, I know Singing
Waters has never led an easy nor a tranquil life. She was a
Kiowa captive, and very badly used as their slave and woman
of pleasure. When Mr. Rawlins first saw her she was thin
unto death with great weeping sores on her body. She still
bears those scars of her captivity. Without considering why,
Mr. Rawlins bought her and proceeded to nurse her back to
health. When she was better he offered to take her back to her
people. She declined and has been with him ever since. They
are as devoted a couple as ever one would hope to find. This
makes her death sentence so much harder for all to accept.*

*But while the rest of us bewail her fate, she is busy about
the camp, always working on something. She is a silent
woman who moves as quietly and gracefully as a cat. Or a
wraith. Yes, perhaps wraith is the better image, for when she
passes now, I've seen some of the men cross themselves as if
she had already crossed the River Styx.*

*So, what has occurred in these two days I have been loath to
touch pen to paper?*

*We buried Mr. Grady the same day he died. Mr. Rawlins
said a few Christian words over his grave as rain began to fall.
No one seemed to even notice the rain. We all stood staring
down at the grave, each man to his own thoughts until we
were soaked through. When the dirt covered him up, they
brought the animals to the grave area for their corral. It seems
barbarous and disrespectful of the dead to use their last resting
place for animal grazing, but it is just the opposite. The
animals are picketed over the grave site in the hope they will
pack down the earth so tightly that no scavengers may dig him
up for their feasting.*

*As we turned to leave the grave the wind increased and the
temperature dropped. Though several hours remained until*

*nightfall, the sky turned dark as night. Great rumbles rolled
over the prairie, each growing louder than the one before.
Flashes of light cracked the sky. I had almost made it to the
supposed safety of my tent when the wind tore it from its
moorings and ripped it apart. Instead of gaining the safety I'd
envisioned I was instead employed in rescuing my belongings!
We flung things higgledy-piggledy into the back of the big
Conestoga, then sought relief from the drenching rain in one
of the Dearborns, and there we spent the rest of the day and
night, eating cold rations and shivering.*

*The next morning we woke to discover many of the animals
had broken loose during the night and had wandered away.
While the last of the repairs were made to the damaged wagons
the bullwhackers went in search of their lost stock. By late
afternoon all save three oxen and two mules could be found
and herded back to camp. The stock, I'm told, had a mind to
return to Independence.*

*This morning we left Council Grove. I remember when we
came here I felt excited, like a foolish school girl, seeing this
spot as a milestone for my journey. Now I see it only as a spot
I am thankful to leave. Isn't it odd how our ideas and
perceptions change? We did not make the traveling time my
little party was wont to do because of the logistics of moving a
large party and, perhaps more a factor, the state of the Little
Arkansas River.*

*We are camped on the far side of the river, but getting here
was a struggle. And through this struggle, I believe I
understand where the term "bullwhacker" for oxen driver
derived.*

*At the place where we crossed the river it ran only five to
six yards wide; however, its banks were steep and the riverbed
a miry mixture of mud and sand. To enable us to cross the
river Mr. Rawlins sent a team of men ahead of the wagons
with picks and shovels and axes. The men cut into the river's*

steep banks to form ramps on either shore. These ramps leading into the water were of miry earth, much too soft to support a loaded wagon's weight. To compensate, the ramps were cross-laid with willow and grass. Fresh dirt was shoveled on top and, if necessary, another layer of willow and grass laid down until a secure roadbed could be established.

It was hot, exhausting work made worse by the onslaught of mosquitoes. Yes, the pests that Mr. Gaspard warned me of descended upon us in so thick a swarm that never was one threatened by just one mosquito at a time, but by hundreds!

Their whining buzz told us of their approach. But soon there were so many the air was brown with their presence. I hid behind my veiled riding habit and, despite the heat of the day, made certain every inch of skin on my body was covered.

The men cursed louder and worked harder to get us out of that benighted area. In a way, I would venture to say the mosquitoes aided the bullwhackers efforts to get the oxen and mules across the river. The bullwhackers used their whips to goad the animals forward into the water, and then once in the water to goad them to pull the wagons out. It is easier on all if the animals continue to move forward without stopping. The swarm of mosquitoes acted like a thousand whips to the beleaguered animals. They pulled hard in their yokes in an effort to get away from the little pests.

This evening we camp in a valley beyond the river. A breeze has blown steadily so we are mercifully without mosquitoes here, but the effect of their presence is seen in the welt-sized bites on many. Singing Waters has been busy this evening applying poultices to these welts and murmuring soothing words of comfort. Pedro and Manuel Gutierez say the poultices do sooth the bites and take the itch away. I should ask Singing Waters for her recipe.

Oh! I am yawning and my eyes want to close. It is late. I have written more this evening than is my wont to do, but I

wanted to let you know what has transpired in the last two
days. Has it only been two? It feels like a lifetime.

CAROLINA WATCHED YOUNG Juniper Robles swab out his tin
plate with the last of his biscuit. He grimaced as he popped the
drippings-laden bread into his mouth. She shook her head. "You're
a mystery, Mr. Robles."

"Me, ma'am?" With only the campfire to illuminate him, the
Missouri youth looked skinnier, younger.

She nodded as she sipped her coffee. "You eat like a ravenous
man starved for days, yet with every bite a profound dislike travels across your face. Why is that?"

He set his plate down on the ground by his feet. "I want me
a taste of buffalo meat. I'd thought we'd be getting some buffalo
by now."

"Soon," Mr. Gaspard said as he sat down beside Carolina. He
nodded his head toward the prairie beyond their camp. "Have
you noticed how the grass has begun to change? It's getting shorter
and curly. That's buffalo grass. And those crazy winding paths cut
through it? They weren't made by any soused bullwhacker."

"But, seeing buffaloes also means Indian hunting parties,"
Rawlins added from where he sat on the other side of the fire. In
the darkness, his voice assumed a somber, foreboding tone.

A quick frown crossed young Robles's face.

Gaspard nodded. "We're not a big enough party to travel without concern."

Juniper Robles scowled at Gaspard, then rose to his feet. "If
you'll excuse me, ma'am," he said to Carolina, "I think I'll go clean
up my kit and stretch my legs a bit before turning in." Several of
the other young men murmured agreement and rose as well. The
weathered trail veterans didn't move more than to sip their coffee
and lean back on their elbows or saddle packs.

When Robles and the other men were beyond the circle of the
wagons Egan Bush slapped his hand against his thigh and

laughed, sputtering with too long contained mirth. "Well, now, seems ya got those youn'uns goin' right good."

"What do you mean, Mr. Bush?" Carolina asked. She owned that her own heart beat harder and faster at the thought of Indians in the area, but why should concern engender humor with the trail veterans?

"Don't go outta the light of the fire, ma'am, or you're like as not to git yourself shot. Those boys jest come down with a touch a Injun fever," he cackled.

Next to her, Mr. Gaspard nodded. "Better to let them get the spooks outta them now before we really come into Indian country," he explained.

"You mean this really isn't where Indians and buffalo can be found?" Carolina asked, confused.

"No, ma'am," Gaspard answered. "We don't mean to say that at all." He leaned forward to snag the coffeepot from the fire and re-filled his tin mug. "It's just that they haven't been here in a while and probably won't be for a while longer."

"Why?" she persisted. These veterans of the trail were too la-conic for her. They didn't understand that a little knowledge held a thousand fears at bay.

"On account of the burned prairie," Gaspard said.

"Oh, you mean the wide burned swath we crossed today?" She turned back toward the old wagoneer. "You told me, Mr. Bush, lightning sometimes sets the grass on fire."

"Yes, ma'am. And that burn got pushed 'cross the prayrie on a wind outta the nor'west. Didn't burn itself out until the sandy hillock area along the river here. Red buffler, that's wot the Injuns call a prayrie fyar. Red buffler sweeping 'cross the prayrie."

June 8, 1846. Day twelve.
Today we crossed a desolate wasteland painted in shades of brown and black and gray. What trees we passed were dark twisted bones silhouetted against a cloudless blue sky, burned

lifeless. It was an otherworldly landscape such as the devil himself must favor. I saw several of the Mexican drivers cross themselves and murmur prayers. I said one of my own, for the living and the dead.

Crossing this nightmare terrain so quickly after our sadness in Council Grove is disquieting. The party was strangely subdued all day. I think the moodiness of the party has led Mr. Rawlins to request Sibby and myself to help Singing Waters prepare supper for us all. He does not want the men to spend too much time whispering among themselves and building upon their own fears. A community supper does much to dispel the evening horrors.

Normally in caravans of this size and larger, the men are divided into units, or messes. These messes have a semblance of military units that is useful for maintaining order and delivering commands within a large company. Each mess elects their own leader, cook, and guard delegates for the caravan. Usually, each mess is responsible for its own cooking. Under the circumstances we find ourselves in, it has been decided that the entire company will sup together rather than in their individual mess. Supper supplies have been transferred to one of the Dearborn wagons. Breakfast continues to be prepared within each mess.

I own I quite enjoyed the evening meal, and slowly I am learning the names of the men in the company and a bit of their history. I have not as yet been able to glean any more information from Mr. Gaspard other than what he told the Oregon-bound immigrant children, but I will persevere.

Singing Waters remains smiling and serene. Perhaps she may be one of the blessed ones that are reprieved. One may only pray.

CAROLINA SPOONED A second helping of beans onto Jedediah Rawlins's tin plate.

"Singing Waters says you have family in New Mexico," he said.

"Yes. From both sides of my family," she said as she set the bean pot back near the campfire.

"Both sides?

She nodded. "My mother's brother, Elliott Reeves, lives there."

"Reeves! I knowed him!" Egan Bush said as he poured himself another mug of coffee. The firelight on his stubby features gave him an elvish appearance. "Didn't he marry a cousin a Beaubien's wife?"

"Yes," Carolina said eagerly, pleased to learn he knew her uncle. "Estafina. But she died last winter."

"I'm right sorry to hear that. She war a right fine woman. Kept Reeves in line, too."

Carolina laughed. "I'm beginning to believe you know everyone and everything, Mr. Bush. And keeping Uncle Elliott in line is a necessity! Unfortunately, her dying left him with three young children to care for. And if you know my uncle, then you probably have some idea of what prompts me to go to Santa Fe!"

"Hell, yes. Beggin' your pardon, ma'am, but Elliott Reeves has about as much sense as those oxen over there," he said, jerking his head in the direction of the animals. "Prob'ly less."

Carolina sighed. "As much as one might wish one could be proud of their relatives, I'll own my uncle Elliot is not a man of sterling qualities."

"You said you had family from both sides in New Mexico?" Rawlins prompted.

"Yes, my father's brother. He lives in Santa Fe, too. I've never met him. My father was from Mexico." She laughed. "A descendant of Spanish nobility, if you will. He and my uncle were never close because of the great age difference between them and because Father moved to New Orleans as a young man and my uncle chose to move to Santa Fe to seek his fortune." She turned to Egan Bush. "Perhaps you know him as well. Diego Navarro?"

"Navarro!" Harry Wells jumped to his feet. He stared down at Carolina.

"What?" Carolina asked.

Wells turned his head and spit in the dirt. There were angry murmured asides beyond her hearing and the Mexicans in the company turned toward her with fear in their eyes.

"Easy boys," Gaspard growled low in his throat. "She ain't her uncle. And by her own words, she hasn't met him either."

"Do you know my uncle?" Carolina asked, incredulous. "What is it?"

"Blood tells," Harry Wells said crisply.

"Now, that's a bloody damned fool thing for you to say!" Gaspard snapped.

"Would someone please tell me what is going on?" Carolina demanded.

Gaspard sighed and ran a tired hand around the back of his neck. "A few years back, did you ever read about the fool's expedition President Lamar of Texas authorized to New Mexico?"

"Yes. Louisiana has a heavy Spanish heritage. It was a prevalent topic in the coffee houses, the market, and social gatherings," Carolina said dryly.

Gaspard leaned forward, resting his forearms on his thighs; his hands dangled tiredly between his knees. "I reckon it would be. Well, then, did you hear tell of the executions that came from that?"

"A Mr. Baker and a Mr. Howell?"

"Howland. Baker and Howland. Rosenberg, who had been captured with them originally, was killed after they escaped."

"I remember. A series of articles was published about the expedition, done by a journalist who'd traveled in their merchant train."

"Kendall. Yes. But what wasn't written was the name of the man who ordered their execution."

"I thought the New Mexican governor ordered them." Carolina picked the coffeepot up from the fire and silently offered refills.

Gaspard straightened and reached for his mug. "Officially it was Governor Armijo," he said as she topped off his coffee. "But it was another of his officers who first arranged for Baker, Howland, and Rosenberg to be captured, arranged for their escape, and then participated in the battle for their recapture."

Rawlins nodded. "He took great pleasure in laying open Howland's face, and he thought it fitting that the other Texans who'd surrendered, after accepting false promises sent to them in Armijo's name, were kept in a rough, foul-smelling pen of a prison that wasn't fit for animals."

Carolina shook her head. "I don't understand. Are you inferring that my uncle was this man?"

"I'm not inferring nothing," Rawlins said. He took off his hat and combed his fingers through his hair. "I'm telling you. Furthermore, Mrs. Harper, his part in the disaster of the Texas expedition is the mildest of his activities. It is well known that he delights in torture, in causing pain. Especially with a whip. People see Diego Navarro in the plaza, they go the other way. It's also well known that he hates Texans, but truth is, United States citizen, Texan, or some other citizen from across the Atlantic or Pacific oceans wouldn't make much difference. Just be something other than Mexican and you're fair game."

"Mexicans, too, señor," put in old Manuel Gutierez, his expression as solemn as a priest's at a grave. The other Mexicans around him nodded.

"I see," Carolina said slowly, a frown settled on her face. She sighed. "It will be interesting, then, to see what kind of reception I receive from him. He and my father were younger sons with twelve years difference in age, so there was never a question of jealousy or animosity."

"Diego Navarro don't need no reason for cruelty," Harry Wells said bitterly.

Manuel Gutierez hobbled over to Carolina. Into her hand he placed a crucifix. "I pray for you, señora. I pray," he said. He then turned and walked away to where his blanket and packs lay. He wrapped the blanket about himself, then lay down, his back to the fire, the subject of Diego Navarro closed. One by one the other men slipped off into the velvety night until only Gaspard, Rawlins, and Bush remained. The men exchanged glances reflecting concern. Gaspard looked as if he would like to say something more, but changed his mind. Bush spit a wad of tobacco into the fire, sending sparks popping and winging upward.

Carolina sat for a few minutes more by the fire. She looked down at the crucifix Gutierez had pressed into her palm. The fire in front of her burned hot, but inside she shivered.

June 9, 1846, along the Arkansas. Day thirteen.

It is late. I stayed sitting by the campfire far longer than my habit. I stayed until only a glow remained and the wind had begun to carry the light ash away.

It is amazing how many ideas—fantasies—we carry around in our heads, fantasies we treat as the truth. Normally they aren't harmful. But when we base our actions on them we can lead ourselves astray. Certain things said this evening have led me to wonder if I have not been guilty of following my fantasies.

When I decided to travel to New Mexico to care for Uncle Elliott's children, I knew I was doing so to regain purpose in my life. I am not a woman to live off others, though I have that experience in my past. But I must be busy. It is the only thing that keeps the demons at bay. It is the only thing that saves me from myself. So we have often discussed. But there is a restlessness within me. I cannot be indolent, for then I am truly locked within my own mind.

Just thinking of the word "indolent" reminds me of Great-aunt Henrietta Winston, who used to scold me when I was a child for my restless ways.

But I digress again. Fatigue is partly to blame; more is the jumble of thoughts that ricochet about in my mind.

I rationalized my journeying to New Mexico without waiting for acceptance or rejection of my plan from Uncle

Elliott. I thought if Uncle Elliott became difficult I could stay with father's brother, Uncle Diego Navarro. I assumed my half-Mexican heritage would be my guarantee of acceptance in Santa Fe. I may have been grossly naive. We were so proud of Papa. He was a good, learned man. I think I've always assumed his brother would be the same. Certainly father never said any differently to me. Did he to you? What an absurd question. Of course not, else you would have told me.

Today I learned that the Navarro name is a respected name in New Mexico only because it is a feared name. It is a name synonymous with cruelty and pain. And now knowledge of that connection has several members of our caravan looking at me askance as if I should magically turn into this greatly feared man. Or perhaps that I am his spy, or could be his spy.

Why must I always battle for my sense of self apart from others?

It is little wonder that Uncle Elliott has never mentioned Diego Navarro in any of his infrequent letters. Now I shall have to place all of my expectations on Uncle Elliott. What a frightening thought!

Ah! I'm glad I can start to laugh again. Laughing is necessary lest I cry.

7

June 10, 1846, along Cow Creek. Evening, day fourteen.
Buffalo!

The majestic prairie beast with his broad noble brow and thick coat of fur has been spotted!

Actually, I do not find the animal "majestic," as some newspapers have described the beast. Odd, certainly. But with its thick coat of wavy, matted fur, its broad beetling brow, and its shambling movement across the prairie, I think the buffalo more malevolent than noble or majestic in appearance. Ugly would be an apt description.

What I have found fascinating is the behavioral changes I've observed in the men of this caravan. At the sight of a buffalo they run mad like a school of boys let loose on holiday. The greenhorns scrambled to mount their horses and mules to run the buffalo down. Whooping and hollering in such a fashion I swear their purpose was to frighten the animal to death, whereby he might die either by a heart attack or by exhaustion from running to escape their banshee cries.

One young man, Louie Belmont, a shy yet personable

young man from Kentucky, came near disaster by his antics
when chasing buffalo and earned himself a prodigious dressing
down from Mr. Rawlins. He galloped in pursuit of a large
prize buffalo, his attention centered on his prey. Suddenly his
horse stepped into a hole, an animal burrow, most likely. I am
told that a loud "snap" was heard by those behind him. Down
the noble horse went to his knees, its leg broken. Mr. Belmont
flew over the horse's head. He threw out his arms to break his
fall, landed awkwardly, and badly sprained one wrist. But that
was not the end of it. The buffalo, perhaps maddened by the
pursuit, turned and proceeded to run straight at the injured
Mr. Belmont! Mr. Belmont swears the beast's eyes glowed red
with demonic light. In shock and in pain he lay in the buffalo's
path. Behind him, his horse whinnied and frantically tried to
rise. Mr. Gaspard and Mr. Rawlins rode straight for the
maddened buffalo. At the last possible moment the old buffalo
veered off and Mr. Belmont was safe. Regrettably, his horse
had to be put down. As part of his punishment for his wild
carelessness, Mr. Rawlins made the boy walk back to camp
carrying his saddle and packs on his back. I must admit I wish
I might have seen the drama. Mr. Gaspard and Mr. Rawlins
are reticent. It was from others in the party I heard the entire
tale.

In contrast to the impetuousness of the greenhorns, the trail
veterans do not run wild at the prospect of hunting buffalo;
nonetheless, their enthusiasm is just as strong. It is merely
tempered by experience and therefore channeled into time-
proven methods for success.

It has become my understanding that the sport in buffalo
hunting is derived from two aspects, used either together or
independently. These aspects are the use of a planned strategy,
or the ability to deliver a swift, killing blow.

I shall address the second aspect first as it is the easier to
explain. The buffalo has a thick hide and an even thicker layer

of fur on its body. Unless a bullet is delivered into a vital area it is probable that a buffalo wounded in the flesh may carry around spent bullets in his body for years without them unduly affecting his activities. I have listened to campfire arguments as to the relevant benefits of one or another location for delivering that fatal blow; however, so far no one has been able to agree as to how best to achieve these vulnerable spots.

Buffalo have poor eyesight, Mr. Bush tells me, but they have an excellent sense of smell. If the hunters can stay to the leeward out of their scent, they have a high probability of achieving their target. Therefore, a planned strategy involves, from what I have observed, men crawling on their bellies toward the buffalo while making sure the wind is in their faces. They crawl as close as possible to the beast before rising in the grass to bring their rifles to their shoulders and deliver the killing shot. I do not see how this method of buffalo hunting is in any way less foolhardy than Mr. Belmont's method, but they tell me, quite strongly, that it is. If I live to be one hundred I swear I shall never understand a man's mind.

Juniper Robles led a string of mules back to camp laden with buffalo meat. When he arrived Sibby's and my education began. Singing Waters had us stringing strips of meat on ropes to dry in the sun. This meat will feed us all when we are no longer in range of the buffalo.

Little of the animal is wasted. Most of the liver, I am told, is eaten raw at the site of the kill. It is considered a delicacy and the prize of the man who brought the animal down. Additionally, liver is mixed with fat and buffalo brains to form a compound used in tanning the buffalo hide to soft flexibility. The marrow makes a delicious butter, the rib meat from the area of the hump is a flavorful cut for soup. The stomach is used as a cooking pouch for three or more days until it becomes too waterlogged, then it is eaten. What is not eaten of

the buffalo is used for clothing, weapons, or household
purposes. This evening my hands and arms ache from
scraping buffalo hides using a curved, dull-bladed knife made
with buffalo horn handles.

Since our forefathers first came to this land Indians have
taught the white man how to live off the land and its bounty.
Now Singing Waters is teaching me. It is the most amazing
thing, but did you know the rough side of a buffalo tongue can
be used as a hairbrush! Every day I learn how little I know! It
makes each day that much more precious.

SOMETHING WASN'T RIGHT. It was nothing that could be seen, or heard, or touched. Carolina felt it.

She looked over at Sibby. Her maid was sleeping, as was often her habit in the afternoon. Sibby never seemed to be bothered by the wagon jolting across deep ruts. Carolina envied her.

Sibby wasn't the source of the odd feeling.

Curious, Carolina quietly shifted position to try to peer out the opening of the wagon's canvas covering. The back of her driver, Jorge, blocked any view outside. She climbed over the boxes at the front of the wagon and tapped his back.

"Move over, please. I'd like to join you outside. Away from Sibby's snoring!"

Jorge jumped, startled by her light touch, but he quickly moved over to make room for her on the platform seat. Carolina gathered up her skirts and stepped out onto the front of the wagon, then settled down beside Jorge.

The sky in the west was the color of dark steel.

"There's a storm approaching."

"*Sí*, señora. A big storm. I pray we stop soon. I do not like it."

Up ahead, Rawlins, Gaspard, and Bush had ridden their horses together for a conference. Every once in a while they glanced up at the darkening sky and frowned, then returned to their conversation.

In the distance lightning cracked the sky, too far for thunder to follow; however, the air already smelled of rain. The animals were growing restive and harder to manage.

Mr. Gaspard rode down the wagon train. "Tighten up! Tighten up, there!" he called out. "Keep them moving!"

"Mr. Gaspard!" Carolina called out. "What's going on?" She used a free hand to hold the wild, dancing wisps of her hair back from her face.

"We're going to try to make the river crossing before the rain hits. We wait too long, we could be here for days waiting on the river to subside."

Carolina nodded and turned her face into a wind that rose to life out of nothing. She could feel the temperature dropping. She rubbed her hands over her upper arms. Dust began to swirl upward in clouds, choking her and stinging her eyes.

"Señora, you go inside!" Jorge said as he dug a large kerchief out of a waistcoat pocket. He tried to hold the reins between his knees so he could tie the cloth over his nose, but the mules were too skittery.

Carolina shook her head, not daring to open her mouth to the sand and dirt in the air.

"Jorge! You're next across the river. Keep them moving. Don't let them stop," Mr. Rawlins called out to them. "Hee-yah!" He swatted a recalcitrant mule's rump as he passed.

Carolina looked over at Jorge. He was struggling against the dust, and the fear. She remembered his cowardice at the Narrows and damned herself for the forgiveness she'd extended, which allowed him again to drive her wagon. There was nothing she could do now but help by bolstering the man.

Quickly she grabbed the reins from him, squinting her eyes to slits. "Get your kerchief on," she yelled, then fell to coughing against the dirt in her mouth.

Jorge quickly tied the cloth over his nose and mouth, then took the reins from her. "Señora! Please!" he said, jerking his head in the direction of the wagon.

Her eyes were beginning to burn and her lungs ache. She turned to go back into the wagon to fetch her hat with its enveloping veil. Thunder now came with the lightning.

Inside the wagon Sibby was awake, her eyes wide with fear. When she saw Carolina looking at her she licked her lips and compressed them tightly. "I'm all right," she said.

Carolina didn't know for whom Sibby intended her words but she had to smile at the effort Sibby exerted to be "all right."

"We're trying to cross the river, but there's a storm approaching. We're being hit with the dust and wind pushed before it."

Sibby nodded.

"I need my hat with the thick veil."

"It's right here," Sibby said, uncovering a large hatbox beneath a stack of blankets. "But what do you need a hat for?"

"I'm going to sit with Jorge. I'm not confident of his nerve." She fastened the hat to her head with a large hat pin.

"You think he'll jump?"

Carolina stared at Jorge's hunched back. She shook her head. "I don't know what I think. I just know I should keep him company." She draped the veil over her face and tied it behind her head.

"You be careful yourself, Miz Carolina."

"I will, Sibby," she said, ducking back outside. She waved Jorge's protests aside when she came back to sit beside him.

Up ahead one of the big wagons wasn't moving, stopping the whole train. Men ranged on each side of the eight oxen harnessed to the wagon and whipped the animals across their backs until flecks of blood spattered their whip tips red. The oxen leaned into their yokes and with a precarious lurch pulled the wagon to the other bank.

Up ahead she could see the rain falling in sheets across the prairie. Slowly they were coming together. The first fat drops reached them as her mules slid down the sandy riverbank. The wagon skidded sideways, then hit a rock or rut and bounced back into line.

"Madre de Dios!" Jorge yelled.

Carolina clung to the narrow wooden seat rim. She could see white all around Jorge's eyes. Sweat ran down his brow.

"Keep 'em going! Don't let 'em stop!" Rawlins exhorted.

"Hee-yah!" Gaspard yelled, coming back up the line of wagons. "Mrs. Harper," he hoarsely called out as he came alongside, "best you get back in the wagon.

Mutely Carolina shook her head. Now wasn't the time to tell him Jorge was terrified and most likely only Gaspard's presence kept him on the wagon seat with his hands holding the reins. Jorge looked like he could break at any moment. She felt for the man, for she was scared, too; but she had too much invested in the wagon to risk losing it.

A tangled bolt of lightning hit the ground less than fifty yards away, blinding, the boom of its thunder felt as well as heard. Carolina found her hands pressed against her ears before she even realized what her hands were doing.

Jorge screamed and tossed the reins aside as he jumped off the wagon seat into the stream. Carolina cried out and lurched forward to grab the reins. She managed to catch one of the reins and Jorge's whip, balanced precariously over the wagon edge. The other rein fell, trailing from the mules into the water. She stared down at the rising, swirling waters, then looked up at the backs of the mules. She wasn't going to lose the wagon, she vowed to herself. Every breath she took hurt. Fear threatened to choke off her breathing. Resolutely, she fought it back.

She bit her lip between her teeth, then sat back down and cracked the whip over the mules' heads. The animals were frightened. They tossed their heads and side-stepped agitatedly.

"Get going! Come on now, move!" she yelled, snapping the whip over the animals. Wind tore at her veiled hat. The temperature had dropped more. The steady spatters of rain touched her hands.

The mules dipped their heads and pulled harder.

"Miz Carolina?"

"Not now, Sibby," she said between deep breaths. She didn't have time for any of Sibby's hysterics. The mules were flagging. "Come on! Move! Keep going!" She flicked the whip again.

"Mr. Gutierez, he say you cain't be nice to mules. They responds best to swearing," Sibby said over Carolina's shoulder.

Carolina turned her head quickly to look at Sibby, then turned back to the mules. Her thoughts stumbled. She cracked the whip again and licked her lips.

"Move it, you damn flea-bit devil's plague!" She flicked the whip over the lead team's head.

"Don't stop!" Sibby cried.

Carolina took a deep breath. "Pull, damn you! Pull until you drop or I'll slice your knees and leave you to the wolves! Pull!" she screamed.

The water rose frighteningly fast. The scattering drops of rain increased to a blowing wall of water before Carolina's eyes. Her soaked cotton dress weighed heavily on her body. The cold chill from the wind cramped her fingers around the rein and whip. A rising hysteria felt like a tightening band about her chest.

Anger burned cleanly through Carolina, engulfing the hysteria. Hysteria was not a part of who she would let herself be. Ruthlessly she pried the singed remnants of hysteria out of her soul. She had never been a woman given to hand wringing and she was not about to start being one! She took a deep breath.

She cracked the whip again, touching the rump of the lead animal, whose rein had fallen in the water.

"That's it, Miz Carolina! That's it!" Sibby cajoled from behind her.

Suddenly Carolina felt lighter, renewed. Sibby, her dear friend Sibby was back! "Move you lop-eared miserable excuse for an animal. Get along there, damn you! Hee-yah!" she yelled as she flicked the whip again, this time with more bite and balance than she'd achieved before. She wanted to throw her head back and laugh until tears streamed down her cheeks. She wanted to hug Sibby, to revel in her support.

Mr. Gaspard's horse splashed through the rising water to her side.

"Where's Jorge?" he shouted.

"He jumped off."

"Again," Sibby added ungraciously. Carolina turned her head to frown at her, but quickly turned back to the mules.

Gaspard cursed loudly and, Carolina thought bemusedly, quite eloquently in French. He rode up alongside the lead mules, grabbed a harness strap, and pulled himself onto the back of the lead mule. His heels kicked into the side of the animal. The wagon moved forward deeper into the swirling waters. Carolina feared she and her entire wagon would soon be flooded out and swept down the black, swirling stream. Instead the mules finally found purchase on the far bank and started the hard pull out of the water, the wagon creaking and groaning in protest.

When they reached the top bank and turned to join the other wagons gathered on a small ridge, Carolina discovered hers was the last wagon to make it safely across the stream. The company was divided. Nineteen wagons had crossed the stream. The Dearborn wagon behind Carolina's had foundered and been swept downstream. The last eleven remained on the far side, among them Carolina's other two wagons. And Pedro!

8

June 12, 1846. Morning, day sixteen.

Yesterday the rain came in a storm unlike any I have ever experienced. Or hope to again. For hours we watched the storm come toward us from out of the west. We watched the sky turn to dull lead. We saw rain in darker gray streaks like an old woman's wind-whipped hair. The rain came toward us slowly, and we toward it.

Mr. Rawlins, Mr. Gaspard, and Mr. Bush intended for our company to cross the river before the storm reached us. They harried everyone along with what I thought, in my naivete, unnecessary forcefulness. How wrong can someone be?

They harried us along for our lives!

The storm met us as the lead wagon in our caravan crossed the river. Before the storm came a wind stirring up dust and gritty dirt that stung the eyes and made breathing heavy and difficult without a kerchief over one's nose and mouth. The temperature dropped.

Jorge drove the wagon in which Sibby and I traveled. Remembering his fear at the Narrows quagmire, I sat next to him on the wagon box. I wanted to bolster his courage, and

*my own, while reminding him of his responsibilities.
Ultimately I discovered my fears were appropriate; my
precautions were not. My meager companionship efforts
neither bolstered Jorge's courage nor fostered within him a
sense of responsibility. We were in the middle of the suddenly
engorged river when a blinding bolt of jagged lightning hit the
bank in front of us, spraying upward bits of earth and steam.
The boom of its thunder deafened me for a moment, my body
shrinking as if it would curl in upon itself for safety. I would
that I could have commanded my sanity better, for I looked up
only in time to see Jorge jump from the wagon.*

*Instinctively, I think, I reached for his reins and whip as he
jumped. I caught the whip, but only one rein. The other rein
fell into the swirling, rising waters. Now I was truly terrified,
but I was determined not to lose my wagon. If I did, I stood as
good a chance to also lose the lives of Sibby, her unborn child,
and myself. To say nothing of the lives of those others who
might feel bound to attempt rescue. I am not a woman to
scream and wring my hands, else I should have gone mad in
my youth. I couldn't allow death to win too easily. I shall
always fight and rail against death until it takes my last
breath. Death has taken too much from me in my life and I
cannot abide greed.*

*Somehow, I had to get the wagon across. I had taken it for
granted that I should always have someone to drive my wagon
for me. How naive. Now the responsibility fell to me.
Whipping up the mules and calling to them I realized how
inadequately I was prepared.*

*It was then, when my own fears and uncertainties
threatened to stand in my way, that Sibby came to my rescue.
She called encouragement over my shoulder and reminded me
how the best mule drivers handled their teams. Together we
got the mules moving; but each step took an eon and still the
waters rose. Then Mr. Gaspard rode up and jumped onto the
back of the lead mule. Together, we got the wagon across.*

Mine was the last wagon to safely cross the river. The wagon behind me did not make it. The rising waters swept it downstream. I do not know yet whether its driver made it to safety or not, just as I do not know the fate of Jorge. I pray he made it back to the other shore, for he is not in this camp.

By the time my wagon cleared the river and drew into the circle of the other wagons that had made it across, I was exhausted. I felt so drained, I would have gone to sleep in my wet clothing if Sibby hadn't bullied me into changing, all the while pulling at the sodden material of my dress.

As if in a dream, I heard people talking in low voices outside my wagon. Their voices rose and fell, hardly more than murmurs. I fell asleep within moments of laying my head down, too tired and chilled to investigate. I fell asleep to the soft murmurs as easily as if they were a child's lullaby. When I awoke this morning, I awoke remembering those voices and wondering if I'd missed anything.

Gracious, that sounds like a child determined to miss nothing!

But, as I look out from my wagon, I see the rain clouds have vanished from the horizon as if they'd never been, though the ground is wet and everything glistens like diamonds. Perhaps we will not have long to wait for the other wagons to cross the river. The air smells fresh and cleansed. As I inhale deeply I cannot help but smile.

Well, enough of my ramblings. I must get up and about to see what needs to be done and discover the fate of Jorge, and the driver of the wagon behind us.

June 12, 1846. Evening.

Jorge is dead.

They discovered his body this afternoon when two men traveled downriver to judge crossing conditions, hoping to find an easier passage across the river for the rest of the wagons. They were unsuccessful in their search; but they did find Jorge, his poor, water-swollen body caught in a tangle of branches from trees fallen into the river.

I'm not surprised at his fate. I feel a curious ache in my chest at the reality of this death. But I think I knew, somehow in the depths of my soul, that when he jumped out of the wagon that I wouldn't see him again. I'm not claiming prescience or latent gypsy blood. The man lived as a bundle of nerves held together by thin strips of sinew and muscle. Nonetheless, like Mr. Donne wrote, any man's death diminishes me. I felt again that hollow, numbing ache I experienced after Edward's death. Only this time, strangely, it was accompanied by tears slowly coursing down my cheeks.

I pulled my Bible out of my pack this afternoon and read for an hour.

For Jorge.

For myself.

Today was an odd day in its entirety; the river too muddy from the storm for washing purposes, the ground too soaked for walking or laying out the wagon goods to redistribute the load. There's nothing remaining to be mended and all the leathers we might work are with Singing Waters across the river. From the smoke I see rising from a separate fire removed from the cook fire, I believe she is smoking some of the leather to make it waterproof and more supple. That is a procedure I wanted to learn.

Now I sit here mentally "smoking" as much as that fire, but I don't suppose I shall become more supple. Quite the opposite! Is it any wonder that I should be tired of my own company? Oh, Sibby has been a good companion when she can, but she suffers from morning sickness. Now, when I realize why I never could find her in the morning, I'm embarrassed to admit I never considered breeding to be the source of Sibby's difficulties. The close air in the wagon often brings on her feelings of discomfort. It is not so bad in the

*wagon when we are moving, for we can have the canvas
curtains open to allow whatever breeze blows across the
prairie to join us in the wagon. But at night, she suffers so. If
the weather allows, she sleeps outside under the wagon to ease
her discomfort. It makes it lonely in the wagon for me. I miss
my tent; but Mr. Rawlins calls it a time-consuming nuisance,
which on our push out of Council Grove he'd rather I do
without. Besides, it is still in need of repair. I have mended
some of the tears, but my fingers protest at sewing canvas.*

*I'm feeling petulant. Actually, it is a luxury to indulge in a
bit of petulance. For so long, it seems, I haven't felt anything.
I have been accustomed to being the one to soothe troubled
waters, to quietly continue working for the benefit of all while
men rant together over one issue or another. We clean, we
cook, we sew, we nurse, we sow, we harvest, we listen. But
sometimes, for one's own mental as well as physical health,
one must consider oneself first before others. I consider my
private petulance to be my own small act of defiance, feeble
though it might be. I suppose that is what I am doing at the
moment as I indulge in this spot of petulance.*

*What an odd flight my mind has taken this evening. It
must be a result of this long day. I—*

"MIZ CAROLINA!"

Carolina looked up. "Yes, Sibby?" She arched her neck to re-
lieve the cramped aches from bending over her journal. Sibby
pushed the canvas open wider and climbed into the wagon.

"Mr. Gaspard, he wants you to come out for a meetin'."

"A meeting!" Carolina laid her pen aside.

"Yes'm. That's what he say."

She closed her journal. "Gracious." Her fingers curled around
the edge of her book. "Did you receive the impression that anything is wrong?"

Sibby shook her head. "No, ma'am. Leastwise, not bad wrong.

He were a mite serious, though. Looked like he had a heap on his mind."

"Well, then, I believe I should accommodate him immediately," she said. She returned her journal to her lap desk and placed the box in the corner of the wagon where she kept her toiletries. Glancing down at her comb and brush, she ran a hand over her hair, feeling for errant wisps. Her hair felt smooth and tightly drawn into its bun at the nape of her neck. Satisfied, she stood up, shook out her gray-and-red-plaid cotton skirt, and climbed out the back of the wagon.

"Let me help you, ma'am."

Startled, Carolina turned her head to see Juniper Robles reaching up a hand to help her down. She smiled slightly at him and laid her hand in his.

"Thank you, Mr. Robles," she said as her feet touched the ground and her hand slid from his. "Have you any idea why Mr. Gaspard has called a meeting?" she asked as they walked together toward the big campfire, where other members of the party gathered.

Juniper stuck his thumbs in his waistband. "Not directly, ma'am. But he and Egan, they been conferrin' across the river with Mr. Rawlins. And now Mr. Tidewell, he just come back from scoutin' on down the trail and they been talkin' to him, too."

Carolina nodded. "Hopefully, then, we shall learn when we might be on our way again."

"Yes'm. We're all anxiouslike to be on with it. We've had our share of disaster. Makes folks suspiciouslike and jumpy. Them Mexes is crossin' themselves every time you look at 'em."

"Surely that's a bit of an exaggeration, Mr. Robles," Carolina laughingly chided.

Juniper stuck out his chin. "Seems like," he said tenaciously.

Carolina let the matter go, though Mr. Robles's observations bothered her. The company was on edge and the series of mishaps encountered by the enterprise *were* of too high a number and too diverse to totally ignore. They were the stuff that bred fear. Whispers of a cursed expedition could prove self-fulfilling.

The circle of men around the campfire parted slightly at her approach. A murmur of greetings and tipped hats acknowledged her presence. She smiled and nodded in return, warmed by the overall reception she received from these same men who were originally taciturn and suspicious of a white woman in their party. Mr. Gaspard raised his voice to speak to them all.

"Mr. Rawlins, Mr. Bush, and I believe the river will be low enough in the morning to bring the wagons across. It'll be miry, though, so we'll need every man available to make certain we don't lose any more. As soon as they're across we're going to head out, so set your goods and belongings to right before the crossing."

He removed his hat from his head and turned to look at Carolina. "Mrs. Harper, instead of each mess cooking breakfast in the morning, we're wondering if you and your woman might not do it for all so as the men can get to the river and to seein' that those wagons get across."

Carolina felt a curious lump of satisfaction settle within her. She smiled. "Certainly, Mr. Gaspard. I consider it the least that I could do."

"Thank you, ma'am." He replaced his hat on his head.

Carolina took a step closer to the fire. Her gaze swept the company before coming back to face Gaspard. "And I think it would be best if I collected supplies from each mess this evening so we might be cooking at first light. The kind of work you're looking to do requires a hearty breakfast," she added.

"Yes, ma'am." Gaspard concurred, grinning his odd, lopsided grin. He saluted her with two fingers against his hat brim, then his smile faded and he turned serious again.

"There's reason for pressing on tomorrow," he said. He turned to include the rest of the men in his comments. "Reason that is too early to say if it be good or bad. Mr. Tidewell has just returned from scouting our forward trail. He says there's sign that there's a large party not more than two days ahead of us on the trail. We're going to get this caravan moving tomorrow to try to catch up with them. If not tomorrow then the day after."

"Why?" Harry Wells asked. "What do we need with another caravan now?"

Several men agreed and echoed his words.

Gaspard waited until the men settled down enough to listen again. "There's soldiers in the party," he said. His voice held a curious flatness that intrigued Carolina.

"Soldiers?" one of the young men parroted.

"How many?" a veteran trail driver asked. He spit a wad of tobacco into the fire. Sparks flew into the darkness, then winked out.

Max Tidewell stepped out of the shadows into the firelight. "At least a dozen. Maybe more," he said softly.

Carolina heard sudden swears and more odd knots of conversation swell up among the men. "I don't understand. What's the matter?"

"Soljers always means some kinda trouble," Egan Bush said, shaking his head.

A chorus of begrudging agreement went round the campfire.

"Indians!"

The word, spoken once from the other side of the fire, hung heavily in the night air.

Carolina shivered. *Indians.* She wiped the palms of her hands down the front of her skirt, then folded her hands before her.

Gaspard took a deep breath and nodded slowly. "Might be Indian trouble," he conceded. "Might also be marauders, or might be that war with Mexico or England has finally come," he said. "We just plain don't know. But I say it's best we find out fast."

"Mr. Gaspard and I will ride out at first light to scout the situation," Tidewell said.

She looked from Mr. Gaspard to Mr. Tidewell and back. Their expressions mirrored the possible seriousness behind the reason there was a company of soldiers on the trail. "But if it's Indians . . . " she protested.

"If there are Indians, they're likely to be before the soldiers," Mr. Gaspard said firmly. His tone brooked no argument.

Carolina nodded, but her mind shrieked a thousand fears, fears laid there at St. Louis parties and parlor get-togethers. She knew many of the tales she heard were embroidered for the audience; still, there was truth behind each exaggeration. She bit her lip against her own voice.

"Best we all get some shut-eye now. Tomorrow's going to be a hard day," Gaspard said. "Robles, help Mrs. Harper gather those supplies."

"Yes, sir," Juniper Robles said.

The rest of the men began to drift off toward their bedrolls and packs, talking quietly among themselves. But now there was a tenseness in their quiet discourse, and often they looked out past the camp periphery as if they could see into the night and all that the darkness hid.

The hoot of an owl could be heard nearby. The howl of a prairie wolf floated in on the wind. Carolina shivered at the eerie sounds. It was as if one answered the other. She hoped they weren't an omen for tomorrow.

9

CAROLINA SLOWLY SWABBED out the gravy pot in the river water, her attention centered on the activities of the men as they harangued the oxen and mules to pull their wagons across the still swollen river. Those men who weren't driving the wagons either walked through water more than knee deep alongside the animals to whip them forward, or they scoured the riverbank to cut what sparse brush and saplings could be found to lay crosswise in the mud as a makeshift road for the wagons coming out of the water and climbing the bank.

No job was easy.

Though the morning sun hung low in the sky, sweat trickled down Carolina's forehead and between her breasts. She raked the back of her hand across her brow, pushing sweat-soaked black strands of hair away from her eyes.

Curses saturated the air, harsher and grittier than the men's common coarse talk, and punctuated with grunts and groans. Carolina grimaced at the language, but she understood the mingled feelings of anger, frustration, and impatience the men felt with the animals and their situation. Any possibility that Indians were the cause of soldiers on the prairie unsettled everyone, making tempers short. The cicadas in the grass along the bank droned. Water gurgled and splashed, mud sucked at animal hooves and wagon wheels, while the crack of whips added sharp, staccato accents.

Inch by inch the wagons rolled forward. A low huzzah sounded when the first wagon crossed the river and climbed the bank to join the circle of wagons. But each wagon's crossing increased the difficulty for those that followed. The churned river mud fought for possession of the wagons. Men trudged farther downriver to cut more trees to lay in the mud to give the wagon wheels purchase.

Another wagon joined the circle.

Carolina twisted the square of cloth she'd used to swab out the pot. Water ran down her bare arms, dribbling onto her skirt, which was nearly as wet as the cloth she rinsed. She looked across the river to the wagons still on the far shore, each patiently awaiting its turn in the slow march to the other side.

Singing Waters sat at the front of one of the wagons, holding the reins. She held her body stiffly upright as she waited for her turn.

Carolina frowned. She turned to toss the cloth into the willow basket Sibby and she had brought down to the river to carry their cooking utensils.

"Sibby, I'm going to help," she said as she sat down on the bank and unlaced her shoes.

"Ma'am?" The soapy wooden bowl Sibby had been scrubbing fell into the water. Flustered, she picked it up.

"Don't look so startled. I'm going to help Singing Waters." She pointed across the river toward the Rawlins's wagon.

Sibby followed the line of Carolina's hand with her eyes. She clucked her tongue and nodded. "Yes, ma'am. She done look like a woman holdin' on by her fingertips."

Carolina sighed. "Can you blame her?"

"No, ma'am," Sibby said vehemently. "But if'n it had been me as her, I'd prob'ly have scaret myself to death just a thinkin' on it. Damn phoby cat." She shuddered and crossed herself. "Shor' do make a body thankful," she finished softly as she stared across the river at Singing Waters.

Carolina felt her throat muscles constrict painfully. She blinked away the sudden tears that sheened her eyes. "Yes. Yes, that it does," she said briskly as she rose to her feet. "Would you take my shoes back to the wagon?"

"Yes'm."

Carolina stepped into the river, slick cold mud squishing upward between her toes. The water climbed to her knees, her skirts wicking it higher. The material in her wide cotton skirts became heavy, forcing her to throw each leg forward one after another in a rocking fashion as she fought the water's resistance and the leaden weight of the drenched fabric. Halfway across the river, she looked up to see Egan Bush riding toward her on Rawlins's big sorrel gelding.

"What in thunderation are ya doin'?" he bellowed.

Carolina stumbled and grabbed for his horse's reins to steady herself. The animal shied sideways, nearly pulling her off balance. She let go of the reins and fell against Egan Bush's leg. The man flinched as if he'd been stung.

"I'm going to help Singing Waters," she snapped as she struggled to regain her balance.

"Easy there!" Bush said.

She stepped back a pace and shielded her eyes from the sun with the back of her hand as she looked up at Egan Bush. "Singing Waters should be resting, not driving a wagon through this muck."

He shook his head. "Dang fool woman. Singing Waters is Injun! She don't need no help," he said waspishly.

Carolina stared at him in dumb shock, then her eyes narrowed and she shook her finger at him. "I thought better of you, Mr. Bush. I really did. Singing Waters is a woman, and that should be re-

membered before all else. She is a woman approaching her time!"
she retorted, her voice tight and guttural with fury.

She was pleased to see the man look abashed. With grim satisfaction flowing through her, she turned away from him and took
a step forward, intending to swing wide of him.

Bush muttered a string of curses without apology, then reined
his horse around to come up beside her. "And if'n you get yorself
hurt I'd shor' as hell want to be in the next territory when Gaspard
returns."

Carolina took a step sideways away from him. "Mr. Gaspard,
may I remind you, is in my employ. It is not for him to question,"
she said austerely. She lifted her chin and one brow arched upward as she assumed her haughtiest Louisiana attitude, daring
him to argue.

He opened and closed his mouth twice, but no argument came.
Frustrated, Bush yanked his hat off his head and hit his knee with
it while one of the more colorful curses Carolina had yet heard
slipped out between his clenched teeth.

Carolina was hard pressed not to smile. When he didn't argue,
she nodded to herself, satisfied, and took another step forward.
And slipped.

She fought against falling face forward into the water, swinging
her arms wildly to counter the forward momentum. The sorrel
gelding whinnied and shied away from her. She fell backward, the
cold river water closing over her head.

"Miz Harper!" Egan Bush yelled. "Miz Harper!"

Carolina flailed in the water a moment before she could bring
her feet underneath her again. She tried to stand, but the slick footing and the weight of her wet clothes undermined her effort. She
fell back into the river again. When she struggled upright, sputtering and dragging her arm across her face, she discovered Mr.
Bush's horse alongside her. Bush leaned down to grab her arm to
steady her.

Carolina leaned wearily against his horse for a moment. The

water had pulled her black bun loose. It hung at the nape of her neck, dark strands clinging to her face and shoulders. She pushed them back as she glared up at Egan Bush.

"Aw, hell, damn fool woman," he muttered. "Put yor foot on mine and I'll pull ya up afore me," he said.

"What?"

"Well, do ya or don't ya wants to git to the Rawlinses' wagon?"

Carolina stared at his hand a moment, then she pulled her sodden skirts up higher than what she could have countenanced a scant week previous, revealing an ample portion of her lower limbs. She disregarded that knowledge as she reached up to grasp his gnarled hand. She placed her right foot on his stirrup and shifted sideways as he helped her up.

"Thank you, Mr. Bush," she said sweetly as she settled herself before him on the saddle.

Mr. Bush eyed her askance, but other than his mustache twitching, he made no recognition of her response.

June 13, 1846.

I apologize for ending my writing so abruptly last evening. So much has happened between now and then. Where do I begin? I scarce know, for tonight I fairly quiver with fatigue; yet I run on like a seven-day clock to the next minute, the next hour. Dragging my pen across these pages is almost more than my muscles may contrive to do. Yet I persist. My mind is alive, darting hither and yon like the prairie rabbit.

Yesterday evening I was called to attend a meeting. Mr. Tidewell, a pleasant though rather taciturn man who has acted as our company's scout, brought news of another company on the trail ahead of us. This company, he said, has soldiers in its party. From my limited understanding I was given to know that soldiers on the trail is a matter of concern. They are rarely about when all is peaceful. Their presence could mean some form of danger lies in our path.

Mr. Gaspard and Mr. Tidewell went before us today to attempt to catch up with this party and ascertain the nature of the danger we might face. Despite the muddy riverbanks, Mr. Rawlins would bring the rest of the wagons across the river for we are much stronger and safer when our numbers are greater. It was requested that Sibby and I see to the men's breakfast as this would save time over the traditional separate morning messes.

I, naturally, agreed.

No, more than naturally, I joyfully agreed. I do not know what is happening to me. This journey is changing me in ways I'm only beginning to notice; but I do perceive they are profound changes. Old notions and perceptions are being blown away. A feeling of deep dissatisfaction for myself, for the way I've lived my life is creeping over me. Too much of my life has been lived as an observer, as a member of the audience in some grand play. I cannot allow that to continue. I will not!

It was known that bringing the wagons across would be no easy task, that every man would have to work as if the demons of hell nipped at their heels. And perhaps they did, for they nipped at mine.

There is not a muscle in my body that is not reacting to this day's work. My entire being tingles with awareness. My chest rises and falls with each breath, my heart beats steadily. I am cognizant of all this in a manner never approaching my consciousness before.

You may say it's strange, but I confess this fatigue-born awareness is a glorious feeling! Oh, how I want to laugh giddily. I'd like to twirl about in a waltz, sway to the music and sing loudly, if not well.

I am alive!

No, I have not run mad; however, for the first time in months—or is it years?—I feel alive.

And worthwhile.

Ah, yes. There lies the nugget of truth. As I have written before, I am not a woman for idleness; yet so much of my life has been led in idleness or idle activity. All that I have done to be busy exists as shadows of usefulness. To perspire from heat is common to me, to perspire from exertion is alien. Too easy has it been to send Sibby, Pedro, or some other minion to do that which would require those extra efforts.

I never thought myself above labor; but I see now that I labored when I wished to, not of necessity. It is, in some ways, a lowering understanding. This day I labored before sunrise to after sunset cooking, cleaning, driving wagons, tending animals, gathering dried buffalo chips for our fires, and mending torn shirts. Not a moment have I been idle that my eyes have not turned to another labor that must be done this day and so I began again. Now, when I should sleep, for tomorrow will bring the same, I find my mind running hither and yon in a kind of wonder for all that my labors have done today. A greater sense of peace and purpose fills me than I have felt in a long while.

I am not foolish enough to glorify the daily labor that some must do merely to live, for I have seen the years it has added to their faces. And I know that hard, grinding necessity obscures, and may make a lie of, a sense of worthiness to those who live with it every hour of every day. Participating in life here on the trail I feel I am a naive child. What makes life so different here than from my existence in Louisiana? In Louisiana, with its trappings of civilization, I thought I was safe. But here, on the prairie, the word "safety" takes on new meaning and I feel safer in the company of these rough and experienced men than I ever felt in one of the grand Harper family houses with all their doors and windows locked.

Perhaps notions of life and death change. Perhaps of necessity.

When I think of the formal funerals I have attended with

wailing, prostrate relatives of the deceased, I am reminded of the ancient practice of hiring professional mourners. Here, away from the cities with their encumbrances of form before function, death is starker and at the same time more calmly accepted. There is grief, but there is also the knowledge that wailing won't change death. Such is it with Singing Waters.

I spent much of my day in her company.

This morning I saw that she was to drive her own wagon across the river, for all the men were otherwise engaged in driving wagons, harrying the wagon teams across the river, or cutting brush along the river to lay on the riverbanks. The banks were still saturated with rainwater to such an extent that they were muddy quagmires nearly as bad as those we encountered at the Narrows. To traverse this mud the men again cut brush to provide some measure of purchase for the oxen, mules, and wagons as they came out of the river. Unfortunately, the brush is sparser here than when last we had to contrive a road out of a miry riverbank. The work, therefore, was harder and longer.

When I understood Singing Waters' intentions, I attempted to wade across the river to go to her aid. So late in her time, and with her other affliction coming at any moment, I did not think she should put undue exertions upon herself. I was dismayed when Mr. Bush, a man I had thought more forward thinking, attempted to tell me to desist because Singing Waters is an Indian and therefore did not need my aid. I consoled myself with the knowledge that Mr. Bush does not know what it means to be a woman, particularly a woman near her time who fears for her unborn child's well-being. Nonetheless, Mr. Bush did see that I crossed the river safely. Singing Waters was glad for my aid. Though she said little, I could tell her back was paining her. I made her lie down in the back of the wagon while I drove the wagon across. After my harrowing experience the night of the storm, the effort was minimal. Though I will confess you would be shocked by the language I have developed when urging recalcitrant mules to move! Young Juniper Robles was.

After all the wagons were safely across the river we broke camp and pressed on down the trail after Mr. Gaspard and Mr. Tidewell. Despite our late start, we made good time and mileage for the day; still, there is no sign of the party before us or our men. No one is worried about this, but there is much continued speculation in the party as to what lies before us. For myself, I admit I'm concerned by the speculation. It has developed almost to farcical proportions. I worry that should we come upon another party there are those in our midst, particularly certain Mexicans and all the young men who have just left their mothers' sides, who would act upon their speculations without proper knowledge. I believe Mr. Rawlins shares my concern, for on more than one occasion I heard him sharply call to task a man for some ridiculous comment that others were rapidly and volubly developing to be truth. I intend to remain vigilant for I believe more harm comes to those who see ghosts at every turn. Since we continue to dispense with individual messes for any meal, mealtimes will be advantageous for hearing and controlling such nonsense.

I cannot believe I have written so much this evening. I did not think my fatigue would permit me more than a few lines. Nonetheless, I must quit now though there is much more in my mind. I need sleep. Tomorrow will be another long day.

June 14, 1846, Ash Creek, "Dog City."
We've camped not far from the amazing sight of a prairie dog city. The prairie dog is not actually a dog. It is more like a large rodent, being not much bigger than a well-grown New Orleans–bred rat. The animal is nearly as golden as the ground it burrows in and has a blockish build. His house is a

burrow in the ground with a tall conical tower opening
created when he dug his home, heaping up the excavated dirt
at the mouth of his burrow.

The prairie dog's city is a sea of conical tower houses, each
house cheek-by-jowl to its neighbor, spreading outward in a
circle for at least one hundred yards. And like any city
neighborhood, its residents visit one another, running between
houses, or they watch the world pass them by as they peek out
from their own homes. From one end to the other of their city
can be heard sharp barking, no doubt their commentary on the
ways of men who pass by them.

The area around the prairie dog city is alive with other
species, particularly the rattlesnake. I'm told that the
rattlesnake feeds on young prairie dogs and sometimes usurps
a prairie dog burrow as its own, and yet to my eye, they
appear to coexist, each ignoring the other. Perhaps in this area
they have achieved some measure of mutual respect which
precludes enemy behaviors. I know I have not been sanguine
about the great quantity of rattlesnakes that are about. Near
hysteria might more accurately describe my attitude toward
the loathsome creature. Earlier, when I walked about the camp,
I carried a gun loaded with shot, ready for any rattlesnake in
my path. By the end of my walk my wrist ached from trying to
carry the gun up and ready.

Another prey on the prairie dog is the hawk, and their
numbers in the sky have been remarked by several men as they
soar above on the warm air, their feathers gently flaring in the
afternoon breeze. There aren't many trees about, but when a
lone tree appears on the prairie it is not uncommon to see a
hawk perched at the top of the tree, only his head turning from
side to side as he stares off intently across the landscape.
Watching the hawk, I find myself glad I do not number among
his prey.

I did hear one disquieting comment about hawks. One of

the teamsters likened Indians to hawks. The imagery sends shivers up my spine.

The landscape we are crossing now has more of a golden than green cast. The land is full of yellow sandy ridges and hillocks. I swear one might ride not far from another party and not see them at all for the little dips and valleys that sculpt the land.

June 15, 1846, Pawnee Fork.

We have stopped to noon it. As of yet, there is no sign of Mr. Gaspard and Mr. Tidewell. Either the party before us pushed ahead of us farther and faster than Mr. Tidewell anticipated or—no. Any other possibility does not bear thinking.

And yet we do think of it; I drive the wagon with a rifle laid across my lap. This morning we passed too near a famous landmark not to think of Indian attacks.

Pawnee Rock.

Sibby and I rode out to this trail landmark. We had one of Mr. Rawlins's men for guard. The fact that we needed a guard was almost enough to dissuade me from visiting the site. And to some extent, I find I am still unsettled afterward.

Pawnee Rock is merely a high mound with one side of sandstone. It derives its name from a battle that was fought at the site with the Pawnee Indians and some company of Santa Fe merchants. The Pawnees are known for being the most treacherous of tribes that Santa Fe merchants must contend with on their journeys between Santa Fe and St. Louis.

I carved my name upon Pawnee Rock, joining hundreds of names already there. I was surprised to see Mr. Gaspard's name along with the names of men I've read about in newspapers, or that Mr. Gaspard has mentioned. But while carving, I felt a distinct unease between my shoulders, as if someone watched me from behind.

Sibby and I had intended to take our time at Pawnee Rock.

We'd even secured a picnic lunch for ourselves; but as we
thought upon the history of the rock, we forswore our picnic.
I have induced Singing Waters to take a nap while we rest
the animals. She protested, claiming a dozen things that must
be done. I overrode her with a reminder of her desire to protect
her unborn child's life. Was that cruel? I do not know. I do
not even know if it would be better for her to rest or not. Will
that hold back the disease more or foster it sooner? All I can
do is act as I feel is right. Perhaps that is all anyone can do in
life. Sibby is with Singing Waters at the moment and that,
too, eases my heart. I should see to her chickens while we're
here.

MR. RAWLINS'S SHRILL whistle broke through the sounds of the
caravan preparing to break camp. Carolina looked up from the
mule harness she was tightening to see him gesturing to members
of the company to gather. The brown mule turned his head and
nipped her arm.

"Ouch!" She pushed his head away. "Stop it, Beelzebub," she
said irritably. This mule was the most contumacious mule of the
entire string and worthy of his name. He required her complete attention when harnessing or unharnessing or he was likely to move
just enough to trod on her foot or swing his head around to bite.
And he was cagey enough to take advantage of her wandering attention. She rammed a knee up into his side to get him to blow out
the big breath the old devil was holding, then she pulled the cinch
tight.

"Sibby! Watch the mules!" she called out as she ran to the circle
of men gathered around Mr. Rawlins.

". . . two men riding this way," she heard him say.

"Is it Mr. Gaspard and Mr. Tidewell?" she asked.

He turned toward her. "We don't know yet, ma'am. I've sent
Bush riding forward to meet them. We'll know within the hour."
He turned his attention back to the knot of men standing in front

of him. "Bring the wagons into a double line. We'll head out immediately."

"But . . . " Carolina began as the men turned away. All her fears and uncertainty were mirrored in her eyes.

"They're not hard riding, Mrs. Harper," Rawlins said in a gentler tone than he was wont to use.

"What? Oh!" Carolina said as understanding grew in her mind. She blushed. "If there was danger they would be hard riding?"

"Yes. And Mrs. Harper," he said before he turned to go. He touched her forearm with the tips of his fingers. "Thank you for your care of my wife."

Carolina smiled. "It is my pleasure, Mr. Rawlins."

He compressed his lips and nodded curtly.

"I'd best bring your wagon into line," she said into the awkward silence. She picked up her skirts and turned to run toward the wagon with its devil mule.

She shooed Sibby into the wagon with Singing Waters, then stepped on a wagon spoke with her right foot, pulling up on the wheel rim as her left foot found the narrow running board of the Rawlins's wagon. She untied the long reins from around the brake as she released it and grabbed up the long thronged whip. Wryly she realized her movements had become second nature; yet before the storm the only vehicles she'd driven were carriages with well-trained horses and small wagons pulled by sturdy farm horses. She'd never handled a heavy wagon and a full team of mules—let alone harness one—and if it had been suggested to her, her likely reaction would have been a polite laugh. Another change wrought by the land and circumstances. No, coming west was not as simple as traveling from New Orleans to St. Louis, or from one end of a state to the other. Water roads and dusty dirt roads crisscrossed the United States, but beyond, in the territories, roads were little more than faint depressions in the grass and a recitation of landmarks passed verbally from one traveler to another.

She flicked her whip and called out to the mules. The wagon creaked and groaned as it began to roll forward. She played out the whip again over their heads and braced her body to ride with the bumps and sways of the wagon.

"Turn out!" shouted Mr. Rawlins and immediately his words were repeated down the line of wagons cumbersomely maneuvering into two lines.

Carolina was pleased to see Pedro pull up alongside her driving one of her Dearborn wagons. She waved at him. He bobbed his head respectfully in her direction.

June 16, 1846, beyond Coon Creek.

Mr. Gaspard and Mr. Tidewell have returned to our company hail and hearty, though I detect some measure of disquiet in their eyes. They are often in private discourse with Mr. Rawlins and Mr. Bush, the latter gentleman spitting out his tobacco with an uncommon look of distaste upon his face that I cannot convince myself is caused by the tobacco!

They have been forward enough with facts; but I believe there is much behind those facts they are not saying, and as yet I have not puzzled the entire matter through myself, nor have I had the opportunity to ask.

So, what are the facts? Briefly: The party before us is but a splinter of a larger whole. The main personage in the party is Mr. George Thomas Howard, who says he has brought news all the way from Washington of war with Mexico! His retinue is small, but he has traveled swiftly ahead of a Captain Benjamin Moore commanding two companies of the First Dragoons! Mr. Howard has blown his animals attempting to catch up with the same caravans I, in my naivete, had also tried to meet. Mr. Howard's mission is, ostensibly, to warn merchants of the war.

Captain Moore pursues a more militaristic end. He desires to halt all traffic to New Mexico. He follows behind, led by

Tom Fitzpatrick. Mr. Fitzpatrick is well known by the men in our company. His trail name is Brokenhand.

Captain Moore will proceed down the Cimarron crossing in an effort, they say, to warn caravans ahead of what lies before them. Personally, I find myself remembering my conversation with Mr. Gaspard that first day out of Westport. He told me then that one of the early caravans carried munitions to New Mexico and that the merchandise was owned by the governor of New Mexico.

It is my belief that it is that particular caravan that Captain Moore searches out. He will not find them unless they have encountered mishaps such as have befallen Mr. Rawlins's company.

But there is more to this, of that I am certain. In the past weeks I have become fairly well acquainted with the tenor of the men with whom I travel. Their current manners tell me there is more to know. The next few days should prove interesting. If nothing else, they will take our minds from the dark cloud that hangs over our heads.

Mr. Gaspard says we shall come upon Mr. Howard and his small company about noon tomorrow. I admit to a feeling of anticipation for that meeting, so much so that I shall put aside my book now and turn down the lamp so that I may sleep and that much quicker turn tomorrow into today.

10

Mr. George Thomas Howard surprised Carolina, and her surprise carried with it an unsettled feeling. She did not know what to think of the man. He exuded a curious blend of self-importance and timidity, a blend she would not have thought found in any man engaged in U.S. government business in the far-flung western territories. It was a blend found in petty tyrants who clung to their fiefdoms of power. She'd had too many experiences with the type not to recognize their ilk.

Just the hint of that memory made her stomach muscles tighten.

On the other hand, she mentally amended, striving for dispassionate objectivity, men like Mr. Howard, who thought of power and aggrandizement for their imaginary fiefdoms, jumped the quickest and proclaimed loudest this thing they called Manifest Destiny.

Who put the name to this impulse that drove men to claim a land they had never seen? To fight for a right they had no basis for claiming? Did that unknown soul know what, have any idea what he was proclaiming? Did he understand the power of words?

Manifest Destiny.

Poetry and power resided in those two words. They conjured visions in fevered brains of some long-lost or maybe dimly remembered paradise. Adam thought if he looked hard enough, long enough, he'd stumble upon Eden again. Carolina smiled to herself. Maybe that was why they didn't like women on the trails out west. Men were afraid the women, like their universal ancestress before them, would get them banned from paradise.

Could they honestly believe that stealing another's homeland would bring them that much closer to paradise?

Probably, she privately conceded, if you equated paradise with plundering gold, silver, and furs, as they equated plundering Mexican territories.

No. That was too harsh a condemnation. At least she hoped it was.

They'd caught up with Mr. Howard's party just after noon, and in the time since she'd begun an afternoon meal for their company, Mr. Howard had been hovering near her fire. To Carolina's surprise and amusement, it appeared to her that members of her company were determined she not spend any time alone with the man, though why that would be the case, she could not conceive.

She studied Mr. Howard as she added salterous to the biscuit dough. "They've been talking of war with Mexico for over a year now," she said matter-of-factly.

"That's true, Mrs. Harper. Only now, the talk, it's over. It's a fact."

The hint of satisfaction in the man's voice had Carolina lifting her chin in her haughtiest New Orleans manner. The realization brought her chin down and drew her brows together in frowning surprise.

Seated across the fire from her on the makeshift bench, she saw Mr. Gaspard grin. She struggled to rein in her own answering grin. That gentleman was becoming entirely too knowing for her peace of mind. She tried to glare at him, then turned her attention back to Mr. Howard.

"How are you involved, Mr. Howard?" she asked. "That is, if you don't mind me asking such a forward question," she finished, smiling at him.

"Not at all, not at all, ma'am," he said heartily. "But it's a nasty business all around." He shook his head. "Doesn't show some of our own too well, sorry to say." He took a sip of coffee, then a deep breath. Next to him Mr. Gaspard cocked his head and pulled on his chin; Egan Bush spit tobacco and looked up.

"Immediately after war was declared in Congress on May thirteenth, I was sent from Washington to try to catch any of the spring caravans destined for New Mexico," Mr. Howard said gravely, full of his importance. He frowned and shook his head. "Many have pressed ahead faster than we anticipated. We didn't catch them this side of the crossing. To warn them, that is. But Captain Moore, he'll pursue them down the Cimarron cutoff to see if he can't negotiate some justice there."

"Justice?" Carolina repeated in a musing tone. When did war and justice ever walk hand in hand as far as people—apart from soldiers and politicians—were concerned, she wondered.

He smiled patronizingly at her.

Carolina looked back down to the biscuit dough she mixed. She was rapidly developing a sour distaste for Mr. Howard.

"I understand that it might be difficult for a refined gentlewoman such as yourself to understand; howsomever, Mrs. Harper, some of the merchants in those caravans place personal interest above national interest."

Carolina looked up at him, her facial expression bland. "You surprise me, Mr. Howard. I'm certain I've never heard such a notion." She did not dare look at Mr. Gaspard, for she could hear him swallowing laughter. She didn't know what strange demon drove her to her outrageous behavior; but there was no ending, for she was well caught up in the moment.

Mr. Howard nodded gravely as he held out his coffee mug for a refill. "I know, Mrs. Harper. Hard for any God-fearing man, or woman, to fathom."

She wrapped the corner of her apron around the handle of the coffeepot and picked it up to refill his mug. "And just what are our national interests with regards to New Mexico, Mr. Howard?"

"Trade and freedom. Freedom to travel, hunt, and settle God's great land."

"Even when it is not our land?" she asked tightly as she returned the coffeepot to the fire. She heard Mr. Gaspard clear his throat. She didn't look at him.

"This land from the Atlantic to the Pacific oceans is our nation's destiny. It is not for a mere man or woman to question."

"Mule piss. This war is nothing more than a contrived, trumped-up affair," Gaspard said caustically before Carolina could argue. He picked a twig up off the ground and tossed it into the fire. His gray eyes met Carolina's, but she didn't know if she wanted to heed the warnings there. Or if she would. She looked away.

Egan Bush nodded in agreement to Gaspard's comment. "Hell, everyone knowed this hyar country be stitched together with cotton thread."

"What do you mean, sir?" demanded Mr. Howard, rising from the makeshift bench.

"It's a damn conspiracy of slavies, that's what it be," Bush returned, rising to stand toe to toe with Mr. Howard, his eyes narrowing, his hirsute chin thrust pugnaciously forward.

"Easy, Egan," Gaspard said as he grabbed the wagoneer's arm and pulled him back down to sit on the bench.

"Nonsense," Mr. Howard returned. He sniffed loudly and proceeded to pace the ground between them and the fire. "In the couple hundred years that parts of these southwestern lands have been in Mexican and Spanish possession, little more than mining and building missions has been accomplished."

"Gold, silver, and God," Bush said with a dry, cackling laugh. He spit toward the fire, mere inches in front of Mr. Howard.

Mr. Howard didn't notice the implied slight for he'd obviously become consumed with his own view of the world. His color and voice rose as he spoke. "It's a waste. A sin to let God's great creation go so unappreciated!"

"I doubt the gold and silver have gone unappreciated," Gaspard observed dryly.

"We would do so much more!" Mr. Howard exclaimed. His hands sliced through the air to punctuate his impassioned speech. "These western lands can grow our economy, give our farmers more markets for their goods and more land for our people to settle. Young people won't be forced to move to the cities to make their way in the world. Our country was agrarian based, and agrarian based it must and shall stay!"

The heat of Mr. Howard's passion sent a cold chill through Carolina. He believed in these goals with a ferocity to rival an old Spanish inquisitor. A wild light shone in his eyes, the light of a believer in one's own inner light, a believer in every man's light coming from the same place and holding the same meaning. She handed the large bowl of dough over to Sibby and rose to her feet as she wiped her hands on her apron.

"But at what expense?" Carolina demanded, disgusted by Mr. Howard's sanctimonious tone. "I have relatives in New Mexico, sir. My uncle is—"

"Elliott Reeves," Egan Bush said suddenly. "You ever met that palouse when you was in New Mexico, George?" he asked.

Carolina scowled at him. "I meant—"

"Mrs. Harper, I just saw Jed waving toward us to get your attention. Might be something with Singing Waters," Gaspard said.

Carolina turned her head. "I don't see Mr. Rawlins."

"He went back toward his wagon. Come, I'll escort you," he said, getting up from the bench and crossing to Carolina's side of the fire.

"Really, Mr. Gaspard, there is no need. And if it was urgent, I'm sure Mr. Rawlins would have done more than wave." She turned back to Mr. Howard. "My father's brother—"

"You best hie yourself to Rawlins, ma'am," Mr. Bush said quickly. "I knowed your uncle. I'll tell Mr. Howard, here. Give him a laugh. No offense, of course."

Gaspard grabbed her elbow and propelled her in the direction of the Rawlinses' wagon. Behind her she heard Mr. Bush launch into a wild tale about Elliott Reeves. Carolina allowed Mr. Gaspard to lead her away from the fire though she kept her posture rigid. As soon as they were around the supply wagon she shook free from his grasp and whirled to face him.

"What did you do that for? Why are you and Mr. Bush so determined that I not speak with Mr. Howard about my family?"

"Hush! Keep your voice down!"

She tucked a lock of hair that had pulled free from her bun back behind her ear. "Perhaps I don't wish to keep my voice down," she said sarcastically, but in a lower, though still mutinous tone. "Perhaps I want everyone to hear me. What is going on?"

"Don't be a fool!"

"What?" She planted her hands on her hips.

He grabbed her elbow and pulled her farther into their own camp, away from Howard and his soldier escort.

"Remember some of the men's reaction in our party when they learned of your relationship to Diego Navarro?"

"Yes."

"About his being directly responsible for the executions of Baker and Howland?"

"Yes again, but I weathered their narrow-minded attitudes. It didn't take long for them to realize I am not my uncle and can not be judged by his actions."

"For some it'd be harder."

"Are you saying Mr. Howard would be worse than the wagoneers? Surely that cannot be. Mr. Howard is obviously a man of education and experience with the world. And Mr. Polk did send him to intercept the merchant trains."

"But you don't see him none too eager to push on to New Mexico. He's content to let Captain Moore push ahead and himself stay behind in safety."

"Are you calling Mr. Howard a coward?"

He shook his head. "No, ma'am. But he's a man plagued by ghosts."

"Ghosts?"

"New Mexican ghosts."

"Mr. Gaspard, if you have something to say, I wish you would say it. I do not understand your meaning."

"To put no bark on it, Mrs. Harper, Mr. Howard was there."

"Why do I feel I am in one of those nonsensical traveling comedy plays? All right, I'll ask. What do you mean by *there?*"

"When Baker and Howland were executed."

Her mouth formed a silent *Oh.* Her eyes grew wide.

"Back then he was Major Howard of the Texas Army and under orders from Lamar, the president of the Texas Republic. He was one of the leaders of that Texan expedition. He didn't have much good for Mexicans after that."

"My God!" Carolina whispered.

Gaspard nodded heavily. "My point, ma'am."

June 18, 1846, Arkansas River, lower crossing.

The lower crossing is the first of three common branching-off points for the southern Santa Fe Trail known as the Joranda, or Cimarron cutoff. It is a trail shortcut; but it is a dry trail, hard on man and animal. Still in all, we would have gone down this trail if it weren't for the news we received today. We will continue down the mountain route, if we are allowed to do so.

We have met with Mr. Howard and his party. From him we learn there are soldiers coming behind us whose intent is to

close the Joranda trail. But God willing, we will be gone in the
morning before the sun clears the horizon, heading west for
the mountain route. Swiftly we will press on as if the devil's
hounds chased us.

Perhaps they do. Or, if I am to believe Mr. Gaspard, Mr.
Rawlins, and Mr. Bush, they would chase my heels to hold me
hostage for the deeds of others. Through birth they would have
me a traitor. My mind reels at the inanity.

I am reminded of the melodramas played by traveling
players from town to town. They feature the wicked villain,
the damsel in distress, the hero. I, naturally, am cast as the
damsel. My hero is not one, but many. The villain—ah, the
villain. How simple it would be to say it is Mr. Howard, but
that should be a lie for he is as much a pawn as any of us.
Could we say all my Spanish ancestors? No, for that is too
broad and nebulous. The United States government for their
declared war against Mexico? That is merely a reflexive
action. Then who, or what, is the villain?

Fear and fascination.

Fear of the unknown, of those somehow different by
language, looks, and culture. And fascination with those
differences. Differences, hmmm. They'd best be careful not to
hold a mirror too close.

Now I begin to understand why Grandmother and
Grandfather Reeves never visited us. Now I understand why
Papa was always too busy with work or his studies to
accompany us when we visited them. I feel as if I have worn
blinders my entire life! They never approved of your marriage
to Papa, did they? How did you stand it? Love flourished in
our household. So much so that in my naivete I assumed all
marriages were created equal. When I consider my childhood I
realize there was much I took for granted. I didn't see the
prejudice. It was always "over there" somewhere, not around
me. It is no wonder they showered me with gifts and good

wishes when I married Edward, the epitome of American gentility and good family. And it is probably no wonder that they, and Edward's parents, blamed me first for Edward's mania and for our business failings and later for the deaths of my precious David and Edward, so close together.

Strange. For a long while now I have been silently, secretly ashamed of my marriage. When I married Edward I expected too much of him. I wanted him to think and feel a certain way. I wanted him to be like Papa. When he wasn't, when his behavior became erratic and the family business floundered, I expected him to pull himself together and to try again. He didn't. At least not with his whole heart. Truly he couldn't, not with those wild episodes that when spent left him limp and crying like a baby. I didn't understand that he was ill. And ultimately, I didn't understand, or perhaps refused to understand, that business failure, and personal lack of control, was, for him, devastating. He came from a family of successful, strong-willed people. For him, failure was anathema. He ran from it straight into a liquor bottle. I didn't help by alternately harping at him to try something else and maintaining a tight-lipped silence. Why couldn't I see how he felt?

He became a Mr. Howard, a man bitter and resentful of the past.

Oh, dear. That is a non sequitur. Forgive me. So much is on my mind tonight. So much has happened over the forty-eight hours since last I had opportunity to write in my journal that my mind wanders off into odd fits and starts!

The United States is at war with Mexico.

Of course, I know you know this, and have known it long before I. You probably wring your handkerchief between your hands when you think of me off on this mad start to New Mexico. Do you turn your eyes to the west and pray for me? There was a time when I would not have understood. Having once been blessed as a mother, I more than understand. I find myself wondering what are the thoughts of the mothers of the young men of our party. And, I admit, I wonder at the thoughts of the mothers of the seasoned men, too.

I fear I have been too much in my own company this day. My thoughts turn sour. This is not what I would have for myself! I must marshal my lowered spirits with their caustic tenor. Tonight I shall again be with the company; but I shall stay silent in the background. Listening. Learning. If I can.

Nothing must stand in the way of our continued progress down the trail. For the sake of my little cousins, for the sake of Singing Waters. I shall do whatever needs to be done to see us on the trail tomorrow.

Whatever.

War.

The thought of it makes my stomach twist. I could not eat this afternoon. My family is at war, each against the other. And who is right and who is wrong? Can there be any clear answers? I do not agree with "Manifest Destiny." But neither am I fond of Mexican politics.

I find I am now more than ever anxious to get to Santa Fe. We must protect the children alive today, for they will be our tomorrow. Mr. Howard believes that the Manifest Destiny credo is for our children's benefit. I pray he is right.

CAROLINA WRAPPED HER hands around her coffee mug as she sat by the fire. The evening meal was over and put away. Most of the men had wandered off to their bedrolls or a hand of cards around one of the other fires that dotted the campsite. A few remained to discuss the war, each man ready to conjecture on its cause and outcome. Each man ready to listen to another man do the same.

"There's some in Washington been preparin' fer this war fer years," Egan Bush said.

"Why do you say that?" Carolina asked. For a man with a

mountain dialect and manners, she'd always found Mr. Bush an intelligent, intuitive, worldly man.

He snorted. "Stands to reason with anyone has a nose on his face."

Carolina laughed. "Well, I admit I have a nose, but I don't see."

"John C. Frémont."

Carolina looked at him quizzically. "What about Captain Frémont?"

He opened the possibles pouch slung around his neck and reached in for a pinch of tobacco. "This hyar coon'll never believe he's jest a fancy mil'tary surveyor," he said as he shook loose a clump. He tucked it into the corner of his mouth.

"I think Captain Frémont prefers to think of himself as an explorer. After all, isn't he the Great Pathfinder?"

Bush shook his head. "An explorer that's under orders that don't come from the mil'tary. He's Benton's boy."

Carolina laughed. "Oh, really, just because he married Benton's daughter—"

"And how d'ya think it come about he could know Miss Benton so well? 'Course, that must a come as quite a surprize to Benton when his tool run off with his daughter like he done, but ol' Benton, he's a wily one, and he turned that marriage to his advantage, tied Frémont tighter to him than ever," he said, talking around the wad of tobacco in his cheek.

"Oh, really, Mr. Bush."

He spit into the fire. "Take that scoutin' trip he set off on June a last yar. They give over they war goin' to survey the Great Basin, but everyone knowed thyar real destination war Californie."

"So?"

"So, with this war and all, I say timin' war jest a tad too convenient fer this'un. Especially since they ain't back. Leastwise, they warn't when we left Sin' Louie."

Carolina laughed indulgently. "Mr. Bush, I'm convinced you are as skittish as a colt."

"Mrs. Harper, Egan may not be speaking wrong," Gaspard said slowly. "Frémont hired a number of good, savvy mountain men to go with him on this last trip a his. Why would he need so many men of their experience? Then when he got to Bent's Fort, he chose thirty-five men to go back to Fort Gibson by way of New Mexico. I heard that was his way of culling out those he couldn't trust to see things and do things his way only."

"Ridiculous," Carolina countered.

Mr. Gaspard shook his head. "I know one of the men who went with him. I heard from him that Frémont made every man jack of them agree not to keep a journal or any other written record of the trip. His is to be the only written record. Now, I ask you, why lay that heavy a rule? Why make it a rule at all?"

Carolina laughed. "He did do rather well for himself by the last book he wrote after his travels. Maybe he didn't want the competition."

"Or maybe he didn't want too close a record of what their activities were. I wager we hear he tries to stir things up in California, get the residents to think about revolting from Mexico's control. Probably draw parallels to our own country's history. Might be successful, too," Gaspard finished quietly.

A night wind swept through the camp, sending the campfire flames wildly dancing. Carolina shivered, but she wasn't entirely certain that was in reaction to the cold wind. All this talk of war, of complicated machinations and people dancing like puppets to another hand distressed her. After all, she was half-Spanish, from Mexico. Part of her felt a kinship with the people of that country. They were her people. Yet she did not like the notion of some other country trying to wrest a part of the United States away; too many battles had been fought already. She took pride in the United States, in where it had been and what it was becoming. Though she had never visited the birth land of her father, she had family in Mexico. Might they not feel the same way for their country as she felt for the United States?

Politics.

She looked at the gleam in the men's eyes as they continued their speculations and discussions of what they felt the country should and shouldn't do. It was especially clear in the eyes of the younger men. They shone in the firelight with excitement. They probably hoped to see a bit of war.

Carolina frowned.

"It distresses me to see a pretty woman frown."

Carolina's head snapped up. "What?"

Mr. Howard hunkered down by her side. He smiled at her and touched her cheek with his finger. "I said, I don't like to see a pretty woman frown."

Carolina leaned away from him and picked up the coffeepot. "I was merely lost in thought. Coffee, Mr. Howard?"

Carolina got up to fetch another tin mug from the kitchen box. Behind her she heard Mr. Rawlins ask Mr. Howard a question. To answer him Mr. Howard got up and walked over to join Mr. Rawlins where he sat on one of the makeshift benches. Carolina poured him a cup of coffee and handed it to him, then retreated to the far side of the fire. She sipped on her coffee as she listened to the men discuss Captain Moore and the two companies he commanded. There was a great deal of speculation as to the captain's intentions. Mr. Howard laughed the comments aside.

"Captain Moore is just an advance detachment for Colonel Kearny. He's preparing to march on Santa Fe."

"And what is Colonel Kearny's objective?" Mr. Rawlins countered.

Mr. Howard looked at him in surprise. "Why, conquest, of course."

"I see," Rawlins said.

Carolina saw Rawlins and Gaspard exchange quick glances, their expressions neutral, but Carolina thought she detected a bit of tightness in the set of their lips. After her days of traveling with these men she was becoming acquainted with their habits and thoughts.

"More coffee, gentlemen?" she asked.

Gaspard looked up at her then, his expression almost one of surprise that she still stood by the fire. He frowned quickly, then smiled and nodded. "Yes, ma'am, I could use another cup."

"Me, too," Rawlins said.

Mr. Howard shook his head. "No thanks, ma'am." He patted his chest right below his heart with his fingertips. "Too much coffee gets me right here. But I do thank you for the meal tonight." He laughed. "Better than what I'd get in my mess. Think I'll turn in. See you folks tomorrow." He rose to leave.

"Think we might just push on tomorrow," Rawlins said casually.

Mr. Howard frowned. In the flickering campfire flames his expression looked ghoulish. "Captain Moore wouldn't like that. Best stay here and wait for him to get here. I believe his orders are to stop all caravans from heading toward New Mexico."

"We need to press on as far as Bent's Fort," Rawlins said.

Mr. Howard shook his head. "Captain Moore is bound to consider that a motion of support for the enemy."

"Then we'll have to trust in you to set him straight," Carolina said.

"Me?"

"Certainly, Mr. Howard," she said and walked around the fire. "You will tell Captain Moore how near her time Singing Waters is and of the terrible rabies curse she lives under."

"I will?"

"Mr. Howard!" Carolina raised an eyebrow and folded her arms across her chest as she stared at him.

Mr. Howard coughed. "I mean, of course. Yes. Bad for morale to see someone like that."

Carolina winced at his quick rationale and glanced at Rawlins. His head was bowed; he seemed to stare into the coffee mug he held loosely between his hands. She looked back toward Mr. Howard and opened her mouth to sharply protest, but Gaspard waved her to silence.

"Well, good night, again," Mr. Howard said. He turned and sauntered toward his tent at the other side of the camp.

Rawlins, Gaspard, and Carolina watched him go.

11

A HEAVY, OPPRESSIVE fog hung low over the predawn campsite. Men rising from their bedrolls to stretch out chilled muscles appeared as ghostly silhouettes in macabre dances.

Carolina rhythmically stropped her Green River knife against the whetstone while her mind roamed past the dawn's oppression, and past memories, to find a place within herself as still as the dawn. The morning dew on the grass soaked the hems of her dress and petticoats, weighing down the fabric, reminding her of the river crossing when she'd defied Mr. Bush to aid Singing Waters. Despite her stockings, her legs felt cold.

"Coffee ready?"

Carolina looked up into Juniper Robles's young face. She laughed lightly at his rumpled, sleepy appearance. She nodded and pointed to the coffeepot on the fire. "Should be. Help yourself. You, too, Mr. Wells," she added as she saw that man step into the glowing circle of firelight.

Her fingers tightened around the handle of the big knife. She didn't understand why her stomach clenched with a sickly wariness whenever Harry Wells came around. It was illogical. Most of the men liked him well enough. In the evening, and at every noon stop, several men joined him in a hand of cards, others lounged nearby, their raucous laughter carrying clearly across still night air or in the fetid heaviness of noon.

A large, blockish man, his neck appeared nearly as broad as his thigh. His manners made no attempt to be other than what they were—rough and crude. Indeed, Carolina thought she detected some delight on his part for displaying a want of manners around her. Since he'd discovered her relationship to Diego Navarro, he'd persisted in his attempts to discomfort her and draw others of their party into a like-minded attitude. For the most part, he'd failed, owing to the respect the men had for Jedediah Rawlins. Also, his behavior toward the Mexican teamsters was nearly as bad. Oddly, his surfeit of animosity toward Carolina and the Mexicans engendered a good attitude among the other men, for none of them were comfortable with general condemnation.

Harry Wells's thank-you grin for the coffee more resembled a smirk. He took a sip, then hunkered down to face her at eye level.

"Yes, Mr. Wells?" Carolina prompted, inordinately nettled by his steady, silent regard.

He grinned again, his broad cheeks bunching, squeezing his eyes to beads. Carolina felt unease shift through her, but she refused to move, to give him that satisfaction. Instead, she resumed stropping the knife with long, caressing strokes. Her breath rose and fell heavily within her chest.

"You're a mighty fine-lookin' woman. Real easy on the eyes."

"Thank you, Mr. Wells," Carolina said as matter-of-factly as she could. Inside, thousands of needles pricked her senses.

He sipped his coffee. "Probably none to good for Mr. Howard to hear you was related to that Mexican bastard Navarro."

"My uncle is Spanish."

Wells shrugged. "Makes no matter. They's all a bunch of bloodthirsty papists." He laughed crudely. "That sure don't seem to matter none to Gaspard, neither."

"Mr. Wells, I find this line of conversation offensive. My father was Spanish. I am half Spanish. And I do not see where either fact should make a bit of difference to Mr. Gaspard." Carolina was distressed to note the rising tone in her voice. She could feel the tension gathering within her. It was palpable now. Like roiling dark storm clouds. She took a deep breath to try to master the tension. "If you will excuse me . . . "

"Gaspard, now, he's downright cagey. But we've all seed where that li'l darkie of yours sleeps lately."

Carolina's head snapped up. "I beg your pardon!"

He laughed and held his hands up before him as if to ward off her blows. "Just makin' an observation."

"Perhaps, but your inference is unfounded."

"Now, what inference might that be, ma'am?"

Carolina glared at him but refused to be drawn further. She tested the edge of the knife.

"That's a mighty big hunk a knife for a li'l gal," he finally said.

"Yes," Carolina answered noncommittally.

"Whose is it?"

She paused and looked up at him. "It's mine."

He laughed. "You don't say. Well, fancy that. Let's have a see." He grabbed for the knife.

Faster, Carolina flipped the knife forward, its point flashing upward just below his chin.

He jerked backward, falling on his backside, spilling hot coffee in his lap.

"No," she said flatly as he shouted curses and flailed like a turtle on its back before he could struggle up again. When he finally stood, he towered over her, his face mottling red with rage.

"Señora Harper?" called out Pedro Perales. He trotted bandy-legged toward her. Manuel Gutierez and Hector Garcia followed closely behind.

Harry Wells looked from the three Mexicans to her and back. "Damn Mexes," he muttered. "Too goddemmed high and mighty.

You'll regret that," he said, his voice rising. He shook his fist at her. "See if'n you don't. I'll show you not to trifle with Harry Wells." He turned and stalked away.

Carolina sat back, letting the big knife fall across her lap. She ran a shaky hand over her severely pulled back hair.

"Señora?" Pedro repeated, his expression anxious.

Carolina looked up at him. "I'm all right. It was just a misunderstanding. A silly misunderstanding," she repeated softly as she stared off in the direction Mr. Wells went.

She chewed on her lower lip. Mr. Wells had headed for Mr. Howard's tent. And she knew what he was doing as surely as she knew her own name. She sighed and shook her head. She looked up at Pedro. "You'd best fetch Mr. Rawlins," she said. "Right away."

"*Si*, señora."

The other two Mexicans stared at her uncertainly. She stood up. "Help yourself to coffee," she said, her voice dry and flat. She returned the knife to its leather sheath and tucked it away in her kitchen box. Then she turned to walk toward the wagons to meet Mr. Rawlins.

Rawlins, with Gaspard close behind, met her as she rounded the first of their wagons.

"Mrs. Harper?" Mr. Rawlins began; twin furrows carved deeply over his nose pulled his tawny eyebrows together. "Pedro came running. Said you need to see me. Something about Wells?"

"I'm sorry, Mr. Rawlins, but I'm afraid I might have jeopardized our plans to leave this morning," she said on a heavy sigh. She glanced over her shoulder in the direction of Mr. Howard's tent, then back. "I should not have acted as I did. Truly, I know that, but when he grabbed for the knife—"

"What knife?" Gaspard demanded, shouldering past Rawlins. He grabbed her elbow, his lopsided gaze checking her for cuts or bruises.

"My Green River. I was sharpening it. Mr. Wells said he wanted to see it and grabbed for it before I could say yea or nay. I'm afraid he startled me." She shook her head. "I don't quite know how it came about, but one moment he was grabbing for the knife and the next I've got the point pressed against his neck. He was so startled he fell over backward."

Rawlins laughed. "I'll bet he did!"

"Did he hurt you?" Gaspard asked.

"No, no. But I'm afraid I've angered him. He said he would get even and when he stalked off he was heading for Mr. Howard's tent."

"You think he's gone to tell him about Navarro?"

She nodded. "I'm sorry."

Mr. Gaspard smiled, but the smile failed to reach his silver eyes. "I've been expecting him to before now."

"I beg your pardon?"

"Wells has been spoiling for a fight since Council Grove."

"Why?"

Rawlins swept his hat off his head and scratched his scalp. "Grady and he went back a long way. After that wagon fell on Grady, Wells has been as ornery as that she-bear that lit into Gaspard here. Seems as if Wells blames us all for living while Grady died." He shook his head. "I don't know."

"I hadn't realized . . . "

"No reason you should," Gaspard assured her.

From the other side of the camp, they could hear Mr. Howard calling his handful of soldier escorts to order.

"You go on back to your wagon," Mr. Gaspard said. He gently pushed her toward one of her Dearborn wagons.

Carolina refused to let herself be pushed into the background. "Mrs. Harper!"

"No. I cannot allow Mr. Howard to make an issue of who my uncle is. It's entirely too ridiculous."

"Beg pardon, ma'am, but it really ain't. There's many a family has those kinds of sight-unseen loyalty, and I'd be the last to say otherwise myself. And how are you to say you'd choose if you were directly faced with a choice—some American stranger's life for your uncle's life?"

Carolina pulled free. "Right now, Mr. Gaspard, family loyalty is not an issue! Neither is death. Life is the issue!"

She walked across the camp to meet Mr. Howard, her stride brisk, masking the quivering she felt inside her body. Her stomach churned, throwing a foul taste into her mouth. She swallowed it down.

From her right and left men stopped what they were doing. She sensed the tensions rising from every man, a tension made palpable by their stillness. She increased her pace until she reached the edge of the picket line where the two camps met. Her heart hammered in her chest.

Mr. Howard approached from the opposite end of the campsite followed by several soldiers and Harry Wells. As they passed Mexican members of the Rawlinses' caravan tending the animals on the picket line, Mr. Howard shouted that they were under arrest under martial law.

Outrage swept through Carolina, burning away the cold fear that had settled in her stomach. "What is the meaning of this? How dare you!" she yelled.

"Now, hold on there, Howard!" Rawlins shouted.

Howard ignored Rawlins, his attention on Carolina. "Wells here says you're that bastard Navarro's niece."

She nodded and crossed her arms over her chest. "Yes, if you are speaking of Diego Navarro, I am." Her chin thrust forward as she tossed her head back.

"Oh, Lordy," muttered Gaspard from right behind her. She hadn't realized he'd followed so closely behind, but she drew strength, and daring, from his presence.

Mr. Howard's face turned choleric. "You, madam, are under arrest! Sergeant!"

"For what? I cannot help my relations, just as you cannot help yours." She unfolded her arms and pointed her finger at him. "Tell me, Mr. Howard, for what am I arrested?" She stepped toward him, punctuating the air with her finger. Her voice rose. "And do not tell me it is strictly because some of the same blood runs in our veins! I have never even met or had any communication with Señor Navarro, so tell me," she said, stepping close enough to stab him twice in the chest with her finger, "what is my crime?"

He stepped a pace back before her onslaught. "That bastard—"

"Yes, yes," she said acidly, "I am well aware of my uncle's perfidy." She stepped closer, stabbing him again in the chest as she spoke. "What I fail to grasp is my own. I am not even journeying to New Mexico to see my uncle Navarro, though I do attest to some small curiosity to see my father's younger brother."

He backed up again and she followed. "I am going, Mr. Howard, as I told you last evening, to New Mexico to see my maternal uncle, Elliot Reeves, who, I believe, you discussed with Mr. Bush. He has three small children much in need of care."

"Madam." He backed up again until he stumbled on the toes of a soldier behind him. Carolina followed, her voice thick with rage, her posture radiating disdain.

"You may have your little wars and battles back and forth across New Mexico and down into Mexico, for all I care, so long as you leave the children alone. Do not mix them up in your grand schemes for domination."

"Domination! My dear lady—"

"And do not mix me in either!" She plunged on, ignoring his interruption. She shook her finger at his nose. "I was born and bred in the United States; it is the only home I know. I have never visited Mexico or New Mexico, so do not attribute Aaron Burr domination attributes to me. Look within yourselves for that!"

"My dear lady!"

"How dare you even threaten to arrest me or any man working on this train!"

"These are New Mexican nationals and we are at war with their country."

"Which you knew when our party encountered yours." She shook her finger at him again. "Do not try to turn pious and prosy now, Mr. Howard."

"But—"

"There are no 'but's," she countered.

Satisfied she had Mr. Howard on the defensive, she deemed it time to change her tactics. She stepped back a pace, her voice dropping. "Mr. Wells here came running to you because his wishes were thwarted," she said.

"What do you mean?" He squared his shoulders. He stood straighter as she stepped back another pace.

Deliberately she sighed heavily, allowing her shoulders to slump as she clasped her hands before her. "Mr. Howard, I am the only white woman in this caravan."

"Ah," he said paternally. He swung his head to the right to glare at Wells.

"Now wait a goddamn minute!" Wells bellowed. He took a step toward Carolina, his large hands bunched into fists.

Gaspard stepped in front of her, but Howard thrust his arm out to block Wells. Gaspard stared hard at Howard, nodded, then stepped back again, though his eyes never left Wells.

"Regardless of what you think of me . . . " Carolina continued when she saw the men had stayed Mr. Wells's retaliation. Her voice was soft now and those standing more than ten feet away had to strain to hear her words. She spread her arms wide, palms up as she spoke. ". . . our haste to Bent's Fort has nothing to do with politics, wars, or even mercantile avarice. Our haste has to do with *life*. Can you understand that, Mr. Howard? We spoke of it last night."

"Now, hold on!" Mr. Wells sputtered.

"Stubble it, Wells!" Howard barked. Then he smiled at Carolina, and took her arm to lead her back toward the Rawlinses' camp. Gaspard and Rawlins stepped back as they passed them.

"Well, now, Mrs. Harper," Mr. Howard said, "I suppose it's true we don't pick our family. I got some I'd just as well not say were kin, myself. And, if even half of what Bush told me of that uncle of yours named Elliott Reeves is true, then I'd say if ever there was a man in need of help, it's probably him, and that's the God's truth."

"I do worry for my little cousins," Carolina said.

"And well you should. And it's quite proper in my mind that a widow woman such as yourself would want to care for the defenseless little ones."

"You are very understanding."

He nodded.

"You do understand our need to press on to Bent's Fort?"

"Having met you, Mrs. Harper, I could scarcely expect you to do less."

She looked to the east. The rising sun had finally chased away the morning fog. A pale golden glow bathed the landscape. "It is getting late." She chewed her lower lip. "I did hope to make good time and distance today. . . ."

"You shall, my dear. I'll have my men help harness the animals."

"That would be a help. Sometimes it takes so long. It seems an entire morning can be spent just making ready to leave a campsite! And you will have breakfast with us, won't you?"

Rawlins clapped Mr. Howard on the back as he came by. "Of course he will!"

Mr. Howard nodded. "That's one thing I will hate with your leaving," he said to Rawlins. "I'm going to hate to miss out on this lady's fine cooking."

Rawlins and Gaspard laughed with him in agreement.

"Not mine alone," Carolina corrected. "Singing Waters and Sibby contribute as well."

Mr. Howard shook his head. "But I am certain it was only your hand and watchful eye last night that made supper as delicious as it was, gracious lady."

Carolina merely smiled politely.

Mr. Howard promised to be back for breakfast, then turned and sauntered toward his tent at the far opposite end of the camp.

"That was slicker than bear grease," Mr. Gaspard said so softly she felt the breath of his words more than heard them.

She turned to look at him and smiled.

12

June 19, 1846.

    I have so much to tell you of today that I scarce know where to begin or what to say. And it is still morning!

    As I wrote yesterday afternoon (was it only yesterday?) I was determined to do whatever I must to ensure our continuance down the trail. To that end I have truly become one of those traveling players and my melodrama turned around our familial relationship to Diego Navarro.

    Papa would have been heartsick and confused by the fervor. His gentleness must have been in direct opposition to the composition of his younger brother's disposition. Is a murderer's family as guilty for a murder as the murderer because they are family? It would seem so. Once again emotions ran hot at the knowledge of my connection, only this time I was nearly arrested!

    Yes, arrested. Arrested by representatives of the United States Army! That one man should be the author of an animosity so intense that any who might know him is touched by his evil is awesome and frightening. I, at one time, thought

*I should like to meet my infamous uncle. I am now of a mind
to remain as far from him as possible!*

But I am drifting from my tale.

*Very early this morning when the camp had just begun to
stir I was up honing my Green River knife before cutting
chunks of dried buffalo meat for breakfast. I had already made
a fresh pot of coffee and expected the aroma to draw the early
risers to the fire for their first mug. This it did in the persons
of Juniper Robles and Harry Wells.*

*Mr. Wells is the gentleman who first exploded with
animosity toward me for the connection to Diego Navarro.
Since that time Mr. Wells and I have contrived to form an
awkward truce; we stayed away from each other.*

*I don't know precisely what was in his mind this
morning. I think he may have wanted to create an unsavory
situation, perhaps with blackmail in exchange for favors that
should put me beyond the pale. I think this is a circumstance
in which Mr. Wells views me, anyway. He cannot conceive
that any proper lady would undertake a journey to Santa Fe
or anywhere in the western territories without all her family.
The only women who go west unaccompanied are women of
uncertain virtue. At one point he even made vulgar
allusions about Mr. Gaspard and I. I did my best to fail to
respond to his gibes. Perhaps I was too successful. I was
nervous, afraid of the man. When he made a grab for my
Green River, I panicked. I drew the knife on Mr. Wells! I
still cannot fathom my actions! Regardless, they were the
impetus he needed to feel justified in bringing my familial
relationship to the attention of Mr. Howard and his military
escort.*

*When I informed Mr. Rawlins and Mr. Gaspard of the
situation they would I turn the matter over to them to handle.
This I could not do in good conscious. Instead, I directly
approached Mr. Howard.*

What happened next I am ashamed to admit, and my cheeks flame at the memory. I played upon my womanhood.

First, when Mr. Howard declared I was arrested, I railed at him like a common Louisiana fishwife, then I played the helpless female, victim of a covetous man's appetites. I displayed unscrupulous behavior unbecoming a lady. I might as well have been a strumpet on the stage. In a manner of minutes I turned an arrest into an offer of help to see us on our way.

I am so unnerved by my effrontery that I wish all could have been taken in by it. It wouldn't seem so damning then. Isn't it curious how the mind works? But no, I did not take all in. Mr. Gaspard remained too knowing and afterward commended me for being "slicker than bear grease." The encomium is a whip upon my conscious.

Nevertheless, we shall be on our way within the hour, minus Mr. Wells's company, for Mr. Rawlins would not allow him to continue with us. He paid Wells his wages and bought out his trade goods at too high a coin, just to be parted with the man. To my relief, it does not appear his absence displeases anyone in our company. When we leave, we shall push up the trail swiftly, for Mr. Rawlins and Mr. Gaspard do not trust Mr. Howard to hold faith with his promises. So we fly.

"MRS. HARPER!" MR. Rawlins called out to her as he rode up alongside the wagon she drove. "Mrs. Harper, I want to say thank you for convincing Howard to support us in our plans to push on, both last night and this morning."

Carolina felt a warm blush on her cheeks. "I was worried you'd take offense."

"For your bamboozlin' Mr. Howard?" He shook his head. "That's for city folks to condemn. You won't get that out here."

"So I've been learning. But I didn't think anyone else knew. I mean, Mr. Rawlins, did you . . . " Carolina broke off.

Rawlins saw her attention shift and turned in his saddle to see what had captured her interest.

Max Tidewell galloped toward them. "There's a party of about twenty men coming this way, fast," he shouted as he pulled up his horse sharply. The animal pirouetted, then came down hard beside Rawlins's horse, his sides heaving.

"From the west?"

"Yes. I was too far away to see clearly, but I think one might be St. Vrain. I recognized his favorite horse."

Rawlins nodded curtly, then turned to shout and raise his arm to signal the train to halt. Then he turned back to Mr. Tidewell. "Get one of the greenhorns to see to your horse, then get yourself a fresh mount."

Carolina reined in the mules, set the brake, and scrambled down off the wagon perch just as Mr. Gaspard rode up. "What is it?"

"Riders. Coming this way," Tidewell explained curtly as he whirled his mount about and headed for the rear of the train.

"Tidewell thinks one of them might be St. Vrain," Rawlins explained.

Gaspard rubbed the edge of his chin with the back of his hand. He nodded. "Ever since we heard about the war I been expecting to meet up with someone from Bent's Fort sooner or later."

"Will they try to stop us?" Carolina asked.

"Shouldn't think so. Not without damn good reason. Question is, will they stop long enough to tell us what they're riding from?"

"Or to," Carolina suggested.

Gaspard nodded slowly. "Or to."

Other men rode up. Rawlins turned in his saddle to hail them. "Bring those wagons around in a circle," he said. "We'll noon it here."

Mr. Gaspard got off his horse and handed Carolina its reins. "I'll get the wagon into the circle, ma'am." He jumped up onto the wagon with an agility few men possessed. Carolina silently shook her head and clucked her tongue as she led Gaspard's horse over

to the area where two of the young men of the party were secur-
ing a picket line. As she turned to walk back to the wagon she
paused for a moment to observe the activity around her. From the
moment Mr. Rawlins signaled a halt, the entire company had
moved to form camp with a swift precision that few army companies could match. Though every man was curious as to the reason
for the early halt, each saw to the setting up of the camp before
looking for answers. They were a disparate lot: grizzled mountain
men and greenhorns, Mexican teamsters and merchants and the
odd others that defied definition. To see the men working
smoothly together gave Carolina hope. If these varied men could
come to terms with one another enough to share a common goal,
might not Mexico and the United States come to do so?

She walked back to the wagons. Mr. Rawlins was helping his
wife down from their wagon. Singing Waters moved slowly, more
ungainly now that the child had dropped. It wouldn't be long before the babe was born. Carolina marveled at the Indian woman's
continued serenity. And it humbled her.

The need to be active and productive swamped Carolina. She
hurried forward to help Sibby unload the kitchenwares. Juniper
Robles helped them. Carolina smiled her thanks, though she did
wonder at his helpfulness over the past few days. Then she caught
him hesitating by Rawlins and Gaspard as they talked, and she understood. Rawlins and Gaspard often stood near the women when
they talked. Mr. Robles volunteered to help so he might eavesdrop
on them. Though she understood the young man's desire, she
didn't think Rawlins and Gaspard would. She called young Robles to her side away from the other men as she unpacked coffee
and sugar and salt from one of their food storage trunks.

Carolina glanced up at the sky. The sun shone directly overhead, washing out the blue sky. It was early for their noon stop,
and too close to Mr. Howard and possibly Captain Moore for Carolina to be relaxed. She knew it had been Mr. Rawlins's intention
to push them all hard for mileage today.

She looked to the east, back the way they'd come. The empty, rolling landscape seemed to go on forever, and Mr. Howard's camp now no more than a figment of the imagination. She unbuttoned the cuffs of her dress and rolled the fabric up to her elbows. A gentle wind swept across the prairie, ruffling the wagon canvas, mules' tails, and Carolina's skirts. The wind mitigated the worst of the heat, but the day remained far from its hottest hour. Resolutely she shook off the ennui heat brought and turned back to the kitchen staples. Their stores had dwindled. There should be enough to last them until Bent's Fort unless there were more additional guests, as there had been the night before. Singing Waters' beloved chickens might have to provide more than eggs; the pemmican Singing Waters taught her to make, along with rock-hard johnnycakes, might soon be all their daytime trail food.

Large pots of rice and buffalo meat with gravy were cooking on the kitchen fires when the lookout gave a shrill whistle announcing they had company approaching.

Carolina patted her wide skirts, hurriedly untied her apron, and tossed it aside. Her hands flew up to touch her hair, to smooth it. Then she realized what she was doing. She laughed softly to herself, turned away from the speck in the distance the guard had indicated, and resolutely returned to her cooking pots. Still, she strove to listen intently for the strangers' approach.

June 19, 1846.

Twenty-three men rode into our camp today. They rode in from the west, unencumbered by pack mules and wagons, a band of men riding hard and fast for the United States.

Our forward scout, Max Tidewell, thought one of the men approaching would be Mr. Ceran St. Vrain. And Mr. Tidewell was right. St. Vrain was one of the party, as was Charles Bent and Jared Folger. All are hardened, experienced mountain men and traders with weathered complexions and deep-set eyes that blaze with intent. They slid off their horses as if one, their supple leather clothing swishing as they walked their horses to the picket lines, expecting aid and nodding silent thanks to the young men who jumped forward to grab the reins and stammer promises to rub the animals down.

The leaders sat on the benches near our cooking fire with Mr. Rawlins and Mr. Gaspard. Sibby, Singing Waters, and I passed out mugs of coffee and fresh-made biscuits along with tin plates of buffalo meat with gravy and rice.

Anti–United States sentiment is running high in New Mexico. So much so that these hard-bitten merchants and mountain men worry for the safety of their families in Taos and Santa Fe. Particularly Taos, for there is a priest in that village, Padre Martinez, who speaks openly about his dislike for American merchants and mountain men in his country. At least in Santa Fe, the United States consul, a Spaniard named Manuel Alvarez, has managed to maintain some semblance of control and rationality toward the United States from the New Mexican leaders.

These men had heard the rumors of war, they were riding to Fort Leavenworth to ascertain its truth, and to discover, if they could, the army's intentions. When Mr. Rawlins and Mr. Gaspard informed them of the true existence of war, a profound silence settled over the men, a silence that disturbed me the most for its length.

I hurriedly refilled coffee cups as I waited to hear their reaction.

Ponderously, Mr. Bent commented that he thought it could be immediately profitable for Bent's Fort, but in the long run, it could mean the end of their business. Mr. St. Vrain said they should offer their knowledge and services to the military. It would be the only way to protect their interests. They would have to trust in Tom Boggs, a man whom by previous agreement they'd requested to watch out for their families if they weren't about.

They all agreed and determined to push on immediately after their meal, their desire to reach the United States burning hotter.

But before they left, Mr. Bent drew me aside for a word about Uncle Elliott and his family. My young cousins are in Taos in the care of their maternal grandparents and their extended family. It was a gentle way of telling me I would not be needed, and perhaps not wanted, for my aunt's parents were not happy with their daughter's husband and blame him for their daughter's illness and death. Mr. Bent urged me to remain at Bent's Fort; he said his brother William would see to my comfort and arrange for me to travel back to St. Louis. I do not know what to think. Mr. Bent was serious, and I have no doubts as to his sincerity. The news of war weighs heavily on him. But I do not want to believe I have traveled all this way in vain, in some frivolous desire to be needed.

For the time, I am keeping Mr. Bent's words to myself. If I told Mr. Gaspard or Mr. Rawlins, they would insist I do as Mr. Bent suggested. As I know you would, too. But I don't know if I want to, or if my spirit could. I shall keep this to myself for the time.

June 23, 1846.

It was dark before we camped tonight. Perforce, dinner was hasty and light. As I page through this journal I realize it has been days since last I wrote. The days have gone by quickly, yet at the same time I confess to a mind-numbing sameness to each. We've pushed hard up the trail during the past week, so hard that I've collapsed in my bed almost immediately after cleaning up from dinner, only to rise the next morning before the sun to prepare breakfast and get us on our way again. Tomorrow we shall cross the Big Sandy Creek and reach the Big Timbers area. Mr. Bush tells me I'll find Big Timbers a veritable oasis after our long pull through the prairie. We will

rest the stock there while the men hunt to replenish our meat
stores.

I'm looking forward to the break, for both my mind and
body remain troubled by Mr. Bent's words and need time to
rest and think.

June 24, 1846, Big Timbers.

We reached Big Timbers this afternoon and it is everything
Mr. Bush promised and more, venerable tall cottonwood trees,
rippling clear water, sunflowers, and game!

Everyone seems lighter in spirit and revived in intent.
Most of the men will go buffalo hunting tomorrow. And they
are as giddy at the prospect as young boys on their first hunt!
While they are away, I shall sit by the stream listening to the
birds and watching the tall trees' shadows shorten then
lengthen again. Perhaps I will do laundry, too. Perhaps not. I
don't know and do not intend to plan. Right now I must go to
sleep early for I intend to enjoy tomorrow to its fullest extent!

13

"YA SHOR YA don't mind, ma'am?" Louie Belmont asked as he and Juniper Robles packed johnnycakes and pemmican in their saddlebags.

"No, Mr. Belmont, we don't mind," Carolina said, laughing. Young Belmont and Robles tried to appear dubious at the prospect of leaving the women alone, but their bodies quivered like hunting dogs keen to a scent.

"We promise we'll stay in rifle-shot range should you need us," Juniper Robles hastened to assure her. "We'll just be over that ridge."

"I know, and I believe you, too."

" 'Asides which, Mr. Rawlins and Mr. Gaspard would have our hides staked out if'n we didn't!" Louie Belmont exclaimed.

"That's God's truth," Robles fervently agreed.

"I know you'll be close enough," she assured them. "I'm only sorry you had to miss the big buffalo hunt."

"Oh, well, shucks, ma'am, that's all right," Louie said. " 'Asides, I gotta be honest wit'ya, ma'am. I ain't a fan a that raw buffler liver that they all thinks so mighty fine. No, ma'am!"

Carolina laughed at the expression on his face.

"Huntin' grouse and rabbit, that's fine by us."

"Well, you boys enjoy yourselves. You've worked hard the last few days. You deserve it."

"Thank you," Juniper Robles said. He swung up into his saddle. "But you be sure now to fire that rifle should you need us."

"I will."

The two young men touched the brims of their hats, their expressions solemn, before they turned their horses' heads away to the north. They were scarcely beyond the boundaries of the camp when Carolina saw them kick their spurred heels into their horses' sides and let out two loud whoops. They galloped up the small ridge, then down the other side, to quickly vanish from sight.

Coming up to stand behind Carolina, Sibby clucked her tongue disapprovingly. "Mr. Gaspard, he ain't going to like to hear they rode off like that."

"What Mr. Gaspard and Mr. Rawlins don't know won't bother them."

"Miz Carolina! Is you fixin' to lie?"

"No, Sibby. I'm fixing not to mention the boys' jaunt. I trust you won't either?"

"No, ma'am. Not me," Sibby promised.

"Good. Then let's carry those baskets of clothing down to the river and get to washing. I confess I'm just as glad to have those boys gone because I have to wash my underpinnings and I've no mind to have them gawked at by boys masquerading as men!"

Sibby giggled. "I heared you, Miz Carolina." She picked up an overflowing basket. "That I do!" She walked down to the river. Carolina followed behind her with a similarly full basket.

"Have you seen Singing Waters about?"

"Yes'm. She say she got washing to do, too, and she be down to join us directly," Sibby said. She set her basket down and turned toward Carolina. She looked worried. "But Miz Carolina?"

"Yes?"

She twisted her fingers together. "She looked mighty odd."

"Odd? What do you mean, Sibby?"

"Well, she were distracted like and scratchin' her hand 'nuff to draw welts."

Carolina dropped her basket of clothes and grabbed Sibby's arm. "Which hand?" she asked. Her voice sounded unnaturally harsh to her own ears as cold foreboding filled her. She tried to corral the spreading coldness within her. "Which hand?" she repeated, more softly.

"Her right," Sibby said, her brow furrowing.

"Oh, my God," Carolina whispered. "No! Please, no!"

"What's the matter, Miz Carolina? What is it? Is it . . . is it . . . "

Carolina swallowed. "Mr. Bush told me that often the first symptom of hydrophobia is extreme itching at the site of the bite."

Sibby's eyes widened. She clapped her hands together. "Sweet Jesus, help us!"

"You mean, help her!" Carolina snapped. "Come on, we have to go to her!"

"But, Miz Carolina," Sibby protested.

"Don't dally!" Carolina said sharply as she raised her skirts to her knees to run up the riverbank.

At the top of the bank Carolina stopped. The camp looked deserted and unnaturally quiet. Only the grazing mules and oxen moved.

"Singing Waters!"

There was no answer.

Carolina ran to the Rawlinses' wagon. "Singing Waters!" she yelled again. She frantically pushed aside the canvas covering, but the Indian woman was not inside.

"Miz Carolina!" Sibby motioned her to come to the Rawlinses' merchandise wagon.

Carolina ran to the bigger wagon. The foreboding chilled her senses. She stumbled over a rock and fell, sprawling in the coarse grass. Dazed, it took her a moment to catch her breath before she could push herself up and run again, ignoring the pain that shot through her knee.

Carolina rounded the big wagon, her breath coming hard. She willed calmness as she looked up at Singing Waters.

Singing Waters sat at the back of the wagon using her knife to saw awkwardly at a tanned buffalo hide. She looked up at Carolina's approach, but her eyes appeared unfocused. Carolina reached out to gently touch her hand.

"My hand. It itches." Singing Waters' voice caught in her throat. She blinked away a quick sheen of tears.

She grabbed Carolina's forearm, her grip as tight as the metal rim to a wagon wheel. "Please," she said, "please, you tie me up." She grabbed one of the tanned buffalo hides and frantically tried to saw strips from it. "Must tie. Tight!" she said, her voice quivering.

"Don't. Don't, Singing Waters. Stop!" Carolina begged, grabbing her hands. Tears pooled in her eyes, blurring her sight.

Singing Waters pulled her hands free. "I must . . ."

Carolina wiped away her tears with her fingertips. "No. Calm yourself," she said.

"No! No time!" Singing Waters wailed.

"Let Sibby do it," Carolina coaxed. She tried to keep her voice even and gentle, but even with her own ears she heard the ragged edge of hysteria. "Sibby will cut them, won't you, Sibby?" She took the knife from Singing Waters.

"Yes'm." Sibby said, though her voice shook and her eyes showed white all around their dark centers. She quickly took the knife from Carolina's outstretched hand before Singing Waters could grab it back.

Carolina lifted the buffalo hides off Singing Waters' lap and handed those to Sibby, too.

"Let me help you down and to your own wagon," she told Singing Waters. Gently she handed her down. "Come on, Singing Waters," she cooed, then gasped when she saw that the back side of the Indian woman's dress was wet. Her waters had broken! Carolina stared at the damp evidence, her mind reeling.

"Sibby, fire the rifle to call back Mr. Belmont and Mr. Robles," Carolina said grimly as she guided the Indian woman to her living wagon.

Halfway to the other wagon Singing Waters moaned and grabbed her stomach. Carolina took more of her weight as the contraction gripped her. Carolina's knee protested, but she ignored it. When the contraction had passed, Carolina hurried Singing Waters as fast as she dared. They had almost reached the wagon when they heard Sibby fire the rifle. Both women flinched at the sound.

Singing Waters grew frenzied. She started babbling at Carolina in her native tongue. Then she started laughing hysterically, a high, maniacal laugh. It sent shudders down Carolina's spine and fear burst from cold foreboding. When Sibby came tentatively up to the wagon, Carolina drew a small breath and relaxed. No matter her fears, she knew Sibby would stand by her.

"You'd better go ahead and cut those leather bindings," she quietly told Sibby.

Singing Waters' strange laughter cut off as suddenly as it started. Another contraction had claimed her.

After the contraction let up, Carolina and Sibby got Singing Waters into her wagon and got her wet dress off.

"Sibby, fetch me one of my nightgowns," Carolina told her. "And you'd better set some water boiling, too."

When Sibby returned, it took both of them to get Singing Waters into the nightgown, for it seemed that her muscles were never still, that she was constantly in motion. A whirlwind, laughing wildly all the while.

Carolina knew Singing Waters had spoken the truth. She needed to be bound for everyone's safety. And so she told Sibby. Wide-eyed, Sibby merely nodded. She thrust a rag in Singing Waters' mouth so she could not bite them while they tied her. Carolina knotted the leather thongs around her wrists while Sibby held her down by the simple expedient of lying across her chest. Still, Singing Waters almost got away from them, the hydrophobia giving her an unnatural, wild strength. Finally, it was the advent of another contraction that stopped Singing Waters' struggles against them. While she whimpered and writhed in pain, Carolina spread her arms wide from her body and tied the ends of the leather strips to either side of the wagon around the ribs supporting the wagon's canvas covering. Tears nearly blinded Carolina as she tied the knots. Angrily she dashed them away with the back of her hand. She removed the rag from Singing Waters' mouth. Sibby got off of her and backed away. Singing Waters was quiet for a moment, then she screamed, bucked, and fought against the leather bindings and kicked out with her legs, catching Sibby in the face.

Sibby fell backward and grabbed the edge of the back canvas covering to keep from tumbling out of the wagon.

"Sibby! Are you all right?"

Sibby's nose dripped blood. "I—"

"You're bleeding!" Carolina exclaimed in dismay. She grabbed the handkerchief from her dress pocket and held it up to Sibby's nose. "Hold that there, tightly," she told her.

She looked back at Singing Waters. The Indian woman watched them like a predator watched its prey. Sweat dripped off her face, her hair clung to her cheeks, and her dark eyes glowed with an unnatural light. She did not know them.

Carolina suppressed a shudder. She turned back to Sibby. "We'll need to tie her legs, too."

Afterward she sat back on her heels as she dragged the back of her hand across her forehead. "Go see if there's any sign of Mr. Belmont and Mr. Robles yet." She slowly got to her feet. "If not, run up the ridge and fire another shot. We need them back here!"

Sibby nodded and jumped down from the wagon.

Carolina watched Singing Waters, careful to stay away from her flailing feet. She searched her friend's face for any sign of the gentle woman she knew. There was no resemblance until the next contraction came and passed; then, when she panted with exhaustion, her face relaxed and once again Carolina saw the true Singing Waters. She smiled tentatively at her.

"You must be thirsty. I'll get you some water."

Singing Waters nodded weakly.

Carolina got a dipper of water from the water barrel lashed to the side of the wagon and brought it carefully back into the wagon. She looked to see first if Singing Waters remained calm, then brought the water toward her mouth. "Here, this will help."

But when she brought the water closer, Singing Waters suddenly scooted back, as far from Carolina and the water dipper as her leather bonds would allow. Her mouth dropped open and her face contorted into a silent scream. Every cord and muscle in her neck and face stood out. Her eyes bulged as she fought to get far away from the water.

"Singing Waters! What is it?" Carolina asked, horrified beyond measure at her reaction. She pulled the dipper away and was relieved to see Singing Waters relax a little, though her expression remained fear-struck until the next contraction.

"Miz Carolina! They comin'!" Sibby yelled from across the camp.

Carolina poked her head out the wagon. It was true, the two boys were riding hard toward the camp. She looked back at Singing Waters, wishing there was something she could do for the woman, but knowing the best she could do would be to be there for the baby. As close as the contractions were coming, it wouldn't be long, unless the madness gripping Singing Waters claimed her life before the baby could be born, in which case they'd have to cut it out of her.

She climbed down from the wagon to greet the two boys. "The baby's coming!" she called out as they rode up to her.

"Ya-hoo!" Juniper Robles yelled. He jumped down off his horse.

Carolina shook her head. "No, it isn't that easy. Singing Waters has the madness!"

Away from Singing Waters, away from the immediacy of reacting to her, the awful reality hit Carolina. Her chin quivered and tears welled in her eyes and streamed down her cheeks. She couldn't see. She could scarcely talk. "She's mad and I don't know what to do!" she choked out.

The two boys stared at her in dumb horror, then Juniper Robles stepped forward to grab Carolina to hold her against him. She clung to him, sobs wracking her body. Sibby and Louie stood uneasily beside them. Then a high-pitched scream had them all looking in horror at the Rawlinses' wagon.

Carolina stepped away from Juniper and grabbed up a corner of her apron to blot her face and eyes. "I'm going to need one of you to help Sibby and me with her while the other rides off to find the others."

"I'll help you, Mrs. Harper," Juniper Robles said. "She were always kind to me and taught me a lot. I'd like to help her like she done me."

"Thank you, Juniper." She turned to Louie Belmont.

Young Belmont nodded awkwardly, his lips compressed tightly. "I'll find Mr. Rawlins. I'll find him fast. I promise," he said as he threw himself back into the saddle. "I'll git him here." His horse nearly pivoted on his hind legs as Louie pulled him around and kicked him into a gallop in the direction the hunting party had taken that morning.

"Juniper, the first thing I need you to do is to help make more room in the wagon. We need to move out some of the Rawlinses' household goods to give us room to work."

"Yes'm."

"Sibby, we'll need plenty of clean cloths, boiling water, and my Green River knife. But see that you clean the knife well."

"Yes, Miz Carolina!"

Sibby ran off immediately, anxious to do any chore that kept her away from Singing Waters. Carolina didn't blame her and wished she could be busy elsewhere, too. She took a deep breath and walked back to the wagon. Silently, Juniper Robles followed.

When she threw back the wagon canvas Carolina was relieved to see Singing Waters again exhausted and in a semilucid state.

"Juniper Robles has come to help. Right now he's going to move some of these things out of the way to give us more room."

Behind her she could hear young Robles swallow convulsively. She looked back at him to find him staring in horrified fascination at Singing Waters, who now looked so unlike the sweet, gentle woman known by everyone in the caravan.

"If you'd grab that box there, Mr. Robles," she said, reminding him of his chore.

His head bobbed as he recalled himself and agreed. She saw him set his jaw forward as he bent to lift the first box. Carolina fought her own silent battle, tossing her head up and biting her lower lip until she drew blood, but she did blink back the tears.

When he came back for the next box Carolina saw he had himself well in hand. Quickly the wagon was emptied around Singing Waters and mercifully the entire time she remained quiet or caught in contractions.

The day grew warmer. Sweat trickled down Carolina's face and dampened her dress. "Mr. Robles, would you draw up the wagon canvas sides a bit to see if we might get some air?"

"Yes'm," he said, jumping out of the wagon. As the canvas sides came up, Carolina blessed the slight breeze that stirred the air in the wagon. She breathed a sigh of relief.

"No!" Singing Waters screamed. "No!" She tugged on the ropes frantically, trying to pull away from the light breeze. The leather chafed her wrists, drawing bright red lines around them. "No!" she repeated as she tried to pull herself into a tight ball.

"Singing Waters! What is it?" Carolina cried out.

Singing Waters thrashed from side to side. "No!"

Juniper Robles ran to the back of the wagon and stuck his head in.

"What? What is it?" Carolina cried helplessly.

Singing Waters merely screamed again.

"I bet I know!" Juniper said.

"What . . ." Carolina began as she turned toward him, but he was already back at the sides of the wagon. With a loud *thwack*, the canvas fell down back against the wagon, first one side and then the other. "What are you doing?" she demanded. "It's stifling in here."

"I know," he said, coming back into the wagon. He was careful to put the canvas flap back down. "But I remembered when one of the folks down in the next valley from us was bit and got the madness. Ma and Pa talked about how he couldn't stand no breeze on him, nor drink a water 'cause it only made the madness worse." He shook his head. "No air, no water. Truly is hell's curse."

"Yes, but why couldn't hell reserve its curse for those that deserve it," Carolina said bitterly. She leaned forward to mop Singing Waters' brow, but jumped backward when Singing Waters began to thrash about again. She sat back and helplessly watched until the Indian woman quieted.

And so it continued.

The baby boy was born when the sun was high in the sky and Carolina thought she would die of suffocation in the hot, airless wagon. When the babe let out a lusty wail, Carolina saw and felt Singing Waters relax. As she held the child in her arms, she looked down at Singing Waters. The Indian woman smiled and nodded. She looked normal again, her face glowing, the wild light gone from her eyes.

Carolina remembered how she felt, the tide of emotion that had swept her when she held her own child for the first time. She remembered the sense of a miracle in the small life. She smiled at Singing Waters.

"Would you like to hold him?" she asked. "We could undo the wrist straps just for a moment and—"

Singing Waters head snapped up. "No! No, it not safe," she said weakly. "The demons, they hide. They would kill my son! You, you take him away now before they find him! Go! *Go!*" she screamed. Tears trickled from the corners of her eyes.

"Best do as she says, Mrs. Harper. I'll stay with her," Juniper Robles said softly.

She looked at the young man. His haggard face revealed a new maturity. He'd stayed with Carolina during the long morning. Carolina would no longer think of Juniper Robles as a boy, nor, she thought, would he.

Singing Waters closed her eyes. She sighed deeply, seeming to sink into herself. The labor, with her madness, had exhausted her. Her complexion turned a sallow color. But the ordeal of birth was not yet over and Carolina knew she would have to coax Singing Waters to finish it though her residual strength had vanished.

She bit her lower lip. "No," Carolina said suddenly, swinging back to face Juniper. "You take the baby."

"Mrs. Harper?" he lamely objected as she laid the baby in his arms.

She nodded in Singing Waters direction. "I have work here yet," she said, her voice husky. "Just keep the baby warm."

Juniper Robles looked at Carolina askance, but did as she directed. Carefully he climbed down from the wagon with his fragile burden tucked securely in his arms. The expression on his face tore at Carolina's heart for it revealed his shock, awe, and his fear. Yet these emotions were all overlaid with an intuitive knowledge that he'd crossed some invisible barrier between being a boy and being a man.

"Sibby!" Carolina called from the wagon opening.

"Yes, Miz Carolina?" Sibby called out as she came around the wagon. In her arms were a bundle of soft clean cloths.

"Give those cloths to me, then take the baby from Mr. Robles."

"Yes'm," Sibby said. "But how we going to feed it?"

Carolina shook her head, her expression bleak. "I don't know. I suppose we could boil up some more dried apples and see if we can dribble some of the sweet juice into his mouth."

The unspoken knowledge that Singing Waters would never be able to care for her child tore at Carolina's heart. She sagged against the wagon's side. All morning she'd managed to separate her feelings for Singing Waters' fate from the task at hand. Now it overwhelmed her. Fresh tears welled up in her eyes and slid down her cheeks. Helpless, she lifted her face to the sun and silently raged at heaven. The sun warmed her skin, but it couldn't reach the cold heavy spot inside where despair dwelled.

"Carolina."

She turned toward the ragged thread of sound. Singing Waters struggled to sit up. Carolina ran to her side.

"No, no! You must not. Lay down, please!"

Singing Waters shook her head. "Kill me," she whispered.

"What?" Carolina's hand flew to her throat as she scuttled backward. Her eyes widened in horror.

"Kill me!" Singing Waters repeated, her voice stronger.

Dazed, Carolina slowly shook her head. "No. I . . . I can't!"

"You wound my spirit."

"Singing Waters . . . "

"I no want him see me mad." A slight shudder passed through her body. "Leave him good memories," she pleaded.

Fresh tears coursed down Carolina's cheeks. All she could do was shake her head.

Singing Waters sighed and lay back.

Carolina leaned back against the side of the wagon and closed her eyes as she dragged the back of her hand across her perspiring forehead. A part of her wished she could do as Singing Waters requested, wished she were not such a coward.

From outside the wagon she heard Sibby singing to the baby. She took a deep breath. They had to save the child's life! It was what Singing Waters wanted most. That she could try to do. She needed to think, to come up with ideas for feeding the child. Her mind felt as thick as the quagmire at the Narrows.

She heard a low-throated sound, like a growl. She opened her eyes to see the horror returned. Foaming spittle dribbled from the corners of Singing Waters' mouth. Her eyes were wide open, unblinking and protruding from her face while her neck and facial muscles tightened, standing out under her skin like cords. There remained no vestige of humanity in the woman, only feral animal. She pulled wildly against the leather wrist bindings and Carolina heard one of the wooden wagon ribs crack. She looked toward the ominous sound and watched as the wood finally splintered and the leather thong was free.

Fear choked Carolina. The being before her was not her friend. It was not Singing Waters! "Juniper!" she screamed. She edged toward the back of the wagon. "Juniper!" She scrambled over the back of the wagon. Her foot caught on her skirt and she lost her balance, tumbling to the ground. She tried to get up, but she'd landed on the knee she'd injured before and now it wouldn't hold her. Above her, the noise in the wagon grew louder.

"Miz Carolina!" Sibby yelled, coming toward her with the baby in her arms.

"Stay back! Get Juniper!" Carolina yelled. She used her arms to scuttle backward, dragging her leg. Pain shot through her leg and up into her back. A wooden box they'd left in the front of the wagon came flying out, just missing Carolina's head. It was followed by other items. Frantically Carolina pulled herself farther away and damned herself for cowardliness. From behind her came a roaring sound like thunder.

She turned her head toward the sound. The hunting party was returning at full gallop. Great gulping sobs shook Carolina, choking her. The sobs came one after the other, making her chest hurt and her throat raw, but she couldn't stop. She couldn't pull herself backward any farther, either. She collapsed against the prairie grass and let all the horror she'd fought against swamp her.

She didn't know how long she lay there, sobbing, when suddenly she felt strong arms lift her from the ground and heard soothing assurances whispered in her ear again and again. Her sobs lessened and she drew a clean, deep breath between hiccups.

She gave a tiny mew of protest when the arms lowered her back to the ground. She opened her eyes to see Mr. Gaspard bending over her. When he started to draw away she frantically grabbed his hand.

"No, please, don't go," she whispered past her rough, raw throat. "Please!" Tears welled in her eyes again and a shudder swept her body.

"Shush," he said. "Easy now." Gently he brushed her hair away from her damp face. He opened the water pouch he had slung around his neck and held it to her lips. Eagerly she sucked down the water. When she'd had enough, he pulled a large, dirt-streaked bandanna from his pocket and poured water over the cloth. He gently dabbed her fevered forehead with the damp cloth. She sighed deeply.

"Rest," he said, his voice a gentle command.

Her eyes blinked, fighting against the command, but they lost the battle and closed. A slight breeze blew across her skin, cooling it. All around her were the rising and falling murmurs of subdued voices. They sounded like a lullaby. She wouldn't have to deal with Singing Waters now. For once in her life she could turn a problem over to someone else.

She sighed deeply and slept.

14

June 25, 1846, Big Timbers.

It is the screams I hate the most. It does no good to clamp my hands over my ears. I still hear them, and they echo within me as if I were an empty room.

As if? I should laugh at that. I am empty. Drained. A husk of walking flesh. Soon, no doubt, I shall collapse in upon myself into a little ball of nothing. Perhaps then I won't hear the screams.

What screams, you ask? What has transpired to reduce me to nothing? I forget you do not know. Was it merely yesterday that I wrote of peace and rest? Of arriving at our oasis for renewal? Such naive thoughts. One would think that I would not be so naive. I am not a young miss from the schoolroom. I have lived through too many broken promises, too many lost opportunities, too many bad decisions.

From what does my eternal optimism spring? I would crush it under the heel of my boot. How can I continue to believe otherwise? How is it that I hold out for that one chance against all odds no sensible gambler would take? Why do I

*believe in good and goodness? Why do I continue to believe in
Divine Providence?*

*There is something within me that burns bright even when
my life and everything within it lies in shambles at my feet.
That brightness forces me to look up, to push forward, to
believe in new undertakings.*

*Therein lies my strength. And, equally, my downfall. So
when that hope is shattered, I shatter. Of what do I ramble?
Surely you may guess.*

*It came today, and it came swiftly. The devil's curse has
visited itself upon Singing Waters and it is worse than any of
my remotest imaginings.*

*It is her screams I hear tonight and feel within me. Her
screams, to my ear, are more frightening than any night
sound. They are wild, beastlike sounds devoid of humanity.*

*I sit here in my wagon within a small circle of uncertain
lantern light, an unwilling listener with a heart too heavy for
tears. The night presses in around me. I would that it were a
cloak I could pull over me, that I could burrow into until
morning. But it isn't. And for all my desire to hide away, I
won't, for life, demanding life, lies within my reach.*

A baby.

*Huzzah! The devil has not claimed total victory! I must
take great comfort from that truth.*

*Singing Waters' baby was born today. He was born amidst
awful seizures from that wretched disease. But he was born
alive and well. I know better than anyone this truth for he was
born straight into my arms. The glory of it overwhelmed me,
while the reality of Singing Waters' struggles against her
disease humbled me. Blessedly, Singing Waters experienced
moments of sanity through which to see her son. Truly God
smiled down amongst us for that.*

*I fear those precious moments when the baby was born were
among the last of Singing Waters' sane moments.*

I cannot bring myself to write of it here. I know I promised

to tell you all that occurred, but to say it would bring back the
horror, which is not something my mind can accept.

To my dismay and shame, the strain of caring for Singing
Waters during her labors taxed my strength of mind and body.
I collapsed this afternoon and slept, leaving Sibby to care for
the baby. But now she sleeps, so the child is with me.

CAROLINA REACHED OUT to lightly stroke the baby's cheek with
the back of her finger. His skin felt silken. He opened his mouth
and yawned, then settled back into sleep. Soon enough he would
wake again, hungry, and she would try to get him to drink more
of the apple juice she'd contrived from the dried apples.

Mr. Gaspard has managed to surprise me. He has proven
himself a most resourceful and clever man, although he
attributes his cleverness totally to his Indian friends. He has
fashioned a feeding pouch for the baby. He took a piece of the
leather Singing Waters had smoked (to make the leather soft,
supple, and waterproof) and fashioned it into a baby's bottle.
For the nipple he inserted a small piece of hollow bird's feather
quill into the soft leather to prevent it from collapsing in upon
itself as the baby sucks. All the seams have been sealed with
buffalo grease.

The bottle has been successful. Earlier today I was
uncertain how we could keep the child alive without a wet
nurse; now I am more confident. I will need to experiment
with different liquid diets; but I feel certain we will be
victorious for the child is healthy and shows no sign of
Singing Waters' disease. I will admit I worried for that, but
Mr. Bush told me he's never heard of a woman passing the
disease on to her unborn child. I pray he is correct.

THE BABY TWITCHED, then whimpered and screwed up his face
to cry.

Carolina capped her ink bottle and set her pen and lap desk

aside. At the baby's first demanding cry, Carolina smiled. She picked him up. It felt good to hold an infant's body next to hers once again. This time, when the memory pang for her lost child came, it was softer, more bittersweet, for here was life.

Quickly she changed his soiled swaddling clothes, murmuring softly to him as she worked. He cried and fussed louder. Carolina's smile grew broader and more tender. When he was clean and dry, she cuddled him close to her, her cheek stroking his as she savored his touch and infant smell. Then she settled him in the crook of her left arm and brought the bottle Mr. Gaspard made up to his lips. She lightly brushed the side of his cheek with a fingertip. His little birdlike mouth opened and clamped hungrily around the bottle's nipple.

She sighed deeply.

"Mrs. Harper?" A man called to her from just the other side of the canvas curtain that shut out the night.

"Yes, Mr. Gaspard?" she said, recognizing his soft, gravelly tone.

"May I speak with you, ma'am?"

There was that odd distance in his tone again. The distance she hadn't heard since before Council Grove. She frowned and felt a little disappointed.

"Yes, of course, Mr. Gaspard. Come in, please," she replied as she settled the baby higher in her arms, close to her heart.

He pushed aside the wagon canvas and climbed up into the wagon. Amusement touched her as she watched him tie back the canvas curtain sides so anyone walking by would clearly see them and the proprieties. He sat down on a low crate packed with cutlery, his back resting against a larger crate filled with calicoes. He looked at the infant in her arms and a frown creased his brow.

"How's Singing Waters?" Carolina asked, realizing she hadn't heard the screaming for some minutes now.

Gaspard raised his eyes to look at her and slowly shook his head. "She's not going quick, nor easy. Jed, he's staying right with her, though. If the disease were to have its way she'd probably last another day, if not two. Her lucid times is getting fewer and shorter."

"If?"

Gaspard looked at her steadily.

Remembering Singing Waters' plea for death, Carolina turned her head aside. "Probably be easier on him if she stayed out of her mind," she murmured.

Gaspard sighed heavily and shifted position. "I'd say that's right." He paused. "But the last time she was herself, she asked Jed to take his son to a Cheyenne village, find an Indian woman there with milk enough for two."

The emptiness Carolina had felt all day yawned wider. She looked down at the child in her arms. Her arms had felt empty for so long. It felt right to hold a baby again. So right. But the child wasn't hers, and so the universe cruelly reminded her. An iron band encircled her heart.

"I see," she said. She felt a freshet of tears prick her eyes. She blinked them away. "Is there an Indian village nearby?" she asked, hoping to maintain a neutral voice.

"About two days southwest of here."

"Will we be going there tomorrow?"

Gaspard shook his head.

Carolina felt the band around her heart loosen.

"No, ma'am," he said. He awkwardly cleared his throat. "The caravan will be settled here until . . . well, until afterward."

He paused and shifted position again, coming close enough to gently cup the baby's dark-haired head with his hand. "Carolina," he said softly, her given name rumbling out on a breath.

She looked at him, his face just inches from her own. His gray eyes were dark with compassion and sorrow. Her breath caught in her chest, the band around her heart tightened again. Tighter. She knew, but she searched his ravaged face for another answer.

"Carolina, I'm sorry. I'm taking the child tomorrow."

Knife-edged pain caught her throat and robbed her of breath, then twisted, cutting deeply into her soul. She couldn't talk. She couldn't think. She merely looked at him. Her eyes glazed over. Tears trickled down her cheeks, then slid in a steady silent stream.

The baby fussed when the tears touched his head. Carolina's arms tightened around him, pulling him closer to her as if she could pull him inside herself. She licked her lips. They were wet and salty. Her heart shattered beneath the tightening band, flying off into thousands of needlelike slivers to plague her soul; but she nodded, her head bobbing like a marionette's.

She understood. It was right. It was best for the baby. For Mr. Rawlins. For Singing Waters. She did understand.

But it hurt. *Dear God, it hurts!*

She pressed her lips tightly together against the sob that rose in her chest.

"Ah, damnation," she heard Mr. Gaspard say. Then he was beside her, pulling her and the baby back to lean against his broad chest. He murmured softly in her ear assurances and understandings as he stroked her hair.

Just like he had that afternoon. He was a good man. And perhaps he did understand, a little. Perhaps he cared, too. But even if he didn't, it didn't matter.

Some of the pain and tension slowly leached out of Carolina. She relaxed against him. She didn't care that anyone who walked by the end of the wagon could see them. It felt good to be held again, to be cared for. She closed her eyes, luxuriating in the feelings she hadn't had in years, not since before Edward's business had gone bad.

Yes, Gerard Gaspard was a good man.

And she was a fool.

The baby slept again.

Carolina lifted a hand to her face to wipe away the tears. She'd cried too much today. She thought she'd long ago learned the futility of tears. Maybe one never did. Her head ached.

"Mrs. Harper?" Gaspard said, seeking her state of mind.

A part of Carolina silently raged against his return to formality, but she ignored the voice. It was better this way. Mr. Gaspard was right. She leaned forward out of Gaspard's loose embrace and laid the baby back in the basket she'd made up for his bed.

"Thank you, Mr. Gaspard," she heard herself say in her best formal New Orleans–matron tone. "I won't pretend I'm happy with giving up this child, but I do understand, and it is for the best. You are a kind man to indulge me," she offered lightly. She felt his hard stare, but she couldn't turn her head to look at him. He'd see more in her eyes than she dared to admit even to herself.

"What time will you be leaving in the morning?" she asked. She clenched the edge of the basket as she lifted her head up to stare blindly at the canvas wall.

"As early as I can. First light, if possible."

She nodded. "I'll have him ready."

"Thank you," he said softly. He turned to go.

A gunshot suddenly ripped through the night's silence.

Carolina's head jerked up as a silent scream tightened her throat. She stared at Gaspard. The gunshot was near. Within their camp.

Singing Waters!

"Carolina . . . " Gaspard began, reaching toward her.

She turned toward the direction of the sound. Toward the Rawlinses' wagon, where she knew Jed had done what she'd lacked the courage, and the love, to do.

Her head dropped, her shoulders slumping.

Carolina felt Gaspard behind her, felt his tension. She expected him to say something else, but he didn't. He rose and left the wagon, pulling the canvas curtains closed tightly after him.

Carolina stayed frozen in position for a moment more, then she collapsed in upon herself next to the basket. She collapsed, a near hysterical portion of her observed, just like she'd written in her journal.

There were no more tears, but an ache that pierced her soul

stayed with her all through the night as she stayed by the baby's side.

June 26, 1846, Big Timbers.

> *Last night saw Singing Waters freed from her earthly hell.*
>
> *Sibby and I assisted Mr. Rawlins in laying her out this morning. Though we tried, we could not smooth from her once beautiful face the feral animal snarl. The knowledge that Divine Providence received assistance I will keep within the leather covers of this journal. Providence must understand, and so Sibby and I pray.*
>
> *This morning Mr. Gaspard took Singing Waters' baby to a Cheyenne village in search of a wet nurse. It is what Singing Waters and Mr. Rawlins wanted. It is the right thing to do. I helped Gaspard fashion a linen sling against his chest in which to carry the baby.*
>
> *His care for the child makes me see that not all men consider children only necessary appendages, to be hidden away until they're grown, as Edward had. This trip has opened my eyes to Edward in ways it may have been best if they had remained forever hidden. This new knowledge only serves to depress me.*
>
> *Mr. Gaspard will meet up with us, afterward, at Bent's Fort.*
>
> *Hunting to replenish our meat stores has resumed today. Already Juniper Robles and Louie Belmont have brought me four rabbits. It is not much, but it is a change in diet. With rice they should make a flavorful stew. Truly, I have never appreciated rice before as I have on this journey. It is a wondrous staple for filling bellies. I'd best leave off my scribbling to see to the rabbits, and see if Mr. Rawlins has any needs.*

CAROLINA READ OVER her last entry and frowned sourly. It read so matter-of-factly, leached of all emotion. She wondered if her mother would one day read it and recognize the pain hidden in her plain recitation.

She felt nearly at the end of her emotional reserves. She did not like to contemplate what would happen to her should they totally disappear. She'd always prided herself on her strength. Where was that strength now? Emotionally she was exhausted, yet she would go on.

But she wished Mr. Gaspard had not gone. He believed in her, and that belief imbued her with strength. Carolina thought she was going to be in need of that strength to see her through the next few days.

She sighed as she put her lap desk away. There was work to be done.

EGAN BUSH HELPED himself to a mug of coffee, then sat down on the bench near her kitchen fire. "That Gaspard, he shor war anxious to git off this mornin'. Cain't say as I blame him. Under the circumstances, he wouldn't want to stay around to see Singing Waters buried."

"Circumstances?" Carolina said. "What do you mean by that?"

"Gaspard, he war married once, y'know," Egan Bush said. He watched her over the rim of his mug as he took a sip of his coffee.

Carolina looked up from stirring a pot of rabbit stew. "No, I didn't.

Egan Bush nodded. "'Bout six years ago."

Carolina looked at him sharply. *Just six years ago?*

"Purty li'l blond gal from Missoura named Sarah Anne," Bush continued. "Born and raised at the edge of the wilderness. She knowed how to live. How to take care of herself and her own."

He stared down at the fire, seemingly mesmerized by the steam rising from a pot of boiling water. Carolina doubted he saw; his eyes were blind while his mind showed a daguerreotype of another time. She tossed cupfuls of rice into the pot, covered it, and removed it to the side of the fire. They really needed another rabbit for a hearty enough stew to feed everyone. She hoped the rice would serve to extend what she did have.

"What happened?" she asked softly as she sat down on the bench next to him.

"What happened?" Mr. Bush sighed heavily. "Same as often happens to women seein' to themselves all alone, with no other woman friend nor husband to care for 'em."

"Was she kidnapped?"

"Hell, no. Though it might a proved better if'n she had been. Leastwise she wouldn'a been alone."

"What do you mean?"

Mr. Bush sighed again. "Sarah Anne and Gaspard, they had them a place down in Arkansas territory. But Gaspard, he ain't no farmer, so he war away mucha the time huntin' or guidin'. Sarah Anne, she war breedin' and not too many weeks from her time when Gaspard had to go on a short guide trip. Leastwise, it war supposed to be a short guide trip but thyar war Indian trouble and animal trouble and weather trouble and all. Any goshdarn thang that might go wrong did jest that with a big show about it, too.

"Anyway, Sarah Anne's time come afore Gaspard come back. It took her so fast, thyar warn't time to hitch the wagon and drive herself ten miles down the road to their nearest neighbor, though that's not to say they warn't the best neighbors anyway, seein' as how if'n they war they woulda been checkin' on her."

"What happened?" Caroline prodded, though in her heart she felt the answer.

Egan Bush sighed and shook his head again. He slapped his hands against his knees and leaned forward. "She had the babe by herself. Took care of the babe. Cleaned the tyke up all fine, but Sarah Anne, she didn't stop bleedin'. She died in her bed, the babe beside her."

"Oh, God, no!"

He nodded. "Gaspard, he figured it war at least two days after that afore he got home. The babe war still alive. Barely. He took the child and rode hell fer leather for help, but the babe, it died in his arms. I guess the young'un jest wanted to meet his pa onct afore he departed this good earth."

"Poor Mr. Gaspard."

"Now ya see why he war so gol'darn fired up to save Jed's young'un?"

"Yes."

"And if thyar be any man that can, it be Gaspard. He'll find that chile a wet nurse, you jest see if'n he don't."

"I think you're right. I would not argue that point." Carolina stared at the fire, which looked like a blur of color through her pooling tears.

15

June 28, 1846. Evening.

Mr. Rawlins is silent, the heaviness in his soul visible in his eyes. He has spent much of the day seated by the river, staring at the water's rippling course.

Our camp is unnaturally quiet. Conversations are in hushed tones. And alas, our beautiful oasis now seems a prison from which we cannot break free too soon.

Today, the men brought in fresh meat—buffalo, deer, rabbit, and grouse. Enough meat to feed us for weeks if I can cure the meat properly, remembering all the Indian techniques Singing Waters taught me. Several men have assisted with the butchering and curing of the meat, others with the tanning of the hides. I am grateful for their assistance, but I know it is not thanks they desire. They desire the speedy departure from this place, and it is for that they so grimly work toward. Still, we shall be here at least another day, but no more, not even if I have to let meat spoil and hides rot!

June 29, 1846.

The tanning and curing is done, after a fashion, though I know Singing Waters would scold me for my less than total commitment to using all the animals, not wasting a morsel of food or scrap of leather. My heart is not in it, therefore my mind lacks the required discipline.

Mr. Rawlins sits again by the river, throwing pebbles into the water and watching the ripples expand. I did coax him into eating some today. Shamed him, more like, for I asked him if he would make his son an orphan and how would Singing Waters care for that.

The men in the camp sympathize with him for his loss, but there are already rumblings of discontent. Life and death are two sides of one coin, but they would play for life. And who can blame them? Mr. Bush has assumed command and so far, there has been no protest from the men that he took it upon himself without an election within the company, as is proper at the loss of an enterprise captain. But have we lost Mr. Rawlins? I pray not.

Tomorrow we leave for Bent's Fort. We should be there in two days. I do not think it can be too soon for anyone in this company.

July 1, 1846.

We arrived at Bent's Fort, the Mud Castle on the Arkansas, late yesterday.

The Mud Castle nickname is apt. It does resemble pictures I've seen of castles, complete with round towers at opposite corners. These towers bristle with weaponry stationed near slits in the tower walls, ready to sweep their adjoining walls with deadly fire to repel any threat posed to the castle and its inhabitants. The "castle" is a massive adobe structure with walls fourteen feet high and three feet thick. The main outer gate, in the north wall, is nine feet high, seven feet wide, and ironclad. Walls that are only six feet high corral the livestock outside the castle and are planted along their top edges with an impenetrable cactus barrier.

Inside the fort, facing the placita, the courtyard, are

twenty-five rooms strung around the quadrangle. Most are dwellings with earthen floors and plaster walls, but along the eastern wall of the fort are positioned the larger trading and storage rooms. In addition, there are second-floor rooms above the southern and western walls of the fort. Mr. William Bent has graciously offered me the use of one of these rooms for the duration of my stay. No doubt he expects an extended visitation. I do not, but I shall not turn aside the man's generosity. The rest of the enterprise remains camped outside the fort.

There are several gens de colour libre at the fort. They have made Sibby quite welcome. Being among them, I sense a return of her former liveliness, which I bless.

There are also Indian and Mexican women at the fort. Though there are no white women here now, and no white women have been known to travel the Sante Fe Trail, this fort has served as host and protector for white women. The mountain men who have used this fort as a base for their travels sometimes return here with white women whom they ransomed from their Indian captors much as Mr. Rawlins ransomed Singing Waters. Mr. Bent told me that sometimes such recoveries are joyful; sometimes they are not, for our society often lacks a compassionate heart for those who have been known by their captors.

Last evening, while my belongings were transferred from the wagon to the room Mr. Bent assigned me, I joined several women in what I take to be a large common room. We sat on rugs and on blankets piled on the earthen floor. The company was quite casual, more in the relaxed manner of a family gathering than a gathering among strangers.

I conversed in Spanish with several of the women, asking questions about their homes in New Mexico, for that is where they originated. From them I learned that the fort is built much like structures in New Mexico, save for the placement of the fireplaces. In New Mexico, fireplaces are situated in the corners of rooms, not in the middle of a wall as is our custom. At the fort, evidently only two rooms have corner fireplaces, the rest are in the middle of walls.

As we talked, we shared a pitcher of water, all using the same dipper to drink from. Water left in the dipper is unceremoniously poured out on the dirt floor in an effort to help combat rising dust. Though you or I may view the living conditions as primitive, these women did not. I am endeavoring to clear my mind of our city and society prejudices and see the fort through their eyes.

There is talk of a rollicking fandango for the July 4th independence celebration, complete with servings of mint juleps. Everyone is awaiting the day with an excitement that has managed to dull the edge of the news we brought to Mr. William Bent of the actuality of war with Mexico.

I hope their exuberance lasts long enough to hush any objections they may have at my continuing on to Santa Fe.

FROM OUTSIDE HER room, Carolina heard a sentry shout that a party approached from Mexican territory. There followed raised voices throughout the fort, and a shrill cry from one woman's throat. Carolina thought she heard someone say "Kit Carson." Another called out something about children. The vociferous activity in the fort surpassed the noise heard at her own arrival.

She capped her ink bottle and carefully stowed her journal in her lap desk and set it in the corner of the room where Sibby had contrived a dressing table from one of their wagon crates. On the makeshift table, Sibby had set out Carolina's silver-handled mirror and brush set. Carolina's gaze rested a moment on the treasured mirror and brush. They were part of her trousseau from her marriage to Edward Harper. They had been packed safely among her more colorful gowns, gowns she still felt reluctant to don out of respect for her husband's memory. But she hadn't been able to part with them either. So she'd brought them with her, and her mirror and brush had come packed among their soft folds. Carolina would have had them stay packed away, but Sibby, glad to be staying in a solid building with some vestiges of civilization, unpacked and settled in like a broody hen.

Carolina picked up the heavy hand mirror to check her hair. Her black hair was neatly pulled away from her face and back into a large twist at the nape of her neck. Satisfied, she started to put the mirror down, then she paused and looked in the mirror again. This time she saw more than neat hair.

Carolina raised her left hand to trace the new strands of white hair that winged outward from her temples on either side of her face. When did those appear? she wondered. She was scarcely twenty-five. She stroked the lines that bracketed her mouth and sighed over the weathered dryness she saw in her cheeks despite Sibby's lotions and liniments, to say nothing of the unfashionable tan on her skin. She grinned at her reflection. Her relatives and acquaintances in New Orleans and St. Louis would surely fail to recognize her, or would cluck their tongues in a disapproving manner.

And she wouldn't care.

Carolina began to laugh. She wouldn't care!

She replaced the mirror on the crate-cum-dressing table. That aspect of vanity, that concern for surfaces versus substance, could not remain vital to anyone faced with the realities of life on the trail. Heavens, Mr. Gaspard's gruesome physical aspect would cause him to be alternately stared at on the streets of eastern cities or, conversely, to be studiously ignored as if he and his ravaged face did not exist. Carolina, however, found herself missing that same ravaged face. She wondered when, and if, he would return to the caravan. She missed his forthright honesty tempered with dry humor. She missed his perspicacity and she missed being able to look his way and know he had seen the same humor in life she had, or drawn the same conclusion.

He was a comforting, personable man to be around.

Her memory smile drifted downward and her brows pulled together. She wondered how old he really was.

She took a dipper of water out of the bucket set near her dressing table. She poured most of it into a tin mug, the rest she poured over a handkerchief. She placed the wet handkerchief alongside her neck, and savored its transitory coolness.

Her mind was shamefully drifting. Quickly, she wiped her face and then her hands with the damp cloth and turned to leave her lodgings.

What would her mother say if she could see her and her surroundings? A small adobe windowless room with a dusty floor. The walls were covered halfway up with calico, the wall above whitewashed. So dark was the room that even in daylight a lantern was needed for any writing or needlework.

Sibby loved their lodgings. Her enthusiasm struck Carolina as abnormally effusive until she looked into her face and saw her eyes. In their dark depths was the awful toll their journey had taken on Sibby. And she wondered for perhaps the hundredth time why Sibby had agreed to come with her.

For Carolina, the journey had been no less hard; however, she'd gathered strength from the hardness. She felt the stirrings of something within her, something that had laid dormant for too many years.

"Miz Carolina! Miz Carolina!" Sibby nearly collided with Carolina as she came out the door of their room. She stumbled backward. Carolina reached out to steady her.

"I heard the men shouting. What's going on?"

Sibby gulped air and tried to get her breath even. "It be Mr. Bent's brother."

"His brother! I thought he was on his way to Missouri! Has something happened?"

Sibby shook her head. "Not that one. This here's Mr. George Bent," she explained as they walked toward the stairs that led down to the plaza. "And a passle a family, too," she added.

"Family?" Carolina asked. She quickly descended the steps to the plaza and wended her way through the chattering knots of fort inhabitants and local visitors to the side of the strangers talking to William Bent.

"In Taos, it ain't safe to be a United States citizen right now. Calf and those brothers of his are stirring the pot agin' us," Carolina heard one of the men say. "Thought we'd best bring the women and children here for a spell. Leastwise, until things quiet down."

"Je-e-sus, George! After what happened to you and Frank Blair at the end of May, I'd say that were a prime idea! What happened this time?"

"When war were announced agin' the United States there were plenty of fancy-talkin' hotheads urgin' the folks to lootin' and murderin' all gringos livin' there. Down in Santa Fe, Armijo put a stop to that kinda talk and action, but up in Taos, well, ya knows what it's like up there."

"Hell, yes! Them Martinez brothers would coordinate the whole of it, too. But outta sight, jest like last time."

"Damn right. And 'cuz one of them's a justice, even if the garrison captain did arrest anyone, he'd let 'em go," another man said.

"You got the right a that, Tom," William Bent said, slowly shaking his broad head. A brooding expression pinched his features for a moment, then he looked up, as if shaking it off. "Come on in outta the sun and rest a bit. We'll settle the womenfolk and children, then looks like there's a might of news to be exchanged. We'd best wait until some of the men out huntin' return. I'd like to ask Jedediah Rawlins and Egan Bush to join us, too."

"Rawlins is here?" the third newcomer asked. He was a short, ugly man who reminded Carolina of some monkeys she'd once seen in New Orleans. "Thought he preferred the Cimarron cutoff. He got that purty li'l woman with him? I keep tryin' to convince her to leave him and come settle with me, but she just laughs."

Carolina felt the cold ache she'd carried in her chest since

Singing Waters' death blossom. "She's dead," she said, before William Bent could answer, her voice coming out on a ragged, harsh breath.

The man who'd spoken quickly spun around to face her. He removed his hat from his head. "Beg pardon, ma'am . . . " he said, his voice trailing off as he looked from her to William Bent.

"Yeah, John, Singin' Waters got bit by a damn phobey cat. She's buried at Big Timbers."

"Damn shame. She were a fine woman," John said, shaking his head. The other men echoed his sentiment.

"Rawlins has got a small caravan camped jest east a here. This here," William Bent said, nodding in Carolina's direction, "is Mrs. Harper. From New Orleans. She's traveling with his party. Mrs. Harper, this here's John Hatcher, Tom Boggs, and my brother George and their wives, my brother Charles's wife, and that there is Kit Carson's wife."

Carolina exchanged greetings. The women were shy and spoke only Spanish, the men effusive at the rarity of seeing a white woman voluntarily this far down the Santa Fe Trail.

Carolina would have liked to stay with the men and listen to their discussions, but the tired faces of the women and children drew at her heart. She urged them to go before them into the big parlor where Carolina had sat on other days with the women of the fort. She asked Sibby if she would go with Black Charlotte and Rosalie, a half-breed woman, to the kitchen to fetch refreshments for everyone, particularly some milk for the children.

"Yes'm," Sibby said. "Poor dears. They do look all done in. We'll take care a them. Now, don't you worry."

Carolina laughed. "I won't."

She turned toward the woman who'd been introduced to her as Ignacia Bent, Charles Bent's wife. She was carrying a young child.

"May I carry her?" Carolina asked her in Spanish.

Ignacia Bent hesitated, then smiled and nodded. She handed the little girl to Carolina.

"What's her name?"

"Estafina," said the oldest of Ignacia Bent's children, a sturdy young boy Carolina judged to be nine or ten years old. "And I'm Alfredo and that's Teresina," he added, pointing to another little girl scarcely older than the first. She clung to Ignacia Bent's skirts and peered up at Carolina through a thick tangle of dark hair.

Carolina wondered if her little cousins would look like these children. Her arms ached to cuddle them all close to her, but she was certain any such behavior on her part would push the children into increased wariness. It would be best if she let them warm to her gradually. This she knew. But it was harder to do than to know. She smiled instead, and walked with the women into the parlor.

Sibby and the others were not long in coming with refreshments. Other women in the fort trailed in afterward. Soon the room filled with chattering women and children. The frontier version of the afternoon social, Carolina thought. Spanish was the predominate language spoken and Carolina was pleased to see Sibby gamely attempting to make conversation in the language. A few women spoke English, and in one corner of the room Carolina heard one of the Indian languages.

In that big parlor, there were no language or cultural barriers, no sense of social strata. Perhaps at other times there would be barriers. But not now, and that realization somehow created a feeling of peace within Carolina.

July 3, 1846.

Maria Josepha Jaramillo Carson is a beautiful young woman. One to cause all men's heads to turn! But there is a wonderful naturalness about her. So unaffected and sweet. My heart quite goes out to her. She is a delight! Tom Boggs says she is taller than Kit Carson, and where that might affect another relationship, it is obvious when Josepha speaks of him that their affections run deep.

I am glad she shares our little dark adobe room. While Sibby has been pleased with our lodgings, I'll own to a dissatisfaction with the closed-in darkness. I long to be back in my wagon or tent. But I would not be an ungracious guest when it is obvious from the comments of others that I should consider myself fortunate to have the room.

Small though it is, Josepha is welcome. We talked long into the night last night as we sat before the fireplace in our room. Unfortunately, my Spanish is not as good as I'd assumed, but with much laughter and giggling at my pronunciation of some words and my request that she speak slower, we did well.

I admit I find it sad that she has no idea when she shall see her husband again. He is off with the "Great Pathfinder" to California. Though she misses him, she does have a large, extended family who keep her in good spirits and well occupied. I envy her. I still find it hard to forgive Papa Harper encouraging me to marry Robert Eddings when Edward, his own son, was scarce cold in his grave. I considered it unseemly. He thought it good business. It is sad to say, but though Papa Harper is a regular church attendee, his true worship is gold.

Perhaps if Edward and I had come west, if we'd left behind the business and property of the Harper family that so shackled us, ours would have been a happier pairing. Perhaps then, too, he might have escaped his odd illness. But who is to say now? That was a lifetime ago.

"MAY I INTEREST you in a mint julep, ma'am?" Jedediah Rawlins asked her the next day as he came to sit next to her on a bench outside the storerooms.

It was the Fourth of July and the entire fort was infected with feverish gaiety.

"A real mint julep!"

"Yes, ma'am," Rawlins said as he held a tall glass out to her.

"I'll own that when mint juleps were spoken of the other day I did not quite believe in their actuality. And in a glass!"

He nodded. "Brought all the way from St. Louis, William tells me, at his brother Charles's insistence. He gave me a full measure of warning against breaking one, too."

"I am not surprised." She took a small sip of the drink. "This is good. Perhaps a touch stronger and not quite as cold as I would prefer, but it certainly goes in keeping with the day."

"That it does."

"So what is the order of the day?"

"A feast and a fandango unlike any you've ever attended before."

"Given our surroundings, I would scarce expect otherwise! Though I did attend a wedding with Mr. Gaspard when we were but a couple of days out of Missouri that was quite exuberant and different."

He smiled slightly. "Yeah, Gerry told me about that one. A couple of Oregon immigrants."

"I still have one or two questions about events at that affair that he has yet to answer." She paused, and frowned. She sipped her drink. "Do you think Mr. Gaspard will rejoin us?" she asked.

Rawlins looked at her in surprise. "Don't you doubt it, ma'am. Don't you doubt it for a single minute. Fact is, I wouldn't be at all surprised to see him ride in today. Gaspard, he always loved a party. Guess it's the damned French frog in him." He shook his head. "And besides, the man's a damn fool when it comes to what he sees as his duty and his honor. Waugh! With Gaspard, you don't mess with either."

"But he wouldn't know there is a party today."

"He knows the Bents."

Carolina laughed. "Oh, I see. Of course." She pursed her lips, silent a moment, then she looked at Rawlins. "Just how old is Mr. Gaspard?"

He raised an eyebrow. "I feared that was the way the wind blew."

"I beg your pardon?"

"You and Gaspard."

"What? No, Mr. Rawlins," she said with a laugh. "I'm afraid you are incorrect."

He looked at her over the rim of his glass. "Gerry's two years younger than me. He's thirty-six."

"Thirty-six!"

Rawlins nodded, then his eyes narrowed as he looked at her. "But something tells me I should have said forty-six."

"I do not know, nor do I think I wish to know, what you mean," Carolina said repressively.

Rawlins laughed suddenly, quite the first time since Singing Waters' death, and startled Carolina by slapping her knee. She jerked backward, spilling some of her mint julep onto the fabric of her wide, dark blue skirts.

She wiped at the puddled spot with her free hand. "That was quite unnecessary, Mr. Rawlins."

"On the contrary, ma'am, it told me all I need to know. For that I'm grateful. But I'm telling you straight out, I ain't going to wish him well. I got my own interests to consider."

"Mr. Rawlins, you are not making any sense," Carolina said, exasperated.

He smiled at her as he rose from the bench. "I've got eyes and ears, same as the next man. And I got desires, same as the next man. And more important, now I've got a son that needs a mother."

A slow blush crept up Carolina's cheeks. "You're unseemly, Mr. Rawlins. Your wife is scarcely cold in her grave! How can you be making such forward insinuations!"

His smile faded, replaced by a melancholy expression. The change startled Carolina in its completeness. "Make no mistake, Mrs. Harper. I loved Singing Waters, make no mistake about that, but civilization's rules for things like mournings and courtships don't hold with life's rules out here. I mourn Singing Waters, and I reckon a part of me always will, but I gotta get on with life now."

"Mr. Rawlins, I know there is much to life out here that I do not know. Cannot know. But I'm also not naive enough to assume life goes on like I've known it to be in New Orleans. That life, for me, is dead. I have no wish for any resurrection. And I see the need and, perhaps, the wisdom of your desires. However, I . . . I knew Singing Waters. I knew her as a person. I knew her as a friend. For that reason, if for none other, I find your hinted suggestions distasteful. It is too mercenary. I'm sorry," she said, laying a hand on his arm.

He looked down at her hand where it lay on the rough cotton material of his shirt. "Forgive me, ma'am, if I say there's more to it than that. You have to look inside yourself a bit deeper. If you dare." He picked up his hat from the bench and settled it on his head.

"Enjoy the mint julep, ma'am. And the day. Ain't many days out here that people hold just for frivolity, but the Fourth, that's sure one of 'em."

She nodded. "I doubt any ball in St. Louis, New Orleans, or any other city could carry as much heartfelt enthusiasm as the celebration here. Which I do admit I find a trifle odd given that the majority of the fort's inhabitants are anything but loyal to the United States."

"Just so, ma'am, just so." He touched his hat in salute, then turned away and walked over to talk to two of the fort's hunters.

Carolina watched the men laugh at some word or quip from Rawlins and all saunter toward the room that held a pool table. The dark interior absorbed them. One moment they were there, bright in the sun, and the next they were gone.

Carolina leaned back against the adobe wall behind her. The sun seeped into her body, pore by pore, until she radiated heat. She felt her heart beat slow and steady, pushing blood through her body. She felt muscles relax that she'd had no notion were tense. As they relaxed, a curious ache spread through them along with a lassitude too strong to let the ache matter. She should have worn a broader-brimmed hat, she decided, or brought out her parasol.

Part of her face and neck felt the sun. She should move to the shade, or lower her head, or . . . Somehow, it didn't matter. Inertia captured her, holding her in place.

Her mother would chastise her if she knew.

Always the lady.

Had it been a natural reaction? Unnatural? She hoped her mother had had to work as strongly as she did to maintain appearances. She could take some cold comfort in knowing that she'd had to expend part of herself to maintain her social mien.

Carolina rolled her shoulders to release the tensions between her shoulder blades. She took another sip of her julep. Anger burned in her stomach. An old anger.

Perhaps too old.

16

As the sun rose higher, washing out the sky, an exuberant festivity pervaded the Mud Castle on the Arkansas, unmarred by thoughts of war. People laughed easily. Children shrieked, giggled, and played games of tag, hide-and-seek, and catch. The men competed in games pitting wit against wit and brawn against brawn. They related tall tales, engaged in games of arm wrestling, knife throwing, target shooting, and footraces. Like peacock-preening storied knights before a joust, they begged good-luck favors from the women. Imitating wild beasts, the men howled as they sought to undermine their opponents' confidence. Then they went into their competitions as into battle, with a ferocious, nigh berserker, intensity.

The competitors churned up billows of dust. The golden clouds hung in the air, forcing many women to use handkerchiefs to cover their noses and mouths. The swirling dust painfully reminded Carolina of Jorge despite the brightness of the day and the clear blue horizon. Tears flooded her eyes. She dashed the tears away with her handkerchief and muttered, with a wry laugh to Charlotte standing next to her, that the dust made her eyes teary.

In the afternoon, as the smells from haunches of roasting buffalo, deer, and antelope pervaded the air, the Cheyenne Indians who camped near the fort joined the party.

Carolina heard William Bent caustically mutter something about them expecting fire water in return. He gave explicit orders against any drinking in the plaza while the Indians were in the fort and assigned extra guards to the storerooms just to be certain no one pressed the issue. They were all going to have their celebration and enjoy it without incident, he declared.

Despite Mr. Bent's sour attitude toward the fort's visitors, Carolina watched the bronze-skinned, sharp-featured Indians with wide-eyed fascination. A group of Indian braves danced in a circle in the plaza to honor the white man's celebration. She enjoyed the Indian dance with its regalia, even though the sight of their scantily dressed bodies caused her cheeks to burn as they had the day Mr. Gaspard had pushed her wagon out of the quagmire at the Narrows. The Indians chanted and bobbed to a steady drumbeat, a beat that echoed within Carolina, that echoed the land she'd crossed and the land she had yet to cross. Unconsciously, she raised a hand to her midriff to hold in the echo, to make it a part of herself.

"Rawlins said I'd probably find you watching the young bucks."

Gaspard!

Carolina whirled around. "Mr. Gaspard! When did you get here? Is the baby all right? Did you find a good wet nurse?"

She hoped he mistook the blush rising to her cheeks to be from the sun and heat of the day, or from embarrassment at enjoying the Indians' dance. Quickly she scanned him, searching out new wounds. He looked well. Too well, she sourly observed.

Gaspard grinned. "The baby's fine. I had no trouble finding him a wet nurse. And as to when I got here, I met up with the caravan about noon. Got cleaned up, then came here. Less than a hundred miles away, I couldn't see a reason to miss the Fourth at the fort."

Carolina relaxed. "Mr. Rawlins told me you'd feel that way."

"The Fourth's a tradition at the fort." He took her elbow to lead her away from the noise of both dancers and spectators. They walked toward the stables at the back of the fort. "Bush tells me you're staying here. Said Bent gave you your own room."

"Yes, but Sibby and I don't have it to ourselves any longer. Mrs. Carson shares the room with us."

He nodded soberly. "I talked to Tom Boggs before I found you. He told me about the trouble down in Taos." He stopped by a bench in the shade of the buildings and invited her to sit down.

"It is all anyone can talk about?" she asked, settling her dark blue skirts about her ankles. "You are familiar with New Mexico. Who is this 'Calf' they mention whenever they speak of past troubles in Taos? Why does he hate Americans so much?"

"The Calf—" He stopped and laughed. "That's Charles Bent's nickname for Father Martinez. The Calf comes from a wealthy family. Story is, he turned to the church after his young wife died, sort of a penance, I guess." He again laughed shortly. "He's an odd sort. Not overly loyal to the cloth, but given to using it, or acting it when it suits his purpose. As far as why he hates Americans, he figures we're corrupting his country and getting too rich off of it."

Carolina sighed. "I don't know about the corruption, but it's true, fortunes have been made in New Mexico trade by men from the United States. Heavens, a good portion of my stepfather's revenues come from the Santa Fe trade!"

Gaspard nodded. "And Martinez hasn't gotten enough of it. Very realistic, is our padre. Actually, his family is old Taos aristocracy and well respected. His family has God, money, and power behind it—at least that's what Padre Martinez would have us think."

"And with that combination, they feel invincible."

"That's just about how it shakes out."

"But surely he doesn't promote violence!" Carolina said.

He looked at her steadily.

"Oh," she said. "Is that another of my naive notions?"

"I wouldn't call it naive, but it sure ain't reality."

"Why should these Taos mobs make life untenable for the women and children? They're their own people!"

"Yes, but to those of Martinez's mind, they sold out. Married the enemy, or at least married a heretic. A worse sin to the good Catholic padre."

"It can't be that simple. Didn't Kit Carson convert to Catholicism to wed Josepha?"

"Yes, but not many men are willing to tread that road, and if they do, there's many as would question their sincerity, with Martinez at the top of that list!"

Carolina worried her lower lip between her teeth.

"And there's others as have adopted Mexican citizenship so they can apply for large land grants, or they've married into a family with large land grants and no sons."

"I am quite conversant with that habit!" Carolina said dryly.

Gaspard raised an eyebrow, but went on without asking her what she meant. "The Martinez family fears New Mexicans are losing control of their land and their heritage."

Carolina sighed. "And they probably are not far out of line, either."

"No, ma'am."

Carolina rubbed her temples with her fingertips. The politics between the United States and New Mexico were a roiling mass of worms. It would perhaps have been wise to remain in St. Louis. But she didn't want to turn back now.

Maybe there was some way she could help. She hoped she wasn't naive enough to think one woman could change the destiny of a country; but she wanted to help heal the breach between the United States and New Mexico. Both sides had much to offer the other in terms of goods, culture, and ideas. Of course, the only thing that mattered to anyone involved in the issue was the goods, and the assurance that the flow of trade between countries would not be interrupted.

If Diego Navarro's influence was as pervasive as the traders believed, perhaps she could trade upon her familial relationship to advantage. Family was important. More important in Mexico and New Mexico than in the United States. How could her uncle repudiate all of the United States if she appeared on his doorstep, the product of the two cultures? She leaned her head back on the adobe walls.

"Tired?" Gaspard asked, his voice a low, gravelly rumble Carolina felt as soothing.

"A little," she said with a smile as she lifted her head to look at him. His gray eyes glowed with compassion, his face revealing a softness to its edges she could remember seeing only in fractured dreams.

"Why don't you take a siesta? You look like you could use it, and besides," he said, compressing his lips a moment, then smiling, "I've a mind to ask you to kick up your heels with me at the fandango tonight. That is, if I get a chance, seeing as how you're bound to be the belle of the ball."

"Belle of the ball?" she parroted back, then shook her head as she laughed. "Hardly." Memories of crystal chandeliers, gleaming, polished wooden dance floors, the heavy fragrance of exotic flowers, and the whisper of costly silk dresses crowded into her mind, only to be pushed aside by the reality of the Mud Castle's smoky candles, dirt floors, smells of unwashed bodies, and the scrape of leather against patched homespun.

Suddenly she found herself looking forward to the evening's fandango. Odd, but she wouldn't change the memories for the realities.

"Perhaps a nap would be appropriate. I understand it will be a late night." She rose to her feet, and he followed. "It is good to see you again, and I look forward to our dance this evening," she said, feeling shy.

"You may not when you find those dainty little feet of yours being trod upon. I'm no fancy dancer."

"That's all right, for I'll tell you a secret, neither am I." She winked at him audaciously, then blushed, and fairly ran across the yard toward the steps to the second level, ignoring the continued Indian display.

July 4, 1846, Bent's Fort.

The Independence Day celebrations here at Bent's Fort are everything, and more, that I've heard them to be. Everyone, whether they are a United States citizen, Indian, Mexican, or foreign adventurer enters wholeheartedly into the festivities. Everyone loves a party.

Yesterday afternoon I helped the women bake cakes and pies and breads in number—too many, I thought, for our population. I worry now that there shall not be enough! Our numbers have been augmented with itinerant traders, mountain men, miners, and Cheyenne Indians. This afternoon the plaza is crowded with people. So crowded that I have retreated to my little adobe room for respite from the dust and the heat below. There will be a party tonight. A fandango, they call it. I have been advised to rest well beforehand. As the only Anglo woman here I shall be besieged with dance requests and most likely, I am assured, several offers of marriage before dawn.

Mr. Gaspard arrived at the fort today. He said he would not miss the festivities here. Mr. Rawlins told me he would think that way. Mr. Rawlins also made an observation that I rejected out of hand but must admit, quite quietly to myself, has some substance of truth in it. He alluded to a relationship between myself and Mr. Gaspard. I rejected it; but there is a portion of me that responded to that suggestion and later responded to seeing Mr. Gaspard again. A curious wild pleasure coursed through my body. Suddenly, I felt like a gauche child, shy and

*tongue-tied. The realization of those feelings, and my reaction
to those feelings, sent me scurrying upstairs to the privacy of
my quarters. I am embarrassed. I must gather my reserves to
ensure that Mr. Gaspard never feels put upon in any way.*

JOSEPHA CARSON STIRRED restlessly in her sleep as Carolina
quietly moved the lantern near the dying fire and arranged crates
around it to shield the room from its soft glow. She drug her pal-
let near the light and laid down on her stomach to write another
journal entry, for though she was tired, her mind raced and she
knew she needed the order of writing to slow her thoughts to
allow sleep to overtake her.

July 5, 1846, Bent's Fort. Before dawn.
  *The sky remains dark. I did not dance until dawn; nonetheless
I do feel as if I have danced for days on end. My dancing
slippers shall never be the same. Foolishly I wore them
(foolishly I packed them!). I should have recalled the fort's dirt
floors. At least the floor was dampened down before the
fandango to keep the dust to a manageable degree.*
  *The dancing here is lively. There is a joy of living among
everyone. I saw no contrived elitism, nor contrived boredom,
nor class snubbing, and the only posturing was done by the
males as they strutted before the women and sometimes vied
with another man for the woman's next dance. Everyone
enjoyed themselves.*
  *The language is rough, and the jokes crude; however, I can't
recall a time I enjoyed myself more. I laughed until my sides
ached and hiccups overwhelmed me, which only served to
increase the laughter of others. Tomorrow—today!—I swear
my toes shall show bruising. I only hope they will not also
swell. The men here are more enthusiastic dancers than they
are skilled.*
  I received three legitimate offers of marriage and five

*drunken ones, which I discount for the gentlemen were
proposing to anything that moved, including Pedro's mule!*

*I danced with Mr. Rawlins early in the evening. He was
smiling and relatively cheerful, but now that I know he would
have me take the place of Singing Waters, I can't be as
comfortable around him as once I felt.*

*Mr. Gaspard nearly did not ask me to dance. As it was, we
did not dance until near the end of the evening. He looked
angry with me; but sometimes it is difficult to read his feelings
for his scarred visage translates differently.*

*He lied, or was being inordinately modest, when he claimed
a lack of dancing ability. He would not appear to disfavor on
any dance floor. But I was flagging by the time we danced and
stumbled more than once. In response he lifted me off my feet
as he twirled me about! We enjoyed two dances, one after the
other, then, when he went off to fetch me a quenching drink, he
had a young trader I did not know bring me the beverage
while he walked on past the refreshment tables and out into
the night. I don't know why. I don't even want to conjecture.
Not now. Not yet.*

*My eyes are drooping. Sleep is finally claiming my
befuddled mind. I'll close for now.*

"YOU'RE UP MIGHTY early, Mrs. Harper."

Carolina slowly turned her eyes away from the misty view of
the Spanish Peaks, blue and purple twin mountains to the distant
southwest of the fort, and turned to look at Mr. Rawlins as he sauntered toward her. "I could say the same of you, sir," she said with
a smile. "And dare I ask how your head is this early morning?"

He grimaced and pressed the heel of his hand against his forehead. "Protesting. Woke me up, in fact." He tried to shake his head.
"Damn, but it would have been best if William had kept the liquor
locked up after the Cheyenne left. Waugh, but there's some mighty
hard heads here!"

"Oh, were you testing them?" Carolina couldn't resist teasing.

"Or them me," he answered morosely.

"Have the cook make you some willow-bark tea."

His lips curled. "Maybe."

She laughed. "Meaning, you won't."

"The cool morning air is physic enough."

"Yes," she said as she turned back to look at the view to the far south. "Yes, it is."

Silence settled between them.

Rawlins joined her at the wall, leaning his arms against the top as he looked out over the countryside. To the east his caravan camped, to the south ran the river, and beyond that a dry, windswept plain until the mountains that stood as a barrier and a gateway to New Mexico.

"So, what are your plans now, Mrs. Harper? Want me to take you back to Missouri?"

Carolina straightened. "No, Mr. Rawlins, I want to continue on to Santa Fe."

"What! Why?" Rawlins exclaimed, then grasped his aching head between his hands at the sound of his own loud voice. "Begging your pardon, ma'am," he continued in a softer tone, "but I don't understand. Bent said he'd buy your goods from you for a fair price. I can guarantee you won't be losin' money trading with him."

Carolina nodded. "I know. Mr. Bush has already assured me of that; however, Mr. Bent will also make a more than tidy profit."

"While he figures New Mexican, and Mexican, demands for U.S. goods are bound and certain to go up now that there's war," Gerard Gaspard said from behind them, his voice flat and laced with cynicism.

Carolina and Jedediah Rawlins turned quickly to look at him. Carolina felt high color flood her cheeks.

"So?" Rawlins demanded. He leaned back against the wall and

crossed his arms over his chest. The big man's brows knitted together as he frowned at Gaspard.

Gaspard sauntered toward them and leaned against the wall on the other side of Carolina. "Be a big black market for whatever goods his men could smuggle in. Also, should the United States take over New Mexico territory, as is talk around here, there will be a tide of settlers coming in needing goods."

He grinned and winked at Carolina with his bad eye. "The Bents have always been successful taking the long view."

Carolina sighed. "I wish more people in our country could take a long view, or at least a broader view."

"You don't think much of this war, do you, ma'am?" Rawlins observed.

"No, sir, I do not."

Jed cocked his head to the side as he considered her vehement expression. "Ma'am, there's a lot of folks who feel the Mexicans were just about begging for this war. As an honorable nation, we couldn't do anything but declare war," he said.

"Honorable to declare war?" She shook her head.

"It's well known that Santa Anna ain't been too keen on observing the Texas border. Many's the time his soldiers have come across the border to kill, loot, and kidnap the good folks in Texas."

"True, but wasn't there an agreement or treaty between Mexico and Texas to the effect that Texas would never become part of the United States? Might not Santa Anna feel entitled to his actions?"

Rawlins scowled and shook his head. "Mexico began pulling their little forays on Texas soil long before Texas became part of the United States."

"Texas was not altogether innocent, either," Gaspard said dryly.

Jed Rawlins turned his head to look at him. "How do you figure that?"

"What about that expedition Mr. Howard participated in?"

"That wasn't Texas, just some misguided few," scoffed Rawlins.

Gaspard nodded, but added, "Under the instructions of President Lamar."

"Hell, Gerry, you know they weren't inciting nothing with their pamphlets. They were merely saying that *if* the New Mexican people were interested in throwing off Mexico's yoke of tyranny, like Texas done, Texas would help."

Carolina laughed. "And as if those weren't inflammatory enough words . . ."

"Hell, no," Rawlins refuted.

"Hell, yes!" Carolina returned, then blinked and blushed. She glanced quickly at one man then the other, but they didn't seem to mind her participation, her vehemence, or her language. Of course, at some point during their journey, they had stopped apologizing to her for their own swearing.

In New Orleans, if Carolina had dared to do more than listen to the men talk politics or war, she'd be roundly chastised by her husband or father-in-law. But to dare speak in return in such an unladylike fashion would have had her banished from company and admonished to read her Bible.

"Don't forget the little matter of the three million dollars the Mexican government owes the United States," Rawlins said.

"Surely, Mr. Rawlins, no one really expects those loans to be repaid," Carolina said a little breathlessly.

An ocean wave of girlish giddiness swept her senses, then swiftly receded; but in that moment she changed. Perhaps only as much as one wave changes the shore; however, nothing for her would ever be the same. For the first time in her recollection she felt treated as a person, not as wife or woman or property.

Rawlins thrust his lower jaw forward. "The American people do."

"*Only* when they can use the lack of payment as an excuse for war," Gaspard fairly drawled. "Hell, money diplomacy, that's a downright contradiction. All we do is throw good money away. I say, if we have given it, we should forget it. There ain't ever any repayments and we ain't going to reap favors for making the loan. Hell, the damn opposite is true. The fact we've made loans makes enemies. Those we would have be grateful are damned jealous that we have the money to give! They're suspicious of us and our purse and only too happy and too quick to cast us as enemies."

"I agree there's jealousy involved, but I disagree as to the cause," Rawlins said. "I think you're forgettin' our freedom. That sticks in the craw of too many outta sheer envy. Any excuse is good enough for a fight or a war when one body of folk gets jealous of another."

"Especially if war creates a nationalistic spirit in an otherwise disenfranchised people?" Carolina asked, then flushed again as both men stared hard at her. Then Gaspard grinned and she relaxed.

"Well said, Mrs. Harper. Damn well said."

Rawlins shook his head and gave a low whistle. "Lordy, who'd a thought. You're a sight knowing for your gender, ma'am."

She stiffened and blushed furiously. "I-I-I'm sorry. I know I . . . Excuse me . . ." she said, stammering. Flustered, she turned to walk back toward her room.

Gaspard grabbed her arm to stay her and laughed. "Don't go getting all flibberty-gibberish now. Jed meant that as a compliment."

Carolina looked back over her shoulder at both men.

"Sure do, ma'am," Rawlins said.

Gently Gaspard pulled her back beside them. "Seeing you take on so, you'd think there were something wrong with a woman having an idea in her head."

She sighed. "To my late husband and all his family, it was not considered seemly for a woman to discuss business or politics," she said stiffly, her lips compressing tightly as unwanted memories crowded together in her mind.

Gaspard snorted. "If I'd thought so, I wouldn't have agreed to take on the job with you in Westport. It's as simple as that. And I figure if you're determined to head on to Santa Fe, then I guess that's where we're going."

"Gerry!" protested Rawlins as he stood up straight and planted his ham-sized fists on his hips. "Don't be a fool. And don't encourage her." He jerked his hat off his head and slapped it against his knee. "Hell, she ain't got no notion of what it's like there. You could be gettin' her and yourself killed!"

Gaspard nodded slowly. "Could be."

"Then why?"

Gaspard looked down at Carolina with a wry grin. "I got an uncomfortable notion if I don't, she'll just up and hire one of Bent's boys."

Carolina laughed and looked up at him. "You're right," she said. Her heart felt lighter than it had in weeks.

Rawlins looked from one to the other, then shook his head. He jammed his hat back on his head. "Damn," he said, under his breath. "I'm damned to be right."

"I beg your pardon, Mr. Rawlins?" Carolina said, looking back at him.

He shook his head and looked up at Gaspard. "Waugh, I don't know whether I outta wish you well or consign you to the devil himself."

Gaspard shrugged. "Don't. Ol' Scratch claimed this soul long ago, my friend. Long ago."

Rawlins stared at him a moment, studied him as if he had just met Gerard Gaspard, then he threw back his head and laughed. "Well, don't that beat all!" he said softly. "Ain't you the pair, without a wit between you!" he said. Then he looked down at Carolina, laughter still dancing in his eyes. "I'll help you get some good fresh mules. Not those broken-down ones we been travelin' with. When do you think you're goin' to leave?"

"Tomorrow, I hope," Carolina said, then held her breath as she looked up at Mr. Gaspard.

He nodded.

Her breath came out in a whoosh and she smiled happily. "I'll go tell Sibby. We have to start sorting through our things right away." She started to walk away, then turned to look back at Mr. Gaspard. "We'll talk later about what of my goods I should keep to take to Santa Fe?"

He nodded. Beside him, Rawlins swore again, but Carolina didn't notice, for she'd already turned to walk swiftly toward her Bent's Fort quarters.

17

"WHAT DO YOU mean, you don't wish to come with me?" Carolina exclaimed to Sibby some two hours later.

Sibby wrung her apron between her hands. "Jest that. I don't wanna go. I wanna stay here. I likes it here. Everyone is nice to me. Especially . . . especially Pete Horsley. He . . . he say he wants to marry me!"

"Marry you!" Carolina echoed. She sank down onto a crate. "Well, I . . . I don't know what to say!"

"It be true, ain't it, that I ain't your slave no more?"

"Yes, of course. I emancipated all the slaves on my husband's death. You know that, Sibby. But I had thought . . ." She paused and shook her head slowly as if to clear her mind. "I had hoped we were always more than mistress and slave," she slowly finished, her eyes looking closely at Sibby's strained features.

Sibby nodded. "You always did treat me fine, I ain't forgettin' that, but . . . but I wanna life a my own. And I don't wanna go down to no New Mexico."

"Oh, dear," Carolina said faintly. She pursed her lips and thought for a moment.

A life of her own.

Carolina would have laughed if it weren't for the fearful look in Sibby's eyes. It was like looking into a mirror. She'd never considered how alike their circumstances were—nor how selfish she'd been in her self-absorption.

She'd never thought of life without Sibby. Though she did give her freedom, she'd never really stopped to think of all that entailed. She'd too easily assumed that nothing would change except that she would pay a wage, which in truth she'd only done on paper. Never had she actually put money into Sibby's hands.

"Well. I don't know what to say. I mean, of course, if that is what you want, it's just that you've taken me quite by surprise. This is so sudden." She looked at her with concern. "And you say Mr. Horsley wants to marry you?"

Sibby nodded. "And he don't care that I'm carryin' another man's get, neither."

"There is no need to get belligerent, Sibby."

"Beg pardon, Miz Carolina." Sibby was nearly trembling. "But I don't want no truck with you tryin' to change my mind."

"No. I would not do that," Carolina said firmly, infusing her voice with sincerity. "Not if this is what you really want to do."

Sibby fell on her knees before her and grabbed Carolina's hands. "Oh, it is, Miz Carolina. It truly is! Mr. Horsley, he makes me feel special. Purty, even."

Carolina pulled one hand free and gently wiped away a tear that escaped. "You *are* pretty, Sibby. And we're going to make you an even prettier bride," she said as she stood up and drew Sibby up with her. "You and I are of a size, let's see what of mine I can give you."

"Oh, no, Miz Carolina! I couldn't."

"Every bride needs a trousseau, Sibby, and if I don't give you these dresses we've hauled from New Orleans, what am I to do with them? I can't pack them all on mules to take to New Mexico!"

"Mr. Bent would keep them for you."

"Yes, I suppose he would, but I don't want to impose on the man any more than I already have. Besides, I want to give them to you. What you don't want, perhaps you can sell or trade to the other women. Consider that a dowry. Along with your wages, of course."

"Oh, no, ma'am! I don't want none of your money. What I done for you I done for love!"

Carolina stopped sorting through the bright fabrics and faced Sibby. She laid a hand against her cheek. "Bless you, my friend. I hope you know I love you and what I do, I do for love, too. It is little enough to give to you. You have so often in the past been my strength. I believe I would have died of despair when my baby died if it hadn't been for you."

Sibby's eyes glistened with tears. "Oh, Miz Carolina!" she wailed. She threw her arms around her and held her close.

Carolina slowly put her arms around Sibby to hug her in return. She felt the dampness of Sibby's tears on her shoulder. She took a deep breath. Her body shuddered as she slowly let the breath out. She closed her eyes and a slight smile curled the corners of her lips as she felt the warmth of her answering tears slide down her cheeks.

July 5, 1846, Bent's Fort.

What am I going to do without Sibby? She has been so long a part of my life. When my life fell apart, she remained there, someone I could rely on, someone to need me and to have faith in me when I had little enough in myself.

Perhaps I should have realized our days together were numbered when she kept the knowledge from me that she was breeding. We had always been honest with each other. Suddenly, she was afraid. Of what? To this day I'm not sure I

*understand. But something changed at some time in this past
year. What was it? When did it happen? Is she afraid of me?
Afraid to tell me? Have I become some bogeyman?*

*I remember how she looked today, how she trembled and
twisted her apron between her fingers. A fine sheen of sweat
beaded her brow as she gathered her courage about her slender
form like a cloak.*

*What am I? What monster have I become that such
nervousness should grip her when she would speak to me?*

When did our friendship die?

*I feel alone. More alone than when David and Edward died.
More alone than ever in my life.*

THE PAGES OF her journal blurred. Carolina laid her pen down and
looked up, staring with unseeing eyes at the low roof above her
head. She blinked hard. She couldn't shake a feeling of betrayal.
Anger wanted to crowd into her heart. Ruthlessly she pushed it
out, back, away from her senses. That was an unfair emotion. Real,
but not worthy of her. Sibby had a right to her own life. Wasn't that
notion just what spurred her to emancipate all the slaves her husband owned? That the Negroes who worked for them had a right
to their own lives? How could she now begrudge Sibby?

She could begrudge solely from fear.

Fear lived in her heart. It had paced round and round within her
like a cat walking in circles until a comfortable situation to lie
down in was found. Once settled, it purred loudly, shattering her
efforts to put the fear away. It echoed in her head, never leaving
her alone. The best she could hope was to maintain the appearance
of confidence.

She picked up her pen again and dipped it into the inkwell.

*I must remain outwardly calm. If I do not, Mr. Bent, Mr.
Rawlins, and others will gain the currency to dissuade me
from my goal.*

I will go to Santa Fe!
There. It is stated. Let no man sway my mind nor my heart.

"WHAT DO YOU mean, Sibby isn't going with us?" Gaspard demanded. He finished tying his pack to the back of his saddle, then turned to glare at Carolina.

Carolina glanced away from him and looked down at her hands as she drew on her leather gloves. The thing about Mr. Gaspard's scarred visage that made it so disconcerting sometimes was how frightening an aspect it could become when he was displeased. So long as she did not look at him she could reassure herself that he displayed more bluster than real displeasure. Though this time she felt certain his displeasure was all too real.

"She's getting married," she said and quickly turned to cross to her own horse.

He caught her arm. "So who's going to be in our party?"

She licked her lips and risked a glance up at him. His expression was as dark and foreboding as she'd feared. "Well, you, myself, and Pedro," she said.

"No one else?"

She hesitated, then sighed and admitted there would be no one else, that she had not asked anyone else.

"Damn." He took his hat off his head and raked his hand through his white hair. "Tom Boggs and George Bent will be taking their families back to Taos in another couple of days, unless they hear any more outta the area." He resettled his hat on his head and rested his elbow on one of the packs. "Maybe we should stay and travel with them."

"No. I wish to go today."

He looked up at the sky a moment, then swung his head down to look at her. "You try a man's patience, Mrs. Harper."

"Staying here I am no more than a parasite upon Mr. Bent's goodwill. And if you are correct as to the military coming this way, he doesn't need another useless mouth to feed."

Gaspard snorted. "You don't eat enough to keep a bird alive. And William ain't begrudging you anything. You get along well with the women here. You don't show any signs of uppitiness. That's impressed Bent."

"But what happens when he learns I am a Navarro? Will he feel the same way Mr. Howard did?"

Gaspard took a deep breath. It whistled out through clinched teeth as he slowly exhaled. "It's true. There's no love lost between the Bents and Diego Navarro. If the Martinez family are their foes in Taos, it would probably have to be Navarro who is their bitterest foe in Santa Fe. Who knows what relations would be like with New Mexico if it weren't for Manuel Alvarez, the American consul in Santa Fe. Navarro doesn't mess with Alvarez, for some reason, and Alvarez has some influence with Armijo. And you know, the more I think on it, if you're going to be so damned muleheaded as insisting on going to Santa Fe, it might be best to take you directly to Alvarez. He'll know what, and who, is safe for you."

"I'll agree to that," Carolina said, glad to turn his mind from refusing to take her on to Santa Fe.

He frowned at her again.

"I'd best see to my horse," she said, slipping away from his side before he could say anything more.

"Miz Carolina!"

Carolina turned to see Sibby running toward her. She carried an Indian parfleche.

"Charlotte, she gave me some trail food to give to you, stuff like Singing Waters used to make." Sibby held out the decorated parfleche to Carolina.

Carolina took the bag from her. Sibby's eyes were bright with tears.

"Now, don't start!" Carolina admonished her. "Or you'll have me crying, too. Just help me mount my horse."

"Let that be my pleasure," said Jedediah Rawlins, coming up beside Carolina.

"Mr. Rawlins!" she said. "I'm glad to see you again before I go. I wanted to thank you for all you've done for me since we met at Council Grove."

"No more than you've done for me, ma'am. Though I guess you know I'd be happy to do much more."

Carolina blushed. "Please, Mr. Rawlins."

He nodded. "I know. I won't plague you again. Here, let me help you up." He grasped Carolina around her waist and effortlessly lifted her into her new Indian saddle.

Carolina quickly twitched her skirts into place, tucking them around her legs. It felt odd to sit astride; however, Mr. Gaspard had been adamant in his insistence that she give up her side saddle. He said it was fine for a few hours a day, but not a full day every day, not on the terrain they were to travel. It would be too hard on her horse.

"Thank you," she said to Rawlins for his assistance.

He backed away from her horse. "My pleasure, ma'am," he said. Then he turned to watch Gaspard ride up beside Carolina. "You gonna take the east trail through Mora and Las Vegas?"

Gaspard nodded. "Even if things have calmed down, people in Taos are damned unpredictable, even for Mexicans."

Rawlins snorted. "That's a fact. Just a word a caution going through Las Vegas. That alcalde's full of himself."

"That alcalde's a blustering old woman," Gaspard said with a grin that bespoke experience.

Rawlins laughed, then sobered, nodding toward Carolina. "Take care of her."

"I intend to."

The two men stared at each other for a moment in some silent communication. Then they solemnly nodded, one to the other.

Gaspard rode out leading five heavily laden pack mules. Carolina quickly fell into line behind him, leading two mules. Pedro followed them with the rest of their pack train.

Carolina waved farewell to Sibby, then turned her face toward the southern plains.

July 7, 1846, Timpas Creek.

Mr. Gaspard continues to wear his displeasure toward me. I am almost regretting this journey, so absolute is his ire. There have been occasions in the past when his manner has been remote toward me, even bordering on rudeness. But never anything like this. I despair at losing my friend, for such I had begun to think of him.

And more.

Damn Mr. Rawlins, to my sorrow I admit it.

It is not to be helped, this displeasure in me. Nor had I adequately considered how Sibby's absence would affect me in everyday small ways. So much did she do for me, calmly and silently, that I am ashamed. How, in my abject ignorance, I have lied to myself for so long is inconceivable to me. I need to look about me—more with my heart than my mind. With a heart turned toward others.

Nevertheless, my errors shall not cause me to change my mind and suggest returning to Bent's Fort even though this portion of our trek is particularly noisome.

I suspect Mr. Gaspard of traveling slower than necessary so that I might experience all the hardships of this landscape and thereby perhaps foster a feeling of regret for my impulsive behavior and insistence on this journey. It probably also accounts for his continued reticence. Damn the man.

No. I do not damn him, though I wish he might understand what drives me.

That is humorous. How can I ask another to understand that which I do not?

The air here is so dry my lips would crack if it weren't for the dollop of buffalo grease I apply to them every hour or so.

*The wind is oddly hot and possesses an unnatural heaviness
that pains my chest as I breathe. Not a blade of green grass
softens this harsh, stony landscape. We cross a wasteland.
This wasteland, they say, is the Great American Desert, except
now we are on New Mexican soil and have been since we
forded the river just beyond the fort.*

*Throughout this journey I sense changes within me.
Changes that have begun to coalesce for good and ill. But why
now?*

*I think it is the solitude, the long times I am forced to live
solely within my head as we travel toward Santa Fe. And it is
the wasteland through which we travel, which contrasts
thoughts and feelings against emptiness and desolation. In the
face of the wasteland, the changes within stand out in contrast
and memory. For so long I lived my life to another's
commands that once, just for once, I want to live life to my
command. That has been the crux of my flight—yes, flight—
from my home.*

*I wrap my desires in a package called duty. Duty to my
family, I said, to care for my uncle's children. Truth to tell,
that has always been an excuse. Witness my insistence to
continue this mad journey when I have been more than amply
assured that these children are well cared for and loved by
their maternal relations! Oh, though I love children and
would adore holding them to my breast, that is little more than
a substitute for dealing with my own grief at the loss of my
baby. Behold my bleak sadness at parting with Singing
Waters' baby!*

*There is a part of me that feels I could have prevented
David's illness, or if not that, his death. And perhaps that
guilt will always plague me. But the fate of Singing Waters
has shown me we cannot alter what to us—mere humans—
must seem as the capricious hand of Divine Providence. And
though I hated Mr. Gaspard for taking the baby from me, I*

knew in my heart and in my mind that I was not capable of properly caring for the child.

So what is there left for me, now that I have chosen my road? Where does it lead?

I do know that I like these wild western lands, and the people who choose to come to them. They are all seekers, like me, though what we seek varies. And they all come to respect the land and what it gives, or takes away. I like the mélange of people at Bent's Fort. Life is not easy for any of them, that is plain to see in their faces; yet they enjoy life.

That, I think, is the gift I seek: the ability to enjoy my life. In some measure this journey has given me that ability. I know never before have I felt so alive and aware of my thoughts and feelings! I feel I've lived my life in a butterfly's chrysalis, hidden from sight and feeling and meaning. I have felt happiness and sadness before; but never with the sharp, cutting clarity visited upon me these last weeks. Always I have maintained a pose of calm. That calm, I thought, was what was proper. No. Beyond that, it was what I was trained to believe was proper.

But is it proper to bury either happiness or grief? Is it right to put a cork into the flask of those feelings? Is that even human? Nay, that is a shadow of a soul, a society's marionette!

No more. Those strings are cut and I pray they may never be restrung.

I do not know what awaits me in the future. I only know I must go out and seek it. Grab it! For good or ill. Isn't that what Sibby has done for herself? I could do well to emulate her sense of self!

Perhaps, when I reach Santa Fe, I shall only stay long enough to sell what goods we've brought and then return to St. Louis. I don't know. But I will have done what I set out to do. That is what is important.

I only pray that my headstrong determination to achieve the goal I set for myself so many months ago in New Orleans will not bring mischief down upon our heads.

July 9, 1846, Rio Timpas.

Mr. Gaspard persists in his brooding. If he were a child I should accuse him of sulking. Am I being foolish, or an unduly unreasonable woman to persist in my desire to continue to Santa Fe without feminine companionship? I'll own that a year ago—nay, less than that—three months ago when I conceived of my intentions to make this journey, I should not have contemplated this endeavor without a full complement of traveling companions. At that time I had no idea that white women had not, heretofore, journeyed down the trail—at least none that any could recall.

My first streak of unreasonableness lay in my persistence in pursuing my goal after I had learned these facts. I am no trailblazer and have no desire to be considered one. I leave that to the John C. Fremonts of the world. However, neither can I be a woman who timidly hangs back from being the first at anything. A man pursues his life. Why not a woman? I cannot imagine myself battening on to you and Mr. Davies or upon Edward's family like some leech. The only patient to die in such a scenario should be myself.

I fear I am a shrew.

Obstinate, stubborn woman.

Actually, I'll confess it. I take some measure of pride in those adjectives. They reveal a will, a sense of self that for too long I have lacked.

It is a will I am in sore need of to survive this last leg of my journey. From here to Santa Fe, the land we cross shall temper my strength and sense of self, or it shall kill me. There can by no half measures.

We are three days out of Bent's Fort, riding alongside the

Timpas River. Tomorrow, Mr. Gaspard says, we shall turn east, at right angles away from the Timpas for an overland march to the Purgatory River and from there turn south again, following its boulder-strewn course until we come to the Raton Pass.

The Raton Pass.

In my mind the Raton Pass looms poetically as another turning point in my life, much like Council Grove. From the wasteland we traverse, it could easily be the gateway to milk and honey, or to earth's hell.

The land we cross now is composed of dry, wind-scoured sandhills. The only plants to thrive are scraggly bushes of silver-green sage, spiky-bladed fans of soap plants, and here and there greasewood bushes growing to a height of five feet. These bushes we gather with a quick twisting motion to the stem so we may have firewood in the evenings. It burns hot and quick, therefore our fires require twice as much wood. Despite my leather gloves, fledgling calluses edge my hands from gathering the wood.

We carried water with us from Bent's Fort, and now I understand Mr. Gaspard's insistence on this, despite the added weight and burden. The water in the Timpas Creek has virtually gone beneath its sandy bottom. It only exists in deep potholes, and what is there is too bitterly alkaline to cook with or use for drinking unless molasses is added to the water. (I thought it odd that Mr. Gaspard had a large bottle of molasses packed among our foodstuffs until my thirst peaked.)

Above us the sky maintains a cloudless bowl of blue which here and there shimmers in mirage reflections across the landscape, promising cool relief from the merciless sun. It is a land to drive men and women mad. That so many have traversed this land, traveling back and forth to "Nuevo Méjico," commands my awe.

Mr. Gaspard looks in my direction with an expression that

*is both an "I warned you" look and sympathy for our daily
discomforts. I do not mind his "I warned you" manner;
however, I find his sympathy nettlesome.*

*His manner has bled into Pedro. He watches me constantly
until, I swear, the furrows between his grizzled brows have
become permanent. His fulsome self is subdued. Even his black
mustache droops!*

*La! I read over what I have written and fear I have become
melancholy. It is this harsh land. I shall recover when the
mountains embrace me.*

18

GERARD GASPARD REINED in his horse and sat back in his saddle. He lifted his head as if to scent the air. A slow smile pulled at the corners of his mouth and that decided twinkle Carolina had seen in his eyes in the past flared back to life. He turned toward her.

"We'll make camp up ahead," he said, his voice leached of emotion.

Carolina could see he was anxious to proceed. A new lightness chased away the morose taciturnity she had too long witnessed. She looked about her for some clue as to the reason for his sudden lightness of spirit. The area resembled much of the land they'd traveled throughout the day—undulating hills and scoured rocks. Clumps of green added ephemeral touches of life to the stark landscape. More life than there had been, she decided, as she looked critically about her noting the size and extent of the grass clumps. Tonight the mules and horses would find enough grass to fill their bellies. Different types of cactus jutted out from between the rocks, and nearby, a scrubby stand of piñon trees added a solid splash of deep green to the landscape. A dark green cedar collar rimmed the top of the sharp-angled pale bluffs, while on the trail large boulders—sheered from the surrounding rock like cheese from a block—required vigilance for discovering safe footage. And from somewhere nearby, Carolina heard water flowing. She scarcely dared hope that that sound heralded good water and good fortune.

Carolina followed Gaspard as closely as she dared, her awareness alive to trail hazards and the behavior of her companions' animals. Mules were cussedly stubborn and on more than one occasion had been witnessed running straight into trouble rather than away.

Gaspard rode off the trail near sheered bluffs that cast long, cool shadows. An errant breeze caressed Carolina's cheek with cool fingers. She shivered, though not from cold, and sat straighter in the saddle. The sound of water rippling over rocks grew louder.

Gaspard raised his hand to call a halt when his horse passed out of shadow and into sunlight, then slowly dismounted from his saddle. Carolina kicked her boots free from the stirrups and slid to the ground. Behind her, Pedro was already off his horse and softly speaking in Spanish to his string of mules as he untied and unbuckled their loads.

Carolina gathered her reins in her hand and walked toward Gaspard. Sunlight touched her face at the same moment she saw the canyon. Rock walls, some nearly eighty feet in height, rose in front of them and behind them. In the middle, dusky trees wound their roots around rock, clinging to the earth. The trees grew along the edge of a brook that purled over rocks worn smooth, disappeared, then reappeared again in shallow pools. Bird whistles and songs came from the wide tree branches. A fat hare darted past, stopped to listen—his ears turning and his nose twitching—then bounded away.

Carolina sighed, letting tension release with her breath. A sylvan grove, she thought, where one could believe magic existed.

"What is this place?" she asked softly, as if afraid it would disappear.

"Hole in the Rock."

She turned to look at him. "Hole in the Rock?"

He breathed in deeply while looking up and down the canyon. He nodded, "Yes, ma'am." He turned back to his horse and began untying his packs.

Recalled to duty, Carolina quickly set about unsaddling her horse and mules. She was anxious to explore the canyon. Tonight, she thought, gathering firewood may be more pleasure than burden.

July 10, 1846, Hole in the Rock.

Darkness comes quickly in high-walled rock canyons. There is little transition time. One moment the sun is overhead and at the next the lengthening shadows paint the canyon walls gunmetal blue, darker than the sky above.

Quickly the rocks lose their sun-baked warmth and the curious wind that comes to play along the rippling stream gets caught between the rock walls and swirls in frustration, growing colder and colder.

Foraging for firewood netted a pitiful mound. I suppose if we hiked to the top of the canyon walls we could find adequate deadfall from the trees growing there, but that would require more energy than any of us can spare this late in the evening.

This, our fourth camp since we left Bent's Fort, is an idyllic place. I know I shall leave with regret on the morrow. I spent much of this late afternoon tramping about and climbing up and down rocks like a mountain goat. I am too tired after that exercise to do more than write a few lines. We had fresh antelope for dinner tonight. They are such foolish creatures, too full of curiosity. This one practically walked straight into Mr. Gaspard's rifle!

"YOU'RE SMILING," SAID Gaspard.

Carolina looked up from the pages of her journal to see Mr. Gaspard standing in front of her with two mugs of coffee in his hands. He held one out to her.

"Was I?" Carolina asked, bemused. She laid aside her pen and accepted the coffee from him. She wrapped her fingers around the hot—nearly too hot—tin mug and breathed in the rising steam.

"Is this the white man's version of the peace pipe?" she dryly asked.

"Peace pipe? Oh." Gaspard ducked his head a moment as he ran a finger across his wide brows. When he looked up again his face reflected chagrin. "Yes, this is probably the equivalent."

"Well, if it isn't, it probably needs to be," she said tartly. Then she sighed, her shoulders slumping forward. "Regardless, it's your gesture, and I do appreciate it. I haven't liked your remoteness of late."

"Now, ma'am, I hope I've always been respectful," Gaspard said as he sat down near his saddle. He laid the coffee aside as he opened his possibles pouch for a pinch of tobacco.

Carolina laughed. "Oh, Mr. Gaspard, then to what should I attribute your silence since we left Bent's Fort? You were less than pleased with my insistence on continuing this journey without Sibby. Perhaps I was a bit precipitous. But would waiting have changed anything? What would have been the benefit? I only saw more expense and annoyance for everyone."

Gaspard filled his pipe and tamped down the tobacco. "This canyon, it reminds me why I can't disapprove. Why it's not my business."

"I don't understand."

"You see, Mrs. Harper," he said carefully as he chose a long slender branch with which to light his pipe, "here, in the wilderness, death and life exist next to each other as in the Bible."

He drew on his pipe as he laid the lit branch against the pipe bowl. "Beauty and ugliness exist next to each other and each has its place in God's creation, and each has its own nobility, I guess. When that bear attacked me I thought I was gone, but I refused to just lie down, suffer, and die. What was the point? Well, I had a notion to see a bit more of the world, to carry it with me in my eyes and ears and nose, to be all I could be even if only for another minute more. *That* was important."

He threw the branch into the fire and puffed on his pipe. "I don't know if I can make you understand." His brow furrowed. "Don't push yourself. Just be with yourself for all the minutes God grants you."

"I can't!" she said, anguish pulling the words from her soul.

"Why?" he asked. He crossed his arms over his chest as he cradled his pipe in one hand.

She stood up and walked to the edge of the firelight circle. "I don't know who I am." She paused, inhaling and exhaling deeply. "Mr. Gaspard, I'd like to tell you a bit about my life."

He looked up and shifted uneasily. "It isn't any of my concern."

"Please. Just listen." She began to pace before the fire. "When I was a young child I spent much of the time with my maternal grandparents, the Reeves, while my mother and father traveled," she said softly. "My grandparents never approved of their daughter's marriage to a Mexican, even if his family was descended from Spanish aristocracy and was a powerful trading influence within Mexico. My father negotiated many of his family's contracts, which is why he and mother traveled. He would have preferred to live his life solely as a scholar, but if he could not, traveling to negotiate contracts gave him opportunities to continue his studies. A child on such trips was a nuisance.

"After father died, mother married Mr. Davies. Mother and Mr. Davies also traveled so I continued living with Grandmother and Grandfather. They disapproved of my resemblance to my *foreign* father. But they did their best by me, and though they tried not to show it, I often caught them staring at me as if I were some puzzle for which they needed to find a solution." She shook her head, her lips twisting into a wry smile as she thought about her grandparents. She returned to her place by the fire and sat down again.

"When I was sixteen I married Edward Harper," she continued.

She drew her knees up to her chest. "His family thought the marriage politically and monetarily proper. And for my part, as was proper, I presented my husband with a son and heir less than a year after we married. We named him David," she said, her voice softening, a lost smile shining in her faraway expression.

Then the softness in her features faded and her face resumed its matter-of-fact expression. "It wasn't long after my son's birth that I heard the whispered murmurs from Edward's cousins that the relatives hoped David did not develop his father's affliction, for it was in the family coming from his paternal grandmother."

"Affliction?"

Carolina turned away.

Gaspard leaned forward to touch her chin. Gently he turned her face to him. "Carolina?"

She looked down at her hands clenched in her lap, and shook her head. "The whispers I endured. The lies his family told, and the cover-ups they contrived." She shook her head, her expression bleak.

"What do you mean? Was something wrong with Mr. Harper?"

"Wrong?" Her voice rose. "*Wrong?*" she repeated. Her shoulders lifted, then sank wearily. "I believe they sometimes call it melancholia."

"Damn," he said.

"Sometimes it was like Edward was three people." She shook her head. "My husband was not suited to the life his father mapped out for him. He was at heart a farmer forced to be a merchant. He was not talented in business, but he tried hard. The family had him running their trading operations out of New Orleans. It would have been better to let him remain on our small plantation, but no. He was the eldest son and must be broadened and trained as befitted a Harper. One would think he was in training for an actual kingdom! I suppose to the Harpers it was a real kingdom. Edward did fine for a while, but soon his liabilities caught up with him. He did not have a head for numbers and this so embarrassed him that rather than admit his failing, he would scream at whoever foolishly offered assistance. The one time I corrected a column of his figures I was cuffed for my efforts."

Gaspard refilled his coffee. "I've known men like that. Fools who'd cut off their left hand afore they'd admit they were left-handed, as if that were some sin against nature." He held out the pot toward Carolina.

She nodded. "Please," she said, then continued. "That was Edward. Then the business began failing and he began drinking.

"When Father Harper finally noticed that the business revenues were slipping, he came to New Orleans to have a talk with his son. He was bullying and nasty. I was shocked at the words I heard, though I'll own I was not meant to hear them. After that Edward seemed frozen. He could do nothing, and this inability frazzled him. He turned to drinking more and more to calm himself.

"Then one day I came down to breakfast to sit opposite a man I did not know. His eyes were wide and bright. He talked rapidly and without stopping. He was full of solutions to the business problems, full of schemes that I found alarming. He just laughed and told me I could not appreciate his genius, but I would. Everyone would. Then he was up and gone, his movements agitated, quick. He was full of himself and life. I did not know whether to be glad for the change or afraid. I chose glad. I later learned fear would have been a more realistic attitude.

"He was a whirlwind at the mercantile house. He made grandiose buys and sells. One of Edward's cousins, then a junior clerk with the firm, sent a message to Father Harper, who was then in Washington.

"After about a week of this maniacal activity, Edward woke one morning and refused to get out of bed. He hadn't eaten while he was frenzied so he'd lost weight. Now that lack of food weakened him. His skin looked pasty, his eyes sunken. He became sullen and uncommunicative. Sibby and I coaxed first broth and then oats down his throat to give him sustenance; but he wouldn't talk except in a low whine. He wanted his room dark. He wanted to be alone.

"By the afternoon he seemed more himself, even well enough to join me at dinner. I was gratified and I told him so. I felt, or hoped, the past week had been some strange, passing aberration and that my sweet Edward would return. He didn't. A shell of a man now lived with me. Most mornings Edward refused to get out of bed, and only on some evenings, if they were particularly pleasant evenings with pleasant weather, would he get out of bed or even come downstairs.

"I told the clerks in the office that Edward had faith in their abilities to carry on without him, but at the moment he was indisposed with a virulent affliction of some obscure nature. I do not know precisely what yarn I spun for them, but they nodded knowingly enough and wished him well and took themselves off.

"Then Father Harper came to town. The business had lost a great deal of money during Edward's wild, exultant behavior, but evidently his young cousin had taken charge and pulled the business from the brink of bankruptcy.

"Again Father Harper railed at Edward, but this time Edward only looked at him with blankness in his eyes. Father Harper asked if a doctor had been to see Edward. I stammered none had. I got knocked across the room, his backhanded slap was so unexpected. I think I then looked up at him with an expression as confused as Edward's. He consigned us both to perdition and told Edward if he did not pull himself together, or at least see a doctor to physic him, he would disown him, for no son of his could possibly be the wretch Edward had become.

"Edward did see a doctor, one who nodded and gave him pills and nodded some more. Disgusted, Edward threw them away and, to my delight, slowly seemed to be regaining his strength and a renewed will to live.

"I wanted us to go to our plantation to give him some peaceful surroundings to help him recover. Edward insisted he must remain in New Orleans in order to redeem himself. He was very concerned with redemption in his father's eyes. His young cousin taught him a lot, which I took as particularly kind, for if Edward were gone, the business would be this young man's. But I think he knew Edward's improvement would only prove temporary. Toward the end of summer, he became agitated again. This time he spent his time in the coffeehouses debating and participating in wild plans to take over this or that country.

"I hardly saw him." Her voiced hushed and assumed a greater detachment as a ward against the coming memories. "Then yellow fever came to New Orleans as it often did in late, sweltering summer.

"I pleaded with Edward to take me north. He said he couldn't just then, his plans were too incipient. All around us our neighbors fled the city for the country. Then one morning I discovered one of my worst fears had come true. One of our housemaids contracted the disease." She took a deep breath. "She had been David's nanny. Shortly thereafter he came down with it." Her face contorted with pain. "It torn my heart to see him suffering from that devil-spawned affliction! I quickly saw there would be no mercy for my child. The disease consumed him like fire. While David lay pale, sunken-eyed, and dying, Edward again confined himself to his bed and refused a doctor's care.

"When David finally died, I think I went a bit crazy." Carolina's expression cleared, her voice returning to its flat recitation. "But I did everything that needed to be done, though to this day I don't remember any of it. I buried David on the first day a cleansing rain came. That night, Edward hung himself in his room."

"My God," whispered Gaspard. He shifted position to sit beside her. Awkwardly, he draped his arm about her shoulders, pulling her to rest against his shoulder.

"Only with David did I have a bit of myself, for he was of me and for that I could give freely of myself. But to others he was not my son, he was Edward's son," she said softly.

"Gaspard—" She shook her head and then frowned as she stared into the campfire. "Mr. Gaspard, I am an encumbrance," she said brokenly. She turned her head up to look at him in bewilderment and sorrow. "That is almost all I have ever been. I am tired of being a millstone. I want to have value."

"Value? You talk like you want to be put up on the slave block," he said, pulling away from her.

"No, no." She shook her head, then raised a hand to massage her temples. "I don't know why I'm even talking about this."

His eyes narrowed as he looked at her closely. "Maybe because somewhere along the way you got your thinking all twisted up and deep inside you know it."

She laughed harshly. "No, Mr. Gaspard." She sighed and took a sip of coffee before continuing her story. "Naturally, Edward's family blamed me for Edward's and David's deaths. If I weren't around, Edward could have married a woman more suited to him, one who would have known how to keep him from drinking or from going into rages if someone corrected him. They let me know they considered all of Edward's failings my fault. They said I was a millstone around their son's neck. And I guess they were right. I did not know how to stop his drinking, and I was terrified of speaking to him about his mathematics. All I could do was worry and wring my hands, knowing somehow I'd let Edward down, but not certain how!"

"That's foolishness."

"No. No, it isn't. I let Edward down. I was not a helpmate. I was an encumbrance. Oh, I was strong, I took care of everything I could, I kept the estate operating and from that we were able to eke out a living."

"That's more than being an encumbrance. Carolina, I'd say you demand more from yourself than a body should. I don't know what you call being of value, but hell, I saw how you worked with the women at Bent's Fort, you didn't expect to be served. And in the caravan, you kept us fed, sewed many a torn shirt, drove a wagon, and were there for an Indian woman who needed another woman. I sure don't know what else you could be expecting from life or yourself.

"No man nor woman is perfect in this world. All we can do is do the best we can with what God gives us. You expect too much from yourself and from others, too."

He shifted positions, stretching out his long legs as he leaned back against his saddle. "You're going to New Mexico expecting your uncle to need you to care for his children. What if he doesn't?" he asked. "I know the New Mexican people. If his wife's family is alive, they're likely to have welcomed those children with open arms. Hell, it's been what, nine months, a year since his wife died? They wouldn't let those children go unmothered unless Elliott held them off with a rifle and I can't see Elliott Reeves doing that."

Carolina laughed. "No, neither can I."

"Those children are likely settled and happy with someone else now," he said as he stared up at the night sky.

"I know. They are."

His head jerked down to look at her. "You know?"

Carolina nodded. "They're in Taos. Charles Bent told me."

"Bent told you?" he asked incredulously. He drew his feet back toward himself and surged up. "You knew before we reached Bent's Fort?"

"Yes. I knew then that I was deluding myself," she said, looking up at him. "That I had been deluding myself for some time. After all, I never actually received a letter from my uncle asking me to Santa Fe."

Gaspard combed his fingers back through his hair and shook his head. "Then why this damned insistence on getting to New Mexico? Then why the hell are you so fired up to get to Santa Fe? What's in that female mind of yours?" He raised an eyebrow and looked at her intensely. "You ain't thinking of warning Armijo of our intentions, telling what's happening up here."

Carolina blushed hotly. "I am no spy! That was Harry Well's accusation. It wasn't true then and not now!"

"Then why, goddamn it?"

"For the children."

"But—"

"For all the children, for the women, the old people."

"I don't understand."

"There may well be war brought to New Mexico soon. Hotheaded and avaricious men have set a course in that direction. Oh, not just our American men; Mexico, too, with her behavior toward Texas. I know this. And in all wars, it is the defenseless ones who suffer. The old couple whose meager plot of land is trampled into the dirt by thousands of feet, whose food supplies are taken to feed soldiers, whose small home may even be confiscated to house some officer, and all this they must face without complaint. It is for the young girls in the city who fall victim to the victory celebrations of either army, when blood lust turns to carnal lust. It is for the children who get unintentionally trampled by the horses and men, get caught in cross fires, or go to bed with empty bellies because their food has been taken to fill a soldier's belly."

"How can you talk about war? What do you know of it?" Gaspard asked.

She smiled softly. "My father was a scholar. He often talked to me about the cost of war, the costs governments don't calculate. The people costs. It used to fret him when any war was declared. Yes, he still had his merchant's heart, inherited from his family. He understood what depravations war brings to a prosperous land and how this affects trade into and out of a region. But he also taught me the other. The more important aspects of war."

"And by going on to Santa Fe you think you can stop this war?"

"No! No, I know better than that. I cannot stop this war, but perhaps I can pull one child out of the road, one young girl from the arms of victory, one old couple's ranch. It isn't much of a reason, I'll grant you, to risk yours and Pedro's lives to cross this mountain. I realize that now. I'm sorry. It is just something within me. Something I hoped to accomplish."

"Now that you know how things stand in Santa Fe, just what do you intend to do when you get there?"

"I don't know. Perhaps I can hire myself out as a governess or perhaps a cook."

"And risk shaming your family?"

"Shaming them? Now, what are *you* talking about?"

Gaspard scratched his head. "For a woman who claims she thinks too much, I sure don't see evidence of it."

"I beg your pardon!"

"You can beg all you want, you ain't gettin' it. Of all the flea-brained notions for a woman to take to, this does lead the pack. Damn." He sat back down and picked up his mug as he continued to shake his head.

"What are you talking about?"

Gaspard held the mug up close to his face and stared at the steam rising from the hot brew as he thought.

"You're sure full of shoulds and oughts, aren't you?"

"What do you mean?"

"Don't you ever do anything just because you want to? Does everything have to have a greater purpose?"

"I do things I want all the time. It has caused me considerable grief at times as well."

He shook his head. "No, from my observation, I'd say you do things you think you *ought* to do or *should* do, and you kick yourself when you miss something in your list of oughts and shoulds. Oughts and shoulds arc fine for part of the time, but a man—or a woman—needs their own time too. Kinda gives a body evenness," he said, his hand gliding out in an even plane.

She shook her head. "I no longer need to go to Santa Fe, but I am proceeding on because I want to."

Gaspard shook his head and laughed softly. "Ain't that just like a woman. No, I'm not laughing at you. Not precisely. Truth is, I honor you for your gumption. Many another woman would have been hightailing it back to St. Louis."

"I know. And perhaps I should have, but there is really nothing there that I want or that wants me."

He shook his head. "I think you're too harsh on yourself and on others. You're a fine woman, Carolina."

"Thank you."

"I honor your desire. I'll get you to Santa Fe, but I'm staying close by in case you need me. Things might be more complicated than you imagine. When we get to Santa Fe, I'll take you to the United States consul in New Mexico. He'll find you a place to stay and help you get settled. He's a good man. He might even understand your feelings."

"Thank you, Mr. Gaspard, but couldn't I just go to my uncle's house?"

"I wouldn't advise it until we know what the tenor of the land and people are. For all you know, he could have taken himself another wife by now, or some other female to warm his bed. He may not welcome you either."

"I guess I've never really thought this out the way I should, the way I've been taught, but I've never felt so driven. I can't explain—"

He laid a hand over hers. "You don't have to. I think I understand and I respect you for it. No. More than that, Carolina, I honor and like you for it."

"You do?"

"I do."

19

July 10, 1846, later.

    *I had a curious conversation with Mr. Gaspard this evening. I
don't know that we ever came to any understanding as to
what the other meant; however, we talked together, for which I
am delighted. He seems to think I do too much out of an
overdeveloped sense of duty. Much more than my own
interest. At the time I quickly rejected his suggestion out of
hand, but now—now I need to think on this awhile.*

    *Ah, but not now. I am sated, my limbs quiver with
exhaustion, and the fire dies too low for writing any longer.*

CAROLINA LET HER horse pick the path through the boulder-
strewn trail beside the Purgatory River and shook her head. "I see
why we had to dispense with the wagons. Is the whole fifteen
miles of the pass like this?" she asked Gaspard. On either side of
them rock cliffs rose forty to fifty feet. In places there was no room
for a trail next to the river. Instead, the river was the trail, and their
horses and mules picked their way up a rocky channel, only occasionally feeling the lap of cool water on their hooves.

He laughed and shook his head. "No. It gets worse."

"Worse?"

He turned in his saddle to look at her and grinned. "Want to turn back to Bent's Fort?"

She scowled at him, though she knew his suggestion lacked the sincerity it had possessed before they reached the Hole in the Rock canyon. "No, I do not. Lead on!"

He laughed, then waved his arm to point up ahead. "There's a wide, fairly flat spot in the trail not far up on the left. We'll noon it there."

"Flat?" Carolina repeated incredulously as she looked about the rocky landscape. Suddenly her horse stumbled and without thought Carolina pulled back on the reins as she struggled for balance.

Wrong! Wrong! her mind screamed as she felt the horse lurch to the right.

"Miz Carolina!" Pedro yelled.

Gaspard swung around in his saddle.

Her poor horse was going down hard. Carolina kicked one foot free, but the other foot, tangled in skirts tucked around her leg for decorum, was hung up in its stirrup.

The world tilted. The surrounding cliff face swung past her eyes until she saw clouds piling one upon another in the sky. When she hit the ground her breath caught in her chest and pain exploded in her head, radiating shards of blackness before her eyes like so many pieces of broken glass.

Then nothing.

POUNDING, POUNDING PAIN. It pounded in cadence with the sound of rain beating the earth. It filled her head, traveled down her neck, sprang to life in her back and her right leg.

Carolina swallowed a moan that rose in her throat, and tried to open her eyes. They felt weighted. The slightest movement, the slightest flicker renewed the pain in lightning flashes.

A cool wind blew across her face, momentarily dulling the pain. She whimpered and willed the wind back, to take more of the hurt away, but it only teased her senses.

Warmth radiated along her sides and around her. It reminded her of Louisiana and Edward.

Poor Edward, she thought.

Edward!

Her eyes flew open. Sharp, overwhelming pain, too strong to allow a moan to escape her lips, nauseated her. Her eyes refused to focus. Her stomach roiled, then heaved. Desperately she fought down the feeling, fought the acrid taste that rose in her throat. She closed her eyes, then opened them, willing her awareness to extend beyond her body, beyond her center of pain.

Inches away, along her left side lay a snoring man. Slowly she turned her head. In the darkness tempered with predawn light she recognized Pedro. She slowly turned her head to the right. Gaspard.

She sighed softly. She would be well cared for despite herself.

She gasped, then whimpered as nauseating, pounding pain racked her body. She raised her palms to her forehead. Tears gathered in her eyes.

"Carolina?" Gaspard leaned up on his elbow. He touched her forehead.

She winced beneath his light touch.

"Señora?" asked Pedro.

Gaspard slowly pulled his hand away from her forehead and shook his head. "At least there's no fever. That's a relief. How do you feel?"

Carolina licked her dry lips, her breath coming in fast pants as if she'd been running. She closed her eyes. "Hurt," she managed.

"Head?"

She whimpered agreement.

"Leg?"

She gathered her strength to nod. "And back," she managed.

"Damn. Nothing's broken, as far as I can tell," he told her. He looked across her to Pedro. "We've got to keep her warm. Stay close to her while I fetch the laudanum. Should have had it to hand."

Carolina shivered as moist, cold air replaced Mr. Gaspard's warmth. She whimpered again and hated herself for it. Now Gaspard would surely insist they return to Bent's Fort.

She felt herself lifted like a rag doll. Her head lolled against a cool, rain-damp shirt. It felt nice, like the wind on her face. She wanted to say that, but the words wouldn't form.

A hand cupped her chin, holding her steady, and coaxed liquid from a narrow-necked bottle down her throat. Foul-tasting liquid. She wanted to reject it, to turn her head away, but she lacked the strength to even open her eyes to see who would visit this indignity upon her. Docilely she swallowed and promised herself a next time for refusal. *Next time* echoed in her head as she slid again toward oblivion.

SOMETHING SMELLED GOOD. Carolina's nose twitched as she tried to identify the smell. She inhaled deeply. Her head and body responded with their seeming agonies, but the agonies were calmer now, more manageable—at least for a time.

Meat.

That's what the smell was. Meat cooking. Her dry mouth grew moist. She opened her eyes and slowly, testing the movement, she turned her head toward the smell.

Pedro crouched before a fire, stirring the contents of the coffeepot. But Carolina did not smell coffee.

"What?" Her voice came out in a husky whisper too low for Pedro to hear. She swallowed and licked her lips. "What," she began again, "what are you doing?"

Pedro whirled toward Carolina. His face split into a broad smile. "Señora! *Bueno!* I make you good soup!"

"Soup?"

"*Sí*. Very good for you. You see."

In a coffeepot, Carolina mused. She nodded weakly and closed her eyes.

"Here, señora," Pedro said from right beside her.

Disoriented, Carolina looked up at him. She thought she'd just been talking to him while he cooked, and here he was beside her. She must be drifting in and out of sleep. But for how long?

Pedro helped her to sit up. Carolina blushed and quickly pulled a blanket around her shoulders when she realized all she wore was her chemise. And with no other woman in their party that would mean . . . Her mind shied away from completing her thought. But what would she have expected?

She sipped the hot soup Pedro held out to her, enjoying the feel of it sliding down her throat. Flavored with some herb she did not recognize, the thin meat broth tasted delicious and her stomach accepted it without complaint. Suddenly she realized how hungry she was. There was a pang in her middle that had nothing to do with her fall.

"Let me," she said, reaching for the spoon.

He held it away. "No, señora. No. You are weak. Señor Gaspard, he give me orders. I feed you, then you sleep again."

She nodded slightly, pleased to discover her head did not react to the movement with renewed bursts of pain or nausea. "How long?" she managed to ask between bites.

"How long?" Pedro repeated, his brow knitting in confusion.

"Yes, how long have I been here like this."

"Three days."

"Three days!"

"*Sí*. But that is good. Señor Gaspard, he much afraid it be longer before you wake. Me, I say it be this day, and I am right!" He grinned at her, pleased with himself and with her.

Carolina took another sip of soup. "Where is Mr. Gaspard?"

"Hunting."

"Hunting!" She stayed his hand in the act of bringing the soup to her lips. "But shouldn't we stay together? If something were to happen to him . . . "

Pedro looked at her strangely. She flushed and realized she sounded like a frightened child.

"I'm sorry," she said. Her headache began to blossom again. She winced at the pain.

"Eat, señora," Pedro said. "You feel *muy bueno.*"

She opened her mouth for another bite of soup, then lay a hand on his arm when he reached for another spoonful. "No more. Not right now." The few spoonfuls she'd eaten reminded her of her body's other physical needs. Needs for which she'd have to move. Aware how fragile her head felt, she wasn't anxious, though her body might have been.

"Ah! *Sí,*" he said. "The medicine. I get it." Carolina watched him set the mug of soup down and dig into the pack near her head. He pulled out the laudanum bottle. "Here, señora."

"No. Not right yet, Pedro. But soon, I promise you. I need to get up. I need . . . " She waved her hands in the direction of some bushes as her voice trailed off.

Pedro hit his forehead with the heel of his hand and muttered Spanish curses at himself. "*Sí.* Of course!" He scrambled to his feet.

Carolina threw the blankets off her legs and reached up. As he pulled her to her feet Carolina immediately realized two things. First, her right leg could barely hold her weight, and second, the world spun. The feeling made her stomach churn, sending soup partially back up her throat. She choked on the taste.

"Señora?"

"I'm all right. Just a momentary dizziness." Slowly she straightened and felt the world right itself and the dizziness subside to manageable nausea. "See. I am much better now. But I would be grateful for your arm."

With a flourish, Pedro half turned and offered her his arm. Carolina laid her arm on his, then leaned on him heavily when her knee threatened to buckle.

"I'm sorry, Pedro."

"It is nothing," he said quickly.

Her limbs quivered, every muscle in her body screaming in rage and resentment; but her need was greater and she refused to humiliate herself further. Carefully, she tucked each pain away and reached down into herself for strength.

Near a screen of bushes she straightened and dropped her hand from Pedro's arm.

"Señora?"

"It's all right, Pedro. I can make it from here. Give me a moment."

The lines in the old man's face drooped like his mustache. A breeze lifted his thinning, gray-streaked hair.

She hobbled past the bushes.

He's an old man, she thought as she struggled to attend to her body's needs. She did not know why she was suddenly struck by that knowledge. Or how it was that she had not seen his age in the past. He was a faithful servant, but too old for the trials he'd faced with her this journey.

First Sibby, now Pedro. How selfish had she been? What assumptions had she made without concern for their thoughts and feelings?

To honor them, she would be strong and she would get to Santa Fe.

That vow she made as she walked back toward the campfire, and the vow echoed through her like a prayer.

The necessary trip exhausted Carolina. Muzzily, she returned to her bedroll, closed her eyes, and waved away the soup Pedro again offered, but grudgingly accepted the laudanum.

When next she opened her eyes thin clouds scudded before a star-laced sky. She slowly turned her head. No burst of pain now. Just an ache behind her eyes. Gaspard and Pedro hunched in front of a low fire. Gaspard punched at the flames with a branch. Glowing coals popped, crackled, sparked, and shot up into the night sky.

Carolina smelled coffee; it smelled delicious, but it wasn't what she needed. "Water, please," she rasped.

The men whirled about. Gaspard dropped the stick into the fire. They looked like guilty schoolboys.

She struggled to sit up. Her head hurt dreadfully, but not, she thought, as much as before. Unfortunately, her thoughts remained muzzy. It was an odd sensation to be aware that one wasn't altogether sharp and acute. It was frightening, for who could say if it would ever go away?

Wind whipped through the lean-to, reminding Carolina of her attire. She gathered the blanket up to her chin.

"Water," she murmured as Mr. Gaspard brought the water pouch to her mouth.

"Easy, easy, now. Don't gulp it like that. Didn't anyone ever tell you that's a way of getting sick?"

"I am sick. What's the difference?" she croaked.

Gaspard laughed. "If you've your wit back we don't have to worry anymore. You'll do fine."

She laughed weakly. "Don't be quick to think that. Thinking requires effort."

His lips twisted sideways. "Excuse me, ma'am, but if I was a betting man I'd say for you not to think were akin to the day not choosing to begin."

Carolina laughed again, shook her head, and sighed. "You have the truth of it there, Mr. Gaspard. It is a lamentable habit. It would be better for all if I could stop."

"Now, that's a muddle. How do you figure that?"

She looked at him in surprise. "You, yourself, have demonstrated impatience and anger with my thinking."

"With the content of your thinking, that I'll own," he said ruefully, wagging a correcting finger at her. "Sometimes it doesn't seem like thinking at all, so counter it runs from my own."

She grinned. "So man has complained of woman since Eve." She cocked her head to the side, her expression sliding from humor to sadness. "Was it really so incomprehensible to you? My wanting to continue on?"

He shrugged. "I've been thinking on that," he said slowly. "And questioning my feelings . . . I was married once," he confided on a long exhale.

"I know," she said softly. "Mr. Bush told me about Sarah Anne."

His head jerked up, his scars shiny white in the campfire light. "That gossipy old woman!" he said, and swore, calling Mr. Bush nearly every name Carolina had ever heard—and some she hadn't.

She snaked a hand out from the enveloping folds of the blanket to lay on his arm. She tried not to laugh at his vehemence, but she could not forego the sad, rueful smile that quivered on her lips. "I think he told me more for me, as a way to comfort me, rather than as a way to gossip about you. He told me about Sarah Anne, and . . . and your child the day you took Singing Waters' baby away from me."

His lips twisted and twitched as if he were chewing what she'd said and found it distasteful. Slowly Carolina felt the bunched muscle in his arm relax. She quickly withdrew her hand and used it instead to smooth her hair.

"I came near to hating you that day. And hating myself worse," she admitted.

Gaspard nodded. Then he shook his head and ran a long finger along the tracks of the scars on his face. "Bush, when he was young," he finally offered, "trained to be a man of the cloth."

"Mr. Bush!" Carolina gaped at him as she struggled with the idea of Mr. Bush as theologian. She hitched the blanket closer around her shoulders.

He nodded. "He always said he found out before it was too late that he had no calling, but sometimes I wonder if his wasn't a higher calling."

"Yes." She smiled softly. "Yes, I can see that, with the earth at his feet and the sky above as his cathedral," she said, remembering the Oregon immigrant marriage.

He looked at her with surprise. "Yes, that's Bush. But to return to what I need to tell you, not that I'm a man for baring my soul or wallowing in my past, I need to tell you I do know. I understand a bit of the bite of the whip that drives you. I've had it goading me on.

"After Sarah Anne died, I pushed on, explored places I'd never been. Hell, I explored places no white man had ever been! I pushed on because I had to. Here," he said, thumping his chest. "Or I'd as likely shriveled up and died. To this day I carry my load of guilt. So, I push on, looking for only God knows what. Perhaps absolution from God."

"That you have," Carolina said, tears welling in her eyes. She sighed. "The hardest part for me is forgiving myself."

He nodded. "That's the God's truth. And maybe that's why I didn't argue too hard to get you to stop this foolishness. I could have prevented you from leaving Bent's Fort. I could have had Rawlins or Bush loose your horse and mules. They would have done it."

"In a moment!" she agreed with a pained smile.

"And no others would have taken your part if I or Rawlins or Bent told them no."

Carolina bit her lower lip between her teeth, then released it and inhaled deeply. "Yes," she said steadily.

"I do know those damned demons that nip your heels for they've nipped mine a fair amount. I just hope you're not going to be disappointed in Santa Fe. It ain't going to be easy."

"Perhaps not. But the challenges will be my challenges, and as such I welcome them."

He compressed his lips again in the wake of her stubbornness, then laughed softly. "You got more gumption than most men I know. Just you remember, when it comes to battling demons, I'm a veteran. You send word if you need to. Agreed?"

She smiled and nodded. "Agreed."

20

July 15, 1846, Raton Pass.

For four days we have camped at the same spot in the trail. Though I would push on, I admit our dawdling here is my fault. Through a piece of stupidity, I fell from my horse while we were climbing a dry streambed. It was a rocky streambed and therefore I've acquired bruises of all shapes, sizes, and colors. I also suffered a concussion and for a time could scarcely move without becoming ill. But before you moan, lament, panic, and otherwise behave as a mother—no matter the age of the child—be assured that I am recovering swiftly.

It is my horse who will suffer longer. She has a nasty gash on her foreleg. Mr. Gaspard said she should heal with time, that she is not permanently lame, but she cannot be ridden. From here on I shall ride one of the mules.

Mr. Gaspard and Pedro have done all for me they've known to do and have devised beyond knowing. Their care has been prompt and unswerving.

However—Ah, and how do I describe this next? Or should I? This is no delicate manner. Truthfully, you would be shocked at what they've deemed necessary for my care!

During the cold mountain night the three of us lie next to one another sharing warmth. This sleeping arrangement was begun by Pedro and Gaspard while I lay unconscious after the fall, and has continued since for the comfort of all. Mr. Gaspard tells me this type of sleeping arrangement to share warmth was a common practice among the beaver-trapping mountain men who used to be prevalent on the trail.

I have tried to get Mr. Gaspard and Pedro to allow me to take a turn at the outside position, but both gentlemen are adamant in their refusal. Grandmother Reeves would surely die of apoplexy if she saw us, though, and I'm certain that if word of this were ever to reach the Harpers, they would insist they knew all along that I was never as good as others supposed.

I can think of these reactions, but they do not touch me whereas in days past I would have been devastated. Why is that? Have I grown callous?

No, not callous. Perhaps more careworn and therefore more inclined only to take care of those things that are directly within my control, and not to worry about anything else.

Also, I have a growing appreciation for westering man's snubbing convention and his disdain for whispered shock and condemnation. I wish I could discover the strength within me to emulate his disdain, though for now, I'll own that the strength to regain my strength has a greater need for my attention.

July 16, 1846, Raton Pass. Noon.

We departed the scene of my debacle early this morning. We've moved slowly, owing to my still recovering condition. With my diminished strength my explorations of the surrounding lands remain curtailed.

I am exhausted, but please, do not tell Mr. Gaspard! Today, by the time I slid off my mule, it was all I could do to walk to the nearest boulder where I might sit down.

The skeletal bones of wagons, animals, and—yes—a man appear incongruously among boulders and white, yellow, and lavender wildflowers. As if I need reminding as to the harshness of this land! Pedro and Gaspard built a stone cairn for our lost and forlorn traveler. Then Mr. Gaspard pulled a well-worn Bible out of his pack and prayed. He prayed for this unknown soul and for us.

The shell that caught up my emotions all these many months since David's death has been cracking and peeling away as one peels a boiled egg. With the disintegration of the shell something untoward has occurred, something that concerns me; however, I cannot touch it.

The cracking and peeling has not caused a resurgence of my emotions. My feelings still threaten to drain away, leaving only this husk behind, a more fragile and useless thing than any geegaws I could have packed to carry over the mountain.

There is a numbness within me that I cannot shed. I see the beauty of the mountains, the rocks, the trees, the flowers, the little rabbits and squirrels. I hear the screech of the hunting hawk and the nighttime calls of the owl and coyote.

I don't know if the blow to my head is wholly responsible, or if the condition is permanent, but I feel different. And above all else, it doesn't seem to matter. I don't need to analyze it or rationalize it. It just is. Today.

Odd. I've always lived with an eye toward tomorrow. I've missed too many todays in my life. Perhaps, however, a judicious mixture of both is more sensible, with a dash of yesterday for spice and experience, for shouldn't experience stand for something in one's life?

July 16, 1846, later. Evening, beyond the Raton summit.

Ignore every negative comment I've heretofore written about the Raton Pass! Allow old irritations and hardships to slide away!

I am overwhelmed!

I have never smelled air so fresh or seen billowing clouds that appeared close enough to touch. The white clouds' pristine beauty contrasts sharply with the vivid blue dome above and the deep blue shadows the clouds cast upon the earth below.

Everywhere game is abundant. Not many moments ago Mr. Gaspard shot a turkey and a deer to augment our food stores.

Nearby grows a bush with fruit resembling cherries. Mr. Gaspard says when the fruit is ripe it first tastes sweet, but then quickly changes to a mouth-puckering persimmon flavor.

This afternoon we reached the spot on the trail considered the pass summit. The road, such as it is, made a short jog back toward the north. From the cusp of this jog, looking north we could see Pike's Peak more than one hundred miles away. Looking to the northwest we caught a last glimpse of the Spanish Peaks, Wah-to-Yah.

From our vantage point I would have sworn we could see forever. Looking down into the steep valley bordered by gray rock, pine, and piñon we caught glimpses of the stream we'd followed up the mountain. In the sunlight the water coruscated like thousands of diamonds as it alternately tumbled over rocks then slid from view in its headlong journey hundreds of feet to the Purgatory River below.

From the summit, one does not come down out of the mountains so much as one descends a series of hills. Through the spyglass Mr. Gaspard lent me, each fold of the earth revealed signs of human existence: a sheep herder's lean-to, a patch of corn, a cluster of three or four adobe buildings comprising a ranchero or village. For the first time, I am experiencing alienness in this land.

Strange, I never felt this otherworldliness on the trail or at Bent's Fort. Mr. Gaspard and Pedro have been expending more words than either is normally known to have, let alone

*speak. And all words are directed to educating me to the fact
there is a difference to this land! I, in my normal stubborn,
willful manner, did not want to listen. The only differences I
could imagine were differences of language, skin, and
affluence. I begin to sense the breadth of my naivete.*

Too late?

*Too late for taking another road to my future, not too late to
change how I will travel down this road. The key is knowing
how and what to change. Therein lies the rub! Ah, Hamlet.
How well thou spoke. For I see in Spain, Mexico, and New
Mexico Hamlet's family: the murdered father, the uncle, the
mother. And what role is the United States to play?
Fortenbras? And I? I'll not play Ophelia. Instead I should
stand in the back and comment like some Greek chorus.*

*For shame that I should speak of such a famous play, let
alone draw similarities that show this play in an unfavorable
light. Shakespeare's plays are too intelligent and subtle for the
female mind to grasp, Father Harper once decreed.*

*A-A-h! I must desist this petty vanity, for so has
demeaning the Harpers become to me. I give them more
substance than they deserve, and I, alone, may take it away!*

*Mr. Gaspard and Pedro are building a shelter for the night
back against a cliff face above our would-be stream trail. Steel-
blue clouds gather in the mountains to the west and are
rolling over one another in their haste to meet us.*

*You can see where rain falls, for long gray streaks angle
down from the clouds. In other areas, to the south, the sun
shines brilliant gold against the landscape until bit by bit, the
jealous clouds roll over the golden sun there as well.*

Ah! Rain! The first raindrops!

"WHAT ARE YOU doing out there? Did that fall shake out what
was left of your wits?"

"What was left? What do you mean, what was left?" Carolina
bantered back.

Gaspard grinned. "I figured that would get your attention."

"I'm enjoying the rain," Carolina pertly told him as she gathered her writing supplies and walked toward their contrived shelter. However, her supercilious smile threatened to dissolve into a grin.

"Well, enjoy it when someone else has the responsibility for you," he grumbled. "I don't need for you to go and develop pneumonia and folks say it's my fault, just like that concussion."

"Nonsense."

He crossed his arms over his chest and raised a scraggly eyebrow. "You think I want to be anywhere within a hundred miles of Jedediah Rawlins should he hear you died when you were with me?"

Carolina felt a hot blush climb her cheeks. It was both flattering and unnerving to think a man should take an interest in her situation, and for another man to know it! Carolina didn't know how to respond.

"Rooster posturings, Mr. Gaspard," she said with more sharpness than she had intended. She ducked under the roof of the makeshift cave.

"Uo-oh, Pedro, I do believe winter has come," Gaspard teased.

"Mr. Gaspard!" Carolina said in exasperation.

Pedro and Gaspard laughed. Their ease of manner in her company caused Carolina's throat to choke past a sudden lump and her eyes to water.

Camaraderie.

In her heart she felt gifted.

21

July 17, 1846. Noon.

*Coming out of the mountains is nearly as adventuresome as
entering them! The vegetation has decreased almost unto the
death of our animals. Our road is rocky. All signs of game
have vanished.*

*This is almost worse than the Timpas Creek area. If it
weren't for Mr. Gaspard's continued insistence that we
travel slowly for the sake of my health, we should be through
this area swiftly. I have argued until I am nigh hoarse that
we should assume a brisk pace. Mr. Gaspard does not
directly disagree with me; he continues to set a slow
pace.*

Maddening.

"WE'LL BE COMING down into Mora and some of the other villages tomorrow. Since we don't know what they're thinking about
Anglos, Pedro's to proceed us."

"You think that's necessary?"

Mr. Gaspard ran his hand around the back of his neck. "I don't know. But I've always ascribed to the notion a prudent man sees the next sunrise."

"The señor is wise, señora," Pedro interjected. "And me, I am happy to walk and talk among my people again."

Carolina drew her eyebrows together.

"I don't think we'll have a problem." Gaspard said quickly. "More'n likely we'll be met with enthusiasm for whatever trade goods we've brought. But just the same, when we get down to the village, you let me or Pedro do the talking."

She felt they were overreacting and felt she had contended with their nigh swaddling care for long enough! Her lips settled into a straight line. "Why?" she asked.

"We know the people, you don't. . . . Now, don't get your back up. Just because you've got your father's Spanish looks doesn't mean you're going to be welcomed like some long-lost cow or sheep. Your clothes, your accent, your bearing—hell, everything about you screams foreigner! Now there's some," Gaspard conceded, "as who'll be fascinated. But then there are others, the nationalists, who'll not be happy. And frankly, right now I don't know how they'd handle a woman they saw as a threat. They might be gallant and never see it, or they could want to shoot you as soon as look at you."

"Then might this not be an opportunity to use my relationship to Diego Navarro?"

"You stay away from Navarro!" Gaspard snapped.

Carolina's head jerked up and her eyes widened at his vehemence. "Why?"

"The man's dangerous."

Carolina planted her fists on her hips. "How can he be any more dangerous than any others who declare no love lost for the United States?"

"Because he doesn't have life here or here!" He retorted tapping his chest and his head.

"What do you mean?"

"The man lacks a soul."

"*No espíritu. Desalmado*," Pedro said, nodding vigorously.

Carolina shook her head. "He is my father's brother!" she argued.

"Señora, your father, he be a good man. Diego Navarro, he is bad. They are like . . . like . . . "

"Two sides of a coin," Gaspard suggested.

"*Sí*, señor! A coin. Two sides, very different," he said as he held out his hand palm up. "One good, one bad," he turned his hand palm down.

"I find it difficult to believe," Carolina drawled, "that a Navarro could be completely without redemption. But I will accede to your greater knowledge, at least for a time. At least so long as my uncle is pointed out to me at the earliest opportunity."

"Why?" Gaspard asked.

Carolina laughed. "I'm afraid, Mr. Gaspard, I can offer you no greater, or better, reason than curiosity."

He joined her laughter. "At least that's honest. I can deal with that, so long as I have your agreement on the other."

"Thank you. You do. Now, Pedro," Carolina said as she turned away from Gaspard. "Fetch me the pack with the worn silver conch button, and we'll see what I might have to use for exchange in the villages."

July 18, 1846. Evening.

We are out of the Raton and on an open prairie. However, this prairie has sides. Mountainous sides. We crossed an upper stream of the Red River today. Mr. Gaspard tells me that tomorrow we shall come to another area where the available water is saturated with vile salts. Beyond that natural boundary are settlements.

I have been given my orders for proper behavior while in the settlements. They would have me be a silent entity buffeted by life. That is not a role to which I ascribe. It is probably not mine either! Nonetheless, I shall do as they ask. I respect

Gaspard's knowledge of this land and its people. I cannot help
but feel he is exaggerating the danger; however, I do not think
he is making it up.

I suggested that mentioning my relationship to Diego
Navarro could prove beneficial to us. This idea was roundly
dismissed by Gaspard, with Pedro's eager concurrence. And
Pedro hasn't even met Diego Navarro! I think if Gaspard had
his way, I would disavow all knowledge of the Navarro family.
I can't do that. That would be like denying myself and
negating all the thoughts and feelings that led me to make this
journey!

Ever since I fell from my horse, Pedro and Gaspard have
treated me as if I were a delicate piece of Italian glass. They
were never wont to treat me quite so solicitously in the past. I
find I yearn for a bit more of their tempered disinterest. This is
ironic for I also revel in their ability to tease me and grant me
that feeling of camaraderie I saw among men on the trail and
at the fort. Truthfully, I find their easy camaraderie at odds
with their overly solicitous treatment, and when one considers
the two behaviors, they do not go together.

Pedro takes his lead from Gaspard. Noting Pedro's behavior,
at times one would think he were more in Gaspard's employ
than mine! But Mr. Gaspard's behavior? He has ever been an
enigma to me, in the past alternately voluble and reticent. I
never was quite certain where I stood as far as he was
concerned; now he is solicitous and teasing and my heart beats
faster.

But why? Proximity, no doubt. And perhaps I am finally
recovering from my loss only to discover how lonely I am.
Strength, strength of mind, strength of character does not and
should not equate to walking life alone. I know, now, that I
will chance marriage again. At some time. And I also know
that it is the nascent feelings I possess for Mr. Gaspard that
bring this to mind.

But I will not burden Mr. Gaspard with my turmoil. He is

*a good man and a part of me is afraid that if I should in any
way allow him to sense my tenderness, he would rush to
marry me if only to protect me from myself. He is not happy
about my continuing on to Santa Fe and still worries about
where I will stay and if I should not be accepted by the
inhabitants. I cannot let Gaspard be burdened with
responsibility for me. I have too often assumed responsibility
for what is not mine and have suffered for it. I cannot let
Gaspard do that for me. He deserves his own happiness.*

"THIS IS MORA?" Carolina asked. She reined in her mule and
stared down the track at the cluster of mud lumps near the Mora
River, a bright stream.

Gaspard grinned. "This is Mora," he said as he reined in his
horse beside her. Pedro traveled ahead of them and near the largest
building stopped to talk to a man wearing dirty white cotton clothing covered partially by a blanket through which someone had
slit an opening in the middle for his head. The man's face was
shadowed by a wide-brimmed hat such as sported by some of the
Mexican teamsters in the wagon train.

Gaspard urged his horse forward. Carolina followed.

"It's a village only for the convenience of the rancheros tending
the cattle." Gaspard turned his head to look over his shoulder at
Carolina. "But it's not unusual."

Hens and roosters flew up out of the grass as Carolina and Gaspard rode closer to the village. Cattle and sheep roamed among the
buildings, bending their necks to nip at grass right up to the doors
and walls of the buildings. The buildings, made of adobe brick a
long time past, had been eroded by wind and rain until they more
resembled giant prairie dog burrows than human buildings. From
shadowed doorways in the sides of these dirt mounds dark eyes
tracked their progress.

Pedro waved to them, signaling them to join him.

"Señora, señor! The two men in the big house, they are Anglos.

Campadres to Señor Charles Bent. They are not here now, they not be back until tomorrow. But, come, come," he said, grinning broadly, "this man," he said, waving vaguely in the direction of the man with the broad hat, "he says he knows they'd give food in trade for news."

Gaspard laughed. "I hope they consider our news a good trade!"

Pedro shrugged. "It is lonely here." His voice dropped. "Still, I tell him that I am Pedro Perales, a trader, and that Señora Harper, she is my daughter who is with me because her husband, an Anglo, died. You, Señor Gaspard, are my business partner."

Gaspard nodded, but Carolina frowned.

"If these men are friends to Charles Bent, why the deception?" Carolina asked.

Gaspard turned in his saddle to look at her. "To protect you from men who are not," he said.

"Señora," Pedro whispered seriously, "word of your presence, it will travel from village to village like the wind."

"Carolina . . . " Gaspard said warningly.

"I know, I know. I promised to do as you ask. I haven't forgotten." It was rare for Gaspard to call her by her given name. For him to do so stressed to her more than would a lecture on the seriousness of the situation.

"See that you don't," Gaspard said sharply.

Carolina raised her eyebrows, but did not comment.

They dismounted before a mud building surrounded by a fence of sticks. It was only marginally larger than the other buildings. To Carolina's mind it was a mean affair, little more than a hovel. Regardless, she went willingly forward.

The door lintel was lower than she was accustomed to seeing. Reflexively, she ducked her head though she realized she could have walked under the rough wood lintel with an inch or two to spare.

It took a few moments for her eyes to adjust to the dim light and the smells within the building—human and animal. She summoned up a smile for the hovel's inhabitant, a sinewy old man smiling and bobbing his head, motioning her toward the table.

She nodded and approached the table, where the old gentleman had laid out a loaf of hard wheat bread, a smelly, mean-looking cheese, and a jug.

"*Aguardiente?*" Gaspard asked the old man.

"*Sí, señor, aguardiente,*" he said, beaming.

Gaspard leaned toward Carolina. "In the jug is the local whiskey made from corn. Strong. It's known as Taos lightning."

Carolina nodded. She looked at the fare set before them, then squared her shoulders, smiled, and looked up at the old man.

"*Gracias.* May God bless you and yours," she said softly. They had better food in their packs, but Carolina couldn't insult the old man by refusing his food over their own. Quite likely, he was offering them his day's meal. "I have sat in the saddle so much these last few days," she said, rubbing the back sides of her hips, "that I would prefer to eat standing and perhaps walking about your village."

"Ay! *Sí*, señora!" The old man tottered forward, grinning as if his mouth were frozen in position. He cocked his head to one side and nodded again. Only a few teeth remained in his mouth, and all were brown from tobacco spittle. He escorted her to the table and watched with bright, birdlike eyes as she cut a hard crust of bread and a thin slab of cheese. When he held up the jug to her, she declined with a slight shake of her head. He laughed, his eyes closing to slits and his face folding in on itself like a lady's fan. He told Pedro, in a rapid-fire Spanish dialect Carolina had difficulty following, that his "daughter" was wise; but no doubt such wisdom would be met with consternation in Santa Fe!

Carolina didn't know if he spoke of her, or of others upon meeting her, but Gaspard's quick *smirk* followed by an obvious cough to mask his reaction had her glaring at him. He smiled and shrugged. Carolina raised her chin and arched an eyebrow, but did not pursue the matter. The noxious air in the small building made getting outside more important.

Murmuring her thanks again to the old man, she nearly ran out of the hovel. She'd seen many mean and low abodes before in Louisiana; however, she had not considered she should find such equally mean habitations in New Mexico or that she should be expected to enter them.

Suddenly she felt meaner and lower than any abode she'd ever visited. She was nigh to acting as superior as those in Louisiana she'd condemned for superiority!

Balance.

She needed to discover some balance for herself between her American-raised self and her Mexican heritage. She needed to put aside all ideas, all knowledge of society and open herself up to this land and its people. Mr. Gaspard was correct. She could not expect to be any more readily accepted than she was ready to accept.

She was a foreigner, alien to the land of her father.

Gaspard and Pedro remained inside the building, she assumed to relay the news desired in exchange for the food. Outside, she choked down the smelly cheese and hard bread, and did not forage among their packs for tastier fare. By the river, she crouched down to cup her hands to get water to drink. She walked among the buildings, her fingers trailing across rough, eroded mud bricks. She stroked a cow's velvet ear and pushed a nosy sheep away. Tall grass itched her ankles through her stockings. In fleeting glimpses, she saw shy, dark eyes still watching her from the shadows.

She experienced the village and felt ashamed.

July 20, 1846.

I could not bring myself to write yesterday. My feelings were too confused. My sense of self severely disrupted.

But, it served to prepare me for our travels this day.

I do not know that I am as yet ready to commit to paper my

*thoughts and feelings concerning the village of Mora. I
learned a great deal about myself there. Oh! If only you could
have seen this place. Surely our pigs live better!*

*No, I am not condemning. I am stating fact as I observed it
and experienced it. I can neither judge nor condemn anything.*

*Mr. Gaspard had tried to tell me that we are in another
world from what I have known. I see now he was right.*

*I thought my "heritage" should enable me to identify with
these people. I was grossly naive. But I am learning and I hope
I now look about myself with fresh eyes.*

*Today we passed through the village of Las Vegas. To my
eyes, this settlement more resembled a village than did Mora,
though I am thankful for my Mora experience. It enabled me
to be more relaxed and able to communicate with the
inhabitants.*

*As we approached the village my eyes momentarily grew
round and wide as saucers when I saw naked children
running about, laughing and screaming in the way all
children do. This unnatural visage served to remind me that
Mora was not an anomaly and that I should expect to
continue to observe and experience new things.*

*Thus reminded, I girded myself for my Las Vegas
experience, and to my surprise enjoyed myself!*

I am getting ahead of myself. First, the sights.

*This village's dwellings were low, square blocks with flat
roofs that from the road approaching Las Vegas resembled a
brick yard with the "bricks" or adobes being a sun-dried
yellow clay that matched the streets.*

*There is a large square in this village—of the same yellow
hue—into which we rode shortly after noon. Avidly I looked
about me while attempting to ensure I was merely observing,
not judging. Most of the men I saw were dressed similarly to
the old man in Mora. The varied-colored blanket they had over
their white cotton clothes is called a serape. Some of the men,*

like the alcalde of Las Vegas, a position similar to that of a
mayor or constable, wore calico shirts with leather leggings
over their white cotton trousers.

Everyone smokes. Both men and women carry, tied about
their waists, a pouch for their cigarritas. In the pouches is a
bottle of powdered tobacco and a bundle of corn shucks from
the local Indian corn cut into pieces approximately one inch
wide and three inches in length.

The women wear a chemise with a petticoat over it. Over
their heads and draped about their bodies they wear a brightly
colored rebozo, a long scarf that is approximately one half a
yard wide and three or four yards long. This garment they
dexterously maintain draped about their bodies no matter
what they are doing, be it cooking, washing, or nursing their
babies. For this latter, the rebozo serves as their acquaintance
with circumspection and modesty as it amply covers mother
and child.

As you might gather from my description, manner of dress
here is far different from what we consider appropriate. I did
see a few women dressed similarly at Bent's Fort, but I never
considered it worth note for there were so many varied types of
dress at that location. Still, I am surprised I did not see more
outfits such as these while I was there. Mr. Gaspard tells me
that is because the Mexican women have a fascination with
our calicoes, which are readily available to them at the fort. I
think I gave Sibby the best dowry when I gave her all my
fancier dresses!

The alcalde met us in the square and invited us to his home
for food and news.

I was omitted from the ensuing discussion, but as I was
accustomed to this with Edward, I took the opportunity to
study my surroundings.

The walls of the alcalde's house were whitewashed gypsum.
As this substance is susceptible to disintegration at a touch,

the lower half of the wall wears a dress: a breadth of calico tacked to the walls. This protects the clothing of those who sit on the "divan" along the wall. The divan is composed of pillows and coverlets which at night are spread out on the floor for sleeping. The same were used at Bent's Fort, but there I merely thought it for the convenience of the fort!

There is a form of carpeting on the floor: a black and white woven cloth. This cloth, known as jerga, is no thicker than the oiled canvas I used when I still insisted on pitching a tent every night. No pouring the rest of one's drinking water on the floor here!

On the walls are reminders of the devotion of these people to their faith. In specially built niches in the wall are doll-like Virgin Mary statues. Other walls have plain crosses of a rich, dark wood.

The food we ate in Las Vegas was more varied than that in Mora, though its basic ingredients were similar, and I confess, I found it more palatable.

We were served poached eggs, wheaten tortillas (a kind of flat bread), the same cheese we had in Mora, and a mixture of meat, green pepper, and onions all boiled together. It was simple, yet surprisingly tasty.

I am improving in my ability to communicate. Who could believe Spanish dialects could be so different! Of course, they use many Indian words that are foreign to this ear.

July 21, 1846.

We have passed through many small settlements. I confess, my shock as to the behavior of the women continues, though I believe it has evolved into a fascination. And, yes, perhaps an envy. The women do not have the concept of modesty as has been pounded into our being from infancy. When they would cross a river, they raise their skirts to their knees and neither they, nor any chance male observers, take note of their bared

*ankles and calves. If I had lifted my skirts thusly, perhaps I
would not have come to misery at the Arkansas after that
flooding rain.*

*I am developing a fascination with the food served to us
that is made with simple, local ingredients. Today I
particularly enjoyed a soup made of chicken, corn, and beans.*

*Often I feel I am offered a person's own meal, as I felt in
Mora. But the villagers truly want us to eat their food even if
they must go hungry for the day. I am awed.*

*Our scenery is much improved. I've seen wooded hills,
refreshing streams, and natural grassy parks with herds and
flocks on the slopes. This evening we are camped among pine
trees at the foot of a mountain. Tomorrow we enter the village
of San Miguel.*

22

"SAN MIGUEL," GASPARD said, pointing.

Carolina leaned forward in her saddle and stretched her neck as she studied the village ahead of them. San Miguel appeared larger than the other villages; it even had a church—if she correctly identified the towered building—and the other buildings all had a squarer, neater look. But even from a distance, Carolina found herself favoring the other villages they'd passed through. "It looks like a cluster of wounds, or scabs," she murmured.

"Because of the color of the adobe?"

Carolina was surprised he'd heard her. She nodded as she relaxed back in the saddle and turned to face him. "After the bright yellows and tans we have seen, this dull red looks, I don't know, ill somehow."

"Let's hope our reception is not as *ill* as you think this place looks."

She arched her eyebrows. "You think it could be?"

He slowly nodded. "I do." His brow furrowed. "From talk in the villages we passed through, it sounded as if this village *particularly* argued against Anglos, and could prove more than just vocal in their dislike. Like Taos."

"So, what does that mean for us?" Carolina asked.

Gaspard took his hat off, wiped his brow with the back of his arm, and resettled the hat on his head. "I don't know. Just be alert, keep your Green River strapped to your waist, and do whatever Pedro, or I, tell you to do."

"We're maintaining the fiction of father and daughter?"

The hat brim shadowed his eyes. "Yep. I don't see any reason not to. Do you?" he challenged.

Carolina ignored his tone and shook her head as she looked back at the village.

"I ride ahead now, Señor Gaspard," Pedro said as he rode up beside them.

"No," Carolina said swiftly. "This time, we'll ride in together." Her mule shifted its weight from one foot to another and she swayed with the movement.

Pedro looked at Gaspard. Gaspard pursed his lips, then relaxed and nodded. "We go in together."

As they rode closer to the village, Carolina decided that San Miguel looked less like a wound upon the land and more like a prosperous village. Her earlier fancies seemed just that: fancies.

The children who rushed out to greet them were all fully clothed, and many wore sandals or leather shoes made in the United States. They spoke so fast Carolina had difficulty following what they said and asked; so instead of answering, she smiled and laughed. This appeared acceptable to the children as they trotted along beside her mule, each one reaching out to touch the fabric of her dress or to shyly touch her hand.

The littlest boy tripped and fell into the red dirt as he struggled on short legs to keep up with Carolina and the other children. His little face puckered, but with a quivering lower lip, he fought back tears.

Carolina halted her mule and asked an older boy to pick up the child and bring him to her. She took the child from him and balanced him before her on the Indian-made saddle. When she asked him his name, he just looked at her with round-eyed wonder.

"Ramon," the tallest boy said, swaggering toward her. "His name, it is Ramon."

"Thank you." Carolina looked down at the chubby child in her arms. "I'm pleased to meet you, Ramon," she said formally.

The child blinked his large, liquid black eyes, and stuck his thumb in his mouth. Carolina laughed and hugged him. "I once had a little boy just a little younger than you," she said.

"What happened to him?" asked a little girl with a wild mane of thick black hair and a dirt streak on her cheek.

Carolina's throat threatened to close at the innocent question. Her eyes glistened. "He got sick and died," she said lightly and quickly.

The girl's lips pressed tightly together as she nodded in sympathy. A single furrow plowed a vertical line between her brows. "My baby sister died," she said. "She got sick, too."

"I'm sorry," Carolina said.

The girl shrugged. "I don't remember her much, but mí madre, she makes us remember her in our prayers."

Carolina nodded. "That is a good thing to do," she said solemnly.

The girl shrugged again, then danced ahead of Carolina and her mule.

"Do you have any other children?" the tall boy asked.

"No. None," Carolina replied. She looked down at the child before her and ran a hand over his dark head. Waves of emotion threatened to crash over her.

"Señor," the tall boy said admonishingly to Gaspard. "Padre Antonio says a woman without children is like a flower without water."

Carolina jerked her head up, her cheeks staining bright pink.

Gaspard nodded slowly in serious agreement with the boy. His lips twitched against a grin. "Your priest is wise in the ways of women. Señora Harper, here," he said, gesturing in Carolina's direction, "is a widow."

"Ah," the boy said, nodding wisely.

"*And* her husband wasted her dowry."

The boy's lips pursed and his brows drew together as he sagely nodded like the men in the village sagely nodded when confronted with the ill-fortune of others.

"Gaspard!" Carolina admonished.

He looked over at her and winked.

"Señor Gaspard," Pedro said with mock sternness, "you embarrass my daughter."

Gaspard apologized, trying to look contrite, but Carolina saw deviltry dancing in his slate-gray eyes. Against her better judgment, she smiled back at him.

They rode into the central square in San Miguel with their entourage in the early afternoon. As Gaspard and Pedro foretold, word of their coming had swept down out of the mountains, riding on the summer wind. The alcalde and the village priest awaited them in the square. The alcalde's posture was stiff, proud, his head thrown back. His manner reminded her that the position of alcalde was more than just that of constabulary for the area. The alcalde wielded political power that could transcend the bounds of the village. This alcalde looked like a man who could order your imprisonment as easily as he could invite you into his home.

Maybe easier.

During the introductions Carolina found she'd captured the alcalde's attention to a greater degree than she liked. It wasn't common for the New Mexican men to pay attention to a woman, unless perhaps she were dressing and behaving in a manner to cast out lures. Carolina doubted her present travel-stained condition could be considered a form of lure.

She felt like an object under study, like the objects her father had collected and studied. The alcalde's close attention sent shivers down her spine. This feeling intensified when he invited them to dine and stay at his home just as they had been invited by the alcalde of Las Vegas. Carolina wondered if arrangements for their room and board were also carried down the mountain on the summer wind, though she could not think why they should be. Still, this invitation bothered her in a manner she'd not felt from the other villages they'd passed through to get to San Miguel.

Pedro eloquently accepted the invitation, but asked that they might first tend to their animals and goods.

"I don't like this," Gaspard whispered to Carolina as he tied up the mules. "Something's not right."

"Perhaps my fanciful musings when we first saw the village are lingering in your mind," Carolina suggested as she untied the packs from her saddle and set them aside.

"Perhaps."

She pulled the Indian saddle off the mule. "But you don't think so."

"No, ma'am, I do not. And neither do you," Gaspard said pointedly.

Carolina nodded as she stood there holding the saddle. Her shoulders drooped from fatigue. Would there ever be a time when she could stop living like she was on the edge of a precipice?

"Give that here," Gaspard said. He took the saddle out of her arms. "Go get cleaned up. You women always feel better afterward."

Carolina nodded and turned away. She was too surprised and touched by his recognition of her feelings to react in any other way. She dug out one of the remaining slivers of lavender soap from her pack and luxuriated in the smell of lavender and water as she washed her face, neck, and arms from the bucket of water Pedro provided.

The alcalde's house sat on the square looking as drab on the outside as any house Carolina had visited in New Mexico. But it was not a drab box with rooms. The house reminded her of the homes in New Orleans, where the rooms formed the sides for a large open courtyard, just as the village dwellings formed the sides for the village plaza. But unlike the village plaza, this courtyard bloomed with color.

Dark green vines climbed the support posts of the porch roof on two sides of the courtyard. Bright red, pink, and yellow flowers, all with heavy perfumes, bloomed amid the vines and in pots and boxes positioned in corners. Silver-green foliage filled other open spaces.

A baby dozed in an Indian basket shaded by an overhanging plant. A large black dog paced the courtyard. A fluffy tiger cat sat on a rough wood bench, cleaning her fur. She didn't even glance up when they entered the courtyard.

A wizened woman dressed in black appeared from out of the porch shadows. She wore open-fingered black-lace mittens. Between her hands she held a rosary made of silver and bright blue beads.

She tucked her rosary in the waistband of her black skirt as she placed herself between Carolina and the baby in the basket. She lifted a large silver cross from her chest and held it out before her. Her lips moved in a whispered exhortation for demon exorcism.

Carolina gasped, then glared at the woman.

"Leave it, Carolina," Gaspard advised.

Leave it!

Carolina turned toward Gaspard.

"Remember what I said before Mora. Here's an example," he said, waving toward the old woman.

The old woman shrieked at the motion directed toward her, then looked surprised when no ill effects befell her.

Gaspard shook his head. "And I forgot to say they're superstitious, too," he said dryly.

Carolina looked back at the old, wizened creature. She hunched forward as if she would turn and flee at any moment. Her dark eyes darted from her to Gaspard.

"Go! Go to the kitchen!" the alcalde ordered the woman. "These are guests, not demons. Go tell Juana to bring food."

The woman clutched her rosary tighter for a moment, then turned and swooped down to pick up the basket and clutch it closely to her narrow chest as she scuttled from the room.

"I apologize for my mother-in-law," the alcalde said, spreading his hands wide before him. "She thinks all strangers are devils. Ever since she suffered a spell her mind has been broken. She almost died. Unfortunately, her scrawny little body is stronger than her mind."

Carolina schooled her face not to express any reaction to the man's callousness. Not that he would notice, Carolina thought as she turned toward a wooden bench set back against the wall under the shade of the porch.

A heavy-set woman swathed in a dark red rebozo shot with gold thread came out of the shadows of the house into the bright courtyard. Behind her came an Indian woman carrying a bottle of wine and three silver goblets on a large silver tray.

The alcalde introduced the heavy-set woman as Sanchia, his wife. He called the Indian woman Juana.

"Francisco, how is he adapting?" Carolina overheard the alcalde ask his wife.

"Adapting? A coyote would adapt faster! He is hobbled!" his wife returned sharply.

The alcalde's eyebrows climbed his forehead.

After she supervised Juana serving the men, Sanchia invited Carolina to join her in another room.

"Your husband must be an intelligent and powerful man," Carolina said conversationally as they passed through a dim room that looked like a parlor. "You must be very proud of him."

The woman glanced toward Carolina and snorted. "He says to be alcalde, it is a great honor," she said sarcastically. "He says we must live up to his honor. Bah!" Sanchia shook her head.

"Everything is for honor!" she continued as she led the way into the kitchen. She pulled a pouch out from the folds of the rebozo and rolled herself a *cigarrita*. "When he was named alcalde, he told me I would be at leisure with plenty of servants to wait upon me. Now, it is true we have more servants, but who is there to train them? Who is to watch over them?"

She lit a punk from the kitchen's beehive-shaped corner fireplace and raised it to her *cigarrita*. She closed her eyes as she inhaled sharply. When she exhaled, pale blue-gray smoke wreathed her head. She waved a hand languidly about her face to dispel the smoke, silver bangles jangling as her hand moved. Her left hand settled on her ample hips while she held the *cigarrita* with her right hand.

"And this week he brings me another *genízaro*."

Carolina looked at her inquisitively.

"Another *indio de rescate,* a bartered Indian captive," she explained. She drew in deeply on her cigarrita.

"The Indian tribes, they fight each other and take captives. It is God's mercy that in this department, the government and priests encourage captive trading else endless war occur between the tribes. And the priests, they insist that immediately, a new genízaro must be named into the family that bartered them and, of course, baptized into the true faith. This we do. But this one!" she said, waving her cigarrita hand toward the door leading into a back courtyard, "this one is more animal than child, and a boy at that. Of what value is a boy, I ask you? Nothing but trouble and time. A girl would be more useful. But to my husband, the boy is for his *honor.*"

She put the cigarrita between her lips, then reached for a jug and two earthen mugs from a high shelf. She poured liquid from the jug into the mugs, then held out one of the mugs to Carolina.

"I have often observed that it is the wife of an important man who makes it possible for him *to be* important," Carolina said as she accepted the proffered drink.

"*Sí,*" Sanchia said as she nodded her head thoughtfully, "this is so. But this Indian boy he has brought into our home—" She shuddered. "I shall always expect trouble from that one. And for what do I need trouble?"

"Why don't you sell him?"

"Sell him!" She snorted. "If I could. But it is not possible," she said, shaking her head. "He is now Francisco and the priest says he is now of our family, our blood. Besides," she said, shrugging, "who would take him?"

Gingerly, Carolina took a sip of the brew Sanchia gave her. It was mildly alcoholic, nothing like the drink she was offered in Mora. She murmured her appreciation. The woman nodded and smiled at her in return.

As Carolina sipped the brew, she looked about the room. Pottery vessels with symmetrical black designs lay in a pile near the fireplace. Others filled with wheat or cornmeal stood along the wall. Another large clay vessel held water and a ladle to dip it out. In one corner, leaning against a calico-covered wall, sat the old woman. She cringed and made a hissing sound like a cornered cat when Carolina looked at her. Juana stood at the far end of the room mixing a batch of bread ingredients. There was a comfortableness to Sanchia's kitchen that appealed to Carolina. It pulled on the strings of yearnings Carolina had thought long buried.

"Juana," Sanchia called out to the Indian woman, "the first bread, it should be finished by now. Go and see if that lazy boy has taken it out or if he thinks to ruin another loaf of bread!"

Carolina set her mug on the table. "Let me do it," she said to Sanchia.

Sanchia looked at her queerly for a moment, then shrugged and waved her toward a wooden door at the end of the kitchen. "He should have at least one loaf done now. We shall have hot bread with our meal."

Carolina moved around the table toward the door.

"Señora, I warn you. Be careful he does not steal that knife you wear at your waist."

"This?" Carolina said, instinctively reaching for her Green River knife.

"Sí."

Carolina laughed. "I doubt I shall be getting close enough for him to touch me, let alone grab my knife."

"I hope what you say is true, for your sake and ours, señora."

Carolina looked askance at Sanchia, but passed her by as she walked over to the door.

She went out of the house to an outside kitchen. Here there were two large adobe-brick ovens. The boy was pulling a loaf of bread from the oven as Carolina approached. His face was blank of expression, but in the set of his shoulders, the rigidity of his jaw, and the tenseness of his bearing, Carolina could tell the boy was a solid mass of anger.

She studied him closely. Though he looked the height and breadth of a ten- or eleven-year-old boy, Carolina doubted he had seen more than eight summers. It touched her heart to see this boy struggling to maintain his dignity while doing labors he thought beneath him. She refused to add to his burden. She remembered all Gaspard, Rawlins, and Singing Waters had told her about the various Indian tribes. One thing they all had in common was their pride. The work the alcalde and his wife had given the Indian boy cut into his pride like a hot knife.

He was so young. What could be his chances in life? His spirit would not break. He was doomed to die young. But perhaps she could make the circumstances that would claim this young life a little more even.

As soon as she had stepped out into the yard he'd stared at the knife at her waist. She closed her fingers around the knife handle, to assure herself it was safe and it was hers.

His dark eyes flared at her actions, then his lip curled. He started to walk toward her in a parody of a swagger in one so young. Despite his youth, Carolina did not doubt his intentions. She edged backward toward the door until she realized he'd come as far as he could come, as far as his ankle tether would allow.

Her eyes dropped to his ankle. A chain was manacled about his ankle and fastened to a ring in the side of the outdoor ovens. Her eyes swept the range of his captivity. Shimmering waves of heat surrounded the outdoor ovens. By the wall, at the extreme end of his chain length, lay a small pile of feces swarming with flies.

She looked away from the flies back to the boy's face. "Please pass me that loaf of bread," she said.

He stared at her, not moving. The loaf of bread lay on a wooden table closer to him than Carolina.

"The bread, *por favor!*"

He crossed his arms over his chest and continued to pretend he could not understand her.

The boy made her nervous. This surprised her, for she'd never felt nervous around any particular child. This boy sent tingling throughout her body. And the tinglings weren't those of wanting to hold or care for someone else. Children should not know enough to make an adult nervous!

She straightened her shoulders and walked toward the table. The Indian boy did not give ground. Carolina tried to act calm and unconcerned even though she wondered if it was true that an Indian could smell your fear, just like an animal. If one could, then this boy could surely smell hers.

She raised her chin as she reached past the boy for the loaf of fresh bread.

The boy shifted his weight from one foot to another, leaning toward her. Fear swamped Carolina. Her heart raced and her mind reacted. She dropped the bread back on the table, spun, drew the knife, and lunged forward to hold it at the boy's throat.

The boy squawked and fell backward across the table, his eyes as wide as a dollar.

"Señora!"

Carolina turned her head to see Juana at the door to the house, then she turned to look back at the child she had pinned to the table. A sick horror roiled through her. She jerked the knife away and stumbled backward. The child scrambled to his feet, then turned to pick up the loaf of bread and hold it out to her.

Carolina jammed the knife back in its sheath and with trembling hands took the bread from the child. The child's complexion looked ashen. Now she thought *she* knew what fear smelled like!

She turned back to Juana. "He . . . " She looked at the child. "I thought . . . " She shook her head. She didn't know what to say. She raised one hand to clutch her head. Truthfully, she didn't know what had happened or what had triggered her reaction. She only knew it was identical to what had happened with Harry Wells. Unfortunately, judging by the child's reaction, her actions were not in line with his intentions.

A child!

She'd come to New Mexico to protect children, not hold them at knife point! She felt sick.

"Ah, señora, I see," Juana said, nodding. She set a cloth-covered bowl on the table. "The knife, it is too great a temptation for Francisco." She shook her head. "This one, he is a coyote." She turned toward Francisco and spoke harshly to him in their native language. As she harangued the child, Carolina saw the child's manner revert to that of a sullen, insolent youth.

Though the sun blazed overhead and the nearby ovens radiated additional heat, Carolina felt cold. She turned and quickly crossed the yard to the door.

Sanchia stubbed out her cigarrita as Carolina reentered the house.

"The bread smells delicious," Carolina affably told the woman though her heart still raced and the pulse in her neck throbbed. She looked around the little room for utensils to ladle the meaty stew into the bowls. She found them in a rough wooden box at the far end of the long scarred table that took up most of the room.

As she tried to assume everyday duties, blood hammered in her head, her stomach churned, and her breathing refused to slow down. She wiped damp palms against her full skirts.

A child!

Over and over the litany blared in her head. She felt like her entire life had just been turned upside down. And no one noticed!

What would her mother say? What could she write of this? Nothing!

Behind her, the old woman chattered at her like a magpie about demons and sin. Carolina ignored her.

But Carolina wondered.

She carried the tray of stew and Sanchia carried a tray of drinks out to the courtyard. They left Juana in the kitchen making a chocolate cake and watching over the old woman and the baby. The room between the kitchen area and the courtyard was dark and cool. Moving from the darkness to the light, the courtyard took on the aspect of blinding color and light.

In the courtyard the men were sitting on rough benches, Gaspard and Pedro listening to the alcalde. A frown puckered Gaspard's scars. He looked tired.

Carolina's step slowed as she looked at him and Pedro. They both looked tired. She knew that some of their tiredness came from their constant vigilance over her. It was well that they were only two days out of Santa Fe.

There was also a tenseness in them. It was not normal for Pedro to sit so straight, nor for Gaspard to sit with his hands by his knees, grasping the edge of the bench.

And the alcalde looked too relaxed.

Carolina stopped at the edge of darkness and listened.

"This Jesus Perales I know. He says his family has worked for generations for the Navarros. Can you imagine that? Such loyalty! Oh, that I could command such loyalty!" the alcalde said. He inhaled on his cigarrita.

"In this age, that is unusual," Gaspard said carefully.

Pedro nodded.

"So I say to myself, he is loyal to Diego Navarro? Navarro is a man to command respect out of fear. That," he said, slowly nodding, "I understand. But loyalty?" He shook his head.

Pedro shifted uneasily and Gaspard slowly inhaled, then exhaled in a studied fashion.

The alcalde smiled through the blue-gray wisps of smoke that curled up from his cigarrita. "I do not normally trouble myself with speaking to servants, but this one, he was different. So I asked him to tell me of his family and the Navarros. He was anxious to talk, like a dog starved for attention. A loyal dog abused by its master," he said, laughing.

Carolina felt a large lump settle in the pit of her stomach. The smell of the food, which moments ago had been enticing, now seemed cloying.

"One hundred years ago the Perales family came to Mexico with the Navarro family. Always, a son or daughter of the Navarro house had Perales servants. Jesus Perales's brother went with the oldest Navarro son to New Orleans. His name is Pedro Perales. Sad, is it not, this Jesus Perales has not seen his brother since he went to the United States twenty-five years ago."

"Very sad," Carolina said grimly before Gaspard or Pedro could answer. She walked out of the shadows and into the sunlight.

Pedro and Gaspard rose to their feet.

The alcalde laughed.

23

Though she quaked inside, Carolina wrapped herself in her haughtiest New Orleans–matron manner, raised her chin, and looked down her nose at the alcalde.

The man's grin dimmed. He rose slowly to his feet.

Carolina inclined her head slightly, then she turned toward her manservant. "Pedro," she said, holding the tray out before her.

"Señora," he acknowledged soberly. He took the tray from her hands.

Sanchia gaped at Carolina as she swept past Pedro and sat on the bench he had vacated. She sat with her back ramrod straight, her hands folded in her lap. "You may serve us now," she said.

Silently Pedro handed bowels of the aromatic stew around. Carolina maintained a serene expression, ignoring Gaspard's scowls in her direction. The alcalde had questions stamped upon his face.

When they had been served, Pedro looked uncertainly at the remaining bowl of stew.

"Join us," she said. "For outside of this courtyard, we continue as we have begun: you are my father and I your daughter." She looked pointedly at the alcalde. Now butterflies beat their wings against the confines of her already churning stomach. How would this day end? And when? That was all she could ask of it, though she knew it wouldn't be soon enough.

The alcalde frowned at her.

"You are perhaps confused, señor?" she asked.

He didn't agree or disagree. Carolina laughed. "You are a clever man. You guessed what no one before you has guessed. Now you wonder how a Navarro could change places with a servant?"

The alcalde nodded slowly. "Sí, señora. That I do wonder. It is not something Diego Navarro would do."

"Diego Navarro is not a woman."

The alcalde laughed.

Carolina raised a hand to still his mirth. "It is a simple strategy, señor. Even a wise one," she said, remembering her journal entry of two nights ago. "It provides protection and allows me to study my surroundings. It allows me to listen to what is said around me, for what man pays attention to the women who serve him or those that sit at the side of the room speaking among themselves of food and babies?"

"And what woman do you know," Gaspard asked, "would travel with two men who are not family? Necessity drives us all," he said, his lips forming a wry smile.

"So, the loyal Pedro is my father and Señor Gaspard is the father's business associate," Carolina said.

"You are truly the niece of Diego Navarro?" asked Sanchia.

"Yes."

The alcalde jutted his lower lip forward as he nodded, his eyes darting from one person to another. Then he leaned back against the wood column that supported the porch roof. He stroked his chin, then brushed a finger along each side of his mustache.

"I wonder what Señor Navarro will say to a niece coming to Santa Fe, eh?" His eyes narrowed to thin slits. He took another puff on his cigarrita. "Navarro only has three children. Weak, puling girls," he said, shaking his head. "His new wife, she may give him the sons he desires. His first wife, she died. Very sad. She fell and hit her head," he said sadly. Then his eyes lit up. "Or so they say," he added. His lips twisted upward and he smiled.

It was not a smile Carolina trusted. She smoothed her skirt with her hands. "What Diego Navarro says or doesn't say is irrelevant. I have not come to New Mexico to see him."

"You came, perhaps, to spy then, eh? To spy for your birth country?"

"Certainly not! I came here to see my other uncle."

"Other uncle? Señora, do not try to fool me. I am not stupid. There is only *one* Navarro in New Mexico."

"Not Diego Navarro, Alcalde. My mother's brother. Elliott Reeves."

"Elliott Reeves!" The alcalde sat up straight, rocking the wooden bench. "That idiot! He is your uncle? So he *is* related through marriage to Navarro! Navarro threw him in jail once for claiming they were related." He started laughing. He leaned back again, but missed the post and nearly fell off the bench. He scrambled to sit up again, still laughing and unconcerned for his ruffled dignity.

"I hope he is not still in jail!" Carolina said.

The alcalde waved his hands dismissively. "No, no. The United States consul, he complained to Governor Armijo. The governor made Navarro order the release of Señor Reeves."

"Pardon, Alcalde, you sound disgusted at that."

The alcalde snorted. "Señor Reeves would not be missed if he were to disappear from New Mexico. He is the worst kind of gringo."

Carolina looked at him in surprise. "I'll own that my uncle lacks sense; however, I fail to understand why he is the worst kind of United States citizen."

"It is *because* he lacks sense, señora," Pedro said.

The alcalde nodded. "Now, I wonder what Colonel Navarro will think of you."

"I'm sure he and I will meet sometime in Santa Fe. At that point we can determine what will be his reaction. Until then, it is a moot point."

"No, no, señora," the alcalde said, wagging his finger at her. "You will not meet by accident in the street. No. I shall arrange for the meeting. Through the governor. What could be more proper? Yes, through Armijo. And then . . . and then the governor, he will owe me," he said, smiling.

July 22, 1846, San Miguel, at the house of the alcalde.

If I were a woman given to nerves, then at this moment I would be confined to my bed with the affliction and all would worry lest I never recover.

First, I have decided to ransom an Indian boy from the hand of my host and return him to his tribe. Though the priests deem Indian captives as family members of their owner's family and therefore not slaves who may be bought and sold, money speaks louder than the Church.

At least, I shall have him away when I can, for unfortunately, we will be staying in San Miguel longer than we had intended. The alcalde has made us his guests until such time as we may go on to Santa Fe.

Guests? More like captives. It is all very comical, though judging by Mr. Gaspard's pacing before me as I write, he does not see the humor in the situation.

We are pawns in some chess game that is being played here in New Mexico. It is not much different than the games I witnessed men playing in New Orleans. Games that allow them to strut and preen like peacocks.

No matter. Though there is one result of this madness that pleases me. I shall get to meet General Armijo, the governor of New Mexico. I have heard much about him—good and ill. I am very curious. I

"How can you sit there and write in that damn book of yours?" Gaspard demanded.

"Easier than you pace this room," she said dryly.

"Damn it, woman, we could have bluffed it through! Why did you have to tell him you're a Navarro?"

"We have been over this. I told you why, yet you persist in questioning me. Again, then: if he feared Navarro, as so many people seem to, I thought we could use that fear to our advantage."

Gaspard grunted, and then glared at her as he ran his hands through his hair. He shook his head. "You do know about using folks."

Stung, Carolina sniffed, fighting back tears. That was low and she thought better of Gaspard. "How was I to know the man would see me as a potential tool for his own aggrandizement? You must admit, he has proved a very shrewd man," she said levelly, pleased that her emotional jumble did not leak excessively into her voice. "So, what should we do now? Escape?"

"Ha!" He looked about the room with its closed wooden shutters. He shook his head. "Would be easy enough, and that is probably what the alcalde wants, but escaping would sign our death warrant."

Carolina nodded. "Such has been my thought as well. And for some reason, I do not feel like giving the alcalde any satisfaction."

Gaspard reluctantly laughed. "Might as well make him work, eh?"

"Precisely. I doubt he knows how General Armijo will react. From my understanding the governor is often inexplicable in his actions."

Gaspard ran the knuckles of one hand along the edge of his chin as he nodded. His eyes narrowed. "I think," he said slowly, a slight smile pulling at his lips, "I think Armijo is understandable, if you stop thinking of him as a politician."

"What do you mean?"

"General Manuel Armijo's first consideration is to his purse."

"His purse?"

Gaspard nodded, then grinned and sat down on the pillowed divan next to Carolina. "He is a merchant. Everything the man does is tempered with interest in his mercantile expectations. It comes before his country, his people, his wife—hell, probably even before his God!"

"And you think we can use this to our advantage?"

"Not we. You."

"Me?"

"You're the daughter of a merchant, the widow of a merchant whose family has far-flung trading ties, and you're the step-daughter of a prominent St. Louis merchant."

"That's all true, but I don't understand. What does all that have to do with our current situation?"

"Maybe nothing. Maybe everything. Remember, the alcalde is looking to use you for your relationship to a man you have never met. We'll just be using your relationships to men you have met."

She looked at him in confusion, then her brow cleared. "Oh! Dangle trade possibilities before the governor?"

Gaspard inclined his head. "Possible only through you, possible only because of your relationship with people in these trading entities. And even if you could not directly be of help, any harm coming to you would surely be to Armijo's disadvantage in whatever corner of the globe he chooses to trade. Just your presence in his territory will have him twisting in the wind. If we play our cards right."

July 22, 1846, San Miguel, later.

Imagine me grinning.

Mr. Gaspard is a man who thinks in subtleties. I like that.

The alcalde is not a subtle man. He doesn't trust us. He has also deduced my relationship to Diego Navarro. (Gaspard says that is my fault. Sigh.) So, the alcalde is placed on the horns of a dilemma. If he lets us continue on our way, he could be arrested for allowing two "spies" to escape his jurisdiction. If he imprisons or harms us, he risks Navarro's wrath. So he has decided to keep us well guarded until such time as he can turn us over to the governor. Mr. Gaspard thinks that turning us over to General Armijo has a twofold purpose. First and obviously, we become someone else's problem to deal with. Second, the alcalde appears loyal to the locals and to the politicians in Mexico City. Third, and Mr. Gaspard thinks most important, he removes himself from Navarro's path.

I continually find myself astounded at the depth and breadth of emotions caused merely by saying the name 'Diego Navarro.' Did you know Diego Navarro is feared absolutely everywhere? It was made quite plain to me while on the trail that he was a man reviled; but though I learned that, I confess I never truly understood what I was being told.

I remember Papa's gentleness. I have difficulty accepting the notion that Uncle Diego could be so conscienceless, so unredeemable in our Maker's eyes. But enough people have stated it to be fact, so I must put aside prejudices and restrict my viewing to what is.

Because of Diego Navarro, I have adopted the haughtiest New Orleans matron's manner. Shrew is a kind word. This pose is believable because of my relationship to Navarro. To be myself is suspicious. I shake my head at the vagaries of life.

July 23, 1846, San Miguel.

The alcalde has received word from General Armijo. The general will remove us from San Miguel tomorrow. Or perhaps the day after that. Or the one after that. Sometime.

Meanwhile, we are to remain here as the guests of the San Miguel alcalde. Armijo is confident we will be well cared for by anyone's standards: the alcalde's mustache twitched at that line in the missive. Exactly what does that mean? Are we prisoners? Honored guests?

Gaspard frowns and grumbles low in his throat. He paces the room.

He says it is Armijo's way of leaving himself open.

Depending upon what happens when he informs Navarro we are in New Mexico, he can say he meant the opposite in the letter of whatever the alcalde does. The alcalde's mouth was ringed white when he finished reading the missive. His attempt at playing politics has failed. As I stated before, the man lacks subtlety. Now he is stuck with us, and stuck with the cost of covering for our meals. His wife is not happy. We can sometimes hear her railing at him from distant portions of the house, though to us she is unfailingly polite and kind.

Actually, I don't fault the alcalde for trying his hand at the subtle manipulation of events and people. No matter what we are allowed to do, or not do, in New Mexico, not stopping us would have been tantamount to treason. The alcalde was not in a pretty place. He played his hand as well as he could, given the circumstances.

July 24, 1846, San Miguel.

I am becoming as restless as Mr. Gaspard. I would have us gone from this place as quickly as possible. The alcalde's mother-in-law tries my nerves. She continually harps in a shrill voice that grates upon one's hearing that I am some demon incarnation. I find myself gathering my sense of self about me before I must go anywhere within the house that that woman might be.

I admit I am maintaining an arrogant attitude in her presence. I shudder to think of the consequences for any of us if I didn't. However, the old woman has enough of her wits about her to have a certain respect, or should I say fear, for Diego Navarro. Not knowing how he will take the news of our presence keeps her wondering. She did briefly attempt to treat Pedro as a slave. I put a stop to that.

Tomorrow we shall be allowed the freedom of the village, on the condition that all three of us not be out at the same time. I guess the alcalde believes we are closely linked and therefore

one or two of us would not sneak off leaving the others in
danger. Astute gentleman.

I'll close now, for I should offer to assist with dinner.
Walking the line between arrogance and humbleness is
treacherous.

July 25, 1846, San Miguel.

News sweeps down out of the mountains. A large army is
approaching Bent's Fort!

It must be Colonel Kearny and his Army of the West. The
villagers huddle in small knots of humanity as they exchange
information on what they know and speculate on what they
don't. They glare at us as we pass, or go out of their way to be
friendly. They besiege Pedro with questions concerning the
United States and Gaspard with questions concerning our
army and its commanders. I am approached with cooking
questions! I think these women believe the old adage: "The
way to a man's heart is through his stomach."

However, it is through the children and their play that one
can truly see the hopes and fears of these people.

Mock war is the popular game with the village boys.
Tellingly, playing the United States forces is a coveted role.

Unfortunately, their idea of our forces is not a pretty one.
Oh, we are the victors, but we are also the beasts. In their play
the United States soldiers brutally kill everyone in their path,
steal food, and burn villages. I am sick at watching them play.
No protestations on my part can change their perceptions.
They believe we have the brute strength to succeed over all
comers, that we will take without remorse.

I have heard it said that Colonel Kearny is adamant about
the army paying for what it uses. And that he is a stickler for
discipline within the troops. I pray this gossip is true above
what these good people have heard and believe.

July 26, 1846.

> *Today the alcalde received word from the governor. A company*
> *of soldiers will come to San Miguel tomorrow. The alcalde is*
> *to see to their room and board for the night. The next day they*
> *are to escort us to Santa Fe.*
>
> *You should have seen the alcalde's face turn red, veins*
> *bulging from his temples, when he read that he was to provide*
> *for a company of soldiers.*

"POMPOUS DONKEY'S REAR end," Carolina murmured in English. She glared at Lieutenant Ramon Degas's back as he left the fragrant, sunny courtyard and imagined all manner of accidents befalling the young officer.

Gaspard unfolded his arms and straightened his posture from the deceptively relaxed position he'd adopted leaning against a porch roof post. "I'd say the good governor did not tell his faithful dog what he was fetching."

Carolina drummed her fingertips on her knees. "You may be right. Curious, but I do not know whether I am relieved or disgruntled!"

Gaspard laughed, then his face sobered. "Armijo's a clever old coyote. What we have to remember is he never does anything without a reason. A monetary reason." His eyes narrowed. "To figure out how we're going to handle that arrogant pup, we need to figure out the money angle for Armijo." Gaspard rubbed the edge of his chin with the back of his hand as he stared after the Mexican officer Armijo had sent to escort them to Santa Fe.

"Perhaps our officious lieutenant is related to influential people," Carolina suggested.

"Or people at odds with Navarro."

"Possible." Her brow furrowed. "Or the opposite. He is related to people who are Navarro's partners."

"Assuming, of course, that Navarro also has some interest in trade," Gaspard said.

"If he is a Navarro, he is in some form of trade," Carolina said dryly. "Even my father, who was probably the family changeling in temperament, what with his scholarly ways, remained in trade. It is in the blood," she said with some measure of disgust.

"Is it in yours?"

Carolina sighed and ruefully nodded. "How else would I see buying a wagon and goods to trade with as a logical course of action in traveling from Independence to Santa Fe?"

Gaspard laughed as he nodded. "Not many women would have done as you did. That goes without saying, dear lady."

Carolina wrinkled her nose as her lips curled in distaste. "As I said, it's in the blood. As, I'm sure, it is in Diego Navarro's. But, given his behavior toward the Texas expedition participants, I would say there is something else driving him. Some reason for him to be so strongly moved against the Texans. And no, I don't think it was a strong sense of nationalism."

Silently, Pedro came into the courtyard and sat down on one of the long benches.

"Honor. That could be involved," Carolina suggested. "Though I doubt it. I don't think a man could act as my uncle did and still proclaim ringingly that he is a man of honor. . . . You seem to know these people well. From what do they derive their livelihood? The *ricos,* I mean."

"From the land, from their orchards and fields," Gaspard said.

Pedro shook his head. "No, señor. That would not be a Navarro. Farming, ranching, that is a prize to them, not a means."

"Some here did well in the beaver trade, alone or in partnership with a mountain man." Gaspard said. Then he shook his head. "But that's in the past. Most of that trade ended, what with the new silk hats being made for city wear."

"And that's probably more work than he would like. From what everyone has said about my uncle, I gather he is a man of immediate gratification."

"Which wouldn't be realized in the beaver trade. It took a forward-thinking man to make money in that trade."

"Exactly," she said. "A man like my stepfather. Navarro does not sound at all like a man of Mr. Davies's ilk."

"There are some, I hear, who own mines," Pedro said.

"Mines? What kinds of mines?"

"They say this land has gold, silver, and copper."

Gaspard nodded. "Some rich mines, I hear tell. And the owners are very jealous about the business. And it's a business a gringo cannot own, though occasionally they've been supervisors. Mine owners use a lot of Indians and mestizos to dig for them."

"That would appeal to Diego Navarro."

Gaspard looked at Pedro quizzically.

"A mine owner has position. And respectability: Mining is not frowned upon. What is under the ground is a gift, a treasure. Also, using the Indians and others to actually mine for the ore is a source of power."

Gaspard snorted. "Absolute power over others. That would appeal to Navarro."

"But, even if this is true," Carolina continued, "how do mines relate to the governor, or to our new caretaker?"

"Those who trade in ore are highly favored in Mexico City," said Pedro.

"Ah. Politics again," Carolina said.

"So, while Armijo, here, is the governor and wealthy, his wealth stems from trade, not mining."

"Yes," Carolina said slowly. "While an underling derives his wealth from mining and therefore curries more favor with Mexico City."

"And remember," Gaspard said, "Armijo's stint as governor has not been unbroken. Political maneuvering cost him the position last time. It could again."

Carolina nodded. "The governor walks a narrow, slippery road."

"That he does."

"Señora Harper," barked Lieutenant Ramon Degas from the main doorway to the patio. "The alcalde tells me you are related to Colonel Navarro."

Carolina haughtily inclined her head.

"Why did you not tell me this immediately?"

"To what purpose, Lieutenant?"

"Because . . . well, because . . . I mean—"

"I have never met my uncle, Lieutenant. I do not know what to expect and therefore, as you have done with us, I have played my hand close to my chest. Can you blame me, Lieutenant Degas?"

"Blame? No. Oh, no, señora. However, with a proper introduction we could have gotten right to work."

"Work, Lieutenant?"

"I . . . I mean, señora," stumbled the young lieutenant, "we would not have to maintain such formality."

"Nor you treat me quite so much like a spy?"

"Yes, señora. That is it," the lieutenant said, relieved.

"Tell me, Lieutenant, how well do you know my uncle?"

The young lieutenant flushed. "My cousin Carlotta, she was married to him."

"Was?" Carolina probed.

He nodded somberly, his chin twitching against a rush of emotions. "She died last spring. She fell. Fell and hit her head against the oven, Navarro says."

Carolina raised her brows. "But you don't believe that," she stated.

He laughed sharply. "You are right, señora. And I do not trust Navarro. And so I ask myself, why should I trust this woman who says she is a niece to Navarro?"

"I take it, Lieutenant, you've made no secret of your feelings toward Navarro," Gaspard said.

"I am a man of honor, sir!" the lieutenant cried.

"Ah."

The lieutenant thrust out his lower lip as he dipped his head. "And I made a promise to my mother that I would not challenge the jackal. But I shall see him brought down. And you are free to tell your uncle, señora. I do not hide behind a woman's skirts!"

"Lieutenant, Governor Armijo knew of Mrs. Harper's relationship to Colonel Navarro."

"So I understand," the lieutenant said, perplexity snaking a line across his brow.

"Why didn't he tell you?" Gaspard asked softly.

"I do not know," the lieutenant said honestly as he spread his hands palms up before him. "Perhaps he didn't think it of any import."

"But you did when you learned of it. And you can be sure the governor did, too. Think on that, Lieutenant. Ponder carefully your governor's intentions lest we all be victims."

"Victims, señor?"

"Victims of whatever political plans the governor has for, or against, Navarro. Where do you wish to stand, Lieutenant?"

24

July 27, 1846.

My respect grows for Governor Armijo. This is a wary, grudging respect, not one of liking, though Mr. Gaspard says the man can be charming, especially with the ladies.

The escort the governor sent is a young, vocal enemy of Diego Navarro who, I understand, is properly known as Colonel Diego Navarro. Our escort, Lieutenant Ramon Degas, is related to Navarro's late first wife. The lieutenant believes his cousin's death was not accidental.

The governor did not tell our young firebrand lieutenant about my relationship to Navarro. Nonetheless, I am certain the lieutenant was carefully chosen for escort in some form of irony that I do not yet fathom. Plainly the governor did not expect the lieutenant to continue in his ignorance. And he hasn't.

The alcalde moved quickly to end Lieutenant Degas's ignorance. That man is striving to create turmoil! I ask myself, what can the alcalde hope to gain? Does he feed on turmoil like Satan feeds on the misfortune of men?

No answers ride in on the wind, try though I might to listen. But as I listen, I hear the strains of a guitar playing. It is all that remains of the day.

The alcalde's wife turned the advent of the soldiers coming into a community event, a fandango. Every household in the village contributed either food, drink, or music. The young girls blushed at the fulsome compliments of the young soldiers in Lieutenant Degas's company and danced eagerly with every one in turn until perspiration beaded their brows and dampened their clothing.

For the night, animosity and suspicion vanished. I danced with Lieutenant Degas, Pedro, Gaspard, the priest, and others that I did not even know. Such a blessed difference from the past few days.

During the height of the festivities Gaspard spoke to the alcalde of buying the Indian child from him. As he tapped his foot and listened to the music, the alcalde easily agreed. He set the price surprisingly low, though I think I would have paid any price to get the child away from here. The alcalde even laughed and told Gaspard that he had the best over him with this deal. I tell you, Mr. Gaspard must be a gambling man, for his face did not betray what he thought or felt. I am glad the alcalde had not noticed me listening to their conversation, for surely my expression would have led the alcalde to demand more for the child!

Mr. Gaspard has warned me it will be difficult to get the trust of the boy and he will likely prove a handful until we can reunite him with his tribe. We shall have to be on guard against the boy's actions lest he this time in truth attempts to steal a weapon and proves adept with it. I know, for me, this will be difficult to do; consequently I have agreed to allow Gaspard to take charge of the boy. So, once again these arms that ache remain empty.

I should stop these incessant attempts to somehow make up

for disappointments and sorrows in my life. Nay, more than that. It is guilt that chokes me, though in my mind I know this is foolishness. It is my heart I cannot convince. I should let the past be and move on. But it is hard. The guitar playing in the quiet of the night makes it doubly hard. The music has a rhythm to make one sway, and a sound of melancholy to haunt the soul. It is music for memories.

Beautiful though the music is, I've lived too long through memories. Such should be the prerogative of the very old as they stand on the mountaintop of their lives and look out across the landscape of their memories as far as they can see.

I am not old and I trust in God that I am not on the mountaintop of my life. There is much to do from here. I need to wash my mind of notions and live for each day.

"SEÑOR GASPARD, I understood there were to be only three in your party."

"I bought the boy from the alcalde last night," Gaspard said, not turning to look at Lieutenant Degas as he dumped the Indian boy onto the back of Carolina's old mule and tied the boy's hands to the saddle.

The boy squirmed and kicked out at Gaspard. One of his kicks connected with Gaspard's chest, sending the breath out in a whoosh.

The lieutenant laughed. "The cubs can be as dangerous as the bear, señor. They are not worth keeping alive."

"Maybe. But I think this one will have greater value to me traded to the Indians," Gaspard answered the lieutenant. He spoke sharply to the boy in his native tongue as he knotted the rope.

"Ah! I understand, señor! Yes, to an enemy tribe of his people, they may trade well."

Carolina gasped.

The lieutenant turned toward her. "It is true, señora, sometimes the Indians are worse to other Indians than they are to us or the gringos. Myself, I have thought on this before. The priests say it is because the Indians do not yet accept our true God," the young lieutenant said with ponderous sincerity before he rode back to the front of the company.

Behind the lieutenant's back, Gaspard winked at her.

"What did you tell the boy?" Carolina whispered.

He grinned. "I told him to act rebellious to impress the soldiers."

Disconcerted, Carolina's chin lifted as she raised an eyebrow. Gaspard laughed at her expression.

Mulishly, Carolina's chin came down. Then her lips parted in a reluctant smile. "Somewhere in that statement I'm certain there is a bead of logic. However, it alludes me. Elucidate, please," she said with the edge of a laugh.

He nodded. "That boy has got battered pride and shame for being a captive and doing squaw work. He's likely to do himself injury or get himself killed. Unless we can take that bundle of feelings and mold them," he explained, his hands moving as if forming a pot in the air, "that boy, like as not, won't be living long enough to see his tribe again."

Carolina's brow furrowed and she compressed her lips as she nodded.

"Señor Gaspard!" the lieutenant called out. By his expression he spoke sternly, though his tone lacked the depth of command.

Gaspard tapped the brim of his hat with his forefinger and left Carolina's side to mount his horse. Satisfied, the lieutenant nodded and gave the signal for the company to head out of San Miguel.

Carolina turned her horse into line behind Lieutenant Degas. Santa Fe lay more than fifty miles to the northwest. The journey would last two days, or less if the lieutenant pressed them hard. She was glad to be riding her own horse again. The gash in her mare's foreleg suffered when she stumbled in the Purgatory riverbed did not appear to have left lasting damage. This trip would test the mare's soundness.

The lieutenant's haste stirred up uncertainties in Carolina's mind that sank and settled in her stomach as heavy as an undercooked biscuit. She felt old, tired, and incredibly naive.

A rock shifted sideways beneath her horse's hoof. The mare stumbled. Memories of the Raton Pass accident crashed through Carolina's mind as she clung to her saddle. She shivered in reaction and relief as the horse kept moving forward.

She must remain aware of her surroundings. Brooding encouraged accidents. Tomorrow evening she would be in Santa Fe. Soon enough to put speculation aside. Through her long journey her thoughts, her ideals, and her soul had been tested and tempered. Whatever happened in Santa Fe could not possibly bear any greater significance in her life than her days on the trail. The woman who left New Orleans after her son and her husband died no longer existed. Neither did the woman who attended parlors at Dorcas Carr's, nor the woman who bought a Conestoga wagon in Westport, Missouri, and organized a caravan.

Sometimes Carolina felt she no longer knew who she was. And strangely, that didn't seem to matter. The greatest gifts she'd received lay in the people she'd met. Especially Mr. Gaspard.

She understood that he was a loner. He was a man who had found peace within himself, with his world, and with God despite all that had been taken from him. Carolina doubted he was a man to tempt fate twice. And she knew she was not a woman to ask him to. The gift of his friendship would be gift enough.

BY LATE AFTERNOON, sweat trickled down Carolina's body, soaking the bodice of her blue calico dress. Though the dress was not as heavy as it had seemed in the Kansas territory, the days now felt hotter and the sunlight glared off the pale, neutral tints of the land.

She wiped her forehead with the back of her calico-covered arm, then shifted in her saddle, sitting straighter.

They rode along a clear, swiftly running river. Wide, probably one hundred feet across, the water did not look more than two feet deep. The water ran swiftly to join another river. On a hilltop above the merging rivers stood darkly shadowed structures against a rainbow-hued sky.

"Lieutenant Degas! What is that place?" she asked, calling out to him over the steady *clop-clop* of her horse's hooves.

"What, señora?" He turned in his saddle to look back at her.

She waved her hand toward the ruins. "What is this place?"

"Pecos, señora."

"Pecos?"

"*Sí*, señora."

"Pecos Pueblo," Gaspard offered as he rode up beside her. "It's the ruin of an old Indian village that goes back hundreds of years."

"Ruin? How sad. What happened?"

Gaspard shrugged. "Don't know. I doubt anyone really does. I heard some story of a sacred fire going out and when it did, the place was abandoned. The people went to the Jemez Pueblo."

Carolina stared at the twilight-shadowed ruins. "How sad. How long ago did this occur?"

Gaspard scratched the edge of his chin with the tips of his fingers. "I think something like ten years ago. Maybe less."

"We'll camp over there," Lieutenant Degas said, pointing to a broad, flat spot near the river's edge. "If the señora wishes, she may visit the pueblo. All strangers want to see Pecos Pueblo." He shrugged.

July 28, 1846, 30 miles SE of Santa Fe, Pecos Pueblo.
God is a master artist. Those of his children we call great painters pale in humble comparison.

This evening I sat on a rock by the edge of the river and watched the changing canvas shift from bright light and black shadows to darkest velvet night with a magnificent fiery palette of colors in between.

Sun-gilded rocks, as bright as new gold coins, were

*bounded by purple shadows, and around them, red earth
blended into blue. In the sky, colored clouds massed higher and
brighter than the tallest harlequin hat.*

*Throughout the day, hour upon hour, the land displays a
pale, neutral face, a face to wear down a traveler with its
sameness if it were not for the streams and river, blue and
green ribbons woven through the earth. Then, late-afternoon
shadows slash across the land, heralding God's artistry.*

*Today, in the midst of God's display, I walked among
ghosts.*

*Ghosts are all that remain of a once-thriving people who
lived in Pecos Pueblo, a deserted Indian pueblo. The pueblo
sits between two rivers on an elevated ridge. The buildings are
a curious collection of rooms stuck together. Most of the rooms
have fallen in upon each other; however, enough are intact to
discern that many doorways through the roofs allowed the
inhabitants to pull up a ladder when they didn't wish visitors.*

*The most intact building in the pueblo is the church the
priests built when they came to this land to spread
Christianity. Yet it, too, is in near danger of melting away
through rain and wind, or of being vandalized for building
materials in favor of another, newer building.*

*As we walked back to our camp, I looked back over my
shoulder at the pueblo. It looked cold, alone, and near to
vanishing forever into the night.*

July 29, 1846.

*We are near Santa Fe, but have halted for a brief rest. Mr.
Gaspard tells me that travelers often camp here in order to
march fresh into Santa Fe early the following day, but
Lieutenant Degas wishes to press on. I have not had the habit
of late of putting ink to paper at every small stop; nonetheless,
this time I must do so. My thoughts are troubled.*

This day we passed through Glorieta Pass and Apache

Canyon. Mr. Gaspard says this is the route Colonel Kearny is likely to follow as well. I pray this is not so! The road is narrow in places, and turns upon itself with steep ravines falling away from the side of the road. I remained exhaustingly alert during our passage. It is not a location for a complacent, casual ride!

All the while we rode through the pass and canyon, clouds gathered, threatening to release an afternoon shower, as Mr. Gaspard tells me is common in the area. I am thankful the rain held off for I cannot imagine traversing the road we just took in muddy, slippery conditions. Worse yet, when one contemplates this route for an army, one is filled with a sense of fear for our soldiers. Especially at Apache Canyon.

The entrance to Apache Canyon is a bottle-neck passage where, with perhaps only a single cannon, one could hold off an advancing force. It would also prove a perfect location for an ambush. As we rode through the canyon I shuddered and my blood no longer felt the heat of the day.

All for Manifest Destiny.

What can be done to stop the madness? Can Colonel Kearny be persuaded to desist? As I looked down into the ravines falling away inches from my horse's hooves, and as I looked up at the canyon walls I saw in my mind too many lives senselessly lost.

THE LIEUTENANT SIGNALED a halt.

"Is that Santa Fe?" Carolina asked wearily.

The company had traveled over thirty miles that day in Lieutenant Degas's push to achieve Santa Fe. Everyone was tired. Lightning hopscotched through a heavy gray cloud mass and thunder rolled across the sky after it. Then fat drops of rain fell quickly, soaking everything. The weather and the long ride dragged at Carolina's spirits. Without interest, she looked about.

They were halted at the crest of a hill. Falling away before them, the road curved gently to the left, crossed a river, then wended its way into a spread-out jumble of buildings about one mile away.

"*Sí*, señora. Santa Fe, a jewel in Mexico's crown," Lieutenant Degas said proudly.

"I see," Carolina lamely said in response to the officer's pride.

Riding next to her, Gaspard stifled a laugh. She turned her head to glare at him.

"And *el corazón*," the officer continued soberly.

"The heart?"

"*Sí*. Santa Fe, she is the heart of this department of the Republic of Mexico," he said boyishly, seemingly oblivious to the rain that soaked his uniform and streamed off the brim of his hat. He signaled the company to resume the march. Carolina noted he sat straighter in his saddle and took his horse out at a sprightly trot.

"The lieutenant's right," Gaspard conceded. He nodded his head toward the town spread out over the valley below. "I've heard Santa Fe described as a brick kiln yard from a distance, and I'll grant seeing the crops growing to the edge of the buildings and the animals running about nearly as freely as in Mora doesn't give Santa Fe the best of appearances. But like with people, appearances can be deceptive."

"What do you mean?"

He nodded toward the town. "Keep your eyes and your mind open. Don't judge Santa Fe by anything or anyplace in the United States. In some ways it's no different than Mora or San Miguel. In others, well, there's a code—albeit an unwritten code—for behavior that sometimes could rival the society codes of New York or New Orleans or anyplace else you could name."

She lifted her chin. "You're worried that I'll cause offense?"

He grinned. "Yes, every time you lift your chin like that."

Carolina blushed and dropped her head. "I'm sorry, I—"

"I know it's because you're frightened, Well, I guess you've got a right to be. I'm just trying to say that here, humility may get you farther than that taking-on-the-world chin."

"I don't!" she only half heatedly protested, for she knew she really didn't know.

"You have nearly every day I've known you."

"No!"

"Carolina," Gaspard said, casting her a pitying look, "you can lie to me, or to Pedro, or anyone else, but don't lie to yourself."

Carolina's blush faded. She felt the rain drizzle down her neck. She shivered, though she wasn't certain it came solely from the rain.

"Taking on the world," she repeated. "I suppose you're right." She blinked away raindrops as she gazed up at the gray sky. The clouds were thinning, losing some of their grayness. "Every time I get complacent, when I think I've learned all I need to know, some event occurs to tell me I may have judged wrong."

He grinned at her, then indulged in a Gaelic shrug. "As my father said to my mother, 'That is living, *cherí*.' "

25

CAROLINA HATED TRAVELING through rain showers. Particularly afternoon rain showers, even if they did dampen down the dust and freshen the air. Those aspects were well and good; but compared with the feeling of wet clothing steaming in the afternoon sun, those virtues paled. Wet clothing was heavy and clumsy to move about in, it possessed a tendency to smell that, coupled with the smell of wet leather and wet horse, could not fail to offend, and last, once the rain chill and coolness passed, the clothing itched. Dreadfully.

Carolina squirmed in her saddle as the company rode into the plaza in Santa Fe. She desperately wanted to scratch her ribs; however, too many eyes were upon her.

She could feel the curious stares as she rode through the streets and into the plaza.

Small canals planted with rows of cottonwood trees ran along each side of the unpaved plaza. On one side of the plaza was a long low building fronted by a portico. On the other stood a church. Other buildings around the plaza looked like merchant shops and large private residences.

Lieutenant Degas led the company to the portico-fronted building.

Carolina edged her horse closer to Mr. Gaspard. "What is this place?" she asked.

"The Governor's Palace."

Carolina looked at the building in dismay. Though she'd seen and experienced crude living conditions and had mentally prepared herself to discover more of the same in Santa Fe, the reality had not settled within her mind. She halted her horse in front of the door to the palace. Soldiers lounged against the roof posts, Indians and New Mexicans sat against the wall tending goods for sale spread out before them, or smoking cigarritas. This was the governor's palace?

Gaspard came up beside her horse to lift her down. "In normal times, the porch is full of American merchants with their wares spread out around them as they haggle over prices with some stout señora." He nodded toward the small knot of men sitting on the porch. "With the war, it's a mite thin."

"More than a mite, Señor Gaspard," said a deep, full voice.

Carolina and Gaspard turned toward the man. Behind them, the lieutenant saluted crisply.

"Your Excelencia," Gaspard said, acknowledging the man's presence and tipping his head in recognition of his position.

Carolina stared at the large gentleman walking with a slight limp toward them. *So this was the governor of New Mexico, General Manuel Armijo.*

His coloring was a shade darker than what could be considered pure Spanish; however, he was an imposing man. He wore a light blue frock coat with a general's epaulettes. The trousers were a darker blue, which he wore with gold lace and a red sash.

"Señorita Navarro," Armijo said loudly as he approached them. "Welcome to Santa Fe."

"Your Excelencia," Carolina said, following Mr. Gaspard's lead.

She curtsied, but did not look down as she did so. "Your pardon, but it is Señora Harper."

"*Sí*, of course, a widow, I understand. May I offer my condolences."

"Thank you, Your Excelencia."

He turned toward Mr. Gaspard. "I am pleased to see you well, my friend. At some time we must get together to discuss this war business."

"I am at your disposal, Your Excelencia."

"Excellent. Now, I know you wish to attend to your own affairs. I shall see to Señora Harper."

Gaspard rubbed the scar on his cheek. "That's very kind of you, but you see, Your Excelencia, Mrs. Harper's affairs are my affairs."

The governor tilted his head back and raised one eyebrow. "What's this?" he coolly asked.

"Your pardon, Your Excelencia," Carolina said quickly. "What Mr. Gaspard means is that he is in my employ until such time as I release him."

Governor Armijo relaxed. "Ah, of course, of course. A woman traveling alone, or with only servants, would have need of the services of a man such as Mr. Gaspard. But surely, now that you are here, among your own people, you may safely dispense with his services."

"It's okay, Mrs. Harper," Gaspard said to Carolina before she could answer the governor. "I guess I would be grateful to the governor for looking out for you while I go have a chat with the American consul on your behalf, seeing as how you *are* American," he added, looking at the governor.

The governor frowned at Gaspard.

Satisfied, Gaspard turned to go.

"Mr. Gaspard," Carolina called after him, "take Pedro, the boy, and the mules with you. And you have my authority to handle the goods as you deem best. I'll be all right."

"Of a certainty, señora," Governor Armijo said.

Gaspard looked at her for a moment, then nodded. Pedro glanced uncertainly from Gaspard to Carolina to the governor, then gathered the reins of the horses and mules to follow Gaspard.

Armijo raised his hand to wave at the military escort. "You may go, Lieutenant Degas." He turned back to Carolina and offered her his arm. "Come, señora, my wife is anxious to meet you. We shall have a fine dinner this evening and you will tell us all about your trip and your home in America. And perhaps, too, what brings you to Santa Fe."

"Certainly, Your Excelencia. You are too kind," she said. As kind as the snake in the Garden of Eden, she thought as he escorted her into the palace.

July 29, 1846, later, at the Governor's Palace, Santa Fe.

Yes, the Governor's Palace. I'm staying here the night. But lest you envision rococo with white and gilt, I must make a humble effort to describe the surroundings in which I find myself.

The palace at once commands the plaza and is an integral part of the plaza. Under the portico—or portales —which fronts the palace, all manner of men gather for their business and their leisure. Within the palace, it is much like the alcalde's home except that the main hall has a genuine carpet over its earthen floor.

Though the accoutrements of the palace may resemble other homes', there is one accoutrement that I doubt will be found elsewhere. One of the governor's Indian servants told me he has five pairs of human ears strung on a leather thong tacked on his office wall! Texan ears from that ill-fated expedition.

I wonder if the servant told of this barbarous relic of his own volition or if he was told to tell me by the governor himself. I would wager I was told on orders. It is the governor's way of attempting to impress me with his power.

*I believe the governor has numerous reasons for ensuring
I know about the ears, and all of his reasons are
Machiavellian.*

*Don Manuel asked me many questions about my journey
to Santa Fe, and about how—and when—I learned of the war
between our countries. Dona Maria Trinidad, the governor's
wife, voiced suspicious surprise that I should continue my
journey once I learned of the war. I tried to tell her about my
concern for the children, but I could see that I made little
impact on her suspicious mind.*

*The governor's wife has been scrupulously correct in her
dealings with me. Nonetheless, I can tell she feels she is forced
to consort with the enemy. She is a short, stocky woman;
however, her manner and bearing would be the envy of anyone
at any height.*

*Dinner, when it came, was served on silver platters. We
were served mutton, frijoles, tortillas, and fresh fruit. After
dinner we ate chocolate cake and were served whiskey and tea.
I passed on the whiskey. The governor and his wife drank
whiskey and tea while they smoked.*

*I have learned it is a matter of courtesy that a woman is
offered a cigarrita. Unfortunately, I confess my manner was a
trifle snappish when the governor offered me one. Dona Maria
Trinidad frowned mightily. I do not think she likes me.*

July 30, 1846, the Governor's Palace.

*Mr. Gaspard proved true to his word—as always. Early this
morning the American consul called upon me. I don't think
the governor was pleased, but what could he do?*

*Señor Manuel Alvarez is the U.S. Consul. He is a Spaniard
by birth, from northern Spain, I understand. He is a shrewd
man with European manners. I think his success lies in his
clever use of these two aspects of his personality.*

Mr. Alvarez is arranging for me to board with an American
merchant and his Mexican wife.

Everyone is agreed that I cannot stay at the La Fonda
Hotel, though I fail to see why not. I missed noting the hotel as
we rode into the plaza or else I should have immediately
suggested checking into that establishment.

I shall wait upon Señor Alvarez's arrangements; however,
should there be any problem, be certain I shall be ensconced
swiftly at La Fonda.

Both the governor and Señor Alvarez seem surprised at my
desire to see Uncle Elliott and my lack of interest in seeing
Uncle Diego. Truthfully, the stories about Diego Navarro have
been persuasive enough that I am quite frightened to meet
the man.

Regardless, I have secured a promise from Señor Alvarez
that he shall send a messenger to Uncle Elliott, who lives in
Taos.

Señor Alvarez also told me Mr. Gaspard is leaving
Santa Fe today for business in some northern villages.
From his vague comments I believe Gaspard is seeing to
the welfare of our young Indian boy. I am glad he is so
quickly working to solve that problem; but I confess I also feel
bereft.

"Señora Harper, there is no need for you to leave here. Colonel Navarro will certainly return to Santa Fe in the next day or so."

Carolina laughed, but inclined her head respectfully. "My thanks, Your Excelencia, for the hospitality you and your wife have extended, but I do not wait upon Diego Navarro."

"But he is family," protested Armijo.

Carolina shook her head. "I do not even know the man. Elliott Reeves is more my family. And you, Excelencia, are much too busy and important a man to expend your time playing host to me. No.

I shall be better boarding with Mr. Carmody and his good wife. Mr. Carmody numbers among my stepfather's business associates and therefore I have some ties to them. I shall be well content in their company."

"You are an unusual woman, Señora Harper."

"Unusual? Hardly. It is just that I am not Mexican," she said wryly. "I'll own I long thought that my birth made me Mexican as well as American. I have seen, since I've been in your country, that this is not so. I am, perhaps, of neither land. Only time will tell." She stood to leave.

The American consul stood as well. The governor did not.

"So why did you come here, señora? Why come to New Mexico?" Armijo challenged.

Carolina waved the consul to silence as she turned back toward the governor. "Because of the children, Excelencia."

"Children?"

"My uncle's children and all the other children of mixed heritage."

He tilted his head as he looked at her, one brow raising in quizzical inquiry.

"Perhaps . . . perhaps I'll found a Mexican-American school so the children can learn of both their heritages. So they won't wonder where they fit in society."

"And that, perhaps, is what you wonder, señora?"

"I used to, Your Excelencia."

He frowned at her.

"I wondered until I met Singing Waters. She was a quiet, gentle Indian woman who had the capacity to love, no matter what life gave her, and it gave her plenty of misfortune."

"And what happened to this Indian woman?" Armijo asked coldly.

She looked at him directly. "She died. Of rabies."

The governor flinched at the word *rabies*. Carolina curtsied and murmured, "Good day, Excelencia."

She turned and quickly left the room, followed by Pedro and Señor Alvarez.

"You know, señora, the governor was correct in one respect," Señor Alvarez said as they walked down the plaza beneath the *portales*.

"In what way?"

"When he said you are an unusual woman."

Carolina drew back in surprise. "I assure you, I am not."

He smiled faintly. "My business takes me to many places in the United States and Europe. I know of what I speak."

"I don't know what to say."

He shrugged. "There is nothing to say. This next building, it is Mr. Carmody's Emporium."

The building looked much like its neighbors save for the painted wooden sign that hung from the thick beam that protruded from the roof of the building. The white sign proclaimed to all who passed, in bright blue and red script, that this was, indeed, Carmody's Emporium.

Carolina stared at the ornate sign, similar to store signs in New Orleans or St. Louis. To her surprise and embarrassment, her eyes watered.

"Señora?"

Carolina laughed and quickly dashed away the excess moisture with her fingertips. "I'm being excessively silly, but looking at that sign . . . I don't know, it just reminded me of home."

Señor Alvarez nodded. "Mr. Carmody ordered that sign all the way from St. Louis, had it crated and brought as carefully down the trail as if it were a load of the finest china."

"That I did, indeed. Been a good investment, too," said a slender man with wisps of blond hair slicked back over a balding pate. "The name's Benjamin Carmody, ma'am."

"I'm pleased to meet you, Mr. Carmody."

"I'm afraid I must leave you now," Señor Alvarez said. "Mr.

Gaspard gave me news that I must discuss with others in the city. I will visit you tomorrow, Mrs. Harper, if I may?"

"Certainly, señor."

"Good. Good day, then, señora, Carmody," Alvarez said briskly before turning away and hurrying back the way they'd come.

Carolina turned back toward Mr. Carmody, who took her arm to lead her into his shop.

The shop proper was one long, deep room. At the back was a curtained partition to another area. Near the front by one of the shop's two windows stood the sales desk. In between lay a profusion of merchandise: groceries, dry goods ranging from muslins and calicoes to costly silks, drugs, pots and pans, books, tools, toiletries, leather goods, and trinkets.

Behind the sales desk stood a young Mexican attired like a St. Louis shop clerk. He was wrapping a parcel for an old woman with flat features and nervous hands.

"That is Ignacio Ruiz, my assistant. He speaks English. Should you need anything, he will be happy to assist you."

The shop assistant looked up, smiled, and nodded vigorously. The old woman looked over her shoulder at Carmody and Carolina. She looked Carolina over carefully, then sniffed, gestured to Ruiz to hand the package to the Indian girl accompanying her, and left the store.

Carmody shook his head. "Do not mind Dona Lupe Domasio y Garcia."

"I don't. I have received all manner of reception in New Mexico. I think beneath them all is fear of the unknown, the stranger among them."

"Good. But come and meet my wife, Angelina. She is anxious to meet you. She would have been here to meet you herself, however, it is near her time and her legs pain her."

Oh, no! Carolina thought. Not another one! "Gracious! Of course she must rest!" she said.

"This way, please." He took her arm and led her toward the

partitioned part of the store. He pushed aside the curtain and took her out a door in the back that led into a wide, open yard with chickens pecking at grains of corn and an old bitch dozing in the sun.

At their approach the tan and black dog raised her head and thumped her tail a handful of times on the ground; then, as if that action exhausted her, she lowered her head back to her paws and closed her eyes.

Carmody laughed with affection at the old dog. "That is Saber. Nothing bestirs her."

He led Carolina into a house at the other side of the yard. They passed through two dim rooms, then into the light of a courtyard similar to that in the alcalde's house in San Miguel.

"My dear, there you are! Here is Mrs. Harper, who Mr. Alvarez came to talk to us about last night," Mr. Carmody said in English as they approached a chair set in the cool shadows.

As her eyes adjusted to the light, Carolina saw a young woman scarce past girlhood, with large, luminescent eyes and a body well advanced into pregnancy. Her legs were swollen and propped up on a pile of blankets, but she made a move to swing them down in order to get up.

"No, no! Please. You must not get up," Carolina said in Spanish as she hurried forward to lay a hand on the fragile-looking woman's shoulder.

"My wife speaks English," Mr. Carmody said.

"Yes, of course, for I heard you speak to her in English," Carolina responded absently as she smiled at the woman. "And how long is it until your time?" Carolina continued in Spanish.

She saw distress pinch the young woman's face and her glance lift to her husband.

"What is it? Are you ill?"

"Mrs. Harper . . . " Mr. Carmody interrupted impatiently.

"I . . . I am well," Mrs. Carmody said hurriedly in heavily accented English. "And I would please to speak English with you."

"Mrs. Harper, we speak only English in this household," Mr. Carmody said sharply.

Carolina slowly straightened and lifted her head up, then recalled Mr. Gaspard's comment about her chin and lowered it a fraction. She took a deep breath to still the pulse of anger that throbbed within her. "My apologies. Of course."

July 30, 1946. Evening.

I am now ensconced in the home of Mr. and Mrs. Benjamin Carmody. I was uncomfortable staying at the Governor's Palace for I did not want to be a political pawn. Now I am uncomfortable from dislike of my host. I'm sorry. I know he is a business associate of Mr. Davies and perhaps he is an astute businessman. Nonetheless, I cannot like a man who comes to a foreign country to do business but refuses to learn the language of the people.

Not only does Mr. Carmody refuse to learn Spanish, he will not allow Spanish spoken in his house. What arrogance is this? Is it no wonder that some locals hold Americans in contempt? It is not to be borne. I must speak to Señor Alvarez. Perhaps there is another family I may stay with who does not share Mr. Carmody's insularity and arrogance!

July 31, 1846.

Oh! I am quite ready to pull my hair out! And I would leave this place and take up residence at La Fonda Hotel if I were not moved to pity by Carmody's wife. She is a woman-child so heavy with a baby that she can scarce move about. She is also frightened.

As Mr. Carmody will not allow Spanish spoken in his house, Mrs. Carmody is denied visits from her mother and others in her family merely because they do not know English. Even the priest may not visit!

How can this man act in this manner? And what does he

intend to do when it is his wife's time? Deliver the baby himself? It will not be born if that is his intention!

I have spoken to Señor Alvarez about this matter, but he only shrugs. He has offered to find me different accommodations, but what will that serve? Men. Bah!

I did not turn my back on Singing Waters. I will not turn my back on Angelina Carmody.

I wish Mr. Gaspard were about. I believe I could trust him to make Mr. Carmody see the light of sweet reason!

Sunday, August 2, 1846.

Church is an important part of life in New Mexico. It is so important that Mr. Carmody does not dare suggest that his wife not attend a church service even though she will be among Spanish speakers and will most likely discourse in Spanish with one or two individuals.

My tone is perhaps too arch with regards to my host. I shouldn't do that for that is unworthy of me when I recall they have opened their home to me, a mere stranger. I am grateful; I just must confess that I find Carmody's insularism provoking in the extreme.

Nonetheless, I should take this opportunity to talk to you of the church. The building is built of adobe as is every other building in the city; however, it is sufficiently lofty and is therefore seen from every angle within the city and in some areas beyond. The church has two steeples in which hang at least three bells each.

Inside the church are painted carved wood images and wax images of the Virgin Mary and of Jesus. In addition, paintings, complete with gold gilt trim, adorn the walls with further Jesus stories.

Candles burn throughout the church and the smoke from their passing has sadly left much of the intricate paintings marred by accumulated soot. Nonetheless, this does not mar

*the beauty of the church or its services, which this day were
accompanied by violin and triangle.*

*Colonel Diego Navarro returns to Santa Fe tomorrow. This
morning the news was on the tongues of everyone until I came
in view, then all talking unnaturally ceased. It sent shivers up
my spine far more effectively than my uncle's actual presence!*

*Next week there is to be a ball in my honor. The governor
insists.*

26

CAROLINA BENT HER knees and dipped her head from side to side in an effort to look into the low-hung mirror. She was successful in seeing only a part of her face. Enough to enable her to pin her hat on her head. Satisfied, she gave the crown a little pat before straightening and reaching for her gloves.

"Mrs. Harper? Pardon, please?"

Carolina turned around to see Angelina Carmody standing in the doorway. She clutched her stomach, her eyes wide in pain.

"Dear God. The baby's coming," Carolina said. Memories of another birth less than two months ago flooded her mind.

"*Sí*. I . . . I mean, yes," Angelina said anxiously.

"This is not a time to worry about one's language, child. Let's get you settled, then I'll send for the midwife," Carolina said.

"No! You must not! She no speak English. My husband . . . " Angelina gripped Carolina's arm in fear and agitation.

"My dear, this is nonsense!"

"No! *Por favor*, please, no!"

"Hush, hush . . . all right, then," Carolina said soothingly. She bit her lower lip as she thought about what she could do for this child and the child she bore.

If Mr. Carmody would not allow Spanish spoken in this house, then the thing to do would be to take Angelina to another house. In their conversations Angelina had told her that her sister lived in a large house by the river. That is where she would take her.

"Come," she encouraged Angelina. She led her to the door at the opposite end of the house from the broad yard that separated the house from the shop. As they walked she yelled for the Indian servants. She sent one running ahead to the house of her sister to tell them they were coming. She sent another scurrying to gather blankets.

Tears ran down Angelina's face as she protested. She couldn't leave her home, her husband would be angry.

"Men do not have babies," Carolina said tersely in Spanish as she pulled Angelina along.

Outside Angelina flinched at the bright sunlight and Carolina staggered under her weight. She shielded her eyes with one gloved hand as she held Angelina with another.

There down the street, was what they needed and what Carolina had hoped to find, a *carreta*, one of the local carts with solid wooden wheels and crude woven branches for sides pulled by an old burro. An Indian led the burro by a frayed rope tied to its halter. The wagon carried a load of firewood.

"You, there! Stop!" Carolina yelled.

The old Indian looked about for who she might be calling.

"Yes, you. Bring that cart here immediately!"

Confused, he did as she said, then watched in horror as she immediately began dragging the wood out of the cart and scattering it on the road.

"Come and help me," she ordered him.

He gabbled something incomprehensible at her. The servant Carolina had sent for the blankets gabbled something back at him that Carolina figured must be their native language. The Indian helped her clear a space in the wagon for the blankets and Angelina.

Tenderly Carolina settled Angelina in the wagon and cringed as Angelina cried out again in pain. Carolina wondered if she was doing the right thing, then she saw the faith shining in Angelina's eyes. A lump settled in her throat, she swallowed it down. She briskly told the woman servant to walk behind the cart, then she strode back to the burro, picked up the rope lead, and turned the burro and cart about and hurried them toward the river.

It was not to be supposed that their passage would go unremarked; an Anglo woman in Santa Fe leading a peasant's cart carrying a pregnant woman of good birth and followed behind by an Indian servant, but Carolina ignored the stares as she urged the little burro forward.

They were nearly to the river when Carolina heard a loud crack from the cart. She winced. Whatever it is, don't break now, she prayed.

In the cart, Angelina whimpered. Carolina looked down the road. The cart need hold together for only a little farther. And it looked like the servant had relayed the message to Angelina's relatives, for two women hurried toward them. Carolina urged the little burro forward.

"What are you doing with my wife?"

Carolina looked up to see Mr. Carmody riding a mule bareback, his long legs flapping against the sides of the animal.

Crack!

"Mrs. Harper!" screamed Angelina.

Carolina dropped the rope and ran toward the back of the cart just as its off-side wheel broke in two and the cart fell.

Angelina screamed as she tumbled against the cart's rough side, as did the Indian servant trailing behind and the women hurrying toward them.

Carolina compressed her lips as she checked on Angelina. She did not appear to be hurt, only increasingly frightened. And it appeared her time came faster than was common for a first child. The women gathered around her.

"Mrs. Harper!" yelled Mr. Carmody as he dismounted.

She ignored him. "Her time is too near," Carolina told the women.

The older woman nodded. "But there is time enough for both babies."

Two! Carolina looked dumbfounded at Angelina. *Of course!*

"Don't touch my wife!" Carmody yanked Carolina away from the cart. "What the hell do you think you're doing, jeopardizing my wife and child?"

Behind them, the women bustled about and ordered the laughing spectators to carry Angelina to the house, augmenting their orders with a shove and a kick where necessary.

"Jeopardizing? You fool! Angelina needs these women!" Carolina yelled back at him as she twisted free. "Your orders that only English be spoken in your house jeopardizes their lives. I'm trying to save them!"

"What the hell are you talking about?"

"I don't think there are any English-speaking midwives in Santa Fe, Mr. Carmody."

"Midwives? I didn't—"

"How was Angelina to be delivered? By dumb show? Or were you intending to do it?"

"No, I—"

"And the poor child needs to yell out her pain. But you've got her so cowered, she's afraid she'll say something in Spanish that will bring your wrath down on her! No, Mr. Carmody, I am not jeopardizing your wife and babies. You've already done that!"

"Babies?"

"Get out of my way!"

"Babies?" Carmody repeated, his eyes shooting toward the big adobe house into which his wife disappeared.

The men remaining on the street laughed and tossed about

crude jokes in Spanish that Carolina steadfastly chose not to understand.

"Babies," Carolina said flatly.

"But how . . . " Carmody floundered. He turned to look back helplessly at Carolina.

"Mr. Carmody," she chided, but Carmody was not listening to her. Nor were the other men and animals in the street listening to her. Their faces were sober and silent as they looked past her. Even the animals seemed subdued. Carolina turned around.

Black-leather-gloved hands clapped slowly together, their owner smiling caustically, one side of his lips curling upward as he easily sat a large dappled roan. When he saw he now had her attention, he dropped his hands and leaned forward in his saddle.

"It is good to see that the child of my so studious brother has inherited the Navarro fire!"

Diego Navarro.

Carolina felt her stomach tighten, then twist hard. This was not how she'd envisioned meeting her infamous uncle. She raised her hand to shield her eyes from the afternoon sun. "Hardly a child, señor," she said dryly. She felt the past rush in upon her. Her father's face, his laughter, the way he held himself—memories swamped her as she stared at Diego Navarro. Her pulse beat as rapidly as a hummingbird's wings.

"Señor? *Señor?*" He swung his leg over his horse's back, hung upright in the saddle for a moment, then dropped to the ground with an easy, loose-limbed grace and the faint jingle of the large silver spurs on his glossy black boots.

"Your pardon, Uncle Diego," she said wryly.

He crossed his arms over his chest. "I am desolate that I should be out of Santa Fe when you arrived, the only child of my brother! Why did you not send word of your arrival?" Navarro asked.

"Your reputation precedes you, Uncle. You are not known to deal kindly with United States' citizens."

"Never say it, niece! Lies, all lies. I am merely a soldier at my general's command. You must come and stay with me. How would it look for Colonel Navarro's niece to stay with strangers?"

Beside her, Carmody's face grew white. Carolina quickly turned toward him. "Join your wife and family, Mr. Carmody."

"But—"

"Do not be concerned for me," she broke in quickly. "Just go. Go!" she said, shoving him toward the large house his wife had disappeared into.

"Yes, Carmody," Navarro said as he drew off his gloves. "Run to your wife's skirts."

Carolina whirled about to face her uncle. "That is a ridiculous comment, even for you."

Navarro's brows snapped together. A soft scuffling of rope and leather sandals indicated the men left on the street were slinking away. Navarro stropped his gloves through his hands and glared at Carolina.

She lifted her chin.

Suddenly Navarro began to laugh. "Perhaps you are right. I think I like you, niece. Come," he said, smiling at her. "Your aunt wishes you to join us at our home. Come."

Carolina glanced back at the big adobe house by the river, then shrugged slightly. "It would be my pleasure," she said. She clasped her hands together and let them fall against her lap. "If you would give me your direction I can be there in two hours."

"Two hours? You must come with me now!"

"I am afraid that is impossible, Uncle. I must first see to my things and then relay the events of this afternoon to Mr. Carmody's shop assistant and their house servants. They will need instruction for the day and instructions on what to take to Mr. and Mrs. Carmody. After all that is done, I will come."

He frowned slightly, but only as a child whose will has been thwarted, not as the monster people described him to be. Curious, Carolina thought, and relaxed.

He told her where he lived, then he turned on his silver-spurred heel and vaulted into his saddle. "Two hours," he said solemnly to Carolina as he gathered the reins into his hands. "I shall expect you in two hours."

She nodded and raised her right hand in acknowledgment; however, her eyes narrowed as she watched him ride away. Then she turned and walked briskly toward the big adobe house.

August 3, 1846, Santa Fe.

As I sit writing this, my belongings are once again packed in saddlebags and pouches. I am waiting for Pedro to come with my horse and a pack mule. I have been ordered, I can think of no other suitable word, to come stay with Colonel Diego Navarro and his family.

Today Mrs. Carmody's time came. The poor child was dreadfully frightened. I escorted her to her sister's house. While I was standing outside the house, Diego Navarro rode up. I can well see why people are afraid of him. His manner is that of a cat playing with a mouse. He insisted I come stay with his family. His image and honor and all that. Odd, I wouldn't have felt Navarro to care a snap of his fingers for such things.

In all honesty, I confess there is an air of charm about my uncle. And he has Father's smile. Just seeing it played upon my memories. I could not resist his pressured invitation.

Also, unfortunately, I can no longer stay in Mr. Carmody's home, what with his wife staying with her family, which I hazard to guess shall be an extended visit. It would not be seemly to remain here and I do not wish to borrow trouble with rumors. I am too new in Santa Fe and rumors too often develop a life of their own. So what is there to do? I would prefer to go to La Fonda, but once Navarro issued the invitation, to refuse would be churlish. And suspect.

My head aches. There has been too much today. Again I find myself wishing Mr. Gaspard would return to Santa Fe.

*But perhaps he is well rid of me, and his pay willingly
forfeited to stay clear of my orbit. At least Pedro is about. Of
course, he knew before I did that Navarro was looking for me
and intended to have me stay at his house. It was Pedro who
told Navarro I was staying at the Carmodys'.*

*No, Pedro has not turned against me. However, his brother
is something like a steward or a foreman for Navarro. Pedro
was visiting with his brother when Navarro returned to Santa
Fe. So, like rocks rolling down a hillside, one thing rolled to
another and I sit here surrounded by my belongings, awaiting
Pedro.*

CAROLINA LAID HER pen aside and stared down at the words
she'd written. There was so much left unsaid. She didn't like being
evasive in her writing. In the beginning, when she'd started the
journal, she'd been too forthright, leaving herself bare to anyone
who might read her words. Over the past few weeks she found
herself holding more and more back. What held her hand? She
honestly did not know. However, she acknowledged that a strange
disquiet sat in her soul.

"SO, NIECE, YOU have not yet answered me satisfactorily,"
Diego Navarro said as his wife and daughters hurried to clear the
dinner away. He tapped tobacco from a hard leather bottle into a
piece of corn husk, then rolled the cigarrita between long fingers.
His youngest daughter quickly brought him a punk from the fireplace.

"In what way?" Carolina asked as she watched her cousins
scurry. She had wanted to help clear away the food; however, she'd
been overruled. She was their guest, her aunt insisted.

So pronounced were the protestations of her aunt and cousins
that Carolina did not feel comfortable among them. And she
thought the feeling mutual.

Navarro leaned back in his chair as he inhaled deeply. When he released his breath, swirls of blue smoke rose to curl about in the air. "Why did you not contact me?" he asked. "Why did I not know you were coming to Santa Fe?"

"No offense intended, Uncle, but actually, I came to New Mexico to see my uncle Elliott Reeves."

"Reeves!" Navarro threw his cigarrita into the fireplace. "Bah! Do not even whisper that you might be related to that one!"

Carolina blinked at his vehemence. "Why?"

"He is an idiot! How could my brother marry into a family that breeds ones like that?"

Carolina's mouth tightened into a rigid, straight line.

Navarro shook his head, then picked up his silver goblet and saluted Carolina. "In you, niece, ah, in you the Navarro blood beats strong. That is good. I tell you now, if you had been such a one as Reeves, I would have ridden past this afternoon," he said as he flipped his hand up in a contemptuous gesture.

"And then what would people say, Uncle?" Carolina carefully asked, her tone light and even. Her eyes revealed her tension, but Navarro never looked up into her face.

"About what?" he absently asked, his focus on his youngest daughter, whose attention he was trying to gain for her to fetch him his tobacco bottle and corn husk wrappers again for another cigarrita.

"About turning away from your own niece," Carolina said.

He shook his head. "It is not to be considered. The Navarro blood, it is too strong."

The little girl asked her father if she might make the cigarrita for him. Navarro was pleased by her request. He watched her carefully then smiled at the child. That smile surprised Carolina. Her uncle looked younger, more personable, and quite handsome when he smiled like that. He dipped his head to accept the cigarrita from the child, inhaled deeply, then looked up and smiled at Carolina.

Carolina slowly smiled in return. It was hard to resist his smile.

"Yes, Uncle, Navarro blood does run strong. You would do well to remember that," she murmured.

His expression swiftly shifted. His smile changed to a frown. He glared at her, but she merely smiled archly in return.

He stared at her a moment, then his deep smile pulled at the corners of his mouth until his teeth gleamed in the candlelight. "You, niece, are widowed too long. The bit has slipped. I forgive you this time."

Carolina stared at him for a long moment. "Are you threatening me, Uncle?" she asked.

He smiled. "Perhaps."

It was Carolina's turn to smile. "Ah, then you fear me."

"Fear you?" Navarro straightened. "Never! A Navarro fears nothing!"

"Precisely," Carolina returned with bravado and an expression she hoped he would take for sincerity.

He stared hard at her for a moment, then he began to laugh. "If you were any of my daughters I should take a cane to you."

"But I am not. I am a woman of the United States. You would do well to think on that, Uncle. Think on it well."

August 3, 1846, the home of Diego Navarro.

As I write this my newly met cousins Lita and Maria take cushions and blankets that make the divan along the cloth-covered wall and lay them out on the floor to provide our beds. Little Comel, the youngest of Uncle Diego's daughters, kneels before a statue of the Virgin Mary that's in a niche in the wall. Her small hands are pressed tightly together as she says her evening prayers, her eyes focused on the blue-robed and gilt-trimmed statue.

My cousins are shy. They will not look me in the eye, but I know as I look down at these pages to write to you, I know they stare at me. I am a mystery to them.

The feeling is returned for they are also mysteries to me!

They are not mysteries because they are Diego Navarro's daughters, though I'll own that I find Uncle Diego a curious man. No, they are mysteries because they, along with their stepmother, are like most of the New Mexican women I have met or seen since Mora.

Their manner of dress is simple: a short-sleeved white cotton shift, a full skirt of some strong color or black, and the ever-present rebozo. Even young Comel has her rebozo. Currently she has it pulled up and draped over her head as part of her reverence as she prays. The two older girls carry pouches for tobacco and corn husks even though the oldest girl I do not believe is any older than fourteen or fifteen.

The girls are soft-spoken to the point of silence and their manner around their father suggests respect and fear. When they could, they made an effort to walk far around him. This despite the fact they made every effort to second-guess his wishes. One would think Uncle Diego was some sultan or some other outlandish potentate with a harem. And this image of unconditional power over others is reinforced by the bullwhip he hangs on the wall of his library. Nonetheless, I'm sure Father Harper would approve of the demeanor and manners of Uncle Diego's female family members. He'd likely be jealous!

Uncle Diego calls me a true Navarro. If that is so, I pray I am more a true Navarro than he is, for never let it be said that Diego Navarro's more widely reported escapades are more in the family blood than father's quiet style. Still in all, I feel he is anticipating molding me into the demeanor of his womenfolk. There is definitely charm in Uncle Diego. There can be no question of that.

I find it curious, however, that he has yet to question my politics, unless he, like the Harpers, believes politics are beyond women. Or at the least, question me closer as to the *motives of the wagon train or what I might have heard men say.*

Though everyone has been all that is gracious and hospitable toward me since I came to this house, I would like to find an excuse to leave. I am uncomfortable here. It's like spiders crawl on my back. It is all I can do to keep from brushing my hand over my shoulders, so real is the feeling. It sends shivers up and down my spine and makes me want to call for a hip bath.

27

"I HAVE BEEN in this house for days. I'm beginning to feel I am a prisoner here! I need to get out and I am only planning on going to Carmody's Emporium. I do not need a chaperone," Carolina said with forced patience to Rosita Navarro. Carolina's new aunt was her age; however, she adopted the gravity of a grandmother.

Rosita shook her head. "My husband, he say you are to have a duenna or other escort wherever you go."

"That's very kind of him to be concerned for me in that manner; however, I traversed the Santa Fe Trail without mishap. I can risk a trip to Mr. Carmody's store. Besides, if my uncle wished me to always have an escort, he shouldn't have sent Pedro to his Rio Arriba hacienda on a fool's errand."

Rosita adjusted her rebozo higher on her shoulders. "It is not for us to judge a man's mind."

"That's for certain," Carolina mumbled.

"It is merely ours to trust," Rosita explained.

"Trust?" Carolina laughed shortly, "No, Rosita. There I disagree. Trust must be earned. Maybe it's been earned to your satisfaction, it hasn't to mine."

Her aunt compressed her lips and shook her head. "It is God's will—"

Carolina cut her off. "I do not wish to begin a religious discussion. Suffice it to say, my beliefs shall remain different from yours and any religious argument will not sway my mind. Rosita, you are a loyal wife for my uncle, and I respect you for that, but know this: I am going to Carmody's."

"No!" Rosita latched on to Carolina's forearm.

"It is not for you to say. I'm sorry. You should not have to feel in the middle of this situation. I'm certain when Uncle knows me better he will not see anything untoward in my venturing about on my own."

Carolina tried to imbue her voice with kindness to soften her adamant stance. In the few days she'd stayed with her uncle's family she'd come to know and like his young wife. Rosita came from a large, wealthy family who lived near Taos. To them, Rosita's marriage to Colonel Navarro was a coup that brought with it bragging rights. Rosita was valiantly trying to be a good wife to her husband and to make her family proud of her.

"Wait!" Rosita said. "If . . . if you are insistent on going, then take Lita, Maria, and Comel with you," she said as she released Carolina's arm and took a step away from her.

Carolina looked at her. Rosita appeared ready to crumble in upon herself. In a moment she was likely to crush her own fingers with the strength of her wringing and twisting her fingers together. Carolina's heart softened and she took pity on her. "All right, I agree to take them. And don't worry, everything will be fine. When Uncle comes home and he hears all I'm certain you shall see there will not be fireworks. Do not distress yourself."

"Your uncle, we do as he say. It is better that way."

Carolina laughed. "So I gather," she said dryly. "But remember, he is not my father, my guardian, nor my husband. My actions are not for him to say."

Rosita's eyes grew wide. "Oh—oh, please," she said, batting Carolina's arm with her hand. "Please do not say such things to your uncle. It will only anger him. He shall be angry with us all!"

"Angry with you all! That's ridiculous."

"He is a Navarro, the last of the family. He is all those things you named."

"Rosita, I am mistress of my own affairs. While I thank you for having me stay with you, it is not a necessity. I am merely awaiting Mr. Gaspard's return before I continue my journey."

Rosita's face contorted and her lower lip trembled.

"What is it? What's the matter?" Carolina asked.

Rosita shook her head. "I . . . I cannot."

Carolina grew more alarmed at Rosita's expression than she had at any of her words. "You cannot what?"

Rosita's eyes glistened. She raised her hands to her face as tears slid down her cheeks.

"Rosita!" Carolina exclaimed.

"He's not coming back," she said in a strangled voice.

"Who's not coming back. What are you talking about?"

"Your Mr. Gaspard."

"What?" A cold hand gripped Carolina's heart.

Rosita nodded. She sniffed and raised her face from her hands. "Diego, he say he make sure that he leave for good. He say you will soon not be of the United States. He say you be of Mexico, of us, and that he will marry you off advantageously for the Navarros and with much celebration."

"Marry me off?" Carolina paused, then waved her hand. "Never mind. What did he mean when he said Mr. Gaspard is gone for good?"

"I am sorry. I do not know."

"How does he know Gaspard is not returning? Does he mean he's gone back to the United States?" Carolina persisted.

"I do not know! I only know that when my husband say a thing is so, then it is so. I am sorry. I weep because I could tell from our talks that Mr. Gaspard, he is someone special to you, even if he is the enemy of my husband."

"Mr. Gaspard is not Diego Navarro's enemy," Carolina snapped.

At least it didn't sound as if Gaspard were dead or imprisoned. The fear receded.

Rosita shook her head. "He is from the United States. He is then my husband's enemy."

"With that rationale then I, too, am his enemy."

"No. You, you are Navarro!" she exclaimed with a proud toss of her head.

"What a tangle," Carolina murmured. She grabbed the bridge of her nose with her thumb and forefinger and pinched it hard. Yes, she decided, there was pain. She must be alive and awake.

"*Qué?*"

"Nothing," she said, shaking her head. Rosita was loyal to her husband. This was not a conversation with a future in continuance. She would have to see if Carmody or Alvarez knew what was going on.

"If the children wish to go to Carmody's with me, see that they are ready to leave in fifteen minutes," Carolina warned.

A weak, thready laugh spilled out of Rosita. "If I know those children, when I tell them where you are going, they will be ready faster than the chickens gobble the corn."

Glad to hear Rosita's laugh, Carolina smiled back at her. "Come with us," she urged her.

"Oh, no, no. I cannot."

"Yes, you can. Besides, your coming should make Uncle Diego more at ease, for you can act as my duenna."

"I do not think—"

"Do not worry. I shall take care of everything. You will see."

Rosita compressed her lips a moment, then she smiled. "All right," she said. "We all go to this Carmody's Emporium."

CAROLINA STOPPED HER little party just before they got to the shop to stare up at the red, white, and blue sign. The St. Louis sign reminded her of home and made her realize the breadth of difference between the New Mexican culture and the United States culture. Looking at the sign, her eyes watered. Ruefully she dabbed at the corners of her eyes with the rebozo given to her by the Navarros.

"Carolina?" Rosita said.

"I'm sorry, it's just that every time I see this sign I think of home."

"This sign? But it is funny-looking," Comel said.

Carolina laughed. "And the cities at home are filled with just such funny-looking signs. Come, let's go in."

The three little girls stepped cautiously into the shop, then quickly fanned out as different items caught their fancy. Carolina felt a warm glow in her chest as she watched her little cousins. She turned toward the sales counter.

"Good afternoon, Ignacio."

He bobbed his head at her, his expression almost fearful. Carolina cocked her head in puzzlement, then walked toward him.

"Ignacio. What is it? Is something the matter?"

"Nothing, señora!" he said too quickly.

Carolina pursed her lips and shook her head. "No, that's not true. Don't lie to me, Ignacio. You're a poor liar. Is Mrs. Carmody all right? The babies, are they all right?"

Ignacio relaxed. "Sí, señora. The babies, two boys! The babies, they are fine, as is Mrs. Carmody."

"And Mr. Carmody?" Carolina asked, still searching for the source of Ignacio's disquiet.

"Mr. Carmody, he is a man torn." Ignacio grinned briefly. "His wife, she still stay in the house of her sister, a house in which only Spanish may be spoken."

"Ouch!" Carolina said.

"Sí, señora. But Mr. Carmody, he is a smart man. He learn Spanish now. I help him," he said proudly.

Carolina clapped her hands as she laughed delightedly.

"Carolina! Carolina! Come look!" Lita cried out from where she stood by a stack of lengths of calico.

"You found something you like?" Carolina asked, moving away from Ignacio and the mystery of his strange expression.

"Look! Look, is it not pretty?" Lita asked as she stroked the red-and-yellow-print calico.

Carolina thought the pattern a little overbright, but not for the world would she have dampened her cousin's enthusiasm. "Does it call to you?"

"*Qué?*"

Carolina laughed. "Does the fabric say 'I belong to you'?"

"*Sí!*"

"But see this brush!" Maria said to her sister. "It is worth ten lengths of fabric to have a brush such as this!" Maria held up a silver-backed hairbrush. It reminded Carolina of the hairbrush set she had packed in the bags she'd given to Mr. Carmody. It probably was.

Carolina felt a tugging at her skirts. She looked down to see Comel pointing at a porcelain doll.

Carolina sighed. "Let me see what I can do," she told the child and lifted her head to look at the two older girls to convey the same message.

They all perked up and nodded vigorously, then looked at their cousin with adoring eyes. Carolina ruefully shook her head. She turned back toward the sales desk.

"Ignacio, please wrap up these items for my cousins and take it out of my account from the goods Mr. Carmody sold for me."

Ignacio looked pained and shook his head.

"What's the matter? What's wrong?" She walked toward the desk.

Ignacio looked over at Rosita, then leaned toward Carolina. "The account, señora," he whispered, "it is empty. There is no account."

"Empty!" Carolina exclaimed, oblivious to Ignacio's hand motions to be quiet. "That's impossible, Ignacio. I haven't claimed a penny of my money."

"*Sí*, señora, you I have no seen," he conceded, his expression pained and confused, "but another took your money on your behalf. I thought, Mr. Carmody thought . . . " He shrugged helplessly. "We thought you knew."

A chasm opened in Carolina's mind, a chasm with steep walls, swirling winds, and no bottom. She felt as if she stood at the very top of that chasm, at the very edge and that the winds threatened to topple her into the depths. She took a deep breath. "Who?" she asked. "Governor Armijo or Mr. Gaspard?"

He shook his head. "Neither, señora. It was your uncle, Colonel Navarro."

The howling winds shrieked in pitch within her mind. Slowly she turned to face Rosita.

Rosita's eyes were wide and filled with fear. "I did not know. I swear to you I did not know! But," she wrung her hands as she tentatively stepped closer to Carolina, "but is it not better this way?"

"Better?" Carolina parroted back to her in an empty tone.

"*Sí.* Better to have a man in care of your money. A man of your family."

Carolina turned her head to look at Rosita, but she did not see her for her mind stumbled over too many thoughts. Navarro had found the one way to tie her to him. Money. Without money or trade goods she was beholden to him for everything!

Gaspard! her mind screamed. Where are you?

She didn't for a moment believe he was dead, though perhaps if he returned to Santa Fe that would be her uncle's goal. This was her battle. It would be best if she faced it as such. To one and all she proclaimed her independence. It was time she lived it.

"Carolina?" Rosita said. She reached out to tentatively touch her arm.

Carolina slowly closed her eyes then opened them. She shrugged off Rosita's hand and walked past her and out the door of the shop.

"Carolina!"

Carolina ignored her. She walked toward the house of the U.S. consul. She was an American citizen and she needed to report a robbery. Dimly she was aware of Rosita calling the children and following after her. She'd had so many hopes for this journey to Santa Fe. So many fantasies of beginning a new life. It all lay in ashes at her feet.

Up ahead she saw Manuel Alvarez come out of his house. She quickened her pace. "Señor Alvarez! Wait! I would speak with you a moment, please."

"Señora Harper! But of course. What is it?" he asked, alarmed, as she came up beside him. "You are out of breath!"

Carolina glanced quickly back over her shoulder. "In private?"

The U.S. consul followed her glance, then grabbed her elbow. "Come this way," he said, leading her back to his house. "It is not proper to have a young woman here without a chaperone but I get the feeling that any who would volunteer as chaperone would not be welcome."

Carolina nodded, as she paused to get her breath. "Señor Alvarez, I need your help. I have been robbed."

"Robbed!"

"Yes. All of my trade goods, and all of my money that I was to receive from the sale of these goods, is gone."

"I do not understand, señora."

"Mr. Carmody was authorized to act as my agent for all of my goods."

Alvarez nodded. "This I know. Mr. Gaspard arranged this before he went north at my suggestion."

"Mr. Carmody took—without my authorization—he *took* all of my money and goods and gave them to Diego Navarro!"

Alvarez spread his hands wide. "But, señora, was that not the proper thing to do? Colonel Navarro is your uncle."

"No! That was not the proper thing to do! What sort of thinking is that?" she asked, her voice rising. "I hardly know the man. He is as much a stranger to me as you are, señor. But you, you are to keep the interests of the U.S. citizen!" She paused to draw a breath and to quell the fury of the anger that gripped her. "I am not Mexican. I come to you as a citizen needing assistance in a foreign land."

Alvarez spread his hands wide. "In this country, señora, what Colonel Navarro did is considered proper! Have you asked him about the disposition of your affairs and his intentions?"

"No," she said shortly.

"Then you do not know if he would keep your money from you."

"Señor Alvarez, you *know* Diego Navarro. What do you think?"

He sighed. "What I think and what I know often war with each other, señora. But, if it would ease your mind, I shall lend you some money. I know your stepfather would honor the loan, if you are correct, if you have indeed been robbed, and you cannot repay me."

"No, I—"

He grabbed her hand. "Please," he said, interrupting her. "I should rest easier knowing you have money for La Fonda Hotel if you feel you need somewhere to go. If you do, let me know. But I want you to remember, señora, the United States is at war with Mexico. Here, in Santa Fe, you are safer with a citizen of this country."

"Only until Colonel Kearny comes," Carolina said dryly.

Señor Alvarez drew his head back in surprise, then reluctantly nodded. "If the rumors are true, he could be here, in Santa Fe, in two or three weeks. Be careful, señora. By being of both nationalities you bring more hardship upon yourself than if you were only of one."

"I know, señor," Carolina said. "But I am not alone. It is the same for the children of American merchants here, the children of mixed blood."

She thanked him again before he could comment and went outside. She looked up at the broad expanse of blue sky and remembered the time she'd spent on the trail looking up at that same sky. She squatted to pick up a fistful of dirt from the ground. She rose, then let it slowly trickle through her fingers back to the ground. It was the same earth God created, just in different formations. If earth and sky are the same in New Mexico as St. Louis, what of people?

Carolina brushed her hands together to get rid of the dirt on her hands, then she walked back toward Carmody's Emporium to find Rosita and the girls huddled together looking worried and despondent. She smiled at them. Whatever Diego Navarro had or hadn't done, they were blameless.

"Let us return to your home. I am sorry I could not buy you those things you liked in Carmody's," she said as she smiled down on Comel and pushed a wayward strand of dark hair out of the child's eyes. "It appears I no longer have any money."

Rosita winced. The children tried to question Carolina, but Rosita hushed them.

"They aren't asking anything different than what I'm asking," Carolina quietly told her.

"Please, it is for the best, you will see."

"Somehow I doubt that, Rosita, I doubt that very much."

August 6, 1846.

> *Up until now, all I have known of Uncle Diego's infamy is through what others have told me and in his autocratic manner in his household.*
>
> *I have now tasted a bit of his creation.*
>
> *Unbeknownst to me, and therefore without my permission, Diego Navarro has claimed all my trade goods and profits as his—ostensibly for me, but the result is the same: I am without funds. Worse, I am without funds in a land at war with my own country. I see very clearly that though my father was born of the Mexican people, I am not of them. A culture is more than blood, and blood ties do not make for acceptance in society.*

I do not yet know what I am to do. Señor Alvarez would have me discuss the issue with Navarro. He would not have me believe the worse; nonetheless, he did lend me money that I hope I will not have to spend. I wish I could discuss this coil with Mr. Gaspard; but Rosita would have me believe that Gaspard is not returning to Santa Fe, that he has gone back to the United States, or worse, that he is dead. I refuse to believe either possibility. It is not Mr. Gaspard's nature. I would that he return soon!

CAROLINA REREAD HER last paragraph and laughed. She did not know where the certainty in her soul came from, but she truly believed what she'd written. She knew Mr. Gaspard well—better, perhaps, than she'd ever known her husband. He would not abandon her. And more, Carolina felt she'd know if he died, that some shadow, like a pall, would cover her soul.

She sighed deeply, capped her ink bottle, and returned her journal to her lap desk.

Her uncle was due to return on Saturday, the day of the ball. Until then, she would do her best to withhold judgment on his actions and keep well hidden the money Señor Alvarez gave her.

28

August 8, 1846.

Navarro returns today just in time for the baile. *I am nervous. For two days my mind has been devising scenarios for our discussion. But as much as I have planned and speculated, I know that the reality will be far different from any expectation. That is what worries me the most. I hope I am able to quickly, and appropriately, react to anything he says. Too often, in New Orleans when my father-in-law came to visit, I became tongue-tied and failed to properly explain our plight. I would not have that happen to me now. I feel more confident than I did in New Orleans as the young wife of Edward Harper; nonetheless, I cannot shake this feeling of uncertainty and self-doubt. For as much as I've progressed, an equal or greater amount has stayed the same.*

But this is an old theme. I wish I were not so frequently reminded of the foibles of my past. Still, I must take comfort in the knowledge that in some ways I have progressed.

I have learned some interesting facts about the baile *and its location. Here again is a difference between our society balls in St. Louis or New Orleans and what is here!*

Tonight's ball is being held at a gaming establishment. The monte establishment is owned by Dona Gertrudes Barceló, who is more commonly known as Dona Tula. I understand she is quite popular and civic minded. It is common for by-invitation-only balls to be held at the gambling house for the building has a long hall that is, I am told, perfect for dances. Invitations to these balls are coveted and one can discern who is politically out of favor by judging who fails to put in an appearance at the ball. Can you imagine! A gaming house!

I don't have any attire worthy of a ball; however, Rosita has insisted on adding bits of ribbon to one of my dresses to brighten it up. She would prefer I borrow from her wardrobe. This is not something I wish to do. I wish to minimize the favors it behooves me to accept from my Navarro relatives!

There is a commotion outside! Perhaps it is my uncle returned at last.

CAROLINA LAID HER lap desk aside, patted the sides of her head to ensure that not a hair was out of place, then took a deep breath and ran her hands down the sides of her skirts. If the noise was caused by her uncle's return, she knew she was as ready as she could hope to be.

All the noise was coming from the side of the house that faced the street, not the stable area and backyard as she would have expected. She walked through the dim, cool rooms to the front entrance to the house. A dog barked excitedly. She heard Comel call out for her father, followed by childish giggles. She heard Rosita's voice, urgent-sounding though the words were indistinct.

She hurried. She wanted to cut off Rosita before she said too much of what Carolina felt she would say herself.

The door was ajar when she reached it. She pushed the door on its iron hinges aside with such power that it banged against the wall. She scarcely noticed. The sun blazed bright white. Carolina shielded her eyes with her hand. As she watched, Diego Navarro swung down from his saddle with that loose-limbed grace that few men could hope to emulate. He swaggered—there was no other appropriate word—toward Rosita, grabbed her around the waist, bent her over backward, and kissed her. Carolina doubted he'd heard a word of what Rosita had been saying. She breathed a sigh of relief.

Behind him, she saw Pedro dismount from his horse. His movements were slow and stiff. Carolina was reminded of his age and felt a brief chagrin for all he'd done for her in the past months. There was another man who came up beside Pedro, talking to him earnestly. Judging by his appearance and mannerisms, Carolina identified him as Pedro's brother, Jesus. She walked toward them.

"Pedro!" she called out.

He looked up at her, a dim shadow crossing his features. Beside him, his brother increased his unheard importunings.

"Pedro, I have missed you. There is so much I would tell you, that I would have you do!"

"Tomorrow, señora, por favor," he said in a hoarse whisper.

"Are you all right, Pedro? Shall I send for a doctor?"

"No, señora. Nothing . . . nothing greater than age ails me. I am merely tired. I would rest."

Carolina looked at him, perplexed, but quickly acceded and told Jesus to please see that his brother was properly settled.

"Sí, señora. That I will most certainly do," Jesus said with a smirk.

Carolina's brow furrowed. Her eyes followed the pair as they walked into the house. Pedro's movements were slow and studied. Much like hers had been after her concussion.

"Niece!" Navarro's voice called out to her, breaking her line of thought. "Are you not glad to see me, too?"

"What? Oh, yes, Uncle. I am glad to see you," she said, her attention turning back toward the door Pedro and Jesus had entered. "We have much to talk about."

"Yes. Yes, we do," concurred Navarro. "I apologize for being out of Santa Fe for so many days and not talking to you before I left," he said, smiling at her. It was a smile designed to win her trust and confidence. And because it was contrived, it made Carolina nervous. She wrapped her arms across her chest. Her uncle's smile grew.

"You must be hot and tired after your journey, Uncle. Perhaps you would like a chance to clean up and eat before we talk?" she suggested, uncertain how to interpret his mood.

He nodded. "An excellent notion, niece. You are a woman of genteel sensibilities. I like that. But do we not have a ball to attend this evening? One organized by our governor with you as the honored guest?"

"Yes."

"Then you must see to getting ready for the ball, niece! Any conversation we must have can surely wait. It would not do for the guest of honor to be late to a ball in her honor!"

Carolina laughed and shook her head. "Uncle, I do not worry for that. There will be time enough—"

"Precisely, niece," he interrupted, "time enough to talk later."

"No! I—"

"As you suggested, I am off to wash away the travel dirt and sweat, which might irritate a gentle lady's sensibilities." He smiled at her, then quickly brushed by her and into the house. There was nothing for Carolina to do save follow behind him.

"UNCLE!" CAROLINA CALLED out when later she saw him as she crossed from the kitchen to the courtyard. "Uncle Diego!"

He flashed her a grin, waved, and hurried past.

She shook her head. For all his affability, it appeared her uncle was avoiding her. Diego Navarro avoiding anything? Did that equate to fear? She smiled slightly. This gave her a modicum of power. The question became, how should she use it?

August 8, 1846.

Uncle Diego is avoiding me. I am astounded!

And it is all quite disheartening. I'm certain my aunt has told him of my discovery, and that afterward I spent some time

*in conference with Señor Alvarez. Which way he may react—
or strike, for he has much more the reputation of the
rattlesnake, a deadly snake in the desert—is unknown. From
all I have discerned, Diego Navarro is an unpredictable man.
That in itself causes the greatest fear among those who know
him or of him. To me, thus far, he has been all courtesy
mingled with camouflaged threats delivered with ingenuous
smiles. And that makes me nervous.*

*Ah, Rosita is calling for me. Sounds like she has another
suggestion for my evening attire. She is excited about this
evening's ball. She tells me over and over how much of an
honor it is to be invited to one of the balls at Dona Tula's
gambling house. She is determined that everything about this
night shall be perfect. In fact, if I were to let Rosita have her
way I should attend the ball resembling some overly decorated
cake. Restraint, as part of elegance, is unknown to my
erstwhile aunt!*

"WHERE IS MY uncle?" Carolina asked when Jesus and Juana arrived in the courtyard ready to accompany them to the ball.

"My husband will join us at the ball," Rosita said with a gravity beyond her years as she draped her rebozo over her head to rest on the edge of the tall comb she wore in her hair.

"Why isn't he coming with us?"

Rosita glanced up, a mild frown pulling at her features. "I have told you before, Carolina, it is not ours to question. But I can tell you that he received a message he said he must attend to immediately. He will join us at the establishment of Dona Tula. You must be content with that."

"I'm sorry. I meant no offense, Rosita. My question sprang solely from my surprise. I was certain that Navarro was a man to watch over what he would call 'his own' with a hawk's intensity."

Rosita smiled complacently and nodded. "This is so. That is how I know this message must be of some great import."

Carolina did not like the wall of silence she felt being built around her. But further questions or protests would obviously prove futile. "Ah, well, perhaps we will learn more later. Shall we go?"

Rosita nodded and motioned to the servants to follow.

The evening was early, by New Mexican standards. The sun had just dipped behind the mountains, leaving a pink aura above the black-silhouetted crests, and a darkening sky the color of gun-barrel blueing.

The streets were a hive of activity, some activity the residual of the day, some representing new challenges and opportunities. Carolina felt her heart race at the thought of all the people that she passed whom she could be involved with in big and little ways.

There was a crowd gathered outside of Dona Tula's establishment when they arrived. The conversation was lively and Rosita introduced Carolina to those who came to pay their respects to Rosita, which was nearly everyone present because all were curious to meet Diego Navarro's American niece. Carolina smiled, regally nodded, and greeted everyone. This party was a milieu with which she was all too familiar. And while the setting was alien, the feeling was all New Orleans. But her attention focused on the differences between Santa Fe and the United States, not the similarities—though she hoped there were as many as not.

Inside the gambling establishment Carolina saw massive iron chandeliers, each with hundreds of candles, hung from the wooden ceiling beams. The light from the masses of candles reflected like glittering jewels in the tall mirrors that hung all about the walls. Brussels carpeting covered the dirt floor. At one end of the long room were the musicians with their guitars and fiddles, at the other end were the refreshments, which were presided over by dour-faced Indian servants.

Carolina readily identified their hostess by the crowd around her. Dona Tula moved languidly through the guests, speaking first to this person and then to that as if she were granting dispensations. Her black hair was parted in the middle and most of it pulled severely into a large bun at the base of her neck into which was stuck an intricately carved horn comb inlaid with silver and turquoise. The rest of her hair, framing her face, was greased into tight sausage curls. A cigarette perpetually hung from her rouged lips, its blue-gray smoke twirling upward to form a wreath above her head. She was not a handsome woman. Her facial features were strong and showed the beginning ravages of age. However, it was not her facial features that caught and held one's attention, it was her dark eyes. There was a cagey intelligence in their depths along with a sense of humor.

Around her neck she wore many gold and silver necklaces, one with a large silver crucifix that nestled between her ample breasts. Bracelets encircled her wrists, and the rebozo draped casually over her arms was heavily shot with gold. Her chemise was edged with European lace and the royal-blue full skirt she wore was trimmed with silk and velvet.

Dona Tula saw Carolina looking in her direction and she smiled. She casually waved away the person who was attempting to claim her attention and walked over to Carolina.

"Señora Harper! At last we meet. I—"

"Carolina!" Diego Navarro hailed Carolina as he approached from the entrance. "Ah, pardon me, Dona Tula," he said, superficially smiling and bowing to her.

Carolina watched Dona Tula's expression change from warmth to a northern winter's ice. "Diego," she said, acknowledging him.

Her informal address brought Navarro's head up with a snap. Dona Tula raised one dark eyebrow. That these two did not care for the company of the other was obvious. It was equally obvious that each saw the other as a formidable adversary. Carolina looked again at Dona Tula, curious as to how she came to have no fear of her uncle when so many she met did fear him. And equally curious at the obvious respect her uncle accorded Dona Tula in return.

"I wish to have a word with my niece. I shall not be but a moment."

"Of course, Diego, so long as you do not take our guest of honor from us. We have barely had the opportunity to meet your beautiful niece. Such a surprise it is to learn of her existence! And an American! I don't think many knew there were more in your family."

"My father was many years the elder," Carolina said, looking at her uncle out of the corner of her eye. "But perhaps you know my mother's brother as well," she suggested.

"Come, Carolina, I wish to speak with you," Navarro interrupted.

Caroline couldn't suppress a grin.

"Your mother's brother?" Dona Tula repeated, looking from Carolina to Navarro.

"He is of no importance. Come, Carolina," he said, pulling on her arm.

"But I must protest, Diego!" Dona Tula said with a laugh. "You are leaving with a mystery! Ah! I know, it shall be a contest! I shall spread the word among the guests and all shall guess the identity of the beautiful señora's other uncle."

"No!"

"And why not! He is perhaps an American trader?" She shrugged. "There are many in New Mexico despite this war that our government in Mexico City says we are having with the Americans."

"He is not important."

"Then why do you protest against him so strongly?"

"I do not! Please excuse me. I see someone I must speak with immediately. I shall talk with you later, niece," Navarro said, his brows pulled together in a thunderous frown. He slid away from them and quickly crossed the room to talk with Colonel Archuletta, who was in charge of building the defensive works in Apache Canyon in case that was the route chosen by Kearny for his Army of the West.

"You routed my uncle!" Carolina said to Dona Tula. "I had not thought that possible."

She shrugged. "His pride is too big. It was no challenge."

Carolina stared at her in open-mouthed surprise, then she started to laugh. "Now I understand, Dona Tula, why you are one of New Mexico's prize gems."

She laughed. "No, señora. I am merely a business woman. . . . Madre de Dios, I have just thought of who your American uncle might be," Dona Tula said with an arrested expression of surprise and humor on her face. "But of course! The brother of your mother is Señor Reeves, is this not true?"

"Yes, señora. Elliott Reeves is my mother's youngest brother."

Dona Tula shook her head. "It is a wonder that one is not dead. God must surely watch over him."

"Such has long been the thought of many family members," Carolina said dryly. "He is the reason I came to New Mexico."

"*Qué?*"

"We heard that his wife had died and he'd been left with three small children. I had recently lost my only child and husband, so I thought it suitable for me to come to New Mexico to care for my uncle's children. I certainly knew, as did my family, that it was not a task any of us would trust to Elliott."

"Ah. Such was also the thought of his wife's family."

Carolina ruefully nodded. "But at the time, you see, I did not know that her family would assume care of the children. In St. Louis, where my mother lives, we often met with merchants returning from New Mexico. From things they told us, we worried for any child of mixed blood. Particularly in Taos, where Uncle Elliott lives."

Dona Tula nodded. "They are a fiercely independent and suspicious people. This I lay at the door of Padre Martinez."

"I have heard him mentioned before in much the same manner."

She nodded. "Know first that he is a good man. He and his brothers, who are much of the government in Taos, want the best for their people, but they believe the best is a world without gringos."

"And what do you think is best, Dona Tula?"

The woman smiled. "What is there for me to know? I am merely a woman who owns a gambling house that I light candles for in the church and pray I be allowed to continue to own and run no matter the politics.

"But, señora, walk with me. There is a matter I do wish to speak on."

"Of course."

"For all I may bandy words with Diego Navarro, I have a respect for his power. At the moment, as much as I might have him in check, he also has me in check. Neither of us can do anything that would directly jeopardize the other. You understand what I am saying?"

"I think so."

"All right. Now I am going to take you back to my private office. There is someone there for you to see, but please, señora, I did not arrange this meeting. Remember that."

"You're frightening me."

She patted Carolina's hand. "Such was not my intent. I am merely doing a favor for a friend and attempting to protect myself at the same time. *Comprendé?*"

"Yes, of course."

She stopped in front of a heavy wood door ornamented with deep carvings of vines and flowers. "Then, this way." She pressed down on the iron latch and pushed open the door.

29

ONLY ONE CANDLE burned in the dark office. Carolina glanced at her hostess, who nodded. Carolina stepped past Dona Tula as the shadows in the room stirred and coalesced into a man rising to his feet. He stepped forward into the glow of the candlelight.

"Gerry!" Carolina cried out in a strangled voice. She ran the few steps across the room and grabbed on to his arm. "Gerry!" she said again, softer, as she clung to him. Tears flooded her eyes. Behind her, she heard the door gently close. "They told me you would not be back in Santa Fe. They told me you were gone!"

He raised one hand to her face and gently wiped away her tears. "What's this?" he asked, his voice more gravelly than usual.

Mortified, Carolina dropped his arm as if it were a hot coal and stepped back a step. She turned her head away to stare into the single candle flame. "My . . . my apologies. That was ill done of me, I know. Not at all the behavior of a lady."

"Carolina—"

"You may say 'I told you so' if you wish. I was not prepared for Santa Fe. Events here have quite disordered my mind."

"Carolina!"

"I do not intend to place any burden or obligation on you, but in honesty, I fear I must confess that I have missed you," she said. She raised her head. "Damnedably," she whispered.

"Carolina," he said again, this time softer and with a smile playing upon his ravaged features. He grasped her shoulders and pulled her toward him, close, but not, she sadly noticed, into an embrace. "I have missed you as well, and that was not something I expected, nor wanted."

"I know," she said softly.

"Maybe you do; I don't know. All I do know is I should never have left you here in Santa Fe." A light kiss brushed her brow, then he released her and stepped away.

"Alvarez tells me Navarro has claimed all your money and goods."

"Yes, and he won't give me the opportunity to speak about it. In his home I have felt a virtual prisoner, but with Mrs. Carmody having her child I could no longer stay at their home."

"No, I don't suppose you could. I've spoken to Benjamin Carmody about Navarro. Fair near flayed his hide after I heard how you helped his missus when he was acting like a horse's ass." He shook his head. "He's a good man but when he gets an idea in his head, he's worse than an old hound with a bone."

Carolina gave a little watery laugh. Try as she might, she couldn't seem to stop the slow course of tears down her cheeks.

"But Carmody is a businessman. Seems he didn't pay Navarro what he would have paid you, American to American. He gave me the difference for you and some more in gratitude for helping Angelina."

"What! No. That's not right. He doesn't owe me for Angelina and he's already paid Navarro. I do not need his charity. I refuse to be a charity case that people feel sorry for. I would prefer to work to earn my way."

"Now, Carolina Harper, you stop right there with that self-pity. You're a businesswoman. There's no room for pity now. We got enough to take our attention without you wallowing about in self-pity like a pig wallowing in mud. What I'm trying to tell you is that you've got money now and if you want to leave Navarro's you can. But—"

"Yes. Yes, I want to leave Navarro's!"

"But, as I was trying to say, if you could stay on there longer it might be a good idea."

"Why?"

"Navarro's been up north stirring up mischief against Americans. Even tried to have me ambushed."

Carolina gasped and again grabbed on to his arm.

He nodded ruefully. "That's probably how come he was so certain I wasn't coming back to Santa Fe. What Navarro didn't count on was some of those he tried to have kill me are my friends. Friends is the one thing Navarro has always been short on so the idea didn't even occur to him."

"And yet he possesses great loyalty from his family and servants."

Gaspard snorted. "Loyalty out of respect or fear?"

Carolina sighed and shook her head. "I don't know. Still, I don't understand why I should remain in their home. I feel uncomfortable there."

Gaspard ran a hand through his white hair. "I guess what I'm asking you to do is be a spy."

"What? A spy!" she choked out, then looked around the room as if there were others to hear their conversation and condemn them to death.

He nodded. "Kearny is sending James Magoffin, one of the Santa Fe traders, along with one of his captains here to see if they can't parley some kind of deal that doesn't have the Americans and New Mexicans trading hot lead. I'm to meet them in San Miguel and tell them what I know. There's reason to believe many of the *ricos* don't want to fight the Americans. It isn't in their interest. Of course, Navarro hates Americans so he's likely to try to sway the *ricos* to his way of thinking. I'd like you to pay attention to who comes to see Navarro and what they might be saying, if you get a chance to hear. I don't want you to go sneaking around trying to hear. Just let me know what's going on with Navarro. He's too damn unpredictable."

Carolina clasped her hands together and turned away. "I don't know," she said. "Spy on my uncle! I'll grant he is not a good man, but spy?"

"By just keeping your eyes and ears open you could possibly be helping to protect the children, like you said you wanted to do."

She took a deep breath and then slowly blew it out. "Noble words take on a different color in the harsh light of day."

Behind her, Gaspard stayed silent.

Carolina owned that she did not like her uncle. He was too ingratiating one moment, then the next he was cruel. But spy on him? What could be gained from that? The past week he'd scarcely been home. Might that not continue? So what would it matter if she said yes or no? Ultimately it wouldn't.

Gaspard came up behind her and put his arms around her, pulling her against his chest. "I'm sorry, I should never have asked. Your sense of integrity is high. I've seen it in the past, I should have known better than to ask."

She raised her hand to touch his forearm. She smiled. "I don't think it is a matter of integrity. It's probably more fear than anything else. I'll stay at the Navarroses' unless my uncle makes life too uncomfortable there. Somehow I don't think he will, now that he has my money and has his sights set on marrying me off advantageously."

"Marrying you off?"

She nodded as she turned around in his arms to face him. He loosened his embrace, but did not let her go.

"He thinks to marry me to someone who can benefit him, either financially or politically, I'm not certain which. Perhaps to one of those *ricos* he is agitating."

"Now I'm not sure you should stay at Navarro's."

"Why?"

"With a priest in his pocket you could see yourself married any day he chooses."

"But if I object—"

"If you object, Navarro would blackmail you with some threat of harm."

Carolina shuddered. "Yes, he probably would. Still, I believe we are chasing phantoms. My uncle will likely spend his days to the north with the *ricos* just as he has this past week."

August 9, 1846.

The baile *at Dona Tula's was magnificent. I challenge any St. Louis or New Orleans ball to rival it!*

Strong words. I will admit that my emotions color my perceptions of the ball. I am smiling as I write for I discovered last night that Mr. Gaspard cares for me as I do him. Though I confess I perceive he is as uncertain about what to do about that knowledge as I. I suppose this is again something that would be best left to Divine Providence.

At first we met secretly in Dona Tula's office, a small room with little more than a table, chair, and ironbound chest in evidence. Mr. Gaspard arranged this secret meeting because he did not wish Navarro to learn that we might have any feeling toward each other beyond business, which Gaspard feared might become obvious should we meet in a crowded ballroom. His caution was well founded. Rosita had told me that Gaspard had left Santa Fe and wasn't returning. Consequently, when I did see him I was not circumspect in my greeting.

Thankfully, I never imagined Navarro would attempt to arrange for Gaspard's death as a way to prevent him from returning to Santa Fe. I can't imagine what my response would have been had I believed him dead! I had not realized until the moment I saw him again just how deep ran my own affections. The knowledge has shaken me. Never before have I felt such intensity and now I must work hard—for my life and his—not to show one modicum of my true feelings.

Well, I practiced a like deception when Edward was alive and acting peculiar, a deception that nothing was wrong with Edward or our business, so I can do so again, I decided. And proceeded to do so at the baile.

Gaspard timed his "official" arrival at the ball to be just prior to Governor Armijo's, therefore we had only a scant minute or two to practice our deception and act as cordial business associates pleased to see one another again. The governor and his wife quickly claimed all of my attention. (Though I fear Dona Maria Trinidad does not like me. She is an admirer of my uncle.) The governor even danced the cuna with me. This is a dance that is to my mind more scandalous than the waltz. Couples place their arms around each other then lean back, forming a cradle shape, which is what cuna means, and then they twirl about the room. While the upper halves of their bodies may remain apart, I found the lower halves of the bodies becoming too close and often brushing together in too intimate a manner. Of course, I cannot say whether the governor was executing the dance properly or not. He is known to be a man of voracious sexual appetites, which he does not state with his wife or she with him! I certainly do not intend to be a morsel for his devouring.

Talk of the war with the United States was prevalent in the room; however, most I heard prayed it would bypass New Mexico. They saw it as Mexico City's war, not theirs. Still they fear our soldiers are better equipped than theirs and lament all that Mexico City has denied them and what they perceive they would need in order to adequately protect themselves from attack. Observe, they say, how ill prepared they are to stave off Indian attacks on some of the settlements

*and haciendas. Bitterly they claim New Mexico could be too
easily taken.*

*This attitude angered Armijo and he lambasted the
gentlemen there for these thoughts. But there was something
about his harangue that gave me pause. I don't know that I
could quite precisely say what it was, but I think the governor
has actually harbored similar thoughts; but it would not have
been politically expedient to voice them.*

*Throughout the night I was questioned on what I knew
about our military. I could quite truthfully tell them about the
small army detail we met on the Santa Fe Trail and of some of
our naval ships in New Orleans, but that is all. With regards
to Colonel Kearny, they have heard as much—if not more—
than I. Oh! There is pique that the United States is sending
only a colonel to New Mexico and not a general. This is
considered a great insult and it is what, in some measure,
hardens minds and hearts against the United States. Is it not
true that little oversights such as this are what can turn the
tide in battles? The next week or two should prove eventful.
But in this threat of war and battles, where am I? What am I?*

I do not know.

CAROLINA CLOSED THE lid on the wooden chest Rosita gave her
for her belongings and turned around to discover Diego Navarro
watching her.

"Good afternoon, Uncle. I have been wishing to speak with
you."

"As I have been you."

She smiled. "Good," she said, though she felt disquieted by his
shuttered expression. "Shall we go out to the courtyard?"

He shook his head. "Here. We will speak here."

Carolina tipped her head in compliance, sat down on the chest,
and folded her hands in her lap. "I understand you have claimed
my goods and funds from Mr. Carmody."

"Yes."

"Why?"

"Why? But that is an absurd question! I am your only male relative in New Mexico. It is my duty!"

Carolina shook her head. "First, you are not my only male relative in New Mexico, a fact you continually ignore, and second, I am not without some knowledge of the world. I have had a husband, borne a child, and buried them both. I have attended to my family's financial affairs during my husband's illness and after. I bought those trade goods in Independence, Missouri, and hired the crew that helped me take them across the country. Why do you think I did this? To see you? To let you 'claim' what is mine?"

"To spy for the United States, perhaps," he said.

Carolina felt a twinge of conscience, for that was what Gaspard was asking her to do, but that was not why she came to New Mexico, and so she could answer truthfully.

"When I left Westport, Missouri, no one even knew war had been declared. But I knew that my uncle Elliott's wife had died and I knew he had three small children. I know what my uncle is like, why everyone laughs about him."

"The man is an idiot!"

"Perhaps. But he is my uncle, my family, who I have known all my life. And knowing him, I worried for his children."

He snorted. "With just reason. But Estafina's family took the children."

"I know that now, and if I'd truly thought it through I should have realized that would occur. But I had just lost my child and my husband. In my grief, coming to help Uncle Elliott seemed the proper thing to do."

He nodded thoughtfully as he reached into his pouch for a pinch of tobacco to place in a corn husk sheet. "I believe that is what your womanly sentiment deemed proper, but it was a stupid thing to do. What were your male relatives in the United States thinking to allow you to sully yourself in trade?"

"Sully myself?" She laughed, though inside she quaked in outrage. "As heavily into trade as the entire family is on all sides, no
one thought it the least odd or ill bred. Those trade goods were
meant for the Reeves children's benefit, should they need it, and
they are also to help me establish a school for children of Mexican
and American blood, where they would learn of both countries,
both languages." She rose to her feet. "Rather than shipping
money from one country to another, trade goods allowed me to in-
vest my money with the hope that I could ultimately have more
money at my disposal here in New Mexico, something you have
cheated me of!"

"Cheated? How do you claim cheated?"

"When I can't get access to my money, that's being cheated.
Worse. That's being robbed."

He waved the cigarette in the air, dismissing her accusation.
"Call it a trust."

"A trust?"

He nodded. "A trust in Mexico's success in this war with the
United States."

"What?"

He smiled. "If Mexico wins, you get your goods and funds back.
If the United States wins, then consider the property your way of
ensuring the health and safety of your Navarro cousins."

"But this stupid war could drag on for years!"

"This is also true. But this is also my assurance that you do not
help the United States, that you remain neutral, with your only
thought for the children."

"But I need funds now, to live on!"

He shook his head. "Not so long as you remain here, a guest of
your Navarro relations."

"This is untenable. I would be wiser to return to the United
States."

"Without funds?"

"If I have to."

He laughed. "I did not take you for a stupid woman."

"There is truly much that you do not know of me, Uncle. But you are correct in this one thing. I am not stupid. Mr. Gaspard would escort me back, he has offered to do so before this. He knows he would be well paid for his efforts by my relations in the United States."

"You will not go anywhere near Señor Gaspard!" Navarro roared, cords standing out on his neck and his face suffused with dark anger. "That devil-faced monster seeks to destroy New Mexico! I will not allow it!"

"Mr. Gaspard!"

"I know he has ensorcelled you with his devil ways, for so I have been told by the San Miguel alcalde."

"That's ridiculous. He and I have dealt well together as business partners. That is all."

"There were many long nights on the trail traveling here."

"All of which Pedro accompanied. I find your inferences offensive, Uncle, and quite beneath contempt," she said dismissively.

"Perhaps," he said, and finally Carolina sensed doubt in his eyes. "Still, you will stay away from him or else I shall have him arrested and summarily executed."

"You wouldn't!"

"Why not? What do I care about one less American gringo? I have merely to show proof of spying and that I can do at any time for I have only to decide what that proof will be and it shall exist."

Carolina sat back down on the chest, dazed. "I confess I do not understand, at all, your motivations. This is all so ridiculous. Uncle, you are battling phantoms."

"That shall remain to be seen, niece. That shall remain to be seen." He tossed his spent cigarette butt into the corner beehive fireplace, then turned on his heel and left the room.

30

OUT OF THE corner of her eye Carolina recognized the set of the shoulders and the gait of the man who walked past the window.

"Pedro!" she cried out and dropped the chemise she'd been hemming to run through the room toward the kitchen entrance to the house.

"Pedro!" she called out again as she threw open the door.

Pedro Perales set down the pack he'd been carrying, a big weary smile lighting his long face and lifting the corners of his mustache. "Señora!"

Carolina threw her arms around him in a hug. Pedro flinched and stumbled backward out of the unexpected embrace.

"Are you all right?" she asked, for his reaction surprised her.

"It is merely old muscles, señora. They ache an old man."

She relaxed and smiled compassionately. "I am sorry, Pedro, but it is so good to see a familiar face again."

"*Sí*, señora, it is the same for me."

"Are you all right? I admit I am spoiled, I am not used to your being away. I have grown accustomed to your ministrations to my every need."

"I, too, señora, have not felt right being away. Though I do things to Colonel Navarro's bidding, I have not felt right."

She nodded. "We are both of us caught in something beyond our control. This was not what I would have for us."

"This I know, señora. But for me, it is better than for you, for though Colonel Navarro is a hard man, at least for me, I have my brother again."

"Oh, Pedro, I should have taken Mr. Gaspard's advice. When we learned war had been declared I should have remained at Bent's Fort until I could join another caravan returning to Missouri."

"Why is this, señora; do you not like Santa Fe?"

"I like it well enough, Pedro, but not without funds," she said ruefully.

He compressed his lips as a pained sorrow twisted his features. "What is it, Pedro?"

"I am sorry, señora, but that is my fault. I had not seen my brother in so long and I told him all about our journey and about your trade goods and Señor Carmody."

"And he, being the loyal servant of Diego Navarro, told him."

"*Sí*, señora."

Carolina looked at him a long moment. "Are you happy to be in Santa Fe with your brother?"

His face lit. "Oh, *sí*, señora! It has been too many years! As boys, we were much together, for the years that separate us are not the twelve years that separated your father and Colonel Navarro."

Carolina felt as if a part of herself had just broken off and drifted away. "I'm delighted for you," she said, her voice tight in her throat though she kept a steadfast smile on her lips.

"Pedro," she said levelly when she had control of her voice again, "Colonel Navarro has informed me that my business dealings with Mr. Gaspard are at an end and that I am not to see Mr. Gaspard again."

"He has spoken of his dislike for Señor Gaspard," Pedro said slowly.

"Could you please do me a last service and inform Mr. Gaspard of this situation and advise him to contact my stepfather for payment for his services?"

"*Sí,* señora, of course. I shall try to do this. But last service? I do not understand."

"Just as I can no longer pay for Mr. Gaspard's services, I can no longer pay for yours, either," she said, her eyes watering. She tossed her head back as she took a deep breath. "You are officially released from my service."

"But, señora—"

"Pedro, ever since we came to Santa Fe you have been effectively Colonel Navarro's servant. I'm sure he will pay you well," she finished on a strangled sob. She turned on her heel and walked away, ignoring his calls after her. Her heart ached. She'd done that badly, she knew. But Pedro had become Navarro's minion, even if unintentionally. She would not have been forced to stay in the Navarro household or lose control of her money if it were not for Pedro's tongue. And most likely, Gaspard would not be threatened with execution either.

But now she felt more alone than she'd ever felt before. She walked slowly to her room, where she slept, and then opened the chest to pull out her lap desk.

August 10, 1846.
As of this date, Pedro Perales is no longer in my employ.

CAROLINA LAID DOWN the pen. She didn't know what else to write. A great hallow existed in her chest. Her mind felt numb. Slowly, tears slid down her cheeks and splashed on the journal entry. Roughly she shoved the book aside, then buried her head in her arms and wept.

August 11, 1846.
Kearny is at the Cimarron River!
*   The news has been on the tongues of everyone since a*
courier rode into Santa Fe at a gallop last night. He'd been

*sent by Don Juan Dios de Maes, the alcalde of Las Vegas, with
the news.*

*Kearny has ordered his army not to loot. They pay the
villages for food! This is a great wonder to the people here and
they wonder just what sort of man is this Colonel Kearny.*

*Navarro is infuriated by the news and particularly that
Kearny's army is not terrorizing the land they pass through.
This behavior does not help his campaign against gringos.*

*Navarro intends to ride out to Apache Canyon tomorrow to
inspect the defensive works.*

August 12, 1846.

*Pedro saw Gaspard today and gave him my message. Gaspard
said he understood. I gather he and Pedro chatted for a time.
Evidently Pedro told him of Navarro's going to Apache
Canyon. Poor Pedro, he doesn't realize that everyone is using
him for information! I guess I shouldn't be so disappointed in
him. He is an overgrown innocent. I think he and my father
were well matched as master and servant.*

CAROLINA WALKED SWIFTLY out of the Navarro house with a
sense of relief. She'd called out to Rosita that she was going to visit
Angelina Carmody, then, before Rosita could respond, she'd fled
the house.

At the *baile* she'd learned that Angelina was finally at home so
Carolina headed toward Carmody's Emporium. As she walked,
she nodded pleasantly at Señor Alvarez and an American gentleman he was walking down the street with.

"Señora Harper! A moment, please," Señor Alvarez said. "I'd
like you to meet someone."

Carolina stopped and smiled. "My pleasure, señor."

"This is Señor James Magoffin. Señor, this is the Señora Harper
I spoke to you about."

"Mr. Magoffin! My stepfather spoke of you often. I am very
pleased to meet you."

He smiled, his cheeks puffing up like apples. "The pleasure is mine, Mrs. Harper. I knew your father, too, and I've had my share of dealing with the Harpers."

Carolina winced, "Well, I hope you won't hold that against me."

He laughed. "No, ma'am, just as I don't hold Diego Navarro against you neither."

She and Alvarez laughed and she was just about to excuse herself when it occurred to her she'd not seen or heard of this gentleman as being in Santa Fe.

"You are new to Santa Fe?" she asked, not quite keeping the surprise out of her voice.

"Yes, ma'am. I'm here on a mission from President Polk to see if there's not some way we can prevent any fighting. I came here with Captain Cooke from Colonel Kearny's army. Got here right before noon, but if I know the governor, he'll keep us kicking our heels until tonight before he grants us an audience."

Carolina nodded. "I would say that is true." She sighed. "It would be awful if things really did come to fighting. There are so many New Mexican and American marriages here; too many families would be pitted one against the other."

Magoffin frowned. "This is very true. My own wife, may she rest in peace, was Mexican, so my children have ties to both countries."

"But more than the issue of mixed families, the people here are so dependent upon trade with the United States. They don't get half of what they need from Mexico and often what they do get is the shoddy merchandise that did not sell in Mexico."

"You are a very eloquent speaker, Mrs. Harper. Perhaps you should make the appeal to Governor Armijo!" Magoffin joked.

A look of horror gripped Carolina's features. "Please don't even joke about such a matter. As it is, if my uncle discovers I have been talking with you, he will likely call me a traitor. I sometimes think he is looking for a reason to imprison me."

Señor Alvarez frowned. "He would not dare, for I would immediately complain to Armijo."

She stared at him. "And what would that accomplish?" she asked coldly. "About as much as my complaining to you of Navarro robbing me. Now, if you'll excuse me, gentleman." She nodded briefly to each, then hurried on toward Carmody's Emporium. Behind her, she heard Magoffin ask Alvarez what she had been talking about, but she didn't linger to hear Alvarez's reply.

August 13, 1846.

The city gossips are busy today! What happened at the Governor's Palace last night? Speculation runs high.

Late yesterday morning Captain Cooke from Colonel Kearny's Army of the West and James Magoffin rode into Santa Fe. Mr. Magoffin has been directly commissioned by President Polk to see if relations between the United States and the Department of New Mexico might be eased without bloodshed. This, I took to mean, will New Mexico surrender?

I cannot see how Mr. Magoffin could have hope of a surrender. Nonetheless, all eyes and ears are turned toward the Governor's Palace. So far all Governor Armijo has done is inquire as to the progress in Apache Canyon. I take that to mean he does not mean to surrender.

I shudder, however, to even think what war will do to these people. So many have so little already. With war ravaging the land they shall have even less. My heart grows heavy. This morning I walked out with the girls. We crossed the plaza just as Mr. Magoffin and Captain Cooke were preparing to leave. Mr. Magoffin introduced me to Captain Cooke and said something very curious. He reminded me that I have connections to many advantageous trading avenues and that I must not forget that. Then he and the captain with their escort rode out of Santa Fe.

NAVARRO STRODE INTO the kitchen, scowling. "We have been invited to the Governor's Palace this evening."

Rosita and Carolina looked up from the little cakes they were making for the children from a fanciful recipe Carolina knew.

"And he specifically asked that you also attend, niece."

"That is kind of the governor, but I wonder why."

"As do I. What have you been doing while I have been gone."

Carolina looked at him incredulously. "Doing? What can I do?" she asked, her temper rising. "You will recall, I have no money. You took it all."

"Carolina!" Rosita said sharply.

"I beg your pardon," Carolina said.

"I will finish here. You go talk to my husband out in the court-yard."

Carolina untied the knot behind her back of the square of cloth she'd put over her clothes and laid the cloth on the table. "Would you care for anything to drink, Uncle?" she coolly asked.

"Some wine. I will meet you in the courtyard. We have much to discuss, niece."

Carolina sighed and got the bottle of wine from the shelf, then, with a perverseness she could not explain, poured out wine for two. She could feel Rosita frowning behind her, but she did not turn to look at her before she left the kitchen.

"I hear you talked with Magoffin yesterday," he began without preamble as he took his silver wine goblet from her.

"That is true," she calmly replied. She sipped her wine.

"How dare you consort with the enemy!"

"He was a friend of my father. It would have been churlish for either of us to refuse to speak."

"Not when he was here to urge our governor to be a traitor to his country!"

"Urge Governor Armijo? Uncle, my experience with Governor Armijo does not lead me to believe he is a man to be moved by anyone 'urging' him to do so. Furthermore," she continued before he could say anything, "I do not understand why whatever I do is suspect to you! I've told you why I came to New Mexico. My reasons, with hindsight, may be foolish, but they are my reasons. I fail to understand just what it is you are afraid of that I, a woman without money or standing, can do!"

"You can be as unfaithful to your country as your father was."

"Unfaithful? Because he lived in New Orleans?"

"He left the family when Father needed his help."

"Uncle, he was sent away because he was a disappointment to Grandfather. He was sent away to handle the trading interests of the family because he wasn't suited to the rigors of Grandfather's estate. You were likely too young to recall, but my father was a slender, stoop-shouldered man who preferred his books. He was a great disappointment to Grandfather and even the money Father made did not make up for his lack of physical stature and strength. No doubt you grew up hearing what a disappointment he was."

"This is true. And he abandoned his family to live in the United States."

"I think it was the other way around," Carolina said dryly. "His family abandoned him long before he went to the United States."

"That is ridiculous. You know nothing of what you speak."

"Perhaps. But tell me this, Uncle, what happened over the years to all the money my father sent to Mexico? It was never returned, so tell me, what happened to it?"

August 15, 1846.

I attended a reception at the Governor's Palace last night. I never learned the reason for the reception; however, I suspect its actual purpose was to gauge the sentiments of those invited on Mr. Magoffin's and Captain Cooke's visit.

Uncle Diego assumed a belligerent attitude even before we arrived. He frowned and strutted about like a bantam rooster. If any male guest stopped to talk to me, Uncle was immediately at my elbow, listening and answering for me before I could venture a word. I swear he is more possessive than a young man in the throes of his first lust.

*The one time he could not hang upon me was when I
conversed with General Armijo. The governor balefully
frowned at him, then gestured with his chin that he wished
Navarro to go.*

*It was interesting to watch the brief battle of emotions and
thoughts that played across my uncle's features before he
bowed and turned on his heel to cross the room.*

*The governor offered me additional refreshment, then began
talking casually about Mr. Magoffin's recent visit. He said he
understood that Magoffin was a friend of Mr. Davies and my
father. He then spoke about the Harpers and how he hadn't
realized I was related to the Harpers who were in trade and
had their own shipping enterprise.*

*I expressed surprise that he should even have heard of them.
He told me his partner—now former partner—Señor Speyer
often spoke of their far-flung interests. I voiced surprise to
hear that he and Mr. Speyer were no longer partners. He
shrugged and admitted the situation was of recent origin.*

*I answered all of the governor's questions honestly;
however, I do wonder to what purpose was I questioned. This
no doubt harks back to Mr. Magoffin's enigmatic reminders to
consider my connections.*

*Nonetheless, I promised him that when war between our
countries is no longer an issue, I will send letters of
introduction to the Harpers on the governor's behalf.*

*He smiled and looked like the barnyard cat who'd just
captured a delectable mouse. He offered me a piece of chocolate
cake, hailed another guest, and gracefully excused himself.*

THE NEXT MORNING when Carolina walked into the Navarro
house from the sunny, dusty streets, she paused for a moment to
allow her eyes to adjust to the cool dimness. She smiled at the children as they scampered away and promised Rosita she'd join her
in a few minutes.

She lowered her rebozo from her head and savored the peace she'd captured during the mass that morning as she slowly walked to the room she shared with the girls.

The church had been crowded, filled, in addition to its normal parishioners, with families from the countryside who'd come to the city to learn what they could of the American advance.

The priest spoke of peace, patience, and faith.

Carolina sighed deeply. Lately she had not exhibited much in the way of any of those three attributes. She needed to get out her journal to write and thereby attempt to come to terms with those words and what they meant to her.

She removed the colorful rebozo from around her shoulders and laid it down on the bedding placed along the wall. She remembered when Lita handed her the rebozo, a shy smile on her lips along with a tentative look that spoke "I hope you like it" more eloquently than words could have. Despite her negative feelings toward her uncle, his family was charming and she loved them all.

She raised the lid to the chest and took out her lap desk, carrying it over to where she'd laid the rebozo. She sat down on the bedding, settling herself into a comfortable position, then she opened her lap desk.

And froze.

It was gone. Her journal was gone!

31

CAROLINA FELT ALL sense of peace and goodwill leaching from every part of her body. Slowly she closed the lap desk and laid it aside. She did not have to think to know who had her journal. She closed her eyes briefly, then opened them. Likely there was enough in that book to incriminate her and Gaspard. Though as of late she had not written quite as freely as she had in the past, she had written enough. More than enough!

From outside she heard the sound of marching feet. Quickly she got up and rushed to the window to open a shutter.

Outside was a company of soldiers with Lieutenant Ramon Degas leading them. In the middle of them, with his hands tied behind his back, stood Gaspard!

She must have made some sound, for Gaspard's head swiveled to look at her. His expression radiated calmness. It made Carolina's heart ache worse. She was the cause of his arrest. In moments, she would likely be next.

"I have brought the prisoner, as you requested, Colonel Navarro," Lieutenant Degas said stiffly to Navarro.

"Bring him inside."

"Inside, Colonel? Should he not be taken to General Armijo for questioning?"

Carolina saw Navarro stiffen. "I said bring him inside, Degas!" he raged.

"*Sí*, Colonel," Degas said hurriedly. He turned to motion to his men to escort the prisoner inside.

"I'll take charge of Señor Gaspard. You and your men are dismissed. I will send for you when I am done with him."

Degas looked at Navarro sharply. "*Sí*, Colonel," he said slowly. Though his face was somewhat shadowed by the brim of his hat, Carolina could see a pinched look to his features.

"And when you return you shall have another prisoner," Carolina whispered.

She turned away from the window. She supposed she could escape the house, but to what purpose? Where would she go? She could not leave New Mexico without being caught, and to go to anyone else would only brand that person a traitor and leave him or her open to like treatment by Navarro. She had no choice other than to reason with her uncle, and that was not much of a choice.

She tried to think what precisely she had written. She didn't think she had written anything about Gaspard requesting she act as a spy in her uncle's household. She did write of their feelings for each other and their decision to keep this secret. She did write of Navarro's attempt to have Gaspard killed, and—worse for herself—she did write of Magoffin's words and hinted at their possible meaning, although she still didn't know if her interpretation was correct.

She sighed. Perhaps she didn't know, in so many words, what Mr. Magoffin implied, but she knew nonetheless, as would her uncle. And she did write of discussing with Armijo her valuable trade connections.

She heard the soldiers march away. Her heart sank.

Suddenly she felt cold. She picked up her rebozo and draped it about her shoulders, pulling it up close about her neck. She could no longer hide in this room. She could not let Gaspard face Navarro alone She walked toward Navarro's library.

"Señora?"

Carolina turned to see Pedro coming toward her.

"Señora, what is it that is happening?"

"My uncle has had Mr. Gaspard arrested."

"But why?"

"Because of what I wrote of him and everyone else in my journal."

"The little writings that you do for you mother?"

"Yes. I was not discreet. Sometimes the writing was more for my own mind than for my mother."

"This I know. I see that when you are troubled and you write, that this makes you feel better, *sí?*"

"Yes, that's true."

"And so I tell my brother."

Carolina closed her eyes. She felt as if an invisible fist had just punched her in the gullet.

"What is it? What is wrong, señora?"

"Everything you have told your brother," Carolina said slowly, carefully, "he has repeated to my uncle. He is as loyal a servant to Diego Navarro as you ever were to Estaban Navarro."

Pedro looked stricken. "I am again responsible. Like with your money."

Carolina couldn't say anything, she just looked at him.

"I shall go explain to Colonel Navarro that it is all my ramblings."

Carolina laid a hand upon his forearm. "Pedro, enough. He has my journal."

Pedro sagged, as if he would fold in upon himself.

Wordlessly, Carolina patted his arm, then walked on to Navarro's office. Without knocking, she pushed upon the door and went inside.

"Ah! Welcome, niece. I have been expecting you. I have just

been reading to Señor Gaspard from this most interesting document."

"A document you stole," Carolina said dully.

"Stole? From my own home?"

"That journal is for my mother! It is merely a record of what I have experienced since I left Westport, Missouri. It was not meant for your eyes, nor anyone else's!"

"Then it is indeed too bad that your mother shall not see it. There were some quite affecting parts. I particularly liked your description of that Indian woman's death. Full of female sensibilities."

"Why can't my mother see it?" Carolina boldly asked, lifting her chin. Out of the corner of her eye she saw Gaspard quirk a smile and shake his head. Self-consciously, she lowered her chin.

"Why?" he roared. He stepped forward and backhanded her.

Carolina reeled sideways and fell to her knees. Gaspard started toward her but Navarro whirled about and kicked Gaspard's legs out from under him. With his hands tied behind his back, he fell heavily.

"Gaspard!" Carolina cried out as she struggled to her feet.

"Why? You whore, you ask why?" Navarro raged. He kicked Carolina in the face as she tried to stand.

Her face blossomed into agony. She tasted blood.

Gaspard got to his feet and butted Navarro in the small of his back with his head. Navarro grunted as he fell into the wall.

"You shall pay!" he snarled. "You traitors shall pay as all traitors must!"

He grabbed his bullwhip from his desk and snapped it out between them. Then he raised it again and sent it snaking toward Gaspard. Carolina screamed as Gaspard ducked aside. The second lash caught him across the shoulders. The third across the chest. They were not the full force of the whip's lash, but they were blows to sting and draw blood.

Navarro spun and the next lash landed across Carolina's arms. She screamed at the sudden stinging pain and stumbled sideways, away from the lash that next caught her back.

Gaspard charged Navarro before the next lash could descend. Navarro fell backward, but did not lose control of the whip. Instead, with his left hand he pulled out a long knife from the sheath on his hip and grinned. He liked the game. That was all it was to him, a game. He held the knife out before him to prevent Gaspard from again using his body as a ram.

Rage filled Carolina.

Navarro held Gaspard off with the knife as he got to his feet.

"Diego!" It was Rosita's voice. "Diego, are you all right?" she asked as she opened the door to the library.

"Go away, woman!" Navarro roared.

Rosita took in the room and its violence at a glance. "Madre de Dios, what are you doing?"

"Help us," begged Carolina.

"Get out!" he screamed at Rosita, starting menacingly toward the door.

"It is on your soul, Diego Navarro!" Rosita said as she ran from the room.

"Rosita, please!" Carolina begged, calling after her, but the woman was gone.

Navarro laughed exultantly.

Gaspard used his foot to shove a chair at Navarro; unfortunately, as the floor was dirt, it did not slide and instead fell immediately, only the top grazing Navarro's legs.

He easily kicked the chair aside and swung the whip again. This time it caught Gaspard across the shoulders and brought him to his knees. Again and again Navarro brought the whip down, its lash harder now, cutting through Gaspard's leather shirt and drawing blood in long weals.

Carolina screamed and begged him to stop. Navarro only glanced her way and laughed. She picked up the heavy chair that had fallen to the side and suddenly held it out before the snaking lash and caught the whip about it. She tried to pull the whip from her uncle's hand by pulling the chair away; too quickly he had the whip free and whistling above his head.

Carolina tried to hold the chair in front of her like a shield, but the whip's long tongue still caught at her arms and legs.

"No, Uncle! Please! In the name of God, stop this!"

"You are a traitor! You deserve a traitor's punishment!"

"No! You're wrong! I am not a traitor! I care only for those who are like myself, of both countries. I care that the children do not suffer. I would do what I can to keep the children from suffering!" Tears ran down her face.

"Children should not be exposed to a whore," he said, the whip whistling again above his head. He brought it down with a loud crack across Carolina's body.

She cried out in pair and fear. "No!" she screamed. "Dear God, no!"

The whip descended again, cutting deeply through cloth, drawing blood. She fell to the ground.

Gaspard staggered to his feet, blood blinding him. Navarro lashed him twice more, sending him back to the ground. Then Navarro turned to alternate his lighter, toying whip blows between Carolina and Gaspard. Carolina curled herself into a ball, whimpering, trying to cover herself with her rebozo while begging him to stop.

Suddenly Carolina felt a whoosh of air as the door to the office opened.

"No! Señor Colonel!" It was Pedro.

Carolina peeked out from the folds of the rebozo to see Pedro rush her uncle, a long knife in his hand. He sliced the arm that held the whip. Navarro dropped the whip, but stabbed Pedro in the side with the knife he held in his left hand.

"Pedro!" Carolina screamed. She struggled to her knees as Pedro staggered backward with the knife buried in his side.

"Take the knife," Gaspard rasped out at her, indicating with a jerk of his head the knife in Pedro's hand.

"My brother!" Jesus Perales said from the doorway as Carolina helped lower Pedro to the ground.

"Take his knife before the bitch does!" Navarro ordered him.

Quickly Carolina grabbed the knife and held it out before her, both hands wrapped around the hilt. "No. No, I have it."

Gaspard edged his way toward Carolina.

"I'm sorry, señora," Pedro said weakly. "I talk too much to my brother."

"Hush, Pedro."

Navarro laughed. "How affecting."

"I am happy to see him," Pedro went on, driven to explain. He looked up at Jesus. "I am not discreet. And he," he scowled at his brother, then winced at the pain, "he does not care for his family. He is too quick to run to his master."

"This is not so!" Jesus protested.

"Take the knife from the bitch," Navarro said as he tried to bandage his arm using his shirtsleeve. He staggered backward and Carolina saw a large pool of blood where he'd stood. She looked at her uncle closely. He seemed paler and sweat beaded his brow.

With an eye on Jesus, Carolina slipped the knife in the ropes that bound Gaspard's wrists and cut him free. She passed the knife to Gaspard.

"No!" Navarro yelled, finally noticing what they were doing. He staggered forward, his bloodied left hand coming to his forehead. He blinked as if to clear his eyes. "Jesus! They are my prisoners!"

"I do not understand," Jesus protested. He knelt at his brother's side.

"Fool! Leave the traitor be!"

"Traitor? My brother, he is not a traitor. He is loyal to the señora."

"Loyalty is for fools," Navarro spat out.

Jesus rose to his feet. "Then I have been a fool. No more." He crossed to the desk and picked up the journal.

"What are you doing?" Navarro demanded.

Jesus handed the journal to Carolina.

"Fool! Traitor! But I will . . . but . . ." He staggered forward. A look of surprise crossed his features as he fainted.

"Take the Señor Gaspard and go quickly. I will attend to my brother and Colonel Navarro."

"But the soldiers—" Carolina protested.

"All know of Colonel Navarro's temper. If it is seen that the colonel's family knows you are free without comment, they will not make comment. And the colonel has lost much blood."

Carolina nodded, and with a last look after Pedro, she guided Gaspard to the back door of the house. She was thankful not to run into the children for she knew she was cut all about, as was Gaspard, and that blood still seeped from many of the wounds. Now was not the time to stop and tend wounds, but Carolina feared their flayed flesh would stiffen, and they would not be able to move again for a while.

At the back door to the house Carolina met up with Rosita.

"I am sorry for this," she told Carolina. She dabbed her eyes with the corner of her rebozo. "I sent the children away so they would not hear while I remained and listened." She shook her head slowly, her eyes wide. Then she looked up at Carolina. "But I love him, señora."

"I know. And you had best go to him. He is injured."

"My Diego is injured?" Rosita exclaimed. She turned and ran from the room.

Gaspard shook his head. "No accountin' for taste."

Carolina looked up at him and grinned saucily. "Isn't that the truth!"

His lips twitched at her comment. It felt good for both of them, an affirmation of life to be able to joke with each other again.

"Come on, let's see if we can't totter over to Señor Alvarez's home without raising too many New Mexican eyebrows."

"Or collapsing from pain and exhaustion."

"I know. Don't feel it right yet, but it will come soon, like that time that bear like as not took off half my face."

Carolina nodded, then she paused and looked up at him. "Sometime soon, I want the rest of that story."

He laughed. "Sometime soon," he promised.

They walked, each supporting the other, the few blocks to the American consul's house. Every step was an agony and it was only from sheer grit and determination that Carolina made it to the house. She wearily smiled her thanks to the housekeeper who opened the door and then she fainted.

32

"CAROLINA . . . CAROLINA, WAKE up." It was Gaspard's voice.

"Hmm? What?" Carolina murmured, then she moved and her eyes popped open as waves of pain took her breath away. "Hurt," she whimpered. Memory of the events at the Navarro house flooded her mind. She closed her eyes. "Hurt," she said again.

A gentle hand stroked her hair away from her face. "I know. It hurts like hell's fire. But you've got to force yourself to move through the hurt in order for the hurt to get better."

"No," Carolina weakly protested. She felt as if her mind, along with her body, were flayed.

"There's doin's in the world you're going to want to see."

"Doings?"

Gaspard nodded. "You've been sleeping about forty-eight hours."

"Forty-eight hours!" She sat up quickly, then realized all she wore was a thin chemise. She pulled the covers up around her neck as Gaspard chuckled. She ignored him. "Forty-eight hours?" she repeated.

Gaspard nodded. "Consuelo, the housekeeper, patched us up

with some Indian aloe-vera-based salve. She said it will help minimize the scarring." Gaspard traced a fingertip along the whip welt on her cheek. "And she roused you from your faint enough to get some potion down your throat that made you sleep this long."

"Two days." She shook her head in wonder, then she looked up at Gaspard. "Pedro?" she tentatively asked.

"Looks like he'll live. Seems that knife missed any vital parts; still, he'll be laid up awhile."

"And what about us? Are we safe? My uncle—"

"Your uncle is dead."

"Dead!"

Gaspard nodded. "He died early yesterday morning. When Pedro sliced up his arm like he did, he slit along a vein, not across it."

"That's why there was so much blood?"

"That's it. When it comes down to it, Diego Navarro bled to death."

"Oh, poor Rosita and the children. What will happen to them now?"

"Lieutenant Degas said they will be well cared for, that he would personally guarantee it."

"Oh, really?" Carolina laughed. "So that is where our lieutenant's interests lie!"

"It does appear that way. But now it's time to get up." He gathered up a blanket and held it out for her to wrap around herself for modesty's sake.

Every muscle in her body cried out in protest as she moved to stand.

"Do I have to do this?"

"You do if you want to see General Kearny ride into Santa Fe," he said blandly as he settled the blanket about her shoulders.

"What?" She whirled around to look at him in astonishment.

He laughed. "That got your attention. Kearny got the message while he was in Las Vegas that he'd been elevated to general. Don't know if this is just a brevet promotion or not."

Carolina waved her hand dismissively. "What do you mean by 'ride' into Santa Fe? Has there been a battle already? Has General Armijo been defeated?"

He shook his head. "No battle. There were no soldiers in Apache Canyon and Armijo has fled south, probably headed for Mexico."

She shook her head in wonder.

"There's rumor that Magoffin bribed Armijo to not fight. I don't think just a bribe would suffice to sway Armijo. He's a bit more forward-looking than that. I'd say your trade connections were a nice confection on top, and I think that's why Magoffin stressed to you to remember them and why the governor questioned you so closely."

Carolina nodded. "I see what you mean. And you were right to wake me. I do wish to see Kearny—General Kearny—ride into Santa Fe."

"Come on, then," he said as he bent to pick her up.

"What are you about? Put me down! What of your own injuries?"

He strode toward the front of the house with his burden. "My leathers protected me some and this hide's gone through worse. Besides, Navarro was playing with us with those blows. He wasn't trying to kill us. Yet."

Carolina shuddered.

Consuelo hurried to open the door for them.

It was already late afternoon. A light drizzle fell upon Santa Fe from a patchwork of clouds that left odd openings for glimmers of sunlight.

Gaspard lowered Carolina to her feet, then leaned against the door lintel and tucked her into the curve of his arm.

"This is unseemly," she whispered to him, though she made no move away from him.

"This is not New Orleans," he returned.

"No, this is Santa Fe," she said seriously as she watched the blue-uniformed troops ride in a steady stream into the city. "And though I got my wish that there not be any fighting, I wonder at the cost."

"Cost?"

"This is the beginning, again, of Santa Fe. Of New Mexico. Manifest Destiny has cleared one obstacle from its path. But what happens here now?"

"I don't know, Carolina. But I think it's a place for you and me to settle to see if we can't be a part of that answer."

Carolina's eyes filled with tears. "I'd like that. I'd like that a lot."